DAVALYN DURSO

Dangerous Allegiances

An adventure in the world of crime.

Contents

II Acknowledgments

I

Dedication

For all of the girls who ever believed they weren't enough just as they were.
You are enough.

Enzo Berardi: The Interrogation

A blood curdling cry erupted from the room adjacent to Enzo Berardi.

The voice of a desperate man begged for mercy. But none would be found at the hands of his tormentor. Not unless Enzo called her off, but he wasn't likely to.

A small camera sat attached to the upper corner of the room, steadily blinking as it recorded the torture. It fed its view to a small tablet, sitting on a bare card table next to Enzo. The tabletop was cracked, worn with age, having seen many of these interviews and would likely see many more to come.

Enzo briefly looked up from the book he was reading when the man gave another shout. His expression was bored and unamused. The woman had been interviewing the man for hours, and she was starting to pull more sadistic methods from her repertoire. He half pitied the man tied to the chair, he wouldn't want to be on the receiving end of the woman's techniques.

Another man stood against the wall, watching the scene unfold. Tomaso Dante, stared intensely through the window, twirling a butterfly knife around his fingers. His spine was straight and taught, like he was ready to jump in at any moment if necessary.

Tom was taller than Enzo by about an inch, his broad shoulders tensed every time the man in the other room screamed. Everything about him screamed powerful, from the top of his wavy, blonde hair to the tips of his shoes. A shoulder holster rested on his shoulders missing the two usual handguns it normally carried.

Enzo eyed his friend with a sudden smirk and set his book down, "Twenty that she has him spilling everything in the next five minutes."

Tom glanced over, finally breaking his focus, "I'll take that bet."

Enzo dug into his pocket for his wallet and fished for a twenty dollar bill. He lay it on the table and gave Tom a pointed look. The other man pulled his own wallet open and added another bill to the table. Both men turned their attention back on the window, but now watching the clock with bated breath.

The woman sighed, evidently annoyed with the time it was taking her to break the man. Enzo watched her shuffle around in a set of drawers standing behind the interviewee. With each clank of metal, the man flinched, desperately trying to escape his bindings. Finally she found what she had been looking for; an incredibly thin needle that was dangerously sharp on one end. She turned and faced the man. Leaning over his shoulder she showed him the needle with a wicked grin.

Enzo leaned forward, eager to see where she decided to stick her needle. Tom swore under his breath, certain he was about to lose the bet. The woman leaned back and traced the needle over the man's face.

"I know you men seem to have trouble with measurements, so let me help you out," She purred, "This is eight inches. It's rather painful when inserted into your body. Shall we test your pain tolerance?"

Tom sniggered at the comment. Enzo couldn't help but chuckle as well. Amelia Cruz, his interrogator, spy, thief, and pain in his neck, was rather clever when it came to knocking their enemies down a peg or two. He watched as she lifted the needle and pressed it gently at the junction on the man's neck. The sharp point slid smoothly into the man's skin, he grit his teeth and tried to yank away but the woman held the needle steady, continuing to push it further in. Once she had settled it where she wanted, she rounded the man and stood in front of him.

"I am about to send about fifty joules of electricity through that needle," She told him, her tone was sugary sweet, poisonously so, "I would recommend talking."

The door leading into the hallway opened, gaining the attention of Enzo and Tom. Lance Alexander, stepped into the room. He lifted a hand in greeting and with the other raised a beer bottle to his mouth, taking a large swig. Enzo wrinkled his nose, the smell of beer constantly surrounded the man and clung to him like a bad reputation. Lance leaned against the wall to watch Amelia work. For reasons Enzo could not explain, Amelia was dating Lance and had been for a couple of years.

Tom shot a dark look at Lance before removing the money from the table. He tucked it quickly in his pocket to hide it from view. Enzo's own gaze had darkened at the arrival of the third man.

Enzo's focus was drawn back to the interrogation when the man in the next room let out a scream as Amelia connected a wire to the needle. She'd gone through with her threat of using electricity. As he started to scream, a stream of words poured from his lips in a torrent. Enzo set his book fully aside, leaning forward to listen intently, hoping to glean even the smallest bit of information from the man.

"I swear! I didn't know it was your territory! I was told to scope it out because it was unclaimed! I didn't know!" He was sobbing now, jerking as the electricity died down.

The woman rolled her eyes, "Somehow I seriously doubt that. Who told you that? Who was he working for?"

She tapped the metal needle with the copper wire, sending another jolt of electricity through the man.

"It was someone from the Cruzes! I swear, I know nothing else! Please!"

"That's it?" Amelia stepped back in front of him, "That's all you know?"

He looked up at her and spat in her face before beginning to rant in another language. Amelia swore and jumped back, wiping her face in disgust. Enzo recognized it as Spanish, the mother tongue of the Cruz family. Which meant that Amelia could understand every word.

When the man finally slumped forward, having exhausted both his energy and vocabulary, Enzo stood and tapped on the door that joined the two rooms. Opening the door and poking his head in, he beckoned for the woman to follow him out of the room. He stood aside to let her pass before closing the door and looking back at his team of people.

Amelia stomped across the room and snatched a rag from a solitary shelf on the wall. Wiping her face and arms with it, he watched it come away pink from specs of blood. She then took his abandoned chair and scooted it closer to Lance who laid an arm over the back of it. Enzo sighed and grabbed a bottle of water from the shelf and handed it to her, after opening it. This earned him a glare from Lance.

"That was completely useless," Amelia grumbled under her breath. Lance dropped his hand to her shoulder, squeezing it comfortingly.

Tom shook his head, "Was that really only fifty joules? He screamed like it was seventy or more."

Amelia nodded, "He doesn't have much of a pain tolerance. I didn't even push the needle all the way into the nerve bundle. He was acting like I was pulling his nails out and beating his hands with a hammer."

"You don't pull nails," Enzo said from where he stood, leaning against the wall with his arms crossed over his chest.

"It isn't my preference. I have to draw the line somewhere," Amelia smiled innocently.

But Enzo knew better, she wouldn't hesitate to slice a man's throat if she wanted to. She had held back.

"It would be entertaining," Lance shrugged, clearly having missed the sarcasm in his girlfriend's voice. He grinned maniacally, like he truly would enjoy watching the atrocity being discussed.

The young woman wrinkled her nose, "I don't think so."

For a brief moment, no one said anything. The only sounds were the sloshing of alcohol in Lance's beer bottle and the whimpering of the man in the other room. Eventually, Tom sighed and went into the other room. He had disappeared momentarily when the sound of bones snapping came from the interrogation room. He stepped back into the observation room as if there hadn't been any noise at all. Enzo raised his brows questioningly now that there weren't any more whimpering coming from their guest.

"Tom!" Amelia said, clearly exasperated, "You didn't snap his neck, did you? I wasn't done yet!"

Tom shrugged, "Sorry, I'll get you a new one."

Enzo shook his head, a small smile gracing his lips, "Okay, have someone find him a permanent resting place later. Hopefully he gave us something helpful in his little rant before Tom went in there."

The man in question grabbed the tablet from the table and tapped it a few times. The recording of the man's rant began to play from the speakers, filling the room with the desperate cries of a man trying to save his own skin. The buzz of electricity hummed in the background of the recording, a sound that hadn't been heard in the observation room.

Lance leaned forward eagerly listening before looking at his girlfriend, laughing, "You refuse to pull fingernails but you'll stick a needle into someone and electrocute them?"

Amelia tossed the bloody rag at him, "I wouldn't expect someone who has no patience for the graceful art of extraction to understand."

Enzo smirked at the comment and raised himself up from the wall. He wasn't the tallest person, something Tom never let him forget, he was still taller than Lance's five foot ten form. The other man looked like every crime family cliche that Enzo had ever seen. Reddish blonde hair pulled into a ponytail on the back of his head, tattoo sleeves on both arms and scruffy, uneven facial hair. Enzo was a stark contrast to the pale man with his olive skin and dark hair. When he didn't pull his own wavy hair back, it hung into his dark eyes, obscuring his view and irritating him. The two were similar in the fact that they both had several tattoos, Enzo's extended onto the back of his hand. A magnificently detailed image of a bear paw was permanently inked into his skin, reminiscent of the nickname he'd earned over time.

Enzo sighed and pinched the bridge of his nose, "He doesn't say much useful in his little outburst, does he? Although the tidbit about the Cruzes is new. That's helpful, so thank you, Amelia."

She nodded but didn't say anything in response. Instead she pulled her blood spattered coat off and tossed it onto the table. Her black tank top revealed her powerful, elegant form. Enzo had noticed over the years that she moved with the grace of a dancer but also with the speed and cunning of a snake.

Her dark jeans looked as though they too were covered in the blood of men she'd tormented. Enzo couldn't help but feel a bit of pride knowing that he had been the one to uncover her talent of extraction.

"Go and shower," He told her, nodding his head at the door, "We'll sort out the puzzle later. Tom, do me a favor and take Lance with you and get rid of the body. I would rather he not stay there long."

Amelia nodded gratefully and left the room, Lance following after her quickly despite Enzo's instructions. The couple disappeared from sight, leaving Tom and Enzo alone in the room. The former was watching the latter scrupulously.

"Have something you'd like to say?" Enzo asked his second in command.

"When are you going to grow a pair and talk to Amelia?" Tom tucked his hands into his pockets, "You're still looking at her differently than you've ever looked at anyone. I can't be the only one who's noticed, you've been in love with the woman for three years."

Enzo gave his friend a dark look, "She's an intolerable sadist who loves to push my buttons. She lives to torment. I don't understand why you are pushing the matter."

Tom chuckled and moved towards the door, turning back before he left, "If she's a sadist, you are a masochist. You enjoy your interactions, you let her push your buttons because it means that her eyes are on you, not Lance, even for a moment."

"Maybe so, but she *is* with Lance. I have to respect that," Enzo sighed.

"I don't think you should," Tom admitted, "I'll take care of our friend in the other room. Don't worry about him."

"I wasn't," Enzo waved his friend off.

He watched his underboss leave the room. His mind wandered back to the conversation. Enzo would love to be able to talk to Amelia, but she was committed to her relationship with Lance.

Enzo had given her a room in his mansion under the guise of needing her close for work reasons, just in case something came up. Over the years, he'd become less sure of his reasoning and wondered if it was just a way to keep her close.

He thought back to the day he met her, she'd just escaped from the Cruz mansion, seeking shelter from them. He'd seen her potential immediately, or rather, she had shown him immediately.

Three Years Ago:

Enzo sat at his desk, Tom standing behind him, in front of them was a young, pale Hispanic woman. Her green eyes pleaded with Enzo, echoing the words she'd only just spoken. He glanced at his second in command, a silent conversation passing between them. Should they trust her? Was she really seeking asylum or was she a spy?

Eventually Enzo sat back, running a hand over his neatly trimmed facial hair. Tom leaned against the wall, hands in his pockets. The young woman glanced between them nervously.

"Alright, Miss Cruz, if what you are telling me is true," Enzo broke the tense silence, "I will give you an opportunity to prove yourself to me. Earn your place in the ranks, so to speak. I would like to create an alliance with your family."

Amelia froze, "If you're looking for a marriage contract, the answer is no.

Or were you not listening to me?"

"Hardly his intentions. The day Berardi looks for a marriage contract is the day all of hell freezes over," Tom laughed from his spot on the wall.

"An agreement, at the very least and I will grant you safety from them," A small smirk played at his lips, "Can we agree on that?"

Enzo knew that it was unlikely for her to jump at his offer, but something about her made him want to give her a chance. Something about her long hair and curious eyes captured his attention. It didn't help that she immediately had her walls up and met him blow for blow verbally, something only Tom could do. Until now.

She sighed and considered his proposition. He watched her, waiting for her to break the silence. Enzo smirked when her face hardened and she met his eyes with a new fire burning in them.

"Fine!" She snapped, "If that's what it takes, go for it. But, leave me out of your negotiations. I've been their pawn and I'm hardly in the mood to be another man's pawn."

Enzo nodded solemnly, "What if I had you as part of the negotiations?"

Tom stood straighter at his words, frowning down at his boss. Enzo couldn't blame him. In his nearly twenty years as Head of a Family, he had never said something so impulsive. He didn't know where the idea came from.

"Are you trying to trick me into some sort of deal with the devil?" Amelia asked dubiously.

Tom chuckled, looking back and forth between her and his friend, "I don't think so. We're simply not going to underestimate the value you could bring to the organization."

Amelia watched Tom curiously then turned to Enzo, clearly waiting for him to reply. He cleared his throat and leaned on the desk, tenting his hands. Amelia leaned back, crossing one leg over another and staring back at him.

"You made an impressive lift when you came in here, Miss Cruz," His words seemed to surprise her, "I believe you have potential within our world. I think you would make a good asset, if only you are willing to prove yourself."

Tom glanced at his wrist before looking back up at her, "Which reminds me, can I get my watch back?"

Enzo Berardi: The Cruz Brothers

Enzo's office was only a floor above where he'd been earlier, but it was a different world. The room was simple and tasteful with its honey colored wood floors. The upholstery was a beautiful shade of sage green, his mother's favorite color. His father's decor tastes shone through with the sparse crimson accents placed around the room.

Enzo couldn't help but feel calmer in the room, unsure if it was because of the colors or the fact that his father used to sit in the very same chair he now sat in. Everyday he was reminded of fond memories of his parents' playful arguments over the decor. Leon Berardi would tell his wife it was hardly befitting of a mafia boss, while Lucia would tell him that dark colors weren't comfortable and welcoming. In the end, Lucia Berardi got her way and the room was decorated in light colors. Leon had admitted to his son that if his mother had asked for pink upholstery he still would've given in.

"My son, the secret is this; it was never about the color. It was always about what she wanted. As long as she was happy with her choice, I was happy with it."

It wasn't long after that conversation when Enzo and his mother lost his father. It had nearly broken Lucia. In his nightmares, Enzo could still hear the guttural sound that his mother made when they'd been told. She clutched the wall to hold herself up, allowing herself only a moment to grieve before turning to her son. She'd held him close. She'd even held Tom close, raising him as her own from that time on since he had lost his own father that same night.

Enzo would forever admire his mother's strength. He hadn't begrudged her when she'd finally left the city. He understood the desire to leave. There were days when he wanted to escape.

Twenty years later, they had both grown from their grief, but it would never really leave them. Neither would truly heal, the pain of loss refused to leave, they simply grew around it. It lingered and all they could do was cling to one another and take it a day at a time.

Enzo watched the clouds float by from the window, lost in thought. He mulled over the words from the downstairs guest. The man had confirmed a suspicion Enzo held for a while; the Cruzes were starting to play the game. He wondered when they had decided to step up to the plate. For twenty years, the eldest Cruz sibling had played his cards close to the vest and had chosen to carefully curate his image.

Enzo's phone lit up, Tom's name illuminating the screen. With a groan, he answered the call, "Tomaso."

"Hey, I ran down the info from our friend," Tom said. "And? What'd you find?"

"I would guess that you're asking yourself why the Cruzes decided to start moving now, right?" Enzo could hear the smirk in Tom's voice, "Benjamin Cruz has been calling the shots. He's the primary person driving their movement right now. Or at least he was for the past couple of years."

"Where's Angel in all of it?" Enzo asked, his annoyance at his friend's mind reading gone.

"Approving it all. He's still acting as leader, in fact, apparently they've started letting the Hagans into the speakeasy under his approval," Tom told him. He sounded bored, like the information hadn't been worth his time to retrieve,

"There might be a meeting there tonight."

Enzo was inclined to agree. They'd known the Hagans and the Cruzes had been dancing around an alliance for years. Since before Amelia had defected. It had been one of the reasons she'd left. The rumors of the alliance had flared in the past three years, but had never been solidified.

"Anything else?" Enzo asked.

"Nothing that will actually interest you," Tom chuckled dryly.

Enzo cracked a smile, "General work things?"

"Yep," Tom affirmed, "The usual, shipments coming in late, collecting rent, scaring the pants off a few people, etcetera."

"I'll let you handle that," Enzo replied, "But let's crash that meeting later. All four of us."

"Sure thing. I'll let you know when I'm done on my end. Let me know what time," Tom hung up the phone leaving Enzo alone with his thoughts.

He glanced at his watch having gotten it back from Amelia shortly after she'd nicked it in their first meeting. His work day was certainly not coming to an end around five like most people's. Pulling himself up from the couch, Enzo moved to the desk. Taking his place behind it, he rifled through the stacks of papers littering the dark wood. His computer was hardly helpful, since his organization worked primarily in illegal imports; a hackable device was not the best place for paperwork. He often wondered how something that operated primarily under the table could accumulate so much paperwork.

*****

The sun had completely set by the time Enzo pulled his car into the parking lot at the Speakeasy. The drive to Manhattan from his home was a miserable one usually, but due to the late hour, the traffic hadn't made the journey exhaustingly long. As he parked, he spotted Lance and Amelia standing near the former's truck.

From where Enzo sat, it seemed like the two were in a discussion that was irritating Amelia. She was frowning and moving her hands around to emphasize her words. Lance had his arms crossed over his chest, a surly expression on his face.

Enzo rolled his eyes. Removing the keys from the ignition and stepping out of the car, he hoped it would pause the couple's argument. He stayed by his car, straightening his cuffs for a brief moment. The raised voices behind him started to quiet down at his arrival, so he took as his cue to approach.

Amelia greeted him first, smiling and nodding her head at him. Enzo greeted her in a similar fashion before giving her a once over. The crimson silk dress clung to her body beautifully in all the right places. A matching red lipstick applied to perfection made her smile that much more stunning if it was possible. The woman's dark hair hung in elegant waves down her back, stopping at her waist and pinned away from her face. Her signature gold earrings swung back and forth when she moved her head to look back at her date.

Lance cleared his throat and dropped a possessive arm over Amelia's shoulders, gaining Enzo's attention. He was wearing a black suit that had yet to be tailored to fit correctly. He clearly had not bothered to try and fix his hair, it remained in the messy bun from earlier that day. The white button down shirt under Lance's jacket was not buttoned all the way up, leaving the silver chain around his neck on display.

Amelia looked back and forth between the two men before interrupting their silent battle, "Shall we?"

Enzo nodded, tugging at the cuffs of his jacket again, a nervous habit disguised as an act of class, "Where's Tom?"

"He called me earlier, he said he's going to be late," Amelia said, a whisper of her accent coming through as she spoke.

Lance placed a hand on her lower back and steered her towards the door, "Are you coming, Boss?"

Enzo followed the two, an uneasy feeling in the pit of his stomach.

The Speakeasy had been founded during the prohibition and maintained the exterior of an old building. The Cruzes restored it as needed, keeping it up to code in the recent decades. A nightclub and casino now occupied the first couple of floors of the building. They sent music pouring out onto the street, the bass vibrating in Enzo's shoes.

Instead of going towards the entrance though, he led them to a set of stairs on the backside of the building. The damp stone led down to an old rusted door which he knocked on carefully.

This entrance looked as though it had seen better days. Graffiti lined the walls, words and images that made little to no sense to anyone but the artist. Ground up cigarette butts lay in the corners along with shredded magazine pages and a single mousetrap that remained tauntingly empty.

A small flap opened in the door when Enzo tapped on it. He murmured quietly to the person on the other side before the flap shut again and the door swung open. The interior of the Speakeasy was a different world than the one outside.

Solid wood floors that were polished to the point where Enzo could see his reflection in them. Sultry music floated from the small jazz band that the Cruzes employed. They sat on a tiny platform in the corner of the main room. Tables filled the floor, men and women dressed to nines from every Family occupied them. A quiet chatter filled the room and the clinking of crystal and bottles came from the bar. Stocked with only the best liquor money could buy, the Cruzes had spared no expense in making the Speakeasy a place of luxury for the Thirteen Families. Due to its location in Manhattan, it also remained a place of neutral territory, meaning that even if a Family was feuding, they might laugh and drink together like old friends while there.

A waiter approached Enzo, "*Signore* Berardi?"

He raised a brow, "*Si?*"

"If you would follow me, your table is prepared," The waiter led the trio to a spiral staircase that took them to a half floor. A private balcony for those whose pockets reached further than the deepest parts of the ocean.

The waiter continued, "The *Señor* Cruzes would like a word."

He knocked on a door and opened it slowly. Inside were the three Cruz brothers. They rose from the table upon their sister's entrance. Enzo watched her from the corner of his eye, taking in her reaction. The Italian nodded respectfully to the brothers as the waiter left the room with a promise to be back with drinks. He was grateful for that, he was quite certain he would need something to help him through the night. All four of the Cruz siblings being in the same room together was usually a ticking time bomb.

Amelia set her face and went to greet her brothers, kissing each on the cheek out of respect for their heritage. She certainly wasn't doing it out of love and neither were they. They returned the gesture, the oldest two doing so with a disdainful look plastered on their faces.

"*¿Qué tal, mi hermanos?*" She asked politely, her smile forced and stiff.

Camilo Cruz grinned over his glass, he set it down to stand and grabbed his sister's hand "*Me siento increíble!*"

She pulled her hand from his, taking a step back, "*Bueno.*"

Enzo had to resist pulling the woman behind him, the urge to protect her from the inevitable barbs her brothers would throw was overwhelming. Lance seemed to sense Enzo's thoughts and sent him a glare before turning back to Amelia. He grabbed her wrist and tugged her closer to him.

Lance rolled his eyes at the Spanish being used, "English, please. Not all of us speak Spanish or feel the need to show off that we do."

Enzo's gaze darkened, so the barbs would come from both sides tonight.

Angel Cruz spoke up, *"Disculpe, señor,* it is our mother tongue."

Enzo sighed, "Forgive him, *Señor* Cruz. Mr. Alexander doesn't know Spanish, so if we could keep the conversation in a mutual tongue, it would be appreciated. *Gracias.*"

The Italian turned to Lance, placing a hand on his shoulder. Leaning in close, he whispered, "Please try not to be brash tonight. We need to glean information."

Lance shrugged his boss' hand off but nodded. Enzo didn't believe for a second that he was actually going to listen but he turned back to the Cruzes anyway. Rolling his shoulders back, Enzo reached for Angel's hand to shake.

"It is a pleasure to see you again, Angel. I hope all is well."

Angel Cruz was the eldest of the four siblings. Louder and larger than life most of the time. He looked nothing like his sister with his darker skin, brown eyes, and lanky walk. While his facial hair was neatly trimmed, even if patchy in some places, his hair was unruly. Curls stuck out in every direction, not a single one going in the same direction.

As per the dress code of the Speakeasy, he wore a suit, albeit very casually.

He'd slung the coat over the back of his chair and rolled his sleeves up to his elbows. His shirt thankfully was fully buttoned, unlike another man in the room who Enzo was perpetually annoyed with.

The second brother was the tallest of the siblings and even stood a couple of inches taller than Enzo. Leaner and more muscular than his brothers, Benjamin was the one he was most wary of. When Enzo had first met with the brothers, Benjamin hardly said anything and just watched with a grouchy expression from the corner.

He looked more like Angel than Amelia with the same dark complexion and dark eyes. His own curls were gelled back until crunchy. A single diamond stud earring caught the light when he turned to give his sister a once over. Benjamin also wore a suit but had kept his jacket on, surprising Enzo.

"Benjamin," Enzo said by way of greeting. He eyed the new goatee the man wore, he suspected it was an effort to appear more intimidating.

The shortest of the three brothers had flung himself into his chair again after greeting Amelia. His flamboyant nature was apparent when he spread his arms and propped his feet on the table. He wore an indigo tuxedo that washed him out to the point where he looked almost as pale as his sister. She was the fairest in complexion due to having a different mother.

Camilo Cruz was already several drinks in, his cheeks tinted pink by the alcohol in his system. His curly hair was ruffled and wild, much like his personality. He grinned at Enzo but there was nothing amicable about it.

Enzo pulled a chair out for Amelia before seating himself next to her. Lance plopped himself on her other side and laid his arm over her chair. Her shoulders pulled forward, keeping her back straight and preventing contact with Lance's arm. Enzo made a mental note to ask her about that later.

Amelia glanced at her older brother with a sigh, "Camilo, I am well aware that this is your establishment, but please, manners. Take your feet off the table!"

"Relax! I'm fine," He rolled his eyes but moved his feet to the floor.

Enzo chuckled, "Have to remember our manners, mustn't we?"

Before anyone could say another word, a tap sounded on the door. The waiter had returned, drinks in hand and Tom in tow. He stepped into the room after the waiter who carefully placed the drinks on the table. He held the door open for the man to exit through a moment later.
   Tom looked spectacular in his suit, neatly put together and lethal looking. Amelia rose from her seat to greet him with a kiss on the cheek.

Enzo nodded to his underboss, "Dante, glad you could make
   it."

"I'm glad I could. I apologize for my tardiness, there was an unexpected turn of events that needed to be dealt with," Tom eyed his boss, the message in the words clear.

Enzo nodded in understanding. Something might require his attention later. Or Lance's if not a lot of finesse was needed.

"Angel," Amelia caught her brother's attention, "You were expecting us. I don't remember making a reservation, was there an invitation I missed?"

Benjamin answered instead of his brother, "*Hermanita*, you should know we have eyes on everything. We also know when a V.I.P. is on the way."

Camilo jumped in, "You are always welcome here, baby sister. You are *familia* after all."

"*Familia* doesn't try to sell off their sister to form an alliance," She growled.

Enzo held a hand up to prevent her from continuing and potentially turning their situation into an explosive one. The agreement between the Cruzes and his organization was already rocky at best. He didn't want to risk something happening before he knew what was happening with the Hagans.

"*¡Dios mio!* You've got to let that go!" Benjamin said in an exasperated tone.

"Anyway!" Tom interjected, "We came because we heard some interesting rumors and wanted to make sure they weren't true."

"Thank you, Tomaso, for bringing us back on track," Enzo rubbed his temples. The siblings seemed to enjoy being a powder keg ready to explode. The trick was finding the right timing to keep them from going off.

"What rumors," Angel asked, swirling the tequila in his glass.

"The rumors that you are resuming negotiations with the Hagans. And that you are sending men into our territory. Again," Enzo shrugged, nonchalantly, "You know how the Commission feels about that."

Benjamin scoffed, "Two out of the Big Three are involved in the negotiations, so it would seem to me, you are the only person who would object to an alliance."

Amelia sighed, "Benjamin, we aren't the only ones who would care and you know that. The other ten will have something to say, even if they're your tenants."

Angel glared at her, "Amelia, *por favor*, the adults are talking."

Lance laughed out loud, amusement twinkling in his eyes. Enzo shot him a frown before speaking, "I'd watch your language, Angel. Amelia isn't part of your organization anymore. She's part of mine and therefore under the protection of the Berardi family name."

"You've been making friends, *hermanita*," Benjamin groused.

"So have you," She retorted, "The Hagans are dangerous and if you really think that they would hold onto their end of a deal, you are fooling yourselves. Act ignorant and you will become enlightened when you least expect it."

Camilo leaned forward, "The last time I checked, Berardi was the one considered the most dangerous. How is this any different from you joining him?"

"Loyalty," Tom said, "The Berardi family has a reputation of loyalty. Something the Hagans do not have, and you know it."

Enzo chuckled dryly, "Isn't it nice when your people are so loyal that you don't even have to come to your own defense?"

Benjamin glared at him, "Or they're scared of you, so they don't want to-"

A tap on the door called the attention of the room, silencing the rest of Benjamin's sentence. The server stepped inside apologetically, handing a piece of paper to Benjamin. With a nod, the waiter left quickly. The Cruz brothers leaned their heads together to study the note.

"You're either purposely being stupid or you actually are stupid if you're really considering an alliance again," Tom groaned, ignoring the waiter.

Benjamin spared Tom a glance before raising from his chair, "You've made your opinion clear."

Angel looked up at Enzo and his team, "I'm sorry, we'll have to cut this short. Something's come up that requires our attention."

"Please, go, take care of your people," Enzo waved them off like he understood. He had a feeling they were going to meet with the Hagans, "We will show ourselves out."

Enzo stood and offered a hand to Amelia. She took it and rose from her chair gracefully but dropped his hand quickly. Lance once again placed a hand on her back and led her from the room. He lowered his head to her ear and whispered furiously causing Amelia's expression to become stony. Tom and Enzo followed them quickly, bidding goodbye to the Cruz brothers.

Outside in the parking lot, Enzo and Tom could see Amelia standing with Lance by his car. They were speaking too low for the men to understand but as they approached, some of the words became clearer. Lance was very clearly mad at Amelia about something, but Enzo wasn't sure what it was this time.

Tom rolled his eyes, "I'll let you deal with that. I'll see you back at the house."

Enzo frowned, "Thank you so much for that."

"Think nothing of it, I know how much you enjoy breaking up their arguments," Tom grinned and clapped his friend on the shoulder, "By the way, here."

He pulled a couple of bills from his pocket and handed them to Enzo. He looked at them trying to understand before he remembered the bet they'd had earlier. Tom was paying up.

"Thanks," Enzo shook his head, amused, "Have a good night, Dante."

The blonde man waved and walked off towards his own car. He was pulling out of the parking lot in seconds, his car revving loudly like he was gloating to Enzo about not needing to deal with the couple. Enzo flipped him a rude gesture before approaching Amelia and Lance.

"Berardi, this is a private matter if you don't mind," Lance snapped, placing a hand on Amelia's shoulder, turning her away from their boss.

"As much as I hate to break up this joyful little discussion, I am here to take Amelia home. The last time I checked, her residence was in my mansion, not your apartment," Enzo tucked his hands into his pockets and shrugged.

"I'll drop her off," Lance rolled his eyes, "Amelia, get in the car."

Enzo watched the young woman look back and forth between the two men before sighing, "I'll be there in a moment, Berardi. Lance, love, go home. Now isn't the best time for us to talk about this anyway."

Lance glared, "Fine. But we *will* talk about it later."

"I know," Amelia pressed a kiss to his cheek before following their boss to his car.

Enzo stopped at the passenger side and opened it for the young woman. Glancing behind at the other man, he found Lance glaring at him through the open window of his truck. The tires screeched as he pulled it into the night traffic of the city.

After getting into the car himself, Enzo sat for a moment before saying, "I'm not going to apologize for interrupting that."

Amelia waved him off, "You're protective of your people and you got worried. It isn't the first time you've stepped in and it won't be the last."

"I'm glad you're not yelling at me over it," He chuckled. Rubbing a hand down his face, Enzo pulled his car onto the road and pointed them in the direction of home. Hardly taking time away from work had left him with subtle rings under his eyes from lack of sleep.

Amelia seemed to notice it because she asked suddenly, "Enzo, have you been getting enough sleep?"

"I'm fine. Will you be after tonight?" He asked, turning it around on her.

"I'm fine," She echoed his words back at him.

"I have a job for you, by the way," Enzo said, "Should be fairly simple."

"How simple?"

Enzo grinned, "Easy enough that it will be quick, but entertaining enough to keep your little sadistic mind engaged."

Amelia grinned, "What is it?"

Amelia Cruz: The Task

"Easy my foot!" Amelia grumbled, "I'm going to skin Berardi alive for this."

In theory the task was simple, but in reality...

Enzo Berardi had given Amelia a box of bugging devices, cameras and other wiretapping materials with the instruction of putting them inside the Cruzes' house.

The very same house that Manuel Cruz, the founder of the Cruz Cartel had built to keep people in *and* out.

It was a gorgeous *hacienda*, inspired by the family's roots in Mexico. Three stories of brick carefully coated with orange clay. The four walls wrapped around a tile floor that complimented the coloring of the house. In the center of the courtyard stood a large moss covered fountain, perpetually keeping silence away. Vines crawled up the outside of the house, the banisters in the courtyard, and around the pillars framing the door.

Amelia could remember the day her Tio Blas had taught her to climb those very same vines. Her mother had made her swear never to do it again. She'd kept the promise to her mother all the way up until now, those vines would be her way in.

She stared at the house wondering where would be the best to start. The first floor didn't worry her as much as the top two. The top floor held several offices, the Head's and his second in command's usually. The lady of the house also had her own office but Amelia seriously doubted her brothers would say anything interesting in there considering the last woman to occupy the room. Their mother had died and their father had married Amelia's mother less than a year later. Amelia joined the family shortly thereafter.

The second floor was where the bedrooms were. Both family rooms and guest rooms. Amelia felt sorry for the staff of the house, always having to keep the unused rooms clean on top of the rest of the house. Her brothers had never valued cleanliness and often would cause messes just to torment the staff.

Amelia leaned over the front of her motorcycle, using binoculars to scope out the guards. Only four of them could be seen from her position. A relatively easy number to handle if that really was all. It also helped that Tom was sitting on his motorcycle only a few feet away.

She glanced over at him. He was assembling a tranquilizer gun across the fuel tank. The beautiful weapon clicked softly as he slid the clip home. Amelia knew it was filled with darts designed to knock a man unconscious for several hours and she also knew that Tom didn't miss. He was assessing the house from the corner of his eye, counting the guards and looking for her point of entry.

"What?" She asked him when he made a face at the house, "See something?"

"Nothing, just not exactly a fan of this place," He shrugged, hoisting the gun into position.

"That makes two of us. You're staying here though, I'm the one going in," She whispered.

"I never assumed otherwise. I'm only here as backup in the case of an emergency," Tom replied smoothly.

As if to prove his point, he set the gun aside and pulled a tablet from his bag. He showed her that it would connect with the cameras she would be placing. Once activated, he'd be able to see everything. He also removed an in-ear communication device from his pocket and offered it to her.

Amelia eyed her coworker suspiciously, wondering if Berardi had sent him to keep an eye on her rather than the house. She accepted the device nonetheless and was still grateful for the backup. She made a mental note to ask Tom later.

"I think I'm going to start on the second floor in the bedrooms and work my way up," She told him.

Tom placed his own comm in his ear, "I'll be here."

The young woman waited until her friend had raised his gun again before darting across the street to the wall surrounding the house. Even with the vines to provide extra handholds for her, the old brick was worn enough that it was easy for her to climb. She stopped at the top of the wall to observe the grounds, noting the absence of her brothers' cars, Amelia slipped down to the ground.

"Take the guards out," She whispered into her comm.

A moment later, the first guard collapsed, then the second, the third, and the fourth. Each dropped like a sack of potatoes, and each had a feathered dart protruding from their necks. Amelia slipped from her spot next to the wall and crept across the lawn, keeping her eyes open for any other potential threats.

In the blink of an eye, the woman had crossed the yard and was scurrying up the sides of the *hacienda*. The vines assisted her ascent up to one of the balconies. The door standing before her was locked only for a moment. Amelia had learned how to pick the locks to her brothers' rooms from a young age and it had been a skill she had not lost. The door swung open, allowing her to enter Camilo's room.

Enzo had instructed her to place cameras and bugs inside the bedrooms. Knowing their informal approach to conversations, he didn't want to risk missing something. Amelia had cringed at the idea of potentially listening to her brothers' bedroom activities but was following her boss' command anyway.

The floor was littered with laundry and magazines, the covers of which had either cars or half dressed women or both. Amelia rolled her eyes at the disastrous room. Tiptoeing to the bed, she slipped the first bug into place. It was no bigger than her thumbnail, adhering to the frame. Another bug was placed under the bottom drawer in his desk. A camera in the closet, on the light fixture and balanced on the frame of a portrait of Camilo. The portrait was an odd thing, Amelia's brother was posing across a chaise lounge chair wearing a leopard print shirt that fell open revealing his entire torso. One the left side of his chest, over his heart was their family's crest, inked into his skin.

Amelia rolled her eyes at it, half tempted to draw a mustache over her brother's face. The intrusive thought was soon banished from her mind. The faint sound of footsteps echoed in the hall outside of the room.

"Tom, someone's in the hall," She whispered, freezing in place, "Do you have eyes?"

Amelia was met with silence. The comm was eerily silent. Swearing under her breath, Amelia crept to the door, sliding a knife from her sheath at the same time. The footsteps were getting louder, closer to Camilo's room, she silently prayed the person wouldn't enter the room.

Waiting had always been hard for Amelia, the uncertainty of not knowing what was going to happen, it was like a war raging in her head. Two sides fighting for dominance, what was happening versus what could happen.

The footsteps stopped just outside and of course it was that moment the door to the balcony creaked. Somehow Amelia hadn't shut it all the way and the wind was aiding whoever was outside in finding her. The doorknob twisted, the mystery person was coming in.

The door opened revealing a guard that Amelia and Tom had missed. She clocked the moment he saw her, recognizing her as a Cruz but she didn't give him the chance to do anything.

Amelia lunged at the man, knife in hand. Unfortunately for her, the guard was prepared and caught her. His gun slipped from his hands, swinging from its tether around one of his shoulders. One of his hands wrapped around her throat, the other encircled her wrist, stopping her knife from plunging into his own neck.

She didn't allow him to hold her long, swinging her other arm around and clapping his ear, rupturing his eardrum. Instinctively, the guard dropped her and clutched at his ear in agony.

"This could've been so much easier if you hadn't come in here," Amelia sighed like she was bored.

The guard growled at her taunt and reached for her, but she danced out of his reach. Laughing, Amelia darted in at the man and jabbed a hand at his throat. With the wind knocked out of him, the man fell to his knees gasping for air.

"See, this isn't even fun," Amelia whined.

She sauntered around behind the man and rolled her eyes. The challenge was not having to deal with a singular person but rather what would happen when his comrades realized he was missing. Would they swarm? Call her brothers home? What would they do? Since Amelia didn't have answers for those questions, she knew that it was time to pick up the pace.

"I would say I'm sorry about this, but I'm not," Amelia said. She reached around the man's head and jerked his chin swiftly. There was the crunch of bones and then silence. The guard keeled over, dead. She sighed, "You recognized me and I can't have anyone telling Angel I was here."

She slipped from the room and into the hall. It overlooked the courtyard where several other guards were walking around. They circled the bubbling fountain, the only sound was their footsteps and the running water. Amelia realized her brothers were getting smarter by placing guards. Either that or they had been instructed to by their new friends.

Hugging the wall, staying in the shadows, the young woman tiptoed to the next room; Benjamin's.

His room was cleaner than their brother's but it reeked of cologne and hair gel. Posters of cars were pinned on every inch of the walls, polished wrenches sat in size order on the shelves. Model cars arranged like trophies decorated the desk and dresser.

"Obsessive much?" Amelia huffed.

She slipped bugs into the bed frame and desk like she had in the previous room. Finding a small model replica of a GT 40 with that door opened was a pleasant surprise as it allowed her to place a small camera inside. The last camera she set in Benjamin's room was carefully attached in a dark corner, near the ceiling with a perfect view of the bedroom door. With a satisfied nod, Amelia left the room. Outside in the hall once again, she gave the courtyard a once over.

She had originally thought that a viable escape route would be down the stairs and out through the first floor, but with the new guards, that wasn't an option. She needed to be quick if she wanted to be able to leave the same way she'd come in.

But the guards had started congregating in one spot instead of continuing their marching. Amelia grit her teeth, realizing they must have realized that the outside guards weren't replying or that something had happened to one of the guards inside of the *hacienda*.

There were quite a few unattended rooms on the second floor, but only one Amelia had to make it to. Angel's. It was the closest to the master suite which had remained empty since their parents' death several years prior.

Amelia paused, what if Angel had switched in the years since she'd left?

Swearing under her breath, she moved to what she hoped was still Angel's room. He usually kept his door locked out of habit. While it had been a deterrent for her when she was a curious toddler, the locked door meant nothing now. Pins flashed in her fingers when she inserted them into the lock. A few taps and a click later the door gave way. She hesitated, waiting to see if the guards had heard her above their worried conversation. When they didn't seem to move in her direction, she stepped into the room. Sending up a silent prayer of thanks to whoever was listening when she stepped into what was still her eldest brother's room.

It was the largest of the three bedrooms she'd been in so far.

The bed was unmade with the sheets tossed over the side and the comforter thrown over the foot board. Pajama bottoms lay in a pile near the en suite bathroom, the door was ajar, allowing the woman to peek inside. The counter had toiletries strewn across it haphazardly, the toothbrush being the only thing in its place.

Sports balls of every kind decorated the shelves, arranged in size order. Sports jerseys and hats hung in the closet amid the suits and work clothes. On the desk sat an old family photo. It showed Antonio Cruz with his first wife, Carmen, and their three sons. One of Antonio's hands rested on Angel's shoulder, the other on his wife's. He was looking down at the woman lovingly, a look he'd never given Amelia's mother. Camilo sat on his mother's lap in the photo, he couldn't have been more than two years old in the photo. Benjamin was hugging his mother on the side their father wasn't, his hair was wild and untamed, his ear hadn't been pierced yet. Each of the Cruz boys had a beautiful youthful innocence about them in the photo. It must've been taken right before Carmen had passed.

Amelia felt envy rise in herself, she and her mother had never had the chance to have a photo like this. Antonio Cruz hadn't cared to. Growing up he'd made it clear to Amelia that she was going to be married off once she turned eighteen, she would help him form a new alliance. He never praised her the way he would praise his sons. Antonio wanted his daughter to know exactly what her purpose was in life and his sons had followed his lead. When Maria Cruz died, leaving Amelia alone, her father became worse. He grew even colder towards her and she hadn't ever stopped to consider why. So desperate for her father's love, Amelia had been convinced she had deserved the treatment.

"Psst!" A voice pulled Amelia from her jealous thoughts. She set the picture frame down suddenly and looked up, "Are you going to place more cameras or are you calling it quits?"

Tom had been following her movements by using the very same devices she was planting and he'd noticed when she had stopped moving.

"Sorry," She whispered into the comms, "Lost in thought."

"You can't afford to do that right now," He chastised, "Hurry up, the inside guards are mobilizing."

"Yeah, that reminds me, where've you been?" She asked while placing the bugs.

"Dealing with the bodies," Tom grunted, sounding like he was heaving something on his end.

Amelia placed the last bug, "I have to put these in the office!"

"Then you need to get to the next floor quickly," Tom told her like she wasn't already aware.

She glanced around the room and darted back towards the door, locking it just as the footsteps of guards approached the door. The knob rattled when they tried it. Their harsh voices commanded others to move on and examine the next room.

Amelia's heart pounded. Running out to the balcony, she scanned the side of the house, the vines went all the way up to the next floor. She swung herself from the balcony and onto them, crawling at a snail's pace to get to the office.

The upper rooms all connected with one another, each one leading to the next and each with a door to the landing. It made a convenient set up for Amelia to slip through quickly and set cameras. She nestled a few into the books in the library among the Spanish volumes she knew her brothers wouldn't touch. Bugs under couches and desks, stuck to lamp shades and on the back of portrait frames.

Still undetected, she made it to the brothers' main office. It was laid out exactly the same as the last time she'd been in there, three years earlier when Angel and Benjamin had tried to create a marriage contract.

She walked around the furniture, lightly dragging her fingers over it, the memory of that night playing in her mind. With a sigh she shook herself out of the memory, she was there with a purpose. Bugs were placed quickly and discreetly around the study, hidden to the point they would be nearly impossible to find even if someone knew where to look.

With one last look around, Amelia moved to the balcony and froze. Cars were pulling into the driveway. Her brothers were back.

Tom swore in her earpiece, "Amelia, get out of there!"

"How?" She hissed back, "They can see the windows from the parking lot and the guards are flooding the inside route!"

"Then hide!"

A glance around the room told her that there weren't any good options. Without having time to prepare, Amelia tucked herself behind the curtains behind the main desk. The window looked out over the front lawn, she could see the cars in the driveway.

When the door opened and the three brothers stepped in, Amelia had hidden herself as carefully as she could with the little time she'd had. From the sound of their voices, they had been told about the missing guard.

The door slammed open, rattling the frames on the wall. Three distinct footsteps stormed into the room, angry voices following. Amelia held her breath and prayed that the curtain wouldn't sway and give her away.

"How the hell did this happen?" Benjamin was demanding of no one in particular.

"Sweet hiding spot, Cruz," Tom whispered in Amelia's ear. Clearly he had found his way back to the tablet he was supposed to be watching.

"I want to know how we didn't see this coming," Angel's voice grew and faded several times. Even without seeing him, Amelia knew he was burning a hole in the floor from his pacing.

"They came to the speakeasy, we should've seen it coming," Camilo sighed.

There was a scrape of furniture as he flopped onto one of the couches.

Amelia could feel her heart pounding in her chest and wondered if it was loud enough to hear. Craning her neck as far as she dared, she listened intently. Determined to catch every word.

Perhaps if her brothers gave up something now, they wouldn't need to monitor the cameras for very long. The men continued their conversation:

"Speaking of my speakeasy and that conversation," Camilo stifled a yawn, trying to talk through it, "Why did you start the negotiations with the Hagans again? Without Amelia, what could we possibly have to offer?"

"I am curious, Angel, what did you say to them that got them on board?" Benjamin stopped moving around, suddenly curious, the anger ebbing away from his voice.

Amelia could imagine Angel's smug face as he stopped pacing too, "Our beloved sister."

Her breath caught in her throat, had they found her?

But Angel continued, "I offered them Amelia and an opportunity to take down Berardi."

Camilo scoffed, "She'll never do it."

"She doesn't have a choice. By the traditions of our family, she belongs to us until we marry her off," Angel growled, "Berardi was a fool when he placed her so close to power within his organization. We can use what she knows and add it to what the Hagans already know. It's everything we need to rid this city of Berardi for good."

"I thought the Hagans were in the dark too?" Camilo yawned again.

Amelia nodded, grateful her brother voiced her thoughts for her. The Hagans were not usually a family she enjoyed dealing with and yet, she'd run into them on several occasions. They were a ruthless family without morals or ideals.

Angel cackled menacingly and the hairs on the back of Amelia's neck stood on end, "Hagan's had a spy on the inside of Berardi's organization for years."

Amelia's heart plummeted. This was not going to go over well with Berardi or anyone in the organization. Tom seemed to share her sentiments and swore colorfully in her ear.

"How?" Camilo asked, stunned. Amelia couldn't blame him, she wanted to know too.

Benjamin spoke at the same time, "How do you intend to get our sister to join us? She's pretty loyal to Berardi and that boyfriend of hers."

"That's a part of the plan I hadn't gotten to yet," Angel admitted.

Benjamin hummed thoughtfully, "What if you do what our father did with Tio Blas?"

"Explain," Angel demanded.

"Twist the relationship. Father made Tio Blas think the girl he was in love with was only trying to glean secrets to take back to their enemies," Benjamin acquiesced to his brother's command.

Amelia remembered the incident he referred to. She'd been closest to their uncle, she'd seen the personality shift when he thought his love had betrayed him. Blas Cruz had become bitter and cold hearted towards the world, kind to no one except his niece.

When Tio Blas had discovered his brother's treachery, he'd gone to beg his love to come back to him. But she'd married someone else and Blas was met with a bullet. He'd died with the woman's name and an apology on his lips.

"So we twist the relationship and make one of them push the other out?" Angel clarified.

"Yes, and we make it seem like Berardi is aloof to the whole thing," Benjamin said, "It could send her running back to us."

Somewhere in the *hacienda*, a great clock sounded out two tolls.

Angel sighed at the sound, "I like it. But right now I have to deal with the fact that Berardi sent his goons into our home. We'll hammer out the plan in the morning."

Camilo yawned yet again, "Fine by me!"

From the shuffling, Amelia assumed that Camilo had gotten up and left the other two brothers alone. They sat in silence for a moment, the air thick with unspoken words. It seemed like they wanted to say something, but neither could figure out the right way to start.

Finally, Angel yawned and moved towards the door. Just before he stepped through, he said to his brother, "If our mother was alive, do you think she'd be disappointed in us?"

Benjamin murmured softly, "Maybe. But if our father were alive, he'd be proud. He'd say we're finally stepping up. Truthfully, I think Maria would be disappointed too."

Amelia nearly choked at the mention of her mother. Her brothers had never seemed to like her despite the effort she'd put in to be there for them. To hear her brothers consider her disappointment was surprising and even touching.

"I couldn't care less what Maria would have thought," Angel snapped.

Slightly less touching now.

"Maria and our father proved that they were willing to break tradition with our sister!" Angel ground out through grit teeth, "They gave Amelia the same place as me, if she ever wanted, she could try to make a claim to the Headship of our family."

Benjamin sighed, "Angel, have you ever considered that they weren't trying to usurp you but just pick a pretty name for a girl? Have you ever looked at the 'D' names in our family tree? They're not exactly the nicest sounding names."

"She's the first born of another woman, she is technically a first born, she could make a claim," Angel seethed.

Benjamin groaned, "Okay, Angel, whatever helps you sleep at night. I've never known our sister to have Headship ambitions, but, hey, I've been wrong before."

Angel growled and stormed from the room without another word. However, Benjamin stayed back in the study. He moved and came to stand next to the window Amelia had hidden by. She held her breath, Tom urgently whispering in her ear to stay still and not move a single muscle. Her heart was beating so hard it felt like it was going to jump from her chest. Benjamin was so close that she could hear his breathing and smell his cologne.

"Just you wait, Amelia," Benjamin whispered, "We're coming for you and we will get our vengeance."

Amelia closed her eyes, waiting for the curtain to be pulled away. Instead, she heard the door open and close. Then, nothing. He was gone. Amelia let out the breath she was holding. She was in the clear, for now.

Amelia Cruz: A Mole

Amelia didn't breathe evenly again until she was on her bike putting miles in between herself and her family home. Her heart rate didn't slow down until she was pulling into the driveway at the Berardi mansion. Tom pulled in moments after her, casting her yet another concerned look. He'd attempted to check in on her several times on their ride but had been completely ignored.

Amelia pulled her helmet off, releasing her long braid. It fell down her back and strands of hair that had come loose blew into her face. She set her helmet onto the dash and groaned, dropping her head back to stare at the night sky.

"What. The. Hell?" She chuckled humorlessly, "What just happened?"

"I have next to no idea," Tom yanked his own helmet off and dropped it onto the handle of his bike, "But, I have a feeling that our search for this spy is going to derail our surveillance of the Cruzes. I just can't believe they think they can still force you into a marriage contract."

"Without the Commission's approval? Please. It'll never get through," Amelia scoffed, then stopped and turned to Tom, "Right? They can't force me to come back, right? I know the Cruz family traditions, but the Commission can't demand that I follow them, right?"

Tom walked over and placed his hands on her shoulders, "Amelia, take a breath. You're under the protection of the Berardis, they can't do anything without declaring war."

Amelia took a deep breath, trying to steady herself. It was hard for her to remember she was protected and valued sometimes. After a lifetime of being told that she was only around to be sold off, it was hard to remind herself that she had a purpose beyond that now.

"Tonight was a great example of how clueless your brothers are. Six inches away from you and they never knew. They have no idea how this world really works and it shows," Tom threw his head back laughing, "We can't be surprised by their lack of protocol. I would love to know who they plan to marry off when they realize that you aren't coming back to them. Camilo? Benjamin? I'd love to see him in a pretty white dress."

Amelia laughed at the image, "That is an excellent question. But also, who are they bartering with now?"

"Another fabulous question," Tom admitted.

Amelia shook her head, smiling to herself. Glancing at Tom she thanked her lucky stars for him, for his role in her life and for being the older brother she needed.

"If our Tio Blas was still around," She murmured, "He'd knock some sense into them. Not for making a contract, but for not thinking out each step first. He might have taught me to fight, but he was still stuck in the dark ages. I think maybe in part, due to his broken heart."

Tom chuckled, "I remember when he was still around. Mine and Enzo's fathers would always panic. Thinking they might have missed something in their own plans, they would triple check everything because Blas could always find the fault, that singular hairline crack."

She laughed, "That sounds like him. He used to make me do logic puzzles growing up so that I would be able to find faults like he could, did I ever tell you that?"

Tom barked out a laugh, "No wonder you irritate Berardi so much!"

"I don't do it on purpose!" She cried defensively, grabbing the first thing she could and chucking it at his head, "it just happens!"

He caught her keys with ease and held them up, raising an eyebrow, "Really? I don't believe that for a single second."

Amelia frowned and held her hand out, "Give those back!"

"I don't think so, you threw them," He held them over his head, "Finders keepers and all that."

"Tomaso Alessio Dante, give those back!" Amelia scrambled off her motorcycle, nearly knocking it over in the process, and tried to jump to grab the keys, "I need those!"

"For what? You live here and you're not going anywhere else tonight, are you?" He gestured to the front door.

Amelia rolled her eyes and put her hands on her hips, "Yes, I do live here, but that doesn't mean that I wouldn't like to have my keys back."

Still chuckling, Tom finally handed the keys back to her. He sighed and looked up at the house, " You know, given how often we have late nights like these, it's probably a good thing we both live at the mansion rather than someplace where we would disturb the neighbors."

Amelia smiled, "Who says we aren't disturbing the neighbors? I mean, technically speaking, Berardi is our neighbor."

The door opened and out stepped Enzo Berardi, as if he had been summoned, "Yes, I am. And you *are* disturbing the neighbor."

Amelia looked at Tom for a split second before the two of them burst into laughter. Enzo leaned against the door frame, an amused expression on his face. The Hispanic woman glanced his way and chuckled.

Amelia walked up the steps to him and patted his shoulder, "Sorry to have disrupted your beauty sleep, Mr. Grumpy-pants."

"I was waiting for you two, actually," Enzo admitted.

The young woman turned to face him, "Oh really? Well then, get the booze, you're going to need a drink for this one."

Tom stepped into the house and tossed Amelia the bag from her bike, shutting the door behind himself. He moved towards Enzo's office, not bothering to see if the other two were following him. They were, Amelia first, Enzo following steps after, shaking his head. Amelia flopped across one of the couches and propped her feet on the coffee table, letting her head fall back. She let out a sigh, the only thing betraying how tired she felt in the late hours of the night. Tom sat across from her in a high backed armchair, leaning forward and propped his elbows on his knees.

"So, did you learn anything tonight? Or are we waiting to see if the cameras pick anything up?" Enzo asked. His back was to them as he poured whiskey into tumblers.

Amelia looked up at him, "Um, well, I'm really not sure where to start actually."

Enzo approached her, holding a glass of wine out. She accepted it, grateful he remembered her preferred poison. He offered a whiskey to Tom, who took it and held it up as if toasting his thanks. Enzo took a seat on the same couch as Amelia, glancing at her expectantly.

Amelia continued, "the big thing we learned is Hagan has a spy. A mole within our organization. Apparently the information that this guy sends back is more than surface deep."

A muscle twitched in Enzo's jaw but he said nothing. He kept his reactions small and minimal, containing them as best as he could. Amelia watched, hoping for some emotion, something to prove human reactions existed in Enzo. She had warned him about bottling things up before but he never seemed to listen.

Tom spoke up, breaking the eye contact between his boss and coworker, "My best estimate would be around that around the time the original contract between the Hagans and Cruzes was dissolved is when they stuck this guy in."

"That was three years ago!" Amelia exclaimed, "What you're suggesting sounds more like a sleeper agent than a mole."

"That's exactly what I am suggesting," Tom scrubbed a hand over his face.

Before Amelia could respond, her phone began to ring, Lance's name illuminating the screen. She frowned before answering it, "*¡Hola!* Love, why are you awake? It's after two in the morning!"

Tom looked at Enzo, concern written on his face, "Why is he calling her right now?"

Enzo's expression was thunderous, but he shook his head. Amelia pointed a crimson painted nail at both of them, a warning. Tom held his hands up in surrender and sat back to enjoy his drink. Enzo however, leaned forward like he was trying to catch every word spoken on both ends of the conversation.

"You were worried because you saw where I was? What do you mean?" Amelia's brow scrunched, "You have a tracking app on my phone? When did you install that?"

"I've been getting worried about some of what Berardi's been making you do, my love," Lance admitted, "I put one of those family tracking apps on your phone because I was worried about your safety. How am I supposed to protect you if I don't know where you are?"

"When did you do that?" Amelia asked again, not nearly as gentle as the first time she asked, "Don't you trust me to handle myself?"

"Only recently!" Lance snapped defensively, "It isn't that I don't trust you, I don't trust Berardi. He watches you all the time, I swear he's trying to steal you from me. He has you staying at his house when you could and should move in with me! It's my job to protect you!"

Amelia sighed and rubbed her temple as if warding off a headache, "Lance, honey, I love you and I appreciate your concern, but-"

"No buts, Lia!" He interrupted her, "You shouldn't have to do half of what he makes you do for him. It's disrespectful. I have half a mind to take it up with the Commission!"

"Okay, why don't we talk about this in the morning over breakfast?" Amelia sighed again, "I'll come over in the morning and we can make the doughnuts you like so much."

"Okay, I love you," Lance acquiesced.

Amelia hung up the phone and dropped it onto the cushion next to her, "I'm sorry. Do you think we can finish this later?"

"He knows you lived here before you started a relationship with him, right?" Tom asked.

"Yes. But it doesn't matter," She groaned, "It took him over a year to reconcile with the fact that you and I never were and never will be a thing."

"You're kidding," Tom looked stunned, "Seriously? Had he never heard us use the term 'sibling' in reference to each other?"

"Not kidding," Amelia shrugged, "I guess that's just how relationships are. He wants to make sure I'm safe, and that's commendable."

"Amelia, that's not how relationships are," Enzo spoke up, "That is controlling. He went behind your back and put a tracker on your phone, that isn't protective, that's possessive. And frankly, a little predatorial."

"That is protective," Amelia argued, "He's looking out for me."

"Obsessive," Tom countered.

"Loving," She stated.

"Domineering," Enzo shrugged nonchalantly, leaning back on the couch, "We can keep going back and forth naming adjectives all night if you'd like. But it isn't going to change the fact that we have differing opinions."

"Okay, my dating life was not the reason the three of us were in the office talking at two thirty in the morning," Amelia snapped, trying to change the topic. Her tone was defensive and laced with frustration. She left no room to argue. The conversation was either over or switching back to the previous subject.

Enzo looked her up and down and shook his head, "Go get some rest. Both of you. I appreciate what you two did tonight. Tomorrow we'll start our hunt for the mole."

Tom nodded and stood up, stretching his hands over his head, "G'night, Boss. Goodnight, Amelia. I promise that I love you only as a sister."

Amelia waved him off and bid him goodnight. She watched her friend leave the room before looking over at Enzo. He was already staring at her.

"What?" She asked, "Is there something on my face?"

"No," Enzo chuckled, "Not at all. I just wish you understood your value."

"Enzo, I do," Amelia sighed, "But I also have to be realistic. I'm lucky to have him."

The Italian shook his head, "If you say so. Go get some rest."

He stood up and walked around the couch towards the door. As he passed behind her, he reached out and squeezed Amelia's shoulder. If she didn't know any better, she might have said it was almost lovingly. She watched him leave before she groaned and dropped her head back.

Enzo managed to get under her skin every time he made comments regarding her relationship and his opinion of it. And even when it wasn't about her relationship, Enzo challenged her differently than anyone else. He would tease her, test her, encourage her and so many other things that she'd only ever seen him do with Tom. With Lance, Enzo was a menace. The Italian challenged the other man, but not in the same way. It was different, the kind of thing that had Amelia wanting to jump to Lance's defense every second.

Lance said all of the right things, whispering beautiful things in her ear. Loving her, holding her close. He'd been the first person she'd actually been able to choose for herself having never been allowed to pursue relationships growing up. In the Cruz family, it tradition was for the Head to choose a husband for the women, this meant that dating was forbidden. Why risk damaging the product?

Her brothers had tried to marry her off and form an alliance with Narciso Hagan's son three years prior. It had been the final straw for Amelia.

Three Years Ago:

Angel had demanded she meet him in the study at a very specific time. Not a second early or late, precisely on the dot. Amelia hadn't questioned him and swore she'd be there. At the time, she'd been more willing to follow his requests and commands, hoping it would endear her to him. Angel had always been the most harsh with her, especially after her mother's death. But all Amelia had wanted was to be valued by her older brother.

When she'd entered the room, there were two men she didn't recognize sitting and drinking with her brothers. One was incredibly fat and struggled to pull himself from the couch to greet her. What was left of his balding hair might have been red in his younger years.

The second of the two men definitely had red hair. His tall and fit stature was a stark contrast to his companion. His face was drawn and unkind, Amelia had no desire to step any closer. She had to fight the urge to reach for a weapon.

"There she is!" Benjamin had said, and raised his glass to her, "The lady of the hour! The bride to be!"

Amelia recoiled, "I beg your pardon, what?"

The younger of the two strangers finally stood up, "It's a pleasure to meet you, future wife."

He took her hand and bent to kiss it, a cold leer on his face when he looked at her. She snatched her hand back and took a step away. If possible, the man's face hardened more. Angel and Benjamin rolled their eyes, Camilo sat in the corner, blissfully unaware of his surroundings. Too drunk to notice the man staring at his sister like she was a piece of meat.

"Amelia! Be polite!" Angel admonished. He stood and came close to her. Wrapping an arm around her shoulders, he pulled her to the couch across from the two unknown men. Without even an attempt at being subtle, Angel pushed his sister onto the seat, "These are Narciso Hagan and his son, Royal. You, dear sister, will be Royal's wife in a month."

Amelia had, of course, heard of the Hagans before this moment, but she'd never expected to meet them. Their reputation was unpleasant to say the least. For example, Narciso Hagan, was rumored to have killed off his wife but no one could prove it. And the police didn't care enough to search for her, nor did they want to deal with the crime families.

As one of the Big Three Families, the Commission hadn't done anything about it either. The Commission ruled the Thirteen Families and were led by the Heads of the Big Three; Hagans, Cruzes and Berardis. The Commission kept their world hidden from traditional law enforcement with their own laws and rules. But even they were wary of crossing the Hagans.

The family had been rumored to trade in drugs, weapons, and information, anything they could possibly make a profit off of. Blackmail and extortion seemed to be their favorite form of income.

Benjamin stood from his seat at the desk, "Why don't we leave the newly betrothed to get to know one another, the rest of us can iron out the remaining terms of the agreement in another room."

Camilo shrugged and followed his brother. Angel followed on their heels, shooting a wink at his sister as he passed her. Narciso waddled behind them as fast as his pudgy legs could carry him without so much as a glance at Amelia.

This left Royal Hagan alone with her. He leaned back on the couch, arms flung across the back, one ankle propped on his knee, acting as if he owned the place. While his complexion was pale but that didn't hide the pearly scars on his cheeks or neck. Amelia shuddered as his stared, his blue eyes were as cold and sharp as shards of ice, sending shivers down her spine.

"Stand up and turn around for me," Royal commanded, "I want to see what I'm getting."

"No," Amelia didn't move. Maintaining eye contact, she mimicked his position, "I don't think so."

Royal laughed, "You are feisty! I am going to enjoy you. I'm going to enjoy leaving my mark."

So, he was sadistic. She wasn't surprised given the family he came from. He moved off the couch and came closer to her, his hand reaching for her.

Unfortunately for Royal, Amelia was in the habit of carrying a knife. Thanks to her Tio Blas' instruction she also knew how to use it quite well.

Unfortunately for Amelia, the knife only pierced Royal's outstretched hand. He managed to dodge the blade enough that it didn't slice through the delicate skin on his neck. But it deterred him enough to back off and allow her the chance to escape. That night was the same night she found herself seeking shelter and employment with Enzo Berardi. Amelia hadn't looked back since.

*****

It was nearly four in the morning by the time Amelia pulled into the parking lot at Lance's apartment complex. She hadn't been able to sleep after her conversation with Enzo and Tom. Their words circled in her mind endlessly. Finally, she'd decided to hop on her motorcycle and drive over to Lance's. He was waiting for her by his assigned parking spot. She pulled her bike into the spot next to his Jeep and shut it off.

"Hey," She said quietly, pulling her helmet off, "You saw me coming I presume?"

Lance was leaning against his car with his arms crossed over his chest, no amusement on his face at all. His hair was loose around his shoulders instead of the usual tied back style he wore it in. Lance finally stepped towards her and grabbed a fistful of her hair, tipping her head back and forcing her to look at him. Her breath caught in her throat, waiting for him to either smack her or yell at her. She could feel his angry breath on her face. Letting her eyes fall closed, she waited for him to make up his mind.
And nothing.
He released her hair and began to walk towards his apartment. Amelia felt the disappointment rolling off of him and in turn she felt shame in herself. She scurried after him, helmet in one hand, overnight bag in the other.

"Lance, honey!" Amelia called after him.

"Lia," He spun around to face her outside of his door, "I don't understand why you continue to let Berardi disrespect me like that."

Amelia frowned, "Like what?"

"By forcing *my* woman to live with him instead of with me!" Lance yelled and threw his hands up in the air.

Amelia immediately reached for his hands and tried to pull them down, shushing him, "Love, please, it's late, people are sleeping. Please don't yell right now. Let's go inside."

"Fine."

Lance led the way into his apartment shaking his head and running a hand through his hair. He was muttering under his breath unintelligibly. He stopped in the middle of the entryway once the door had shut behind them. His shoulders heaved, tense and angry. It was like waiting for a bomb to go off.

Amelia started speaking before he could, hoping for a chance to defuse the situation, "Lance, I lived in the Berardi mansion before you and I were together. I still live there for nights like these, so that I don't have to worry about waking anyone up when I finally come home. It has nothing to do with you or us or disrespecting us as a pair."

"You are so naive! I love you so much, but you are too trusting!" Lance groaned, "It's not your fault, you were so sheltered growing up."

"Lance! I can handle myself!" Amelia cried, hurt by the assumption that she couldn't.

"Sweetheart, you don't realize what he's doing!" Lance placed his hands on either side of her face then reached for her wrist. Grabbing it and turning it upwards to face him he revealed her initiation and rank tattoos. A simple outline of a bear paw marked her as part of Enzo's inner circle. It rested underneath light, beautiful Italian words that read 'dell'orso' or 'of the bear.' The Berardi family crest had the outline of a bear on it, so for generations, every new person received the making of the Bear. Even Lance had one, just not on his wrist like Amelia's.

"He's claimed you, Lia!" Lance yelled.

"I've never seen it like that," She said, "I have always thought of it as being a part of something."

"That's stupid," Lance laughed.

Amelia took a step back from her boyfriend, feeling like she had been slapped in the face by his words. He looked hurt that she had moved away and the only thing she wanted to do was apologize for offending him. She tried to reach for his hand but Lance held it up, stopping Amelia.

"I need a few minutes," He said. Lance left the room, walking down the hallway to his bedroom. The door snicked shut and the lock clicked a second later leaving Amelia standing stupidly in the entryway.

She walked further into the apartment finding the usual disaster; blankets strewn across the couch and floor. Soda cans crumpled on the desk and overflowing from the waste basket. Red LED lights blinked along the crease of the ceiling rather than the main light causing the woman to squint into the flashes.

It took her several minutes to find the remote and turn off the offending strip of lights. The lightbulbs in the main fixture were coated in dust from lack of use. Once she turned them on, they let off a slight burning smell as they heated.

Amelia moved around the small apartment, tidying as she went. Folding the blankets and gathering the trash from the floor. Stacking dishes neatly in the sink to be done in the morning. Taking the trash out and replacing the plastic liner, sweeping the floors, and when there was nothing else to do she sat on the couch.

She couldn't remember the last time she'd had to clean the whole apartment as an apology. Usually just making him breakfast was enough, but he'd left the door locked. She wasn't welcome in the bedroom. Amelia wrapped a blanket around herself, wondering if Lance was right. That Berardi was using her. Or was Enzo right? She didn't know anymore.

Eventually she fell asleep curled up in the corner of the couch, too exhausted to do anything else.

55

Enzo Berardi: The Start of a Plan

Enzo Berardi's day had already been miserable before he stepped foot in the same room as Lance Alexander.

Having been up all night pouring over employee files, Enzo had suggested the team meet for dinner. An invitation he deeply regretted now that he'd rested a little.

The late meeting offered time for his team to recover from the long night and offered him a reprieve from talking to people.

His stormy mood signified the fruitlessness of his search for Hagan's mole. He'd pulled every file he could think of and gone over them forward and backwards. None had stood out to him, leaving him feeling like he was failing his team.

To make it all worse, Tom had called him earlier in the day to let him know that part of a shipment had gone missing in Lance's district. The three men had spent the better part of the afternoon trying to track it down with no leads. It was like the containers had disappeared into thin air. Enzo had to restrain himself from strangling Lance for not being at his post and not being able to potentially prevent the theft.

The only small silver lining in his day was dinner and the time spent with people he actually liked.

Enzo walked into his kitchen to find jazz music playing lightly over a speaker somewhere. Amelia was at the stove stirring something with one hand, a wine glass in the other. She smiled lightly at him and pointed to the counter where an empty wine goblet stood next to a bottle of white wine.

He poured himself a generous glass and swirled the alcohol in the glass for a moment, observing the movement before taking a deep inhale. He relished the tart scent, picking out the different notes from only the smell the way his mother had taught him to.

Finally he took a sip, savoring the flavor. He caught Amelia watching him, a bemused expression on her face.

"What?" He asked, "Something on my face?"

"No, you look fine," She said, her cheeks tinting pink as she looked away.

"Can I help with dinner?" Enzo changed the subject but enjoyed the satisfied feeling of knowing he'd given her that flush.

Amelia nodded and gestured to the sink where a colander of shrimp sat, waiting to be rid of their shells, "We're having shrimp scampi."

Getting the message, Enzo set his glass down and rolled his sleeves up, ready to help prepare dinner with her. Out of the corner of his eye he saw her pick up a large knife and twirl it a couple of times before slamming it down on the cutting board next to the stove. A moment later, the sound of rapid smack of the blade slicing through fresh herbs filled the kitchen.

"Is that fresh pasta?" Enzo asked her, nodding to the noodles on the stove.

Amelia nodded, "Yeah. I needed to be able to do something with my hands. It was a long day."

Enzo glanced over from the sink where he was deveining the shrimp, "Have a fight with Lance?"

"Not really, just dealing with his understandable frustration," Amelia turned her head away from Enzo but not before he saw her blinking rapidly, like she was trying to prevent tears.

Enzo opened his mouth to speak but was cut off by Tom and Lance traipsing into the kitchen. Neither man had a pleasant expression, the former looked downright murderous. The latter sauntered up to Amelia and turned her around before capturing her mouth in a possessive kiss. Lance then turned and glared at Enzo in greeting. He snagged the bottle of wine from the counter and sniffed the bottle before frowning at it and setting it back down. He walked to the fridge and reached inside for a beer bottle that Enzo didn't remember buying. Tom greeted Amelia with a brotherly hug before pouring himself a glass of wine and leaning against the counter. Lance, however, dropped into a chair at the table, sipping his beer and watching Amelia cook and casting dark looks at the Italian.

Enzo raised a brow at the man but chose not to respond, deciding that poking that particular bear right then, wasn't a good decision. Tom was half watching with an amused expression on his face and partially paying attention to something on his phone, sipping from his own glass. Enzo turned back to the sink and finished relieving the shrimp of their shells. Giving them a quick rinse, he handed them to the Hispanic woman at the stove.

Unable to stay silent, Lance spoke up, "I offered to help you cook and you said no, but you put him to work? Where does the disrespect end, Lia?"

Tom choked on his laughter, turning it into a cough. Even Enzo had to make an effort to hide his own chuckle. But, Amelia didn't seem to find it as amusing as everyone else.

She turned to face her boyfriend, still holding the knife, and said, "Two things; one, you would've griped about deveining the shrimp. Secondly, you are a *gringo* who didn't know salt from seasoning until two years ago. Berardi is Italian and knows how to season food, I can trust him in my kitchen."

"It's not *your* kitchen," Enzo murmured under his breath.

Unfortunately for him, Amelia heard him and whirled around, "Whose the one in here the most?"

Enzo held one hand up and reached forward with the other, moving the knife to the side and away from his face, "Fine, fine, it's your kitchen. *Mi faccia il favore*, let's not swing knives around."

Amelia set the knife down and scooped the chopped herbs into the pan, carefully stirring them into the sauce. The shrimp followed a second later, turning from gray to pink in the heat.

Enzo shook his head at the antics of his team, suddenly feeling lighter than he had earlier. Maybe it was just because for a brief moment he wasn't thinking about all of the responsibilities that weighed on him. Maybe it was simply the laughter, but whatever it was, he was grateful. He watched the three other people talk among themselves, smiling and joking. Teasing Lance's inability to cook, Amelia's Hispanic temper, Tom's obsession with work, just enjoying one another's company and the brief moment of levity.

Enzo smiled and grabbed a stack of plates from the counter. The sizzling sound of searing seafood filling the kitchen made his stomach gurgle, reminding him that he hadn't eaten all day. Continuing to listen to the conversation he passed the dishes out to each of the four spots at the table. Tom pushed off the counter and dug in a drawer for napkins to accompany the plates.

By the time Amelia was pulling the steaming pasta dish off the stove, the two men had finished preparing the table. Enzo pulled the young woman's chair out for her once she'd set the pot down much to the chagrin of Lance.

"It looks amazing, Amelia," Enzo told her.

"You did a good job, darling," Lance complimented, surprising Enzo with the kind words.

Amelia smiled at the praise, but it didn't quite reach her eyes. Enzo looked a little closer and realized the woman had put on more makeup than normal, hiding her exhaustion. He looked up at Tom, wondering if the other man had noticed.

"So, Lance, how was your evening last night?" Tom asked casually, passing the salad around the table as he spoke.

"Would've been better if I hadn't had to call my girlfriend home at two in the morning," He grumbled around a bite of food, grouchy again.

Out of the corner of his eye, Enzo caught a flash of hurt and annoyance in Amelia's eyes, "Still don't live there, so technically not my home yet."

"'Yet' being the key word there," Lance pointed his fork at her as if to emphasize a point.

Enzo set his fork down and wiped his mouth with his napkin. Once he'd set it down and knew he'd gathered the table's attention, he started speaking, "Unfortunately, moving in will have to wait."

"Since when do you get to make that kind of declaration, Berardi?" Lance demanded angrily.

"Since I have a task for her," Enzo said calmly. He crossed his arms over his chest, as if daring the man to challenge him, "I have information I want her to follow up on."

Enzo wasn't sure where the idea he had was coming from. Perhaps he was taking a page from Hagan's book. Maybe because he was considering how he could try to get the Cruzes to show their cards. The wheels in his head were spinning, building a plan, creating contingencies and plan 'B's.

"Congratulations on your breakup, you two," He said, a sly smile appearing on his face.

"I beg your pardon?" Amelia exclaimed, jumping from the table.

Lance followed suit, "You have about three seconds to run before I slug you! This is what I was talking about, Lia!"

Amelia tore her gaze away from Enzo to face Lance. Enzo could see the war in her mind, she was considering the other man's words seriously now. His heart sank in his chest and he sent up a silent prayer that she would let him explain instead of jumping to her own conclusions.

"You two could stop yelling and we could see what this is all about before you decide to threaten your boss," Tom's voice had lost any of its prior amusement, "Sit down!"

Amelia dropped back into her chair, looking apologetic. Lance on the other hand refused to sit down. He crossed his arms over his chest and raised his brows, waiting for the explanation. Enzo chuckled and leaned back, crossing one leg over the other and sipping his wine.

Closing his eyes, the Italian considered his plan, it could very well work if everyone played their part correctly. Setting his glass down and glancing across the table to his second in command, Enzo smiled.

"Sit down, Lance, you aren't really breaking up with your girlfriend," He rolled his eyes.

Lance finally sat down, still glaring at Enzo, "Start talking."

"This weekend is the monthly race weekend in Manhattan and you two are going to stage a very loud, public breakup. Get people's attention, make them think that you are having a falling out with not only Lance, but with me too. Run back to your brothers and beg them for shelter, tell them you made a mistake and want their protection again," Enzo explained. He was cut off by Amelia pretending to throw up.

"I'm sorry," She frowned, "It's just going to be difficult pretending that I made a mistake leaving them."

"I know but, it'll be worth it," Enzo told her reassuringly, "You'll move back in with them, make them show their hand without knowing it. Make them think it's a stroke of luck. Drop info at Luke's."

"Won't they be suspicious of her visiting our mechanic?"Tom frowned.

"Not necessarily," Amelia mused, picking at bits of cheese left on her plate, "Most racers worth their salt go to Luke's. He's genuinely good at what he does, and it benefits him to have people from every family coming, he's never given them reason to question that."

Enzo nodded. Luke Datar hadn't been under his protection for long, he'd been brought in by Tom and Amelia a year and half ago. The two had bonded with the kid mechanic, taking him under their wings and bringing him into the business. Despite physically being on neutral ground, Luke had eventually asked to be part of the organization, claiming he wanted to protect himself and his assets since his shop was a central location for the monthly street racing events in Manhattan.

Enzo had suspected that part of the real reason Luke had asked was out of sheer boredom. Being part of the Berardi organization meant things were always being run through the shop. Money, parts, information, all of it meant more danger and adrenaline for Luke.

The kid was ADHD on steroids, an absolute genius with anything mechanical, be it cars or motorcycles or explosives. His involvement with Berardi had given him the perfect excuse to start carrying explosives in his shop and tinkering with different detonators. Something Enzo regretted allowing, the number of phone calls he'd received regarding explosions were through the roof. Luke seemed to enjoy trying to give him a heart attack. Despite Enzo's best efforts, he was fond of the kid and didn't want anything to happen to him.

"Not to mention you're seen enough in the shop that it won't be suspicious if you continue to go there," Tom conceded, "You and I will need to seem indifferent to one another."

"I wouldn't say no to that anyway," Lance muttered under his breath earning himself a glare from Enzo, "Why is she going to the Cruzes anyway? I don't understand the sudden need for an undercover mission."

"Amelia, you need to be okay with this plan," Enzo ignored Lance and looked at Amelia intensely, maintaining eye contact, "You'll be the one in the most danger, we won't do this without your say so."

"You're- you're actually asking what I think about this?" She looked stunned.

Enzo felt a tug in his chest. He had done his best to respect Amelia as the person she was, his lieutenant, his thief, his friend, but most importantly, her own person. He'd never wanted her to question his motives with her or whether he cared for her opinion.

Enzo broke eye contact to glance at his under boss who motioned subtly with his eyes at Lance. The red-haired man was watching Amelia closely and she was watching him, waiting for his approval it seemed.

"Amelia, it is and has always been your choice," Enzo said, allowing some level of emotion into his voice.

Lance interjected before the woman could speak, "You've always been a controlling bastard, don't gaslight her now into thinking it's all of the sudden her choice."

"It *is* my choice, Lance," Amelia snapped, defiance written in her eyes, "I'll do it, I want to."

Enzo watched as the Hispanic woman charged from the room. Lance made to follow her but Tom leaned forward and shoved his shoulder, forcing him back into his chair.

They could hear the angry stomps of high heels on the stairs followed by a door slamming a few moments later.

"Lance, we need to talk," Enzo's tone dropped, danger lacing it, "Why don't we go to my office and have a bit of a chat?"

It wasn't a question, it was a demand.

He stood from his chair and left the room. A scuffling sound from the other chairs and hushed angry whispers behind him told Enzo that Tom had dragged the third man from his seat. The walk down the hallway from the kitchen to the office was a short journey in reality, but Enzo deliberately moved at a pace that made it take an inordinately long time. He was going to savor this conversation since it would be the last time Lance would have an opportunity to insult his lieutenant before she went undercover. Enzo wanted to hear the man speak without a filter and without Amelia present. He wanted Lance to understand that a protection order went for both threats inside and out of the organization.

Thanks to generations of Berardi men enjoying theatrics, the entrance to the office was a tall set of solid wooden double doors. They swung open grandly and without a single sound. Still not bothering to look behind to see where the other two men were, Enzo stepped further into the room.

Rounding his desk and dropping into the leather chair and pouring himself a whiskey. He chuckled to himself, knowing he was playing into the image of ruthless man, and yet, he didn't care. The point of this conversation was for Lance to understand that he was on thin ice.

A moment later Tom strutted into the room, a fistful of Lance's sleeve in his hand. The latter was struggling to release himself from the former's grip.

Tom was significantly stronger, so the escape was unsuccessful. Once they crossed the threshold of the room, his grip relaxed and Lance stumbled to the floor in a clumsy heap.

Tom turned and closed the doors while Lance stood and straightened his clothing out. He was glaring at Enzo and if look could kill…

"Look here you son of a-!" Lance started his rant. He was cut off by Tom placing both hands on his shoulders and shoving him onto the couch. He moved to stand behind the sofa, hands staying on the other's shoulders to keep him where he was.

Enzo got up from his seat and approached Lance, crouching in front of him, he spoke calmly and clearly, "I will only say this once, Alexander. You will learn some respect. I have never once forced Amelia to do anything, get that through your thick skull. Her living here? Her choice. Her job? Her choice. Her love life? Her choice. Are you seeing the pattern here?"

Enzo sat back on the coffee table before continuing, "You are getting an opportunity here, she's about to deploy. Use that time to learn how to love her the way she deserves."

"Why the hell is she deploying anyway? What could you possibly hope to gain by sending her away to the Cruzes?" Lance demanded.

"That is confidential. Your involvement is one of necessity, nothing more," Enzo leaned back, "Now, get out."

The Italian waved his hand signaling Tom to let Lance go. The man jumped from the couch like he'd been burned. Storming out of the house in an absolute rage, swearing at the other men as he departed. He threw rude gestures in the air when he turned to watch where his feet were taking him, narrowly avoiding running into the door frame.

"That went well," Tomaso sighed when the red haired man finally disappeared from sight and the front door slammed.

Enzo shrugged, "It went how I expected it to, unfortunately."

"Alright man, spill. What was that about?" Tom took Lance's abandoned spot, "You taunted him and warned him at the same time."

"I don't trust him."

"You've made that abundantly clear," Tom rubbed his temples.

"Good, maybe he'll get that his job is on the line," Enzo rolled his neck trying to relieve the tension.

Enzo Berardi: Conversations, Good and Bad

Enzo let Tom go to his own room not long after Lance left the mansion. He'd requested that his friend rest, telling him he needed to be fully aware and awake for what they had planned.

He had not gone to bed himself, he'd stayed in the study, reading a book on the couch. His feet propped up on the table casually with strains of Mozart drifted lightly through the room and his fingers tapped in the air on imaginary piano keys.

A tap on the door drew his attention from the book in hand. He wasn't the least bit surprised when Amelia poked her head in the room. She'd removed her makeup from earlier, gone was the bright red lipstick and the dark eyeliner. Her dark hair was twisted up into a bun on the top of her head, leaving the expanse of her neck visible to him. Enzo found himself wondering if her skin was as soft as he imagined it to be.

Gone were the professional clothes from earlier, she had donned a loose gray t-shirt and black leggings. Enzo felt honored that she trusted him enough to wear them around him. Casual wear was not normal for either of them, so much of their time was spent in dangerous areas that their clothing was, in a way, their armor. A mask to put up, what people were allowed to see and believe. Sometimes, with each other, they allowed the mask to slip and be seen without their armor.

It had been awkward in the first months Amelia had resided in the mansion, not just for her, but for him too. They'd tiptoed around one another, always on edge and unsure how to act. Eventually they'd found a rhythm with each other and formed a friendship.

Enzo had to force himself to stop staring at her, lost in the memories of their relationship. He wasn't sure when their tentative friendship had turned into the bond of trust they had, or when he had started to feel something else, but he refused to jeopardize it.

She was looking at him curiously, crossing her arms over her chest self-consciously. She sat on the opposite side of the couch, her feet curled underneath herself. Enzo placed a slip of paper in his book to mark his place and set it on the table. Turning to face her, he opened his hands as if to say the floor was hers and he would listen.

"Why didn't you go to bed?" He asked when she didn't immediately speak.

"I wanted a straight answer," Amelia sighed and scrubbed a hand over her face, "For once."

Enzo raised a brow, waiting for her to continue.

"Do you purposely torment Lance?" She asked, "You two keep having this stupid measuring contest, which one of you can piss the other off more, but I am so tired of it! Please, leave me out of it. Please."

He sighed, "I won't apologize. I think he's manipulative and you deserve better than that! He started off alright, I'll admit, but over the years... Amelia, I have concerns."

"He's my choice!" She cried defensively, "Trying to put a wedge into the relationship is almost as bad as my brothers never allowing me to make the choice in the first place."

Enzo felt like he'd been slapped. He had never once considered the parallel, he'd only seen his own skewed sense of right and wrong. His greatest desire had been for her to understand what she deserved, not to make her feel like someone was trying to control her actions again. The back of his neck heated in shame and he rubbed a hand over it uncomfortably.

"I'm so sorry. Truly. I never meant to break your trust, Amelia," He apologized. Enzo resigned himself to the fact that there was nothing he could do to change her mind right then, she would have to see it on her own eventually, even if it hurt like hell to watch.

Amelia smiled softly, "I know you didn't. Despite what you say about yourself, you're too honorable to intentionally hurt someone."

Enzo chuckled dryly, "I'm not a good man, Amelia."

"I know, none of us are really 'good,' but you're better than most. Which is why I trust you to have my back in the coming weeks. You're not going to turn a blind eye," Amelia reached out and squeezed his hand, "Nobody is truly good in our world. We live in the shades of gray between black and white, right and wrong. There's almost never a simple solution."

"I think, Amelia, that this time away will help you clear your head of all of the chaos here," Enzo squeezed her hand in return.

She hummed in response, "Perhaps. But Enzo, you have to promise me something."

He leaned closer, "Anything."

"Don't get into petty arguments while I'm away. Don't antagonize Lance because I can't step in," She gave him a pointed look, "I slept on the couch last night because he forgot to unlock the door in his frustration. There's already bumps in my relationship that I need to smooth out, I can't handle your guys' arguments on top of it and this mission."

Enzo opened his mouth to argue but stopped himself. Taking a breath to calm his rising anger at Lance, he nodded, "Fine. I will make an effort. I make no promises at being perfect though."

"I never asked for perfection. Effort, as long as it's real effort, it fine," Amelia said gently. She covered mouth as she suddenly yawned causing Enzo to check the time.

Enzo stood, pulling her with him, "Go to bed, Amelia."

He leaned forward and pressed a gentle kiss to her forehead, unable to stop himself. She surprised him by leaning into it, closing her eyes and accepting the affection. He squeezed her shoulders gently and pulled away, nodding to the door. She smiled tiredly and trudged out of the room. Enzo watched her leave, however bad he thought it was getting with Lance, it had already gotten there.

Shaking his head to force his thoughts elsewhere, knowing that no matter what he did, it had to be Amelia making the decisions regarding issues with Lance. The only thing Enzo could do was be there to catch her when the inevitable fall came. Until then, he needed to lock himself up and keep his emotions under control or he might as well give the Hagans the keys to his organization right there.

*****

The morning of Race Day found Enzo in the boxing ring with Tom before the sun had even come up. Sweating through their shirts and panting from the exertion, they stalked each other in a circle. Tom held practice pads up for Enzo to punch at while they sparred. Even through their panting, they managed to hold a conversation and talk through the plan for the evening.

"So, tonight," Tom grunted at the impact of Enzo's fists hitting the pads, "Are you going to be on the ground or in the lounge?"

Enzo swung at the pads a few more times before answering, "No, I think it'll be better for us to stay in the lounge. We can't act like we're watching. It risks everything. And we have other people in the crowd we need to keep an eye on. Our pick pockets like to go crazy on Race Day."

"Do you want to tell them to stay home so you can keep an eye on everything?" Tom asked, jerking the pad up to block a blow that was aimed for his head, "Jeez, what was that, man?"

Enzo grunted, pummeling the pads in a rapid combination of jabs and swings, "I'll watch what I can from up top. But we have to maintain composure and normalcy."

"What if you're asked about the argument between the couple?" Tom asked, panting. He was beginning to tire himself out. He let go of the pads, letting them fall to the floor.

Enzo shrugged, dropping all emotion from his voice, "What do I care of their personal lives? They're mere employees. Their personal lives are none of my concern, but if you would like to step in, be my guest."

Tom laughed, his head thrown back, eyes lit up, "If I didn't know better, *I* would believe you."

Rolling his eyes, Enzo dropped his gloves on the mat next to the forgotten pads. He flopped down next to them with a sigh. His breathing was still coming in rapid pants and sweat trickled down the back of his neck. Tom grabbed a water bottle from the side of the ring and joined his friend on the floor.

Enzo lifted his head just enough to see Tom staring off into the distance. Nudging him, he asked, "What's up?"

Tom's brow crinkled and he stayed that way for a moment, "Do you ever wonder if maybe the assassinations from years ago are related to anything happening now?"

Enzo propped himself up on his elbows, "I hadn't considered it, mostly because I didn't want to hope."

The Italian understood why his friend asked: their fathers had been among the seven Heads of Families killed twenty years ago. The assassin had never been caught and rumors had circled about the Hagans being involved. It had never been proven but was still a suspicion among many of the Heads.

Tom nodded, "Hagan is still trying to get the Cruzes on his side. What can they offer him?"

"If they form an alliance, then it would always be two versus one on the Commission votes," Enzo sat up, "He would control the Commission and by extension all of the Thirteen."

"It would be quite a coup. It would also make sense for the movements being made in the shadows," Tom contemplated, "It would also explain Angel Cruz's desire of getting his sister back on their side."

Enzo swore, "I hope we're wrong, otherwise, there may be more danger lurking around than we thought."

"That reminds me, of all the women in the world, why pick her to fall head over heels with?" Tom leaned forward, a mischievous expression written across his face.

"Pardon?" Enzo's expression dropped, "Really? You're asking about Amelia?"

"Don't pretend to be dumb, Enzo. I've known you since we were kids, I know your tells," Tom shoved his friend's shoulder, "Seriously, you pick the one woman who is as emotionally unavailable as you. Sister of a rival family, biggest pain in your neck, your employee. And, let's not forget; dating someone else!"

Enzo chuckled dryly, "It's likely that in the years we've spent together, the teasing, poking, challenging and picking on one another, a bond of trust slowly built up. We both learned to be open with someone, but then Lance came into the picture. She started closing herself off again. She let Lance put her into a cage and I don't think she's realized that it even happened."

Tom nodded, leaning against a post opposite of his boss, listening to every word. Enzo found himself *wanting* to talk about it, frustrations he normally would have shared with Amelia and no longer could.

"You know you've got a facade of being cold hearted and a force of nature, but those of us who have the honor of knowing you deeper than that, know that you are driven by desire to protect your people. Likely trying to compensate for the fact that we couldn't protect our fathers," Tom told him.

"When did you become a psychologist?" Enzo chucked one of the boxing gloves at him.

"I'm serious!" Tom laughed, "I also think you chose not to pursue her and let Lance in a misguided attempt to protect her."

"And see how well that turned out," Enzo growled. He stood from his spot on the mat and offered a hand to Tom, pulling the man up was a relatively easy task since he did most of the work, "I'm going to shower and take care of a few things before we need to head to Manhattan."

As Enzo walked away Tom called after him, "Hey! Remember that Amelia doesn't normally go to races without an extra layer of armor! She's changing her usual routine tonight and is putting herself in a vulnerable position for you. Just keep that in mind."

Enzo whirled around, "What are you talking about? She doesn't normally go to race day at all. Period."

Tom laughed to the point where he doubled over and wiped tears from his eyes. When he looked up and saw his boss' confusion, his face dropped, "Wait, seriously? You don't know?"

Now it was Enzo's turn to laugh, "I cannot believe you fell for that."

"Get out of here! You about gave me a heart attack!"

Waving over his shoulder and calling back, "Who do you think bought her that first motorcycle?"

Enzo dodged a boxing glove Tom threw at his head in retaliation to the joke. Waving him off he grabbed his duffle bag from its spot by the door and entered the locker room.

The locker room echoed like any other, but didn't smell nearly as bad as most. Since the gym was one of the establishments Enzo owned, he'd ensured that it was cleaned well. He'd wanted to create a safe environment for his staff to come and have a roof over their head, a warm shower, and take a breather if they needed it. It didn't matter what their rank was, they were protected as long as they were part of his organization.

Enzo lived by his father's words; Take care of your people and they'll take care of you when you're truly desperate.

On the backside of the gym was a much smaller building that his parents had bought and designed. A shelter. Anyone on the run from danger was welcome there, allegiances were disregarded, gender, race, religion, they didn't care. Leon and Lucia Berardi had wanted to build something up, something to stand out in the destructive world they lived in. Neither had passed off the management of the shelter, they were truly involved and they had taught their son to be as well.

Enzo had built on it years ago, adding a deep basement with apartments for long term residents and security to prevent unwanted visitors. He'd found a few people in the county offices who would help change identities when needed. Anything he could do to help the shelter, he'd done.

Now, years after his father's death and mother's departure for Italy, Enzo still ran the shelter and kept it stocked with everything it needed. From cots to water to even keeping a trauma psychologist on staff.

Audra Smith, a friend of his, who now ran the shelter for the most part. She'd been a godsend when he'd found her.

Now that he was thinking about the shelter, he made a mental note to visit soon to check in. To see if they needed anything and ask how Audra was doing.

Enzo approached the showers and flicked one on, the water streamed down smacking the tile floor. He tossed his shirt into his duffle bag on the floor and reached his arms over his head, stretching his sore muscles. He caught sight of himself in the mirror, his black hair was falling into his face, tickling his eyelids. His facial hair was nearing time to trim. The same Italian script that marked his crew was tattooed over the left side of his chest reading 'dell'orso' or 'of the bear.'

It had been his first tattoo but certainly not the last. The most notable were the bear paw consuming the back of his hand and the roman numerals branded into his forearm that translated to the day he took power and his father had fallen. A reminder to seek out the perpetrator and avenge his father. There were others and more he intended to get, but some days he didn't have the time for the proper aftercare thus he'd made the choice not the get them yet.

Letting the water soothe his aching muscles, Enzo dropped his head against the wall. He needed to steel himself, nothing could distract him during these next few days or even weeks. If he stopped paying attention or lost focus for even a moment it could result in a knife to his heart. Or the heart of the organization.

When he stepped out of the shower, his face was hard and set. His dark eyes glinted eerily in the fluorescent lighting of the locker room. He dressed quickly, donning an impeccable suit, tailored to perfection. The hair that had been falling into his face was now combed back, he'd even trimmed his facial hair to a neat scruff. The final pièce de résistance; the sleek black Glock he tucked into his shoulder holsters hidden beneath his jacket.

Enzo had donned his armor and was ready for battle.

Amelia Cruz: Race Day

melia always watched the first part of the race events from the shadows.

Race Day was her favorite day of each month. The thrill of being hidden in plain sight and the adrenaline from the races exhilarated her. The cheering from the crowd and thrum of music pounded through her veins and made her pulse race. And then there was the actual racing. Where the world fell away and there was nothing but the motorcycle and the road. Leaving behind all restrictions and worries, the only goal; to cross the finish line first.

Originally, she hadn't intended to tell anyone that she was even at the racing events, but Berardi had figured it out fairly quickly. Enzo had been the one who'd bought her first bike, so it made sense that he would recognize it in a race.

He'd also given her a strategy for staying below the radar in the future and even helped her a few times. They never spoke about it, the unspoken rule being that it was a secret

and therefore not to be discussed. Ever.

That is, until Tom figured it out. He had introduced her to Luke Datar and when she became a regular customer of the mechanic's, Tom began to get suspicious. He asked questions at Luke's shop and found Amelia's motorcycle receiving modifications. Once he'd seen that, it was easy for him to identify her in a race. He asked her about it later and was then sworn to secrecy.

Luke knew, of course, he worked on her bike, but he also didn't care. The only person he might tell was his girlfriend, Fae Clotho, but she didn't care either. Fae ran a little cafe and bar across the street from Luke's workshop. The two of them were some of Amelia's favorite people to be around, they enjoyed the world without caring what people thought. Always laughing and sometimes blowing things up, the couple were a diamond in the rough.

Engines revved in the distance, a sure sign of a race starting. It would be time to emerge from the shadows soon.

Amelia patted her pocket, checking for the wad of cash she'd pulled from the bank earlier. Without it, she wouldn't be able to race. The young woman wasn't usually worried about pickpockets at races even though it was a prime field for them, but she'd built a reputation for herself and carried a gun on her thigh. People had learned quickly she wasn't afraid to pull it.

Amelia wasn't able to stay long this time, she had to win and disappear quickly. Lance was already at the event but didn't know she was too.

Poor Lance had no idea that she was racing, it was her big secret she kept from him. It was the one thing she wanted to protect and keep for herself. Part of her worried he might not let her race if he knew.

Lance had been sending her messages all night asking where she was and asking why she wasn't replying. Normally she told him that she would be at a shooting range to practice and he would leave it there. This time was a different story because of their mission. She wasn't able to use that lie.

Her phone buzzed again. She picked it up to find several messages from her boyfriend.

Lance: Hon, where are you?

Lance: ???

Lance: Lia? Where are you?! Why aren't you answering me? Amelia: I'll be there soon.

Lance: Where. Are. You?

Amelia: I'll be there soon.

Lance: I'm calling Berardi. If you're with him, Lia…

Amelia rolled her eyes at the last message. Lance had been convinced that she was sleeping with Enzo behind his back for the past year. It was part of the reason she'd started spending more nights in Lance's apartment as an effort to prove that she was loyal to him. Amelia had become intimately familiar with his sofa. Something she had, of course, not told Enzo or Tom about.

Her phone dinged again. Amelia groaned and pulled her glove off to read the message expecting another message from Lance. Instead she was pleasantly surprised to find a message from Tom in a group chat with both herself and Enzo.

Tomato Soup: Good luck tonight, *piccolo fantasma*!

Cranky Bear: We're watching your six from the top. Amelia: See you soon.

Amelia turned her phone off and tucked it away safely. She secured her glove back in place and lifted her motorcycle's kickstand. A moment later the bike roared to life, purring comfortingly beneath her. After confirming her braid was securely tucked into her helmet, she pulled her bike into the street.

Her helmet was the only color she ever wore when racing, its maroon color flashing underneath the black paint on it. Not long after Amelia had begun racing, she'd had a wraith painted onto her helmet in recognition of the nickname the people had given her: the Ghost.

Upon seeing her bike pull up the starting line, the crowd began to cheer, swarming her. They asked the usual questions, what her name was, which Family did she belong to, who worked on her bike, and would she speak. Every time she gave the same answer: silence.

It was part of the routine. They got no answer and she didn't worry about being discovered.

If she ever did need to talk, Luke had installed a voice changer in her helmet. But so far, there hadn't been a severe enough reason to use it.

Keeping her head down and checking over her bike, Amelia eyed the other drivers pulling up to the start line. Each had their own posse fawning over them, girls in tiny shorts and ridiculously high heels. The men leaned against their muscle cars and wore faux gold chains, trying to impress the women teetering in their shoes.

Amelia rolled her eyes. Tonight's crowd was no different than the usual crowd except for the fact that she could see Lance pacing through the crowd. No doubt he was looking for her but he was looking among the groupies, never thinking to look at the racers. He was convinced she was secretly very shy and always wanted to go home. He had no idea she loved the adrenaline rush from racing. It was addicting.

Someone called for the line up, pulling her focus back to the road in front of her. A quarter mile. Such a small distance, but so much could happen. She'd seen bikes flip, crash and go up into flames during the races. Every moment had to be focused, every movement had to be tracked, disaster was always lurking and waiting for a driver to make a mistake, hoping to claim them.

Amelia was going up against four other racers.

One she recognized as one of the lower members of Berardi's organization, another was from the Costa Clan, a group that's loyalty jumped so often she had no idea who they were with anymore. Another racer was a representative of the Connor family; she knew they were loyal to the Hagans. The last racer surprised her, it was Benjamin, her brother. He had never joined the first race before, his times hadn't qualified him to join it.

Amelia frowned, there wasn't a chance that her brother had been able to qualify. He must have paid someone off to join the first race. It was going to be entertaining for her to leave him in the dust. A devious smirk spread across her lips, hidden from view by her helmet.

The officiant cleared the start line of spectators and stood in front of the handful of people who remained, "Are you ready for a street race?"

His call enticed the crowd to cheer. Screaming from every side and even some applause from above. The Leaders' Lounge. A lounge that had been created for the Heads of each Family and their trusted companions and family members. This was where Enzo and Tom would be observing the events of the night. A glance at the balcony told Amelia that they were watching already, Tom dipped his chin to her in greeting. Amelia turned back to the road without a response. She couldn't respond or she might give away who her allegiance was to.

The officiant called the start line to prepare, "Racers, to your mark!"

Each motorcycle revved in turn, each one receiving a cheer louder than the last. Benjamin waved to the crowd when he revved his engine. He blew a kiss to some girl Amelia had never seen before. Another eye roll. Her eyes were going to get stuck in the back of her head if she kept rolling her eyes at her brothers.

It bothered her how he'd been able to join the race. Amelia had worked for the reputation she carried and here was her brother being handed it on a silver platter. It was typical behavior for the Cruz brothers. Amelia vowed she would make this race hell for him.

The officiant raised a green flag in the air. The bikes revved.

The flag dropped.

The racers were off!

The adrenaline flowed through Amelia as she left the start line. Even with a helmet on, wind crept inside and whipped up into her hair. She kept low on the bike willing herself to become as aerodynamic as possible, giving herself the best chance possible. Cars honked on the crowded Manhattan roads, pedestrians yelled out, Amelia wove in and out of the traffic.

A blur. A ghost. Had she really even been there?

And almost as quickly as the race started, it was over. Ten seconds and it was done. Amelia crossed the finish line, clearly marked as the winner. Racers made their way back to the central area where the race had started mere moments earlier. The man from the Connor family had finished second. He gave her a nod of respect when he dismounted his bike and walked it away from the line. Third and fourth were the Costa and Berardi members, fifth and last place was held firmly by Benjamin. He gave the customary nod to the winner and sulkily marched his motorcycle off, muttering under his breath.

Amelia collected her winnings from a race official and left the area. Luke had agreed to let her hide her bike in his shop and let her keep a change of clothes in his office for after her "inevitable win," as he put it.

He was waiting for her at the garage door when she rode up, the chains rattled on the plated door when it slammed shut behind her. She dismounted the bike and tossed the keys to him and dashed into the office. Yanking her helmet and gloves off, Amelia began removing the rest of her protective gear. Nothing could be the same as the Ghost's look, that identity needed to be protected at all costs.

She went from black Kevlar jeans and combat boots to light distressed blue jeans and scarlet high heels. Since no one saw her black tank top underneath her armored jacket, she left it was left on. The padding in the jacket disguised her body type enough that she didn't think it would matter.

Finally she pulled her hair out of the braid it was in and switched the style to a ponytail, adding red lipstick and gold earrings to complete the look. There wasn't a single chance that people would assume that she was the Ghost. Hopefully.

Her phone rang loudly, making her jump. She'd grabbed it after dismounting and had turned it back on, but she was so focused on applying her lipstick that she'd forgotten that the ringer was on. Amelia grabbed the device to find messages from Lance, Tom, and Enzo. She opened Lance's first.

Lance: Did you stand me up for our fake breakup?

Lance: We're going to need to talk about your lack of responding.

Lance: Answer me, Amelia!

Lance: Where the hell are you?

Lance: You'd better be here soon.

His messages continued on for quite some time, all with relatively similar sentiments. She sent off a quick reply telling him to meet her at the Leader's Lounge across the street. Tapping on Enzo's messaging and giving a quick read, Amelia found a message that surprised her.

Cranky Bear: You did good. Now, take a breath and remember we've got your six through this next part of the night.

Cranky Bear: Proud of you.

Tom's texts relayed a similar message of pride in the achievement and that he'd be there if she needed anything. Their messages gave Amelia that last dose of courage she needed to step outside and find her boyfriend to put on a show for the Thirteen.

*****

Amelia found Lance standing outside of the Leaders' Lounge, his arms crossed over his chest and frown on his face. She stopped to take him in.

Taking a moment to admire him from head to toe. He was wearing blue jeans and sneakers, a flannel was tied around his waist and he had on a simple navy t-shirt. He had his hair tied into a bun on the back of his head, a single strand falling out into his eyes.

"Hey, you," Amelia greeted, approaching him and kissing him on the cheek.

Lance reared back, glaring at her, "Where have you been?"

"Classified, you know there are parts of work like that," She shrugged, pretending to be sheepish, "I'm sorry, I can't tell you."

"I can't keep doing this, the not knowing, it isn't going to work if I can't know things," Lance told her harshly, "One of these days you're going to have to pick what matters most to you. Your dime a dozen job, or me."

"I'm sorry, love. I can't tell you everything," She tried to explain, heart sinking in her chest, "It's for the safety of our organization, you know that. I want to tell you, I swear I do."

A few heads poked into the hall, trying to see what the argument was about. Amelia could see her brother, Angel, out of the corner of her eye. Enzo and Tom were still sitting further back in the room, not reacting just yet. Lance seemed to notice their audience too and his body shifted, he wasn't leaning against the wall anymore. He was standing in front of her, staring directly into her eyes. Thanks to her high heels, Lance didn't have to bend to glare at Amelia, they were equal in height.

"If you won't at least tell me where you are when I ask, I can't trust you, Lia," He placed his hands on his hips, like he was speaking to a child, "This sneakiness has to stop!"

Amelia could feel her defenses going up and alarm bells ringing in her head, she had a feeling this wasn't part of the act. Lance continued glowering, waiting for her response, fingers drumming on his hip. She swallowed, suddenly nervous and unsure how to proceed.

Lance gave her an expectant look, "Nothing to say? Good grief, Lia, that tells me everything! You've made your choice then."

He turned to walk away from her, tossing over his shoulder, "When you are ready to be truthful about screwing your boss, you know where to find me."

Amelia saw red, "I am not screwing Berardi! You know that, I've told you a million times. And, it's 'Amelia,' not 'Lia!'"

The man whirled back around and stalked towards her, his voice suddenly filled with exhaustion, "I really, really do not feel like fighting with you tonight, Lia."

"Tough luck, you started this fight in front of a hundred people, you can damn well finish it," It was Amelia's turn to put her hands on her hips, staring him down and waiting for him to reply.

Lance's face softened, "You're right, sorry. I'm sorry I got mad that you wouldn't tell me where you were. I need to be able to trust you."

"I love you, but you need to trust me, and stop accusing me of sleeping with Berardi," She stated bluntly.

"Ha!" Lance laughed in her face, "When he starts respecting me like an equal, maybe then I'll stop asking whether or not he's sleeping with *my* woman."

Amelia sighed, exasperated. His false fight was a repeat of their more recent and very real arguments, "Lance! For crying out loud, you are not his equal!

You work for him! He's your boss!"

Lance crossed his arms over his chest, "Well, if that's what you have to say, then we know where I stand, don't we?"

The young woman felt her heart break a little at her next words, like maybe they were half truthful and half a lie for the act, "Then I can't do this anymore, Lance."

Enzo chose that moment to walk by and give Amelia an exaggerated wink, "I'll see you later."

It was like setting off a bomb.

Lance jumped at Enzo, fist raised in the air, ready to try and pummel the other man but Tom had stepped in and caught the strike before it hit. The Italian thrust the hand back towards its owner and stepped in between him and Berardi. The look on Tom's face was murderous as he stepped closer to Lance.

Amelia forced her way in between them, aware that every eye was on them now. She looked between the two men rapidly, trying to force them apart. Each man was reaching for the other, trying to land a strike. Their fists swung wildly, one blow caught Amelia in the stomach. She doubled over, the wind knocked out of her.

"Berardi, these are your men!" She yelled, still hunched, "Do something about this!"

Enzo leaned against the wall, hands tucked into his pocket, "I can't do anything to help Mr. Alexander's bad temper."

"You can absolutely stop this!" Amelia cried, stood, shoving her shoulder against Lance to force him to take a couple of steps backward before turning to him and begging, "Please! Leave it alone! He's trying to rile you up!"

Lance looked at Amelia with a cold stare and shoved her into the wall next to him, "I don't give a flying eff what you think he's trying to do, woman! He disrespected me beyond belief by insinuating he's been with *my* woman! I will have blood for it!"

"This is not a mutual problem, Alexander, your misfortune appears to be, well, exclusive," Enzo smirked from his spot on the wall.

Lance tried to jump at Enzo again and Amelia flinched when he did. Enzo caught the movement, fire lighting in his eyes. He glared at Lance again, this time stiffer and no longer relaxed. He was prepared to truly pummel the man now.

"*¡Dios mío! Por favor!*" Amelia exclaimed, knowing they wouldn't stop without an intervention.

"ENOUGH!"

The hall went silent. Even the onlookers from the Lounge seemed surprised. Amelia was panting, unsure if what had just happened was real or not. But her anger most certainly was real.
　　The men finally looked at her. Tom's hands held Lance by the collar of his shirt to keep him from jumping their boss. Lance was disheveled and enraged, a snarl formed on his face when he looked at Amelia. Enzo was staring intently, like he was waiting for her to give him his cue.

"Enough! I am so sick of this nonsense! If you two want to keep fighting, fine. But I'm out," Amelia threw her hands up, "I'm done with both of you. Lance, we're over. Berardi, find someone else. I'm out."

Amelia Cruz: Going Undercover

Amelia spent the night in a hotel, avoiding everyone she knew. Her phone had blown up with messages and phone calls from people in the organization who didn't know it was a ruse. There was a single message from Enzo among the hundreds of text messages.

Cranky Bear: You did well. I'm sorry about how that happened. I didn't know Lance intended to throw a punch.

Amelia: I didn't either. I'm not sure what was real and what was fake.

Cranky Bear: Perhaps this time away is a good thing. You can use it to take a step back and figure it out. I have to admit, I thought it was real on his end after the punch.

Amelia hadn't received a message from Lance at all. It appeared as though he was going to treat her time away like a real breakup. The young woman ended up resolving not to spend her one night in a five star hotel wallowing in self pity over her boyfriend's anger.

She ordered a pizza and a bottle of wine to her room. Sitting on the balcony and enjoying both, she watched the busy streets below. The people of New York busied themselves from before sunrise to well after sunset, most unaware of the Thirteen Families and their organizations. So many people passed through the city, but Amelia had never left. It was her wildest dream to escape one day and explore the world. But she knew that she would end up back home, it was inevitable. No one in the Thirteen ever truly left unless Death came to carry them away.

The Hispanic's attention was pulled from the city when her phone rang. Enzo's name, or rather, his nickname, popped up on the screen. She answered with a sigh.

"Enzo, I was enjoying my dinner," She told him.

"I know, I'm sorry," He sounded truly apologetic, "I just needed to ask if you could leave your phone at the hotel. We'll retrieve it later. And Amelia, be prepared for anything. There's a war coming, I'm sure of it."

"I'm going to need it Enzo, you know that," Amelia shook her head even though he couldn't see her.

"I figured you would say that, but I wanted to ask anyway. Be safe."

He hung up without another word, leaving Amelia without answers.

*****

The Cruz Hacienda was just as daunting as it had been the last time she'd been there. Amelia had tried to convince herself that it might be at least partially welcoming. Instead it sent a chill down her spine. She was entering enemy territory and the Hacienda seemed to know she wasn't a friendly. It was as if it was telling her to go away, that she was not welcome. So really, it was no different than growing up here.

Taking the stone steps one at a time and lugging a suitcase up with her, Amelia found herself in front of the grand oak door. The bronze, Gothic style fleur-de-lis knocker seemed to glare at her from its fixed position, daring her to use it, daring her to let the occupants of the house know she was there.

Taking a deep breath, she raised the knocker and slammed it down, once, twice, three times. Glancing over her shoulder at the lawn while she waited, she realized that the garden her mother had planted when she was a little girl had been torn up. Her brothers had hated her mother, so it wasn't a complete shock to Amelia but it was still saddening.

Suddenly, the door opened and Camilo stood in front of her, looking quite surprised. She took in his loud button down shirt, open at the top to show off the Hawaiian style necklaces around his throat. The pale linen pants created a stark contrast of color against his skin and brought attention to the fact that he was barefoot.

"Well, this is a surprise," He stated rather bluntly. He tucked a hand into his pocket and leaned against the door with the other, "What are you doing here? I thought you would be getting into it with either your boyfriend or your boss after last night."

Amelia rolled her eyes, "'Hi sis, great to see you! How are you doing?' Gee thanks, Camilo, I'm fine, it's good to see you too."

Camilo held his hands up as a gesture of peace, "Woah, woah, woah, put down the barbs, I'm just asking. It's good to see you too."

"'Just asking' wouldn't involve the comment about the argument I had with Lance or my now ex boss," Amelia lugged her suitcase into the entryway, "I hope you don't mind me coming here. I didn't really have anywhere else to go."

She did her best to make herself appear tired and defeated, hoping her brother would buy the act. He shrugged and closed the door behind her, "I could've told you that it would end in disaster."

"I don't want to hear 'I told you so' right now, Cam," Amelia sighed, already annoyed with her brother, "I'm going to my room."

Camilo gestured to the stairs, "You know the way. Be sure to stop by the study and let Angel and Benjamin know you're here. I'm going out."

"Don't forget shoes!" Amelia called over her shoulder while making her way to the staircase.

The stairs were covered by an old maroon carpet strip making it easy to keep the wheels of her suitcase from trying to roll back down. As a child she'd asked her father why it wasn't the family color. He'd only said not to worry her little head about it. Her mother had said it was because of her father's work but refused to speak about it any more than that.

But she learned as a teenager why those carpets were the color they were: it was easy to hide blood stains on a red carpet.

Amelia's old room was the only room in the house that had any sort of brightness and life to it now. As a little girl, she had loved the color pink and her room was filled with it, from the curtains to the pillows, to the cushions on the love seat and the comforter on the bed. Three years and nothing had changed in this room. It was still clean too, but Amelia knew better than to think it was because of her brothers. Mrs. Byrd, the old housekeeper probably had kept it clean out of habit and softness for Amelia.

A soft smile appeared as she walked around the room. The sweet little keepsakes from her childhood sat on shelves remembering the time before her mother had died and Amelia had been made to grow up prematurely.

Bookshelves stood proudly next to the window overlooking the back lawn. The books on them were old, and many even had tears from years of being read over and over again. The window seat had a soft blanket folded neatly on one side with a Jane Austen novel sitting on top. She laughed at her younger self's decor style when her gaze landed on the bed.

It was an awful, frilly mess of different shades of pink and white, fluffy pillows and a padded headboard. Little fairy lights decorated the wall behind the bed casting a soft glow around the room when turned on. The hardware on the drawers, doors and in the adjoining bathroom were all a shade of gold that accented the pink beautifully. Maria Cruz had spared no expense in helping Amelia make her room a princess fairy tale dream.

It was a very different image than what her life truly was. Little Amelia wouldn't be able to understand the world that older Amelia was part of. Instead of her fairy tale life in a castle, she was often in the dungeon, torturing men. She had become the dragon instead of the princess.

"This is a surprise," A male voice filled the room suddenly, drawing her from her thoughts. Amelia whirled around and found herself face to face with Benjamin and Angel, "Cam called us to let us know you were going to be crashing with us for a while."

"I hope you don't mind, although you really don't have a choice," She folded her arms over her chest.

"You never need permission to come home, *Hermana*," Angel told her sweetly, opening his arms to embrace her.

Amelia played along and embraced him and then embraced Benjamin as well. After releasing her brothers from the hug she stepped away and set her hand on the suitcase.

"I ought to unpack," Amelia gave them a pointed look, as if to tell them to get going and also not wanting to deal with the false welcome.

Angel nodded and left, Benjamin on the other hand came further into the room and sat on the window seat. Trying to ignore him, Amelia pulled her suitcase onto the bed and unzipped it. She could feel her brother's eyes on her, watching every small movement. Sorting the clothing into different piles and placing them in the dresser felt strange with his eyes on her. Like he was judging her performance.

"Why don't you tell me why you're here," Benjamin crossed his arms and flung one leg over the other.

"Cam told you I was here but didn't tell you why?" She glanced at him, "I don't believe that for a second."

"He may have mentioned, but I want to hear it from you," Benjamin shrugged.

Amelia hummed in response, "You saw the argument last night, I know you did."

"I did," He nodded, picking at an invisible speck of dust on his jeans.

Amelia turned, hands on her hips, "I was done dealing with the lousy lack of respect and the constant petty fights."

Her brother nodded and came up to her, resting his hands on her shoulders, "Well, you at least have a place to go. Maybe you can even help us get rid of Berardi, you know, as payback. Make him suffer the way he made you suffer."

She shrugged his hands off, "We'll see. But I want a seat at the table if I do help. Not just a piece of a stupid contract. Got it?"

"We'll see," He echoed her words, "Enjoy unpacking, but keep the suitcase handy. Just in case there's a contract still viable."

Benjamin left his sister alone in the room to finish the task at hand. With a groan, she threw the shirt she was holding onto the floor and rubbed her eyes with one hand. They were still trying for an alliance with the Hagans. Of course.

It was a risky alliance.

But risk had never really meant anything to the Cruz brothers before, she wasn't surprised that it still carried no weight.

*****

Amelia wasn't the least bit surprised when her brothers decided to have a formal dinner the first night she was back. She also wasn't surprised when they said they were having a few friends over as well. The young woman had a feeling that her brothers were about to spring something unpleasant on her, which was why she had tucked one of her throwing knives under her dress.

The emerald material moved with her, the silk hugging her torso and falling elegantly to her knees. Amelia had deliberately chosen a dress that didn't align with any family colors knowing it would annoy her brothers. She'd opted for black high heels to give her a little extra height and hopefully help her appear more confident and possibly intimidating. One thing Amelia had learned in her time with Berardi was that clothing was armor and she had learned to wield it impossibly well.

Her blood red lipstick caught the eye and demanded attention. She'd sworn to herself that she would walk in like she owned the place, there wouldn't be any hesitation in her stride like when she was a little girl, still scared of her father and his friends. She was a member of the Berardi Family and with that came power and confidence.

It wasn't difficult to command attention when she was walking into a room full of people who didn't know her, especially when she had allies like Enzo and Tom flanking her. But with her brothers, who had spent years tormenting her throughout her childhood, finding every opportunity to shut her out, it was more of a challenge. To walk in and pretend like she hadn't been belittled by them everyday both behind her mother's back and in front of their father's face, she would need a hell of a poker face.

Finally reaching the dining room, Amelia waited a beat before stepping inside and reaching to touch her sheath as a comfort. Male voices could be heard on the other side but she couldn't quite make out what they were saying. Taking a deep breath and steeling herself, she slid the door open quietly. The voices in the room stopped, all eyes on her.

Amelia held her back straight and head high, gliding into the room with an unexpected grace. Out of the corner of her eyes she saw the guests for the evening; Narciso and Royal Hagan. Unsurprising.

"Good evening, gentlemen," She dropped her tone to be sultry and smooth.

Narciso's smile was slimy and creepy, but the young woman returned it warmly. She nodded to Royal who raised an eyebrow at her, she noted that he was absentmindedly rubbing his palm where she'd stabbed in their last encounter. The young man wisely remained quiet this time, although Amelia had a feeling it wouldn't last. Angel was seated at the head of the table, watching her movements, like he wasn't sure what she would do. Benjamin was sitting at their brother's right hand, Camilo on the other side.

Benjamin rose from his chair and pulled the one beside it out for his sister.

"Please, sit by me, little sister," He smiled smoothly at her, but it didn't reach his eyes. Amelia came around the table to his side, taking her seat in an elegant movement. Benjamin slid the chair back into place, "You remember the Hagans? Narciso and Royal?"

She nodded, "Yes, it's a pleasure to see you again."

Royal barked out a laugh, unable to keep quiet anymore, "Is it? Because the last time we met, you put a blade in my hand."

"If I recall correctly, you were using that hand to touch what wasn't yours," She hummed in response.

Royal glared at her, "The contract had been made, you *were* mine!"

Hagan Senior lifted his glass and raised it in a toast, interrupting his son, "Let's not argue tonight. To forming new alliances!"

Amelia raised her glass, copying her brothers. Internally cringing at the moment, it reminded her that Enzo acted with class, whereas the men at the table were crass and uncouth. This cheer was premature, even she knew that. It would have been wiser to toast to a new alliance after it had been set in stone and approved by the Commission. Their excitable behavior made it incredibly evident to her why they could never be as powerful as the Berardis, even if they had more manpower or weapons. Their organizations would never match in strategy or cunning. It made her proud to know who she was loyal to.

"So, Amelia," Hagan drew her attention, "I hear you recently abandoned Berardi's organization, have anything interesting to share? Other than the fact that he was antagonistic towards you? That much was obvious."

She smiled politely, "Nothing in particular."

It was Hagan's turn to hum in reply. Angel looked up at her while serving himself from the platter in front of him, "Nothing at all?"

"I certainly don't believe that," Royal groused.

Amelia chuckled, "Are you sure you aren't just questioning me because of our last meeting, Royal?"

"Amelia!" Benjamin hissed, "Behave!"

She glared at her brother but chose not to keep poking the bear. Instead she filled her plate with the delicious food that the staff had created. There was one thing to be said for her brothers, they knew how to pick their kitchen staff. The cuisine was never lacking.

Benjamin cleared his throat, "My apologies, Mr. Hagan. She's been through an ordeal, it's why she's back with us. But that does not mean that we are not still interested in or hoping that we may be able to renegotiate the marriage contract between our families."

"Ah, yes, we saw the conflict last night," Narciso said with false sympathy then looked thoughtful for a moment, "I suppose we might be able to consider it. But, in light of what happened last time, I would like to make some alterations. A guarantee, a sign of trust, if you will."

Angel nodded, "I wouldn't expect anything less. Did you have something in mind?"

Royal leaned forward on the table, catching Amelia's eyes while his father deliberated. He maintained eye contact over a sip of wine and she didn't back down, mimicking his motions. Setting her glass down, she carefully used a certain finger to wipe the corner of her mouth, like she was neatening her lipstick. Royal's eyes darkened at the taunt but didn't respond.

"I'm willing to honor our previous contract, on the condition that the marriage happens within two or three weeks and she marries my other son. She's mauled Royal, he doesn't deserve that kind of wife," This caught Amelia's attention, her head whipped around, "I want her under control quickly with someone I believe can handle her."

Both Narciso and Royal exchanged looks with each other, wicked delight written on their faces. Like they knew something that gave them an edge. It made Amelia's skin crawl and she felt like ice had been dumped down her back. And the mention of another Hagan that not a single person in the world knew about before this very moment, Amelia could hear warning bells in her head.

"'Under control,' 'handle' me, are you kidding?" She snapped, "I am no one's property and most certainly not anyone's to control or handle."

Hagan laughed cruelly, "Dear girl, you will soon learn that your use is to be quiet and let the men talk. Your father believed something similar, I have no idea how you ended up the way you are, but it will soon be rectified. You will learn that your duty is to join our families. Not just in marriage, but with children as well. You will help make our bloodline stronger."

Enzo Berardi: Puzzle Pieces

The low buzz of a tattoo needle filled the air. Slowly the lines of Gothic style roses and honeysuckle were permanently etched into Enzo's shoulder. The gentle slope of the leaves, the softness of the petals all intricately drawn by the skilled artist.

Franklin Luigi had been a tattoo artist long before Enzo had gotten his first ink. The artist's own dark skin was covered in art he'd drawn, beautiful and impressive line and color work twisted around his limbs. Enzo had come to Frank when he got his very first tattoo, a phrase written over his heart, 'dell'orso' or 'of the bear.' A phrase passed down through the Berardi family, a reminder that they stood together as a family and they would protect their own.

Enzo had been in the chair for all of five minutes when Tom walked in and greeted the artist. He pulled up a stool and sat in front of Enzo after examining the design. His brows shot up so high Enzo worried he might lose them in his hairline.

"You know, Amelia and I had a friendly little wager going on whether or not you would come here on the first day she left," Tom chuckled when he finally looked at his boss, "I said you'd at least make it to day two. Looks like I was wrong."

"You two had a bet on this?" Enzo dropped his head onto the backrest of the chair he was in. The soft buzz of the needle broke the temporary silence. The sting of the breaking skin caused the Italian to wince and took his mind away from his friend's comment.

Tom folded his arms over his chest, amusement written all over his face, "Whose idea do you think it was?"

Enzo sighed, "Hers."

"She enjoys the game," Tom laughed.

"She enjoys tormenting me," Enzo growled lowly, "And having bragging rights when she wins a bet.

Tom laughed harder, "I've said it before and I'll say it again, you're a masochist, so I don't want to hear it."

"I am not!" Enzo denied uselessly.

"Right, and those aren't the June birth flowers you're getting tattooed into your shoulder. Remind me, when is her birthday again?"

Enzo glared at his friend and pointed a finger at his friend's face, "Not one word."

Tom held up his hands, still amused, "Wasn't planning on saying anything else."

"She's with someone else, someone who she chose," Enzo said, he glanced over his shoulder to try and look at his new tattoo, "It's one of the few choices that's actually her own. I have to respect it. Even if I think that he's the wrong person for her."

"The guy is a child trapped in a man's body," Tom scoffed, "He's useful as a blunt instrument but let's face it, he's abusive. And manipulative to boot. I hate using him on projects."

Enzo frowned, "Really? Why?"

"Weaponized incompetence," Tom stated simply, "He knows more than he lets on and acts stupid on purpose."

"You're keeping an eye on that, yes?" Enzo asked.

"Like you need to ask that," Tom rolled his eyes, offended at the question.

Enzo nodded. For a moment there was only the sound of the tattoo needle and the shifting of the artist. His stool creaked as his weight shifted so he could see better.

The Italian found himself remembering one of the first times he'd actually made an effort to get to know Amelia. It had only been a few months after she'd joined the organization and she was still on guard all the time. He hated the fact that she felt so out of place and foreign in what was supposed to be her home.

Three years ago:

Against his better judgment, Enzo had invited Amelia to coffee. On the drive over, he had tried to convince himself that it was just to get to know her better. By the time he parked he was convinced. Mostly.

That particular day was a stormy one. Rain poured heavily from the sky and Enzo couldn't help but chuckle to himself. He'd offered a ride to Amelia but she wanted to walk. He had wondered if she would bail on him, but to his surprise, she showed up only a few minutes late.

Amelia walked into the coffee shop and shook her raincoat off. Her hair was plastered to her face despite the hood on the jacket. He watched her wince every time she stepped, so he could only assume that her shoes were completely soaked through and squishing when she walked.

Enzo could tell when she spotted him, sitting at the booth in the back, his eyes on her filled with mirth. He waved her over to the table and gestured for her to sit across from him. Looking her up and down, Berardi shook his head, unable to hide his laughter.

"You stubborn woman, you chose to walk here rather than accept a ride from me. Why on earth? You knew it was going to rain!"

"Because you like to push my buttons and I didn't feel like dealing with it today," She snapped while wringing out her hair.

Enzo suspected that her crankiness came from being soaked to the bone and how her day had gone. She had been working with a team to retrieve information and had been unsuccessful. He'd heard her mumbling to herself afterwards, beating herself up over it.

Enzo handed her a stack of paper napkins to help her dry off, "I could say the exact same about you, Miss Cruz."

"Why did you invite me here, Berardi?" Amelia asked, rather annoyed and cutting straight to the point.

"Enzo, please," He said, sipping what looked like a tea of some kind, "Because I wanted to get to know you away from the job. I know what you are like at the job, and you're spectacular. I know that your brothers are worse than me, otherwise you'd be back with them. Honestly, I had hoped that by asking you to come here, you might be willing to let your guard down for a little while. And I would like you to be comfortable in the house instead of walking on eggshells."

Amelia stared at him, waiting for him to continue, so he did, "You have more to offer the organization than your skills as a thief, but you need a chance to learn who you are outside of a family name and work. Find a hobby you enjoy, develop yourself, don't let your only definition of yourself be your job. It's okay to have down time. In fact, it's healthy."

She was slack jawed when he finished, "I don't understand why you care."

He smiled sadly at her, "The fact that you don't understand is exactly why I care. Miss Cruz, I am not the Cruz Cartel, nor am I like many of the other big families competing here. I built my organization with people I trust and take an interest in, rather than using nepotism. I try my best to look after my people. So, that being said, tell me about yourself. How can I help you feel comfortable in the manor?"

"You surprise me," She declared suddenly.

Enzo raised his brows, "How so?"

She shrugged, "You care about your people in a way I've never seen. I respect it. A lot. And I admire it."

He smiled, a real smile, "Thank you."

Enzo watched her take a sip of her coffee. She looked thoughtful and even apprehensive. He opened his mouth to speak but she cut him off, starting to tell her story.

"My mother died years ago, I was still pretty young when it happened. My father passed away before I was eighteen, so my brother had custody. I have a pretty strong feeling that my mother's death wasn't entirely accidental, but I don't have any proof," She shrugged nonchalantly, like she didn't care anymore. Enzo assumed it was more likely that she was numb to it. She continued, "I tried to get involved in the family business with my brothers but you know how that turned out. So I learned how to steal information and how to extract it. Learning how to steal actual physical things was a little harder, but I had time on my hands. A lot of time. When my brothers proposed the marriage contract I knew it was time to get out, so I left. After stabbing the guy they wanted me to marry."

Enzo interrupted her, raising a hand to stop her from speaking momentarily, "Hold up, you stabbed your betrothed?"

Amelia held a finger up, "*NOT* my betrothed, I didn't agree to the marriage. But, yes, I stabbed his hand. He was trying to get under my clothes and I didn't agree to it."

Enzo laughed, "I feel like I shouldn't be surprised by that considering your interrogation skills. Well done, very well done."

The two sat in the coffee shop until a server told them to leave. They had stayed until closing time. Amelia let Enzo drive her home and their conversation continued in the car.

Now:

The two Italian men left the tattoo parlor not long after their conversation ended.

Frank had shaken Enzo's hand and given him aftercare instructions for the tattoo. He'd added the cost of the ink to the ever growing tab Enzo had at the shop. Tom booked his next appointment with Frank's daughter who, Enzo suspected, liked his friend quite a bit. She flirted a bit with him as they chatted over the counter and Enzo swore she blew a kiss as the door closed behind them.

Once outside the shop, Enzo shrugged his jacket on and gave Tom instructions for the remainder of the day. The man nodded and gave his friend a mock salute before sauntering towards his car. Enzo rolled his eyes and straddled his motorcycle, watching his friend take off out of the parking lot.

Pulling into the street, Enzo aimed for his manor. There was a stack of paperwork waiting for him on his desk.

*****

The door to Enzo's office opened minutes after he'd sat down, depositing Lance into the room. He looked apologetic with his head hanging. Enzo was immediately standing, heart pounding, hoping that whatever Lance had to share didn't have to do with Amelia.

"Hey, boss man, sorry to bother. I just got a call from my family. There's been an emergency and I need to go home for a bit."

Enzo dropped back into his chair with a sigh of relief, waving his hand, "Go. Take care of your family. How long do you think it'll be?"

Lance shrugged, "Maybe a week or so. My mother is in pretty bad shape. There was an accident, she's got a few broken bones and is in the hospital."

Enzo nodded, "Well, like I said, take care of your family. Let us know if you need anything."

"Will do, thanks!" The man left the room, shutting the door behind himself.

Enzo frowned at the door. Despite Lance's need to leave and care for his family, his behavior suggested there was no true emotion regarding the accident. This wasn't the first time where Enzo had observed the sociopathic tendencies of the other man.

The red haired man had been unusually calm in the recent days without his girlfriend. It almost seemed as if he didn't care that Amelia was risking her life. He hadn't tried to find out more about her deployment or the purpose, there was a distinct lack of empathy that was steadily causing Enzo to become suspicious of Lance.

Berardi groaned, trying to ignore the worrisome thoughts and finally just pulled his phone out. Finding Matteo Hernandez's contact information, he pressed the call button. It rang three times before the Hispanic man answered, "Matteo, tell me you have something on the Cruz household."

"Actually, yes, we were about to call you," Matteo said before pausing. There was an unintelligible voice in the background. Matteo replied, "I am *not* saying that to Berardi, Dude!"

The voice came again and Enzo was still unable to make out what the other person was saying, "How about I just come down and hear what you have to say in person. Does that work for your friend?"

Matteo said something to the second person before answering his boss, "He said 'It's about time.'"

Enzo chuckled, "I'll be there in an hour or so."

Before he hung up, there was an explosion on the other end of the phone. The sound of shouts came through the phone.

"Is everything okay?" Enzo asked, alarmed.

Matteo coughed into the phone, "Luke's here, just so you know."

He hung up without another word and Enzo could feel his suddenly racing heart slow down. It had caught him off guard and his first instinct was to think it was an ambush. He was relieved to know it was his pyromaniac mechanic instead of a rival family.

He thought back to when he met Matteo Hernandez.

Amelia had become friends with the guy through some reading group the former had joined when trying to find a hobby. The two became thick as thieves when they realized that their professional lives both involved the acquisition of information.

Matteo then had become friends with Tom around the same time. The timing had made Enzo do some digging on the him, just to make sure that his people weren't being played. Nothing had come up and it had merely been a random coincidence. It had taken Enzo a while to fully believe it though, but the eager Hispanic had soon earned his trust.

Eventually, Tom had approached him about a job for Matteo. He'd seen what his friend could do with computers and surveillance equipment and thought he'd be an asset. At first, Enzo had been hesitant. Until Matteo had hacked into his computer and locked him out leaving the screen with a perpetual sign reading "please hire me!"

It took less than two hours after that incident for Enzo to change his mind and hire the man. Not only that, but Berardi realized how vital his skills were to helping his organization. Matteo dove right into the world of powerful families, weapons, secrets and hitmen, and he blended in beautifully, playing whatever part he needed and obtaining coveted pieces of information.

Amelia had been bringing Matteo into the fold without telling Enzo, and it led to one of their arguments that could be heard across the house. Followed by apologies on both ends and civilized explanations once Tom was present.

Amelia had been having trouble with a cipher that she'd recovered and had 'accidentally' left it where Matteo could find it. The man had seen the cipher, thought it was a puzzle and solved it in a matter of minutes. Once Amelia realized how quickly her friend was able to solve puzzles, she'd brought several puzzles to him.

Hernandez was one of the best people Enzo knew and he was eternally grateful to Tom and Amelia for finding him and bringing him into the fold. Matteo now ran their surveillance store near the edge of Jersey, leading into the city. He processed every bit of surveillance from cameras Enzo's men placed around the city. With the help of a few specially chosen staff members to assist, Hernandez ran the number one surveillance and camera store in the entirety of the state.

Luke Datar could often be found in the shop on his days off from his own shop. He was usually experimenting with explosives of some kind and in general being a chaotic menace to society. But that same menace always had beneficial information or tools for the organization. He was yet another person Enzo was grateful to have as an ally and friend.

Yet another knock sounded on the office door and Enzo was half expecting Lance to walk in again. But whatever was watching over Enzo offered him some reprieve because Tom stepped in.

He looked how Enzo felt. Exhausted. Rings stood out underneath his eyes, his hair was mussed and he'd shed his customary jacket at some point. He flopped onto the couch and dropped an arm over his face. Enzo looked on with quiet amusement, giving the man a minute to breathe before speaking.

"*Stai bene?*" The Italian slipping out from sheer habit. The two had learned it together as boys, their fathers insisted on it. They had elected to use it only when they wanted full honesty.

"*Esausto, ma vivo,*" Came the muffled reply, "*E tu?*"

Enzo sighed, "I'm concerned, Hernandez said that he already has something and Lance just asked for time off. The timing of it all... something is disconcerting about it."

Tom lifted his arm just enough to peek out at his boss, "How?"

"Lance's mannerisms. He won't ask about his girlfriend, but he will ask for time off for his family who he's never once mentioned?" Enzo said, "It's odd, no?"

Tom raised an eyebrow and sat up, "Want a tail on him?"

"For now, no. There isn't substantial evidence as of yet, and I don't like wasting manpower on that," He replied.

The man on the couch nodded, "Okay, so are you just griping? Or did you want a solution?"

Enzo glared at his friend and looked on his desk for some- thing to throw. His eyes landed on a pen sitting next to the computer, he grabbed it and chucked it across the room. The pen landed on Tom's chest with a quiet *thump*.

Tom sat up fully, grabbing the pen and sent it flying back at its owner. Enzo caught it with a chuckle. He got up from the desk, twirling the pen in between his fingers easily. Taking a seat across from Tom and propping his feet up on the coffee table, he remained silent. Considering the events of the past few months, wondering if the Hagans were trying to stir the pot. With the thefts happening in not just his own territory, but other groups' as well, Enzo had a feeling the Irish family was getting ready for something.

The Hagans were not usually a pleasant group, Narciso was a slimy bastard who disrespected territory lines and got away with it because he held one of the Big Three seats. The Commission was helpless against him unless a unanimous vote came through from the rest of the Thirteen. That wasn't going to happen unless an egregious crime came to light, and thus far, Narciso Hagan had been smart enough to cover his tracks. But he was building up, making bolder moves, hiding a little less.

Suddenly, Enzo sat up straighter. Putting puzzle pieces together in his mind as he sorted his thoughts. He was starting to understand the plan, and if Enzo was right, they had played right into his hand.

"What are you thinking?" Tom asked, breaking Enzo's concentration.

"We just delivered the lynch pin of Hagan's plans to him," Enzo told him, "We need to get to Hernandez's and pray that I'm wrong."

Enzo sprung from his seat, rushing towards the door. Barely stopping to grab a set of keys off the rack by the door, Enzo rushed out to the garage. Inside were several motorcycles and cars lined up next to each other. He grabbed a Kevlar jacket off the wall and pushed his arms through the sleeves before grabbing a helmet and gloves. Footsteps behind him told Enzo that Tom was following behind. The second man also grabbed protective gear and opened the garage.

The bikes roared to life and they took off, kicking up gravel behind them as they pulled out of the garage and onto the street. Enzo leaned close to the bike, swerving through the traffic, trying to reach his destination. If his hunch was right, then he and his organization needed to move quickly or Amelia might not be able to come home to them.

He was going to fight for her, fight for her freedom to come home to them even if it killed him.

Enzo Berardi: The Team

The bell to Hernandez Camera Co. rang loudly in the little store. Glass cases surrounded three sides of the store, filled with camera lenses, batteries, button cameras and microphones. Everything a person needed to either start a photography business or private-eye investigation. A pimple faced teenage boy was sitting on a stool playing on his phone when Enzo walked in. The boy nearly fell out of his chair at the sudden appearance of the two Italian men.

Tom gave the teenager a once over before saying, "Work day's over, kid. Go home."

"Uh, I-I-I can't! My shift isn't over!" He stuttered.

Enzo glanced at the kid's name tag, it read 'Stew,' the man rolled his eyes at it then addressed him, "Get out of here, kid. Store's closed now."

Stew didn't move from his stool, just staring, slaw jawed. A door opened and closed from somewhere further in the shop and Annabelle Hernandez, Matteo's wife, appeared. She looked back and forth between her employee and Enzo, hands on her hips and an annoyed expression on her face.

"You cannot keep coming in here and terrorizing the staff, Berardi!" She told him, she turned, "Stew, get out of here. You'll get your hours for today, just leave."

This got the kid moving. He tripped over his feet in his hurry to get away from Enzo and Tom. He glanced over his shoulder once, wide eyed and morbidly curious.

"Now, Stew!" Annabelle yelled without even needing to look.

No one spoke until the shop's backdoor rattled then slammed shut. Annabelle turned to Enzo, now crossing her arms and giving him a raised eyebrow.

She was a round faced woman with wide brown eyes, blonde hair pulled back into a ponytail. Her uniform consisted of worn jeans and a gray t-shirt that had the shop's logo printed on the back. Silver hoops swung from double pierced ears when she shook her head and her solitaire wedding ring caught the light when she moved to rest her hand on the counter.

Annabelle drummed her fingers, then let out a sigh, "Well, come on. You didn't race to the shop to yell at the kid. Matteo and Luke are in the basement."

She led Enzo and Tom behind the counter and to the basement door. It was rusted metal, coated in a beige paint that was trying and failing to hide the discoloration under- neath. A single light bulb lit the way down the creaking steps. Annabelle motioned for the men to go down.

Enzo went first, as he got further down he could smell gunpowder in the air from the explosions Luke liked to cause. Tom followed behind and chuckled lightly when the pungent odor hit his nose. Behind them, the rusted door clanged shut behind them and Annabelle disappeared from view.

The basement was like a fortress, slate gray walls with computers on two sides, one side showing surveillance footage from both around Enzo's house and in the Cruzes' house. The other side was the Hernandez work space, the desk was littered with notebooks, pencils, and candy wrappers. Enzo wasn't sure how He got anything done in the disorganized mess, but he let it be.

He glanced down the hall to his right, it led to a bathroom and storage closet. He knew first hand the closet wasn't the average janitor supply closet. It held cleaning utensils, yes, but it also concealed explosive materials such as glycerin, gunpowder, contraband fireworks, and other detonation devices that Enzo would never understand.

Down the other hall was Luke's honorary work room. in there they'd installed steel walls for the times when some- thing exploded unexpectedly. Which was every time.

The door to the workroom opened depositing Luke and Matteo into the hall. They saw their boss and both gave him a sheepish smile, as if they were trying to convince him that they hadn't done anything they weren't supposed to. But they were given up by a flash of light, a terrific bang and smoke following them out of the room.

Luke turned and slammed the door shut preventing any more smoke from following them. He gave Enzo another cheeky grin and a wave. He shoved Matteo in the side, a not so subtle hint to wave as well.

Matteo was a Hispanic man with thick black hair and mustache, his glasses were askew on his face. His dark pants hid any indicators of what explosive had just gone off. Like his wife, he was wearing a t-shirt bearing the logo of their shop. Like Amelia, he had an accent, but unlike Amelia where her accent was just a whisper, hardly there, Matteo's was thick and heavy, there was no denying his first language.

Grease stained Luke's clothing and his silver hair. His graphic t-shirt with some superhero that Enzo didn't know, was rumpled and one of his shoes was untied. All in all, he looked exactly like the kid brother they'd all adopted him as.

Berardi raised a brow at them but didn't get a confession because Matteo started tapping on his keyboard and motioning for Enzo to get closer.

"Come check this out."

Matteo had him pull up an extra chair so he could sit and watch the screen.

Luke and Tom came to watch over their shoulders. Both Matteo and Luke smelled of smoke and the latter had grease stains on his hands and clothes as usual. Enzo shook his head at them and glanced at Tom who grinned at the eau de smoke rolling off of his friends. Enzo often wondered if Tom joined their explosive adventures on his off days.

Matteo reached to play the recording but stopped and turned to look at him, "This is a recording, I want you to remember that. It isn't actually happening right now. You can't go big bad mafia boss on them for this."

Enzo glared at the man but didn't get a chance to say anything because he started the recording. In the video, the Cruz brothers were in their study with Narciso and Royal Hagan. Most of them were smoking cigars, lounging leisurely on the furniture without a care in the world. Camilo had even gone so far as to kick one shoe off and was dangling the other on his toes. It was coming dangerously close to falling from his foot.

Benjamin finally broke the silence, "So, Hagan, when are we going to meet this other son of yours?"

Narciso chuckled, "How about next weekend? Bring your family to our home for dinner; I'll make sure the groom is there."

Benjamin shrugged, taking a puff of his cigar, "Works for me."

"We can give my dear little brother and future sister-in-law some private time to get to know one another," Royal grinned, a malicious glint in his eyes, "I'd like to see her try a stunt on him. He'll have her pinned faster than she can blink!"

Hagan, Benjamin and Camilo laughed at Royal's remark while Angel chuckled uncomfortably. He glanced at his brothers and then at the other men, "I do hope that the understanding is that our sister isn't a punching bag."

Narciso waved him off dismissively, "Yes, yes! Don't get your knickers in a wad over a joke."

Angel rolled his eyes, "I don't mean that your son can't teach her to behave, heaven knows she needs an education, I would just rather not deal with her submitting an abuse report to the Commission. They're a pain to deal with."

"You're forgetting that as two of the leading members of the Commission, we'd be able to squash the complaint if it did happen," Hagan reminded Angel.

Matteo shut the recording off, "There isn't much else. Just some more old fashioned B.S.. They don't mention who this 'other son' is at any other point either."

Luke interjected, "We've checked every hospital record, every public and private record we could think of. Whoever this guy is, he's a mystery. There's nothing on him anywhere."

"Great. That's helpful," Tom groaned, "Was there any word on the streets?"

"Nothing that either Fae or I have heard," He shrugged apologetically.

Tom swore under his breath. Enzo stared at the screen in front of him. This confirmed his suspicions; the Hagans were plotting something and they were involving the Cruzes. Enzo suspected that they would drop the cartel once they'd achieved their goal, the Hagans weren't the kind to make an ally if they could be considered equal in status.

"Luke, keep your ear to the ground, and if you can, let Amelia know that she has a very limited amount of time to work," Enzo told the young man, "We need to get her out soon. Tom, meet with our captains. They need to be ready for ambushes and thefts."

Tom raised a brow, "You mean the thefts we've already been dealing with?"

"Yes, exactly like that. The Hagans are responsible," Enzo said, "They have been the whole time."

"How do you know that?" Matteo asked, sheer curiosity on his face.

Enzo looked back at the frozen image on the computer monitor, "It's the only way to explain them renegotiating a partnership with the Cruzes and for even hinting at this second son now. They've got something brewing and I want us to be ready when they finally reveal what it is."

"Why can't you take this to the Commission?" Luke asked. He was frowning at the screen like he was trying to understand what he was looking at.

A look of understanding dawned on Tom's face, "There's never been enough evidence to indict him, only suspicions. Like when people thought he killed his wife, but no one could prove it so he went unpunished."

"I still don't see what we're preparing for," Luke admitted.

"If the Hagans are going to start being more public, they're going to get more aggressive. The more aggressive they get, the more of a division there will be among families. Their usurping will cause strife and commotion," Enzo explained, "It's a good time to build alliances."

"In short they'll disrupt a hundred year balance we've had in the state. They'll gather attention from not just the local authorities but also the people. They're playing with fire," Tom finished.

"What would the goal actually be though?" Matteo asked.

Enzo sighed and thought about it. He never wanted to take his organization to war, he'd done it once before; when his father had been killed. He didn't have to wonder how he would react if Amelia met the same fate.

If the Hagans tried to take the Commission, Enzo would destroy them so completely they could never rebuild.

There was fire in his eyes when he replied to Matteo, "For now, we make an effort to maintain balance. If that's impossible, then we burn them down."

*****

Enzo pulled his motorcycle off the road at the docks, Tom following closely behind. At their approach, a man came out of the guard house and opened the manual gate for them, waving them through with a salute. Their arrival gathered the attention of many dock workers who looked on curiously.

Many went straight back to work, others watched while trying to pretend they were still working.

An older man stepped out of one of the portable offices, the hinges on the metal door squeaking loud enough to send the employees back to work. The man raised a hand in greeting to Enzo and Tom as they dismounted their bikes. He walked up to them and clasped Enzo's hand, shaking it respectfully and promptly doing the same with Tom.

"Hey, Boss," The man said in a thick Russian accent, "How did you know to come here?"

Tom frowned, "Excuse me?"

The man frowned, "I was about to call you. We had another shipment stolen."

"Petrov, please tell me that you're yanking on my chain and aren't being serious," Enzo pinched the bridge of his nose, squeezing his eyes closed.

"No sir, I no kid," Petrov told him earnestly.

"Petrov doesn't have a sense of humor that we're aware of," Tom sighed, "This is great, just great."

Enzo looked around the docking yard. The salty air stung his nostrils and the sounds of machinery filled the air. Hagan was pirating his goods without care and that he was going to pay back with interest. He ground his teeth together so hard he wondered if he ought to keep a dentist on retainer.

Cargo containers were being lifted from a docked ship and set neatly in lines along the dock. Each had an identification number painted onto it on multiple sides. He hoped it meant that it would be easy to find the missing containers.

"What was taken?"

Petrov looked at the clipboard he was carrying. Flipping through the papers, scanning for the answer, "Car parts."

Enzo turned and repeated, "Car parts? That's all?"

Tom seemed to understand where Enzo's mind was going, "Why would they need car parts? The Cruzes import their own. Surely an alliance would mean sharing imports."

"I believe a safe assumption would be they're planning to build an empire, but to do that, they need to stockpile," Enzo rubbed the underside of his chin thoughtfully, "They don't believe the rest of the families will fall in line easily, so they're preparing to survive in case some rebel. That's what we'll need to bank on."

Tom nodded, "I'll call in sentinels to help guard our shipments and stop the thefts."

"Do that. I'm sure Petrov will appreciate it," Enzo said. He pulled his keys from his pocket and moved towards his bike. Tossing the keys up in the air and catching them again. He stood by the bike and observed the yard one more time, a fierce look on his face.

"We're still missing something," He declared.

"Hagan's spy?" Tom suggested, "We still haven't found him yet either. I don't think we'll be able to get ahead of Narciso until we find the rat."

Enzo snapped his fingers and pointed at Tom, indicating he was correct. The spy. For a brief moment he'd forgotten. The rat, the mole, the backstabber, the invisible man. Since they had no clue to his identity, it was time to go digging for a needle in a haystack.

"Ask Luke and Matteo to meet us at the house tonight, we're going through personnel files until we find something that might help us," Enzo commanded, "I'll meet you there. I have an errand to run."

Climbing onto his bike, Enzo left the docking yard. His engine roared as he sped away, angry and frustrated. He needed a little time to just drive and clear his head.

Several hours later, when the sun was beginning to set, Enzo entered his home again. Voices filled the entryway, drifting in from the formal dining area that had been converted into a meeting room. Enzo found the other people already gathered around the large oval table in the center of the room. He shrugged off his jacket, wincing at the motion and hung it over the back of his chair. He rolled his shoulder as if it would ease his stinging skin underneath.

Luke had a large stack of files in front of where he stood at the table, a small cup with markers sitting next to it. Tom was setting a basket filled with little snacks on the table before setting himself in his chair. He even had water bottles and was passing them around, setting them in front of everyone's spot. He stopped when he realized he had accidentally grabbed one to put at Amelia's spot.

"She better get home soon," He grumbled.

"I agree with you there. It's weird without her here, no one is messing with Matteo," Luke teased with a small smile.

Enzo took in the sight before him, these people were family. He was reminded of the impending threat against them and he felt the urge to keep them safe. To maintain their trust in him as a leader.

He loved the meetings at this table usually. Everyone in his inner circle had their own chair that they'd picked, making it their own. This meant Tom, Matteo, Luke, Lance and Amelia all had chairs. Although, he hadn't originally wanted to give one to Lance. Enzo didn't care that the furnishing was chaotic, his group was comfortable.

Tom's was a traditional high back, black leather office chair with thick cushions padding the back and sides. Luke had a stool with a rounded bottom that required him to continually work to keep balanced. He swore up and down it helped him focus and Enzo wasn't going to question it.

Matteo had chosen a red and black gaming chair with cup holders in the armrests that he usually kept a stylus in. His water bottle never went into the cupholders, it stayed on the table at all times, next to his laptop.

Amelia's chair was a weird two-level chair designed so that she could comfortably sit crisscross at the table.

Enzo hadn't put much thought into his chair, he'd copied his father's favorite seat in the house above and had a large armchair. However, his was red leather unlike his father's sleek black.

Lance had also gone the route of a gaming chair. His had a reclining feature unlike the other one at the table. It wasn't uncommon to find him casually laying in the chair and reading a report in one hand, drink in the other.

The snack basket at the center of the table had been Amelia's suggestion as she always liked to have a snack within reach. There were hard candies, gummies, crackers, and protein bars in the wicker basket.

"Shall we begin?" Matteo interrupted Enzo's thoughts, "I've pulled the files from the same year that the Cruzes tried to create a contract with the Hagans. I also still have a program on my computer going through the organization's information so that I can red flag anyone else."

The group took their seats at the table and let the young woman distribute the files to them, "We're going to manually go through these and see if anything pops out at us."

The markers were passed out and two piles of paper set on the table, one for the possible red flags and the ones they cleared. They sat in silence for the most part, only talking to ask questions to one another about a person in the file they were reading. Slowly over the next few hours, the cleared stack began to grow significantly larger than the possible red flag stack.

It was well after midnight when they wrapped up their first round of sorting. They were left with a stack of files that had more remaining in it than they would've liked. But they made progress and they were taking comfort in that.

"So, these are the people we need to fire?" Enzo asked. He scrubbed his hands over his face tiredly.

"I suppose so. I'd rather not have any red flags in the company. But I also think it's likely to happen everywhere, given our organization, unfortunately," Tom leaned back and rubbed his eyes, "My head hurts from reading all of this."

"Same," Luke dropped his head onto the table, "I'm going to order pizza so we can keep working. Any special requests or the usual?"

He pushed up from the table and tiredly walked over to a side table where a laptop lay. Tapping on the keyboard a few times to pull up their favorite pizza joint that found the delivery screen. Luke looked over his shoulder, "You guys didn't answer my question!"

"Just get the usual, man," Matteo called back.

He nodded and proceeded to tap on the keyboard. Enzo reached for one of the possible red flag folders and flipped it open. Inside was a photo and resume of a lower level runner who'd been picked up by the local authorities several times. Reading the charges, he frowned, many of them were for assault and battery and a few breaking and entering, but nothing stood out to him as a major concern. He continued reading through his work reports and that's when he saw it; this particular runner had a pension for running off and disappearing for hours at a time without so much as a word of warning.

"Tom, take a look at this guy and let me know what you think, won't you?" Enzo yawned, handing the file over before grabbing a new one.

Luke came back to the table, "Food's ordered."

"Take a break until the pizza gets here, guys," Enzo pushed himself out of his chair, "We'll come back after we've all had a little food. I'm going to make a pot of coffee."

*****

The next morning came slowly, by the time dawn rolled in, they'd gone through several pots of coffee, their cups strewn across the table, some half full, others empty. Empty pizza boxes were stacked in the corner, paper plates piled in the trash bin. The stack of red flag files had been whittled down even further and yet Enzo still didn't think they had the right person yet.

The group had moved to the living room around three A.M. in hopes that the change of scenery would help them focus, maybe see something new.

Luke had fallen asleep around five, a file still open on his lap. Tom had tossed his jacket over the back of the couch and undone the top button on his shirt, his hair was sticking up in all directions from scratching his head in thought. Matteo was staring at the file in front of him but wasn't actually reading it.

Enzo yawned and took a sip of his coffee. It had been a long night for all of them, whether they had been reading the files all night or checking the video feed at the Cruzes. They were exhausted and were past the point of making progress. He glanced at the tablet set up on the coffee table, the video footage showed a dark room, quiet in the early morning hours.

"I don't know what else we can find, man," Tom hid a yawn behind his hand, "I've read the same paragraph five times and still don't know what it says."

Matteo nodded, setting his file down, "We need sleep."

"Go on upstairs, rest. Recuperate, please," Berardi sighed, completely drained, "Come back in a few hours."

Tom stood from the couch and stretched his arms over his head, "You're not going to sleep, are you?"

"First in, last out," Enzo shrugged.

"Whatever, man," Tom shoved Luke's shoulder to wake him up, "Just try and rest a little, Amelia will have my head if you die while she's gone."

Enzo shook his head with a chuckle as the younger man jerked awake. Luke took a moment, rubbing the sleep from his eyes before focusing on Tom who jerked his head in the direction of the stairs. Enzo had made sure that there were always rooms set up for his team in case of nights like these. He watched the team file out and trudge up the stairs. Three doors opened and closed leaving him alone with his thoughts.

He scanned the room, balls of discarded paper littered the table and floors. Different colored markers strewn across the table haphazardly, the disorganization proof of the team's fatigue.

Enzo stood up suddenly and began to collect the trash, needing to be able to see progress. In his tired state, it took him several trips to the kitchen garbage can to clear up the room. He straightened the stacks of paper and lined the markers up, trying to bring order to the chaos of his living room. When there was nothing else he could do, he stood there, hands by his side helplessly. Unsure of what to do next, he decided to go to his own room and at least change clothes.

His room was neat and tidy, the only thing messy was the bed. He ignored it and made his way into the closet, shoes neatly lined up on the floor, suit jackets hung in a color coordinating pattern. Pants and shirts were hung in the same fashion, the few shelves in the back held t-shirts that were rarely worn.

He found a pair of sweatpants to pair with a soft t-shirt and quickly changed, dropping the dirty clothes in a basket sitting in the corner.

Flopping across his bed, Enzo let out a groan, "What am I missing?"

No one answered him.

Amelia Cruz: A Brief Reprieve

Every day that passed was filled with Amelia's brothers shooting her dirty looks for ruining their dinner, taunts about her time with Enzo, and wedding planning on the Hagans' end.

At one point, Royal had come to drop off an engagement ring his brother had selected. A brother the Cruz family still knew nothing about. Not even his name. It was irritating her that she had yet to meet the man. She couldn't help but feel a pit in her stomach, like her instinct was telling her something. The problem was she didn't know what it was saying yet.

Narciso had given the family an explanation for how his son had remained hidden. He'd supposedly adopted him after marrying his mother. It had been an act of kindness on his part. Amelia didn't buy the act. Narciso was the king of ulterior motives and every one of the Families knew it.

After spending a week with her brothers, Amelia slipped from the house, fed up with the Cruzes. She'd gone about a block before hailing a taxi to take her into Manhattan and towards Luke's shop.

Mrs. Byrd had agreed to cover for her at the house just in case her brothers bothered to ask questions later. She didn't think they would, they were too wrapped up in missing shipments from their docks.

The taxi dropped her a couple of blocks from the mechanic's shop. She thanked the driver and made her way towards her friend's building. The streets bustled with people around her, unaware of the strife bubbling up in their home, unaware that even the crime syndicates were nervous. Amelia glanced down at the jewelry on her hand, it was an ugly silver claddagh ring with a single white sapphire set roughly in the center. The choice of ring was due to the Hagans' pride in their Irish heritage, at least, that's what Narciso had said. For such a rich family, Amelia found herself annoyed, they hadn't even gotten it in the correct ring size. She'd told them. Twice. She rolled her eyes, men, always thinking that something was bigger than it was.

She hoped when the time came for Lance to propose, he remembered her ring size. Amelia glanced at her phone. She had only heard from her boyfriend once since she'd left, he'd told her that he would talk to her when she was finally honest with him. Everyday, she sent him a couple of messages, trying desperately to have some form of a conversation. Trying to explain that she couldn't share what she was doing and that she loved him.

Each day that passed without communication, Amelia found herself not even wanting to try. She was so tired of trying to constantly make up for simply working. She groaned and put her phone back into her pocket. She wished they could go back to the early days of their relationship.

Two Years Ago:

Lance was driving the two of them to their date spot for the evening. He hadn't told Amelia where they were going, just that it was one of his favorite spots in town. He'd been a perfect gentleman, opening the doors, planning the evening, and telling Amelia how beautiful she looked.

When they arrived at the restaurant, he came around and opened her door again, offering her a hand. Amelia stepped out of the car to see the restaurant was a small Irish pub. She'd never heard of it before but it was clearly a popular spot.

As they approached the door she could see people lined up at the hightop bar and servers scrambling to attend to them all. Tables were packed to the gills and waiters wove in between them holding their trays high to avoid being knocked over. A couple of billiard tables in the back had people surrounding them, jeering and laughing at the players.

"Wow," Amelia looked around, trying to take it all in, "This is something."

Lance grinned down at her, "Isn't it great?"

"I feel overdressed," Amelia admitted, looking down at her dress and heels.

"You look perfect," Lance lifted her hand up to his lips and kissed it.

He led her into the restaurant and asked the host for a table. Amelia was surprised when they were seated instantly. Somehow in the midst of the chaos, there was an empty table. Lance reached across the table and clasped Amelia's hand, staring at her adoringly.

"You truly are amazing. How did I get so lucky?" He kissed her hand again.

Amelia's cheeks tinted pink and she ducked her head, "You're sweet, thank you. I can't believe that I am yours."

Most dates that followed were similar. Lance complimenting her and loving her in what felt like an unconditional way.

Amelia found herself falling fast and hard for him. Having never experienced love from her family, she was so grateful for the love she got from Lance.

Everyday she got 'I love you' and 'you are amazing, I'm so lucky,' messages from him. Each one gave her butterflies and made her love him that much more. She was happy to do things for him, whether it was dressing more casually or spending less time exploring the city and being with Fae, Luke, or Tom. He loved her.

But somewhere along the way, he started to worry about how closely she worked with Enzo. He began to get possessive and protective. Amelia had to work harder than ever to keep him appeased.

Now:

Amelia snuck her phone out of her pocket to send Lance one more text as she approached Luke's shop.

Amelia: I love and miss you.

As she approached the shop, a delightful aroma reached her nose, making her turn her head in the direction of Fae's coffee house and bar. The open sign was lit up and through the windows, patrons could be seen at the tables laughing and chatting with one another. Given that she hadn't told Luke she was coming, Amelia decided to cross the street to visit her other friend first. There was no harm in getting a little *café* as well.

A bell tinkled lightly when she entered, the smell of coffee and pastries overwhelming her senses. A few people near the door turned their heads out of sheer instinct but went quickly back to their conversations. A server greeted her kindly from the register, waving and smiling.

Amelia came up to the counter, greeting the server in return, "¡*Buenos dias*! How are you this morning?"

"I'm wonderful, what can I get for you?" The server replied chipperly.

"Is Fae in?" Amelia asked while scanning the menu for any new items she may have missed.

"She is, would you like me to get her?"

"Please, *gracias*." Amelia smiled.

The server nodded and left the register, going into the kitchen through the big swinging doors. A moment later the waitress returned with Fae Clotho, a short, blonde woman. She wore a sage colored shirt covered in flour and baggy, khaki cargo pants. She grinned when she saw Amelia, her nose crinkled when she smiled, making her septum piercing catch the light.

"Amelia!" Fae cried happily, rounding the counter to embrace her friend, "Where have you been girl? I haven't seen you in here all weekend! Not since Race Day!"

"I've been laying low, honestly, needed some time away from the idiots who were always fighting," Amelia grinned, "I'm sure you know who I mean."

Fae threw her head back and laughed, "Of course, I do! Well, don't worry, neither is here right now. Although, I think I saw Tom here not too long ago. I hope he isn't a problem for you."

"Not at all," Amelia replied, "Tomaso and I are still on fine terms last I checked."

"Good, because he's still sitting at the back corner table if you want to say hi," Fae went to the other side of the counter again, "But, for now, what can I get for you?"

The Hispanic woman looked at the menu again before turning back to her friend, "Surprise me!"

Fae laughed again. Her bright smile was contagious, "Sounds good. On the house, purely because I missed you and am definitely *not* trying to bribe you into not disappearing on me again. We'll bring it to you."

Amelia thanked her and went to find Tom. He was sitting in the very back corner, nearly hidden from view. The deep booth he was sitting in was doing well to conceal him.

"Did you want the solitude or may I join you?" Amelia asked.

Tom's head jerked up from his phone when she spoke. A smile spread across his face and he stood from the table, wrapping his arms around her tightly. He took a step back from her, keeping his hands on her shoulders to look her up and down. When he was satisfied with whatever he saw, he motioned to the table.

"Why, pray tell, were you giving me a once over?" She asked, raising a brow.

Tom chuckled, "I promised our boss I would if I saw you. He wanted to make sure you remained uninjured."

She rolled her eyes, "I can take care of myself you know."

"I am well aware, I've been on the receiving end of your punch before," Tom chuckled into his cup, "It's not some- thing I'd like to experience again"

"We were sparring!" Amelia smiled, "It was an accident."

"So you say," Tom smirked.

Amelia rolled her eyes and tried to kick him underneath the table. He winced when her foot connected with his shin and reached to rub it with an exaggerated groan. She laughed at his dramatic reaction.

"We've all missed you this week, Amelia. There's an imbalance without you," He admitted to her softly, "Enzo especially, not that he would admit it. He went to see Frank the first day you were gone."

"I knew he would," Amelia shook her head, "I miss home. It's been a long week."

Tom frowned, "Are you okay? You look kind of pale."

Amelia slumped in her seat, she should have known he would see the weight she was carrying. She looked at her friend before admitting, "My brothers have taken it upon themselves to remind me everyday that the only thing I have to offer is my ability to breed."

"Amelia Rose, you believe them? You cannot possibly believe them!" Tom looked offended, "I'm serious, when you have so many people pulling for you at home and you know we've got your six, how could you possibly believe that for a single second?"

"I don't really think I believe it!" She told him defensively, "It just is hard sometimes. You hear these degrading things about you for hours on end, non stop. You're going to get tired of it and even start feeling like you deserve it."

Tom stared for a moment, pity written on his face. She glared at him, a silent warning to wipe the look from his face. He sat back quickly and tried to don a new expression.

She made a face at him, sticking her tongue out, "How do you play poker? You read like an open book."

Tom laughed, "I can hide my expressions if I want to."

"Can you? Really?" Amelia smiled, mischief dancing in her eyes, "That's news to me."

"Okay, you know what," He didn't finish the sentence, instead just wagged his finger in her face.

The waitress came and dropped a coffee at their table with a smile. As she left, she gave Tom a wink and little wave. Amelia smirked at the blush that rose on her friend's cheeks. She tried to hide her smile behind her mug, but Tom caught it and glared at her.

"So how's this new engagement, by the way?" Tom asked, leaning forward.

"Well, I haven't had to worry about wedding planning. The Hagans have been organizing the whole thing. Unfortunately for them, I won't be going through with it. But the oddest part is, they haven't introduced the guy yet!" Amelia said urgently, "I've never seen his face, I have no idea who he is. No name either. They refer to him as 'my brother,' 'my second son,' or just 'my other son.' Nothing beyond that. Whoever this is, they're still trying to keep his identity hidden. I'm getting worried."

"Wait, you're engaged to a guy you've never met?" Tom asked, both astounded and teasing.

The woman rolled her eyes, "Please! I just said that I am breaking off the engagement before the wedding, not that they're giving me much time to figure out a plan. Although that's kind of the point, they want to prevent me from being able to sabotage them again. The wedding is set for a week from today."

Tom's coffee spewed across the table, "We've had our eyes on the cameras and audio all week, how did we miss that?"

Amelia shrugged, "No idea, but take care how you tell Berardi and Lance. They might blow a gasket and actually end up agreeing on something."

"You think it might actually bring them together for once?" Tom chuckled. Then a crease formed on his brow, "The wedding is in a week? That explains what we've been seeing, I think."

"What have you been dealing with?" Amelia sipped her coffee, enjoying the flavor. Fae hadn't disappointed with the chocolatey drink and pastry she'd picked.

"For starters, our shipments are being pilfered even more than usual. Pretty sure Hagan is preparing a take over," He explained, "Enzo is trying to pull together support from the other families, but that's rather difficult when they believe that the Cruzes and Hagans are in an alliance. They're afraid."

"What's your proof that they aren't actually going to keep the alliance?" She asked between bites of her pastry.

"It's a hunch. But considering what they've been swiping, it's a good guess," He told her, "They're stockpiling to impact supply and demand."

Amelia hummed thoughtfully, taking a bite of her pastry. She didn't reply for a moment, mulling over the information. Tom watched her, waiting for her to say something. When she didn't he continued.

"Lance took time off, said he had to go home to take care of his family," Tom said casually, "So right now, you don't need to worry about him reacting to your brothers signing a betrothal contract."

Amelia frowned, "That's not like him. Which family member?"

"His mother," Tom answered. He watched Amelia's reaction over his coffee. Hurt was written on her face, "Why?"

"Firstly, he's never even mentioned his family to me, secondly, he's never taken time off for me," She sighed, "It's stupid. We're not married, I shouldn't expect that of him. It's fine."

"Amelia," Tom said gently, "I'm going to say this once, and if you ever tell Enzo, I will deny it to the ends of the earth. Your relationship with Lance is not a healthy one. I am concerned for you and so is Enzo. He won't ever demand anything from you regarding your relationships, he's always wanted you to be free to make your own choices. We'll respect that you're dating Lance, but it isn't healthy. And Enzo... it's breaking him slowly. He's so in love with you and won't ever say anything because he doesn't want to take away your choice."

"Tom, Lance is a good guy," She said defensively, trying to ignore the comment about Enzo. It was hard when it struck her like a knife in the chest. But she persisted in defending Lance, "He really is!"

"Who are you trying to convince? Me? Or yourself? Because even you don't believe it," Tom sat back, crossing his arms over his chest, "Amelia, I can see the doubt on your face. Maybe take some time to think about it while he's away and not here to whisper in your ear."

Amelia stood abruptly, "I need to go."

Tom jumped up and caught her wrist, "Just think about it. You don't deserve someone who is *just* a 'good guy.' You deserve that amazing, unconditional, undying love. I don't want to see you lose yourself while trying to justify what you have instead of pursuing what you want."

Amelia blinked up at him before ripping her wrist from his grasp. She darted out the door, not even waving goodbye to Fae at the counter. Weaving through the crowded sidewalk, hardly focusing on where she was, just trying to get over to Luke's shop, where she had originally intended to go. She was regretting going to get coffee.

Amelia glanced at her phone, her heart dropping even lower when she realized she still had no messages from Lance. The young woman hurried in the direction of the mechanic's shop, hoping she could still make a quick stop before going back to her family home. She hoped no one had noticed her absence yet.

In her urgency to get away from the coffee shop, she didn't notice a man wearing a fedora low over his eyes. He bumped into her roughly, slipping something into her hand as he did so. Whipping around and trying to make sense of what happened, Amelia's breath caught in her throat; Berardi was rounding the corner, one hand tucked deep into one of his pockets. He glanced up and tipped his hat at her before he disappeared out of sight.

She stopped in the middle of the sidewalk and looked at her hand. A neatly folded paper sat in her palm. Her name was written in Enzo's neat, tight handwriting. With trembling fingers, she opened it.

Amelia,

I am grateful for what you're doing. I know it isn't easy, I know that your brothers are unkind. I am proud of how you are representing our Family. Not only proud, but impressed.

We miss you here at home. I miss you. I hope that we can get you out this week. We've made some progress on our end.

We think that the Hagans are creating a stockpile so they can take over the Commission. I believe the plan is to use you as a way to get the Cruzes and their allies to support his rise to power. Pray I'm wrong.

Keep your head up. The end is in sight. I hope.

Yours,

L. Berardi

Amelia Cruz: Memories

Since she'd given the majority of the information she'd learned to Tom, Amelia didn't stay at Luke's long. Enough time to say hello and help him by changing the oil on a car. She'd tried to use the conversation about bike repairs to distract herself from the conversation with her other colleague. The paper from Enzo was burning a hole in her pocket, tempting her to reach for it and read it again. BY the time she left Luke's, Amelia hadn't calmed her mind at all. Instead she was even more frustrated than when she'd left.

The *hacienda* was quiet when she got home, not a single one of her brothers' vehicles was in the driveway. Likely out with the Hagans to plot their rise to power. But she could use that time to take a look around the house and possibly find a paper trail.

Amelia walked along the hallway up to the study. Upon reaching the door, Amelia took a breath and reached for the knob. It was thankfully unlocked and allowed her access to the room. Not that a lock would keep her out for long.

Every curtain was open in the study, allowing for natural light to flood in, giving the room a rare but pleasant atmosphere. A few plants sat by the windows adding a pop of color to the orange clay walls. The bottles of liquor on a nearby shelf shone in the sunlight, the crystal cups sparkling in the light.

Amelia looked up to where one of the cameras was hidden and waved at it,

"Hi, Hernandez. I think you're watching right now."

Her phone dinged a moment later with a message from Matteo.

Matteo: I swear, you always know when someone is actively watching. Do you have a camera here that I don't know about?

Amelia: And what if I do?

Matteo: Ha ha, so funny. Do your job!

Amelia looked back up at the cameras and gave a mock salute, "Yes, sir."

She opened a drawer on the desk and pulled out the stack of papers she found inside. Hopefully her brothers kept everything in one place. That level of organization would be surprising for any of them, but they'd shocked their sister before, perhaps they would do it again.

Among the papers she found was a spreadsheet with times on it, some rows highlighted in yellow marker. There were times and coordinates listed in the columns consistent with shipment schedules. The coordinates marked shipyards in the Cruz territory so Amelia set the paper aside and began searching through the stack again. To Amelia's surprise, there were copies of contracts of the suppliers the Berardis used. Private papers she herself rarely saw. Most of the time the contracts were handled by Enzo and Tom and absolutely no one else. The Hagan spy had been busy.

As she went through the papers she glanced up at the cameras again, "How's the missus, Matteo?"

Annabelle: Are you really about to have a conversation through the cameras?

Amelia: And if I am?

Matteo: Are you ever going to answer a message directly? Geez, you're as bad as Berardi when answering something. Always deflecting.

Amelia: You like me though!

Matteo: Humph.

Amelia laughed and set her phone down. The next paper she found had Angel and Benjamin's signatures at the bottom as well as Narciso Hagan's. She studied the paper curiously, wondering what could possibly require all of them to sign. The more she read, the more annoyed she got.

"They set a dowry! Those bastards set a dowry!" She exclaimed, "Those stupid idiots paid the Hagans for the marriage. They signed over parts of their corporation upon completion of the marriage. The Hagans get twenty-five percent of the profits that come from the imports Angel and Benjamin bring in. That's outrageous!"

The phone dinged again from where it sat on the desk.

Matteo: Send me a photo!

Matteo: Are you sure you're mad at the dowry or just that they think you're only worth 25%?

Amelia sent a rude gesture toward the camera before snapping a picture of the contract and sent it to her friend and Tom. Enzo was right, the Hagans were preparing to take over.

Amelia: Oh, hush! It's not funny. This is another piece of evidence that supports Berardi's theory!

Again, she set the paper aside and continued to dig. When she couldn't find anything else interesting in the current pile, she carefully laid the stack back in its drawer. Moving on the bottom drawer she found it locked, she sighed softly at the mild inconvenience.

Slipping a couple of pins from her hair, Amelia inserted them into the keyhole and worked them inside for a minute. The lock clicked and the drawer slid smoothly open , she sat back with a satisfied expression on her face, pleased with how little time it had take her to pick the lock.

Several manila folders were lined up in no particular order. Flipping through them, Amelia found they all had a title, some in English, others in Spanish. The lack of order made it hard to understand what the point of the envelopes were without opening them, but they were completely sealed. She couldn't disturb the seal and risk her brothers realizing she was spying on them.

Ding!

Matteo: Find anything yet?

Amelia: Sealed envelopes. I don't know if I have time to steam them open. Do you know where my brothers are?

Matteo: Yeah, pulling up to the house. You don't have time. Get out of the study!

Amelia's head shot up. In the distance there were sounds of several cars approaching the house. She swore and straightened the envelopes and slammed the drawer shut. She locked it as quickly as possible and rushed from the room. Stopping on the landing to listen for a moment and breathing a sigh of relief when she didn't hear the front door opening just yet, Amelia dashed into her room.

Slamming the door behind herself and grabbing a book from the shelf, Amelia threw herself across the bed. She opened the book to a random page and pretended she was reading. A precaution if anyone stormed into her room.

From downstairs a door slammed and male voices filled the halls. Benjamin was frustrated about something but Amelia couldn't make out what he was saying. Camilo responded in a casual tone and headed up the steps. Amelia knew which brother it was simply by the sound of his footsteps. As a young girl she'd needed to learn how to tell each family member apart without looking, thus the knowledge of their footsteps. The voices at the bottom continued to speak, getting louder as they came up the stairs. Angel and Benjamin seemed to be in a deep discussion about a charity gala the next night as well as the upcoming dinner with the Hagans where they would meet Amelia's betrothed.

Amelia was familiar with the gala. It was a yearly event where the Families gathered like high society and pretended to be civilized. She had attended every year since she'd been sixteen.

"I don't understand why you think we should announce this tomorrow night, Benjamin," Angel was saying, "We haven't met him yet, what if something falls through?"

"That's the point, *Hermano*! By announcing tomorrow, it will force them to keep their end of the bargain!" Benjamin was explaining, he sounded exasperated, like he'd already tried to make his point a thousand times.

The voices stopped moving on the landing. She wondered which way they were going to go. Up to the study or to their rooms? They continued talking, not moving.

"It also has the added benefit of showing Amelia off as being back on our side. Showing that Berardi isn't as invincible as he thinks," Benjamin said. The floor creaked beneath his feet leading Amelia to think that he was leaning against the rail on the landing.

"You make a good point," Angel admitted, "It would make a good statement."

A knock on her door made Amelia jump. She'd been so focused on the conversation she hadn't realized they were actually approaching her door. She moved off the bed and pulled the door open revealing her two eldest brothers.

"*¿Sí?* How can I be of service, brother dears?" She asked like she hadn't been eavesdropping.

Angel gave her a black expression, he knew, "*Hermana*, you may have been living somewhere else for the past three years, but we grew up together. I know you heard at least part of that."

She leaned against the door frame, "Okay, so?"

"You're coming to the gala with us tomorrow. Do you need to go shopping for a new dress? Or did you do that when you snuck out this morning?" Benjamin asked her from his spot on the railing.

Amelia kept her expression blank, "I have no idea what you're talking about, *Hermano*."

She met his eyes, challenging him to cross her. Wisely, he stayed back and lowered his head. Angel however, stepped into her line of sight, a stern expression on his face.

"You can't be sneaking out anymore, Amelia," He told her, "You're going to be married and we can't risk a scandal. It would threaten the alliance."

"Angel, brother dearest, you are not my father, if I feel like going somewhere, I will," She crossed her arms over her chest. Angel maintained eye contact for a minute then seemed to decide that it wasn't worth it to get into an argument with her. He shook his head and walked away, down the hallway to his own room. Benjamin pushed himself off the railing, shot his sister a glare and headed down to his own room.

"Be ready for tomorrow!" He called over his shoulder, "Family colors please!"

Amelia scoffed and slammed her door. Family colors. Their *Abuelo* had decided when he'd first taken over that the Cruzes needed a family color like the other Big Three. Now it was a vital part of their wardrobe, every person wearing the signature Cruz cobalt color at every event.

So she was now required to find a dress that worked, to play the part and she had absolutely nothing. Not one of her formal dresses was the correct color. She had exchanged every bit of cobalt for scarlet, the Berardi family color.

Suddenly, a thought struck her. Amelia opened her door slowly and peeked into the hallway. None of her brothers were in view at the moment so she stepped onto the landing. Tiptoeing down the hallway to their parents' old room, Amelia prayed her brothers hadn't emptied it of her mother's belongings.

The huge room was immaculately cleaned, the bed linens were neat and pressed. Not a speck of dust could be found. Mrs. Byrd hadn't just been keeping Amelia's room clean, the courtesy had extended to her mother as well. And by unfortunate extension, Amelia's father.

Amelia dragged her finger lightly against the soft fabrics of the bedding, still tiptoeing on her way to the closet.

Just as she'd hoped, the clothing inside was untouched. Her mother's gowns hung neatly in their garment bags at the back of the closet.

As Amelia reached for them, she felt a pang in her heart. She wished desperately her mother was still around to give her advice, to hug her, and to love her. Maybe even help her get ready for the gala.

As Amelia riffled through the gowns she was reminded of the last time she'd seen her mother in one. She and her father had come home from the gala, both looking tired but pleased. It was a rare night when the two were being affectionate with one another, so clearly, Antonio had been drinking a bit that night.

Nineteen years earlier:

Seven year old Amelia was supposed to be in bed, but the curiosity of seeing her parents in their evening wear was too tempting. She could see Angel downstairs waiting for his father and stepmother to enter the home, clearly he had something he wanted to say. At fourteen years old, Angel seemed to believe that he was a lot bigger than he was.

The door opened, depositing Antonio Cruz with his wife, Maria, on his arm. They were whispering and laughing quietly between themselves. Maria had on a silk dress that moved like water against her skin, the beautiful fabric shone in the light. Antonio's tuxedo was a crushed velvet with a cobalt lapel that matched his wife's dress perfectly.

A couple steps behind them was Blas, Antonio's younger brother, the children's *Tio*. The man had always enjoyed the parties and tended to stay at his brother's side as an advisor. He spotted his niece in her hiding spot almost immediately and shot her a wink.

The young girl hid her smile behind her hand, trying to keep quiet. She watched her parted move towards the stairs when her brother approached them, hands on his hips.

"Angel, what are you doing up, *Mijo*?" Maria asked gently. She'd tried so hard throughout the last eight years to raise him and love him but he'd refused to accept her.

Angel rolled his eyes and directed his gaze on his father, "I have a question for you."

Antonio looked at his wife, amused before nodding at his son, "Well? What's on your mind?"

"Will I need to compete for my inheritance?" Angel asked, bluntly and to the point.

Antonio was taken aback, "What on earth are you talking about?"

"Our family has traditions, the eldest, the 'A' name receives the inheritance. You remarried and started over instead of following tradition," Angel explained. To his fourteen year old self it must have made sense. He was dedicated to getting his words out, he didn't stop even though their father was holding up a hand, "Will I compete with Amelia for the family business?"

Antonio laughed out loud, throwing his head back. Even Maria joined in the chuckling before her husband tried to explain, "Firstly, I have never once led you to believe you will need to compete. Your sister will have her own purpose later, once she's eighteen. Our family does indeed have traditions, and having a woman take the place of Head is not one of them."

Angel leaned against the stair bannister, unimpressed, "Marriage contract, *sí*?"

"Yes," Antonio was growing irritated. The drunken amusement was wearing off quickly.

Maria looked between the two then to her brother in law, worry written on her face. She turned to her eldest stepson, "Angel, darling, we used an 'A' name for Amelia because any culturally traditional 'D' didn't work for your sister. And she was my first biological child, your father and I felt that it upheld the tradition in this scenario."

Angel rolled his eyes turned to leave, "Fine. Whatever."

"Angel!" Maria called after her step son but was prevented from following him.

Antonio grabbed her arm, "Leave him alone. He needs to work this out on his own, he can't be coddled like a child."

Angel stormed up the stairs and towards his room. His rapid approach got Amelia to jump from her hiding spot and dart into her own room. She jumped on her bed and threw the comforter over her head. She giggled mischievously, trying and failing to muffle the sounds.

The click of her mother's high heels came close to her room.

The door opened quietly then shut. Amelia poked her head out, thinking her mother had just peeked to check on her. She carefully drew the comforter away from her head. She was wrong. Her mother was still there.

Maria was standing inside the room, arms crossed and a look of amusement on her face.

"What have we here?" She teased lightly, "My sweet girl, you are supposed to be asleep! It's late!"

"I know, but I wanted to see you in your pretty dress! I like when you get dressed up! You look like a princess," Amelia copied her mother's crossed arms, "I wish my hair was yellow like yours. It's prettier. And your blue eyes."

Maria gave her daughter a sympathetic smile and kicked her heels off. She came and sat on the bed, gently stroking her daughter's dark hair back.

"Sweetheart, you are beautiful. Your dark hair is beautiful, it's thick and soft, there are a million things you can do with hair like yours. And your eyes?" Maria put her hand over her heart dramatically, "Your eyes are the color of the forest, an amazing, mysterious and magical place. You could get lost in the forest and anything can happen."

Maria stood and kissed her daughter's head, "My beloved daughter, you are exactly as you were made to be. Now, go to sleep, beautiful girl."

Without another word, the pale woman collected her shoes and left the room. She blew a kiss before closing the door behind herself. Muffled voices almost immediately were heard on the other side. Antonio was waiting for his wife outside of the room.

At least Amelia was pretty sure it was her father arguing with mother. She'd seen her *Tío* Blas go to his room, surely he was in bed. The voices got louder for a moment before fading to nothing, covered by a door slam. Amelia didn't know what happened after that, she fell asleep, comforted by her mother's words.

Some nights she wished she'd stayed up to hear what happened next. It was the last night she'd ever seen Maria Cruz alive. It was the last time her mother had held her or whispered sweet words to her. It was the last time she wore a beautiful gown for an event and got called a princess by her daughter. No one really knew what happened, just that the next morning, someone had knocked on the door to bring a death notice and tell the family there had been an accident.

Amelia had always wondered what had happened, but she never got her answers. It was something she had in common with Enzo, neither had ever gotten answers. She was left to wonder and hope that one day she could find out.

Enzo Berardi: The Gala

Enzo usually liked going to the charity galas, he enjoyed the formality and pleasantries exchanged. But this time he was on edge, every leader of the Thirteen was in attendance. Their second and third in commands, their wives, fiances, they were all there and Narciso Hagan looked particularly pleased with himself. Benjamin and Camilo Cruz stood by the bar, whispering to each other, glancing at the Hagans and back to each other. Royal Hagan was whispering with his father and grinning as he looked around the room. They were noticeably without a third companion. The mystery son was still to be unmasked.

Enzo had not yet seen Amelia and it concerned him, if the Cruzes and Hagans wanted to prove a point, she ought to be there.

Tom pushed a glass into Enzo's hands, "Calm down, your unease is wafting through the room like an odor."

Enzo glared, "I'll be fine once we have eyes on our girl. I don't like that I haven't seen her yet."

"She's supposed to come. According to Matteo, the Cruzes were planning to bring her," Tom clapped a hand on Enzo's shoulder, "But seriously, hold it together. You can't risk showing emotion right now."

Enzo shrugged the hand off his shoulder with a wince and rubbed at it, "Fine."

Tom frowned, "I've been meaning to ask, what did you do to your shoulder? Is it just that new ink?"

"Yeah," Enzo said, taking a large swallow of his whiskey to avoid any further questions.

Tom rolled his eyes but wisely chose not to say anything else. Instead he turned to face the room and observed it with his boss. People were talking with each other, drinks in hand. Others were moving gracefully on the dance floor, swaying and turning to the live music playing from the string quartet in the corner. The Thirteen had gone all out for the gala as usual. Enzo wondered which of the wives was responsible for planning the extravagance, he knew none of the Heads would've planned it themselves.

He spotted Matteo standing in a corner, watching the party. The Hispanic man didn't usually attend the galas, but had made an exception given the circumstances. Enzo wasn't sure what it was but decided if it were important enough for him to know, they would tell him.

The room itself was stunning, honey colored wood flooring, a red carpet rolling down the stairs. The curtains on the windows were a crushed velvet material in the most striking shade of crimson. Enzo had to hide his smug smile at the color. It was his family color. Whoever had been on the planning committee was an ally.

The glass reflected the image of the night back at the party goers, the glare of the light making it impossible to see the city outside. Waiters wove through the room with trays of champagne or hor d'oeuvres, looking a bit like penguins in their black and white uniforms.

From where Enzo was leaning against the marble stone of the bar counter, he could see the back shelf stocked with fabulous liquor from only the best companies. Scotch from Scotland, wine from France and Italy, and even vodka generously provided by the Russian families in attendance.

An auction was scheduled to start in an hour or so but Enzo had absolutely no interest in the items for sale. He was here to lay eyes on Amelia, to confirm her well-being himself. It wasn't that he didn't trust the word of his second in command, but he would be comforted to see her with his own eyes.

Benjamin Cruz spotted Enzo and raised his glass to him with a crooked smile. He too seemed rather pleased with himself. Disappointed with the Italian's lack of response, Benjamin waltzed over to him. As he approached, Enzo's nostrils burned from the pungent smell of rich cologne wafting off the taller man.

"Evening, Cruz," Enzo greeted in a monotonous tone.

"Hello, Señor Berardi, Señor Dante," The Hispanic said in greeting, "You two seem lonely tonight, no one to bring?"

Tom growled lowly, "That is not a road you want to travel down, Mister Cruz."

Benjamin laughed, thoroughly amused by the conversation already, "I believe I do, you see, my dear little sister should be arriving any minute on our brother's arm, wearing the engagement ring of Narciso Hagan's son. From where I'm standing, you've been given the short end of the stick."

"Tell me, do you enjoy taking joy away from others, brother dear?" A soft, feminine voice asked.

Enzo's breath caught in his through. Amelia was standing behind her brother in a blue gown he'd never seen before. The cobalt fabric clung to her elegantly, the neckline plunging dangerously low. Her hair was pulled back into a sleek updo revealing her simple golden earrings. She'd done something with her makeup to make her eyes appear even more green than usual. Enzo realized, not for the first time, the woman in front of him was striking. He found himself wanting to reach out and touch her, to make sure she wasn't some figment of his imagination or a trick of the light.

She continued speaking, still directed at her brother, "At what point in your life did you decide to commit to being a killjoy? Please, kindly do us all a favor and be silent. I can't listen to you anymore."

Angel, who was still escorting his sister, pulled her arm abruptly and hissed in her ear, "You are the one who needs to be silent, you menace!"

Enzo glared at the men in front of him and handed his glass to Tom. Holding his hand out to Amelia asked, "Miss Cruz, will you do me the honor of a dance?"

Benjamin tried to step in front of her, "Absolutely not!"

"Benjamin, leave it alone," Amelia sighed, irritation evident in her face and voice, "I'm not going to run away in the five minutes a dance takes. There's no harm in a waltz between former colleagues."

Enzo took the woman's hand and led her away from the gaggle of men watching them. He didn't immediately say anything when they reached the dance floor, instead he placed her hand on his shoulder and wrapped his other hand around her waist. Pulling her closer, he began to lead them in a graceful waltz. Her perfume invaded his senses and he had to close his eyes for a moment to compose himself.

Amelia followed his movements effortlessly, as if she were floating and not touching the floor at all. Enzo couldn't take his eyes off of her even though he knew he was meant to keep his head on a swivel. He was trusting Tom would watch out for them.

Enzo lifted Amelia's hand that wasn't on his shoulder and led her through a delicate turn and brought her back to center. She smiled at him softly, the kind of expression that wasn't usually reserved for him.

He cleared his throat, his mouth feeling very dry all of the sudden, "Are you well?"

"I'm fine," She whispered, "I'm getting tired of my brothers and their hovering, but physically, I'm okay."

He nodded, "Mentally exhausted?"

"Very much so," She admitted to him, her head dropped to his shoulder for just a moment. It was over so quickly, Enzo wondered if he'd imagined it, "Royal Hagan keeps showing up with random needs for this wedding they're trying to plan. He isn't the world's nicest future brother-in-law. The 'needs' are always invasive and rude."

Enzo chuckled, "Well, it's a good thing he isn't really going to be your brother-in-law, isn't it?"

"I still have nothing on the other one, he's as much of a mystery as he was yesterday. At this point, I'm a bit suspicious," She glanced around them, making sure no one else was listening before she continued, "How has no one heard of this man?"

"I'm not sure how Hagan has kept this secret," Enzo said, leading her through another turn on the floor. The skirt of her dress fanned out during the movement before falling back into place perfectly, "This is a beautiful gown, by the way. You look lovely."

"Thank you, it was my mother's," Amelia smiled sadly, "I don't actually own a blue dress of my own."

"I will admit, after years of seeing you in either green or red, it caught me off guard to see you in this," He laughed at himself, "But it was most definitely not a bad surprise. I think if your boyfriend were here, he'd have my head for dancing with you."

"Oh!" She exclaimed softly, "I almost forgot to ask about him! Any word?

How's his family?"

Enzo shrugged, "Radio silence since he left."

"That's unlike him," Amelia said thoughtfully.

Enzo kept his mouth shut. He wasn't sure how out of character it really was.

The two were unable to keep the conversation as the music ended and Angel swooped in. He led Amelia away by the arm, glaring at Enzo over his shoulder. Amelia looked back and mouthed an apology. Enzo waved her off as if to tell her not to worry about it.

Tom walked up to him, "How was the waltz?"

Enzo shook his head to clear his thoughts, "Fine."

"Humph," Tom chuckled dryly, "I don't believe it was just 'fine,' not for one moment. You should've seen the way you were looking at her."

"Tomaso," Enzo warned.

The other man raised his hands in surrender, "Okay, okay! Different topic. I overheard Narciso telling a couple people his second son wouldn't be in attendance tonight. Said he got hung up at work."

"What kind of work? Did he say?"

"No, just that it had delayed him enough to not come."

Enzo walked towards Matteo who was still in the corner. He looked up when his boss approached and whispered, "See if you can get information off of Narciso Hagan's phone. I want to try and find something on this mystery son. I don't like being in the dark."

He nodded and bent his head back down over his phone, this time with a purpose. Enzo walked away from them and started to thread his way through the crowd, engaging with people, holding brief conversations. A kiss on the hand here, a handshake there, the intermittent joke and polite laugh. He worked the room, pulling pieces of information from people without them realizing they were giving it up.

He found more information on people's infidelity than he did about Narciso, much to his chagrin. But he still moved through the room, keeping an eye on Amelia the entire time. She was speaking with Royal Hagan who kept rubbing a scar on his palm and looking slightly nervous.

Enzo made a mental note to ask about that later. He wondered if it was from when she'd stabbed him years ago.

Narciso was talking seriously with the eldest Cruz brother, stern expression on both of their faces. Benjamin and Camilo were raiding the bar, taking shots of vodka like a person would eat candy. They were going to be black out drunk soon enough.

Enzo found a place for himself against a wall to nurse a whiskey and watch the night's events. The auction was drawing closer which meant that anything of major interest

needed to happen in the next thirty minutes or so. Thankfully, they didn't need to wait that long for the commotion.

Narciso Hagan and Angel Cruz moved to the center of the social area. The former raised a glass and tapped on it with a spoon. All eyes turned to the men and the woman being dragged up by one of her brothers.

"May I have your attention!" Narciso called even though he already had it. Being too fat to walk straight, he waddled further into the room, "Welcome, friends! It is such a pleasure to see you all here tonight. Tonight I would like to make an announcement; tonight we celebrate the union of two Families!"

A hesitant round of applause sounded up around the room. People started to murmur with one another curiously. Enzo watched, a hard expression on his face, waiting apprehensively for the next words to come out of the Irishman's mouth.

Instead Angel spoke up, "Tonight we celebrate the return and betrothal of my dear little sister, Amelia. She will be joining the Hagans and Cruzes together in marriage, making the bond uniting the Families even stronger."

Narciso added on, "Unfortunately, my second son, the groom, was unable to attend tonight's soiree, but I am sure you will extend your congratulations to the bride anyway!"

Amelia looked like she was about to stab or punch someone. Her eyes were hard and cold, her spine straight and stiff as an iron bar. Enzo watched as she took a careful step backwards and brought the heel of her shoe down on Camilo's foot. He yelped and let go of her arm, hopping up and down, holding his hurting foot.

"Camilo, are you alright?" Amelia asked, batting her eyes innocently.

Enzo watched as her brother tried to grab her arm again but she sidestepped him, not allowing him to wrap his fingers around her arm. Angel shot the two of them a glare but didn't say anything, he only indicated their silence was needed. Amelia rolled her eyes and glanced over at Enzo. He noted the annoyance and mischief in her eyes and wondered what she was plotting.

Tom stepped close to Enzo, "So this mystery Hagan may not remain a mystery much longer."

Humming in agreement, Enzo checked his watch absentmindedly, "They really should have made sure he was here, they have to introduce him at some point. He can't hide any longer. This is an advantage for us."

Enzo turned and headed for the door, motioning for Matteo to follow him out. Tom was already on his heels, pulling his phone from his pocket to call for their car.

Enzo didn't wait for his people to catch up when he reached their vehicle, he jumped in and told his driver where to go. Matteo and Tom scrambled into the car just before it pulled away from the curb into the night traffic.

Enzo stared out the window for several long minutes before speaking. The lights of the city passed slowly until they reached the edge of the town. Once the car began to pick up speed, he allowed himself to release some of the tension in his shoulders. Facing the other passengers, he found them all pretending to not pay attention to him. Matteo was messaging someone on his phone and given his soft smile, Enzo could only assume he was talking to his wife.

Enzo felt a pang of jealousy, he had hoped for something like that one day. The kind of support and love his parents had too. There was only one person he'd considered that with and she was rather unavailable.

He sighed and leaned his head back, closing his eyes momentarily. He had more pressing matters to attend to than pining after someone.

He lifted his head, "Hagan's second son, did you learn anything?"

Matteo looked up and shook his head, "Not even a whisper of a name."

Enzo groaned and swore, "We need something!"

"It isn't super helpful like a name would be, but I did find out that tailors are being brought in to make the wedding clothes," Matteo spoke up, "Usually tailors have images of the people they make clothes for and if not that, then their measurements. Which could potentially be helpful. If we had even the measurements and went based solely on his family's genetics, we might be able to program a facial recognition software without the face."

Enzo remembered something Amelia had whispered to him at the ball. He shook his head, "We can't use the family's genetic makeup. The second son was from another marriage. A stepson, at least that's what Amelia told me."

Tom scratched his chin thoughtfully, "That could still be useful. Simple background checks will pull up marriage licenses. If we get the name of Narciso's wives we could follow their paper trail."

"Unless of course, they're from a different country," Matteo shrugged. He fished for something from underneath his seat and produced a tablet. Opening it up, the man started tapping on the screen.

"Not helpful, man," Tom rolled his eyes.

"I'm just saying," He shrugged, "I'm running the search anyway. I'll let you know what I find out."

Tom looked at his boss, "Are you alright? You've been on edge since you danced with Amelia."

"I'm fine," Enzo replied, "But, she's not."

Tom sighed, "I'm not sure what we can do for her. So far, we haven't been able to glean much from anyone. Something needs to happen, otherwise we're all trapped in this stalemate."

"We may need to possibly consider waiting for the wedding," Enzo said, "At that point we'd know definitively whether or not the Hagans will drop the Cruzes."

Matteo's tablet vibrated in his hands. Enzo watched his face light up at new information then fall at whatever he saw. He looked up at his boss, distressed and worried.

"Narciso Hagan has had four wives, and each of their records have been cleaned. Someone got to them ahead of time," He said quietly. He swore under his breath.

Tom let out a low whistle, "They've been planning this for a long time."

"He's been planning it since my father and Antonio Cruz were murdered," Enzo realized, "Why else would the Hagans be the only ones untouched? They needed to disrupt the power balance and now they're planning to do it again. I'm positive Narciso Hagan was behind the Massacre."

Enzo looked away, it all made sense. The power imbalance leading to reliance on the one family who would appear strong enough to support all of the Thirteen. It would destroy the credibility of the Commission and lead to a tyrant. Enzo worked to put the pieces together, they would need an heir, hence a marriage contract. They needed to appear strong and like a team player which was why they were creating the illusion of an alliance. But they had to weaken their allies so they were easy to force into submission, which was why the contracts signed over parts of the organizations.

Enzo was now more determined than ever to pull Amelia out and cut off the Hagans at the knees. Dismantle their organization, destroy their reputation, and overturn their whole dynamic.

"Be prepared for a political battlefield," Enzo declared, "We're calling a Commission meeting."

Tom stared, wide eyed, before nodding and making a call. Matteo's jaw hung open for a second at Enzo's word but then he nodded and solemnly agreed.

They all knew it was a possibility they would need to call in the big guns, they had all just hoped that it would never get to that point. But some things are inevitable.

Enzo Berardi: The Commission Meeting

The Commission met at a gorgeous hotel in Central Park, which meant the traffic was a nightmare. The stop and go traffic was enough to make Enzo wish he hadn't called the meeting. Since he was arriving with Tom and they needed to be in suits, they'd had to take a car rather than their motorcycles. Enzo found himself grumbling under his breath the entire time, annoying Tom along the way.

When the car finally pulled up to the hotel and the chauffeur had opened the door for them, Enzo's professional mask slid into place. His face was hard, his posture stiff, and he commanded the attention of everyone in the room. He stood next to the car for a minute, completely ignoring the stares he was receiving from passers by, he straightened the cuffs of his jacket nonchalantly. Tom stood next to him, a briefcase in one hand, phone in the other, and waiting for his boss. When the crime lord began moving towards the entrance, people parted, stumbling over themselves to get out of the way.

The hotel was a grand establishment with a crystal chandelier sparkling in the lobby. The staff wore stiff, starched uniforms of a deep wine color, they bustled around behind the desks trying to care for each of their guests. High heels clicked on the shining marble floor as women brushed past each other on their way to some important place. Men with leather briefcases talked in abrupt and sharp voices as they pushed their way through the door on their way out the door. Signs pointed down different hallways, East Wing to the right, West Wing to the left the boards dictated.

Enzo recognized many of the men strutting through the lobby as captains of some of the Thirteen's men. They were preening like peacocks for the women passing through the lobby. The women didn't seem to be amused by the show they were receiving, they rolled their eyes and rushed out of the building to whatever appointments they had. Enzo couldn't blame them, whoever had told these young men that rubbing their palms together and rubbing their chin was a good move had lied. They looked like they were trying to imitate a housefly.

Enzo scanned the room, there were people from his own organization milling about. None of them were trying to flirt, they'd all been given instructions and had opted to follow them rather than risk their jobs. Enzo had assigned guards to the lobby and the halls near the conference room the Commission would meet in. He didn't want surprises to disrupt how this particular meeting would go.

One of the women at the desk gave Enzo a subtle nod when she saw him. He nodded back, recognizing her as one of his employees who had gotten a job in the hotel to keep an eye on things. She'd been fairly helpful in warning Enzo about meetings between two or three of the Families. He was grateful for her help but he genuinely couldn't remember the woman's name off the top of his head. He knew if he asked Tom he would get the name, but Enzo wasn't that interested in finding out.

When the Thirteen noticed Enzo's arrival, they began filing towards the elevators. The conference room was waiting. The line for the elevators quickly became a ridiculously long trail of people that spilled into the lobby.

Enzo sighed and moved towards the stairs, it was only two floors up. He certainly wasn't going to shove for a spot in an enclosed metal box just for that.

Tom followed without question, head on a swivel on the off chance danger might be nearby.

The concrete stairwell was certainly less luxurious than the rest of the hotel. Eerie echoes sounded from top to bottom. Piles of dirt lay in the corners mixed with little bits of trash. The men took the steps two at a time, reaching their floor before any of the other members of the Thirteen did. Enzo motioned for them to find their place in the conference room and wait.

Enzo pushed open the door and was surprised to find someone already inside waiting for him.

"Amelia."

The woman turned from the window. Her arms were crossed over her chest but the tension in her shoulders released at the sight of friendly faces. She gave the men a soft smile.

"Surprise."

Enzo chuckled, "Definitely. What are you doing here? I didn't expect your brothers to let you come?"

"Since when would that stop me?" She raised a brow, "Even you weren't able to keep me from these meetings."

Tom laughed and quickly turned it into a cough when Enzo shot him a look but even he could see the humor. He gave Amelia a once over, she was wearing a navy blue skirt and gray top, her usual high heels were replaced with flats. Enzo noticed that even her makeup was more subdued. He grit his teeth, a protective instinct rising in him.

This person in front of him was not the vibrant person he'd seen grow over the last three years. He hoped that what he was seeing was part of the act she put on for the rest of the Thirteen and not the fall of the woman he respected.

Unfortunately he didn't have an opportunity to ask because the doors swung open and voices filled the room. The Thirteen trekked in, quickly filling the table and the chairs surrounding the walls. Enzo watched, identifying every person by either their name or rank. Tom sat immediately to his right, also keeping track of who entered the room.

Narciso Hagan lumbered into a room using a wooden cane to assist his steps. He was so large he had to turn sideways to fit through the door. Enzo was afraid the cane might break beneath the man's enormous weight. Royal Hagan was the last person to enter the room, he took the seat near his father and sneered at Amelia. The Cruz brothers had also given her vile looks when they'd come in. Neither family was pleased with her attendance and it gave Enzo great satisfaction that they were irritated.

"No second born son today, Hagan," Amelia taunted, "I'm beginning to think he doesn't exist."

Enzo leaned back in his seat waiting to see where this conversation would go. He was curious if Amelia would snap at them or if her brothers would force her to be quiet. Royal looked ready to stand up and get into her face, but his father held a hand up to settle him.

Narciso sneered, "You ought to hold your tongue, dear girl, you never know what the consequences could be."

"It seems to me, Hagan, you are avoiding answering the actual question," Enzo tented his hands and gave the Irishman a pointed look.

Hagan's face flushed until it was impossible to tell where his face ended and his hair began. Enzo smirked,pleased with the reaction. Royal glowered and crossed his arms reminding the Italian of a petulant toddler.

"It is a family matter, Berardi, do me the kindness of staying out of it," Hagan muttered through grit teeth.

Heads in the room bobbed back and forth between the two men, breaths held as they waited for the next verbal blow. Enzo yawned like he was bored of the conversation, causing the Hagan men's anger to increase. They looked ready to blow their tops but Enzo remained silent. He inspected his fingernails, leaned and whispered to Tom, checked his phone and adjusted his chair, all without saying a word to Narciso.

Finally Amelia sighed, annoyed and irritated she said, "Gentleman, I have things to do today. If you just plan to stay here and argue about whose is bigger, at least give me a warning so I can get a drink."

Petrov interjected in his thick accent, "The lady is right. I would much prefer to get on with the meeting, rather than watching this all day. If I do have to watch, let me do so with vodka in hand."

"Very well, I call for the removal of the Hagans from the council," Enzo stated.

The room was suddenly in an uproar. People jumped up, yelling and slamming their fists on the table. Jeers from those aligned with the Irish family, cheers from Berardi men. Enzo glanced around the room looking for Amelia to see her reaction.

She was in the corner looking mildly surprised and bemused. A glance at Tom told Enzo that he wasn't overly shocked either. He let out a chuckle, of course his two closest companions were unphased.

"On what grounds?" Royal demanded viciously. He slammed his fists down on the table, causing it to rattle.

Another round of voices.

Enzo held his hand up calmly and the room silenced. The men sat back down, giving him suspicious and concerned looks from the corner of their eyes. Hagan had pulled his chair as close to the table as his fat belly would allow. Royal sat dutifully behind his father, waiting for his instructions looking furious. His father had pulled him back immediately after his outburst.

"Tell me, Hagan, has your son ever had an idea of his own?" Tom asked, tilting his head, a crease in his brow. He was staring at Royal like a puzzle that was confusing him.

"This conversation is regarding your boss's ridiculous movement, I pray you stay silent as you should!" Narciso hissed.

Amelia scoffed, "Sir, forgive me, but what are your standards? You first tell me to be quiet, now Tomaso Dante, a second in command. Who *is* allowed to speak?"

Angel stood abruptly and seized his sister's arm. He pulled her close and whispered harshly to her. Enzo could hear him speaking in Spanish in an effort to disguise his words. Enzo had to stop himself from jumping up and stepping between the two. Out of the corner of his eye, he saw Tom tense, wanting to interject as well.

"Answer my question, Berardi," Hagan growled, distracting the Italian man from the siblings' argument in the corner, "On what grounds is your movement founded?"

"You decided to create an alliance without Commission approval," Enzo started, "We also have it on good authority that you are not respecting the boundaries of families' territories. I also have suspicions of your involvement in the Commission Massacre."

"You can't prove anything!" Royal snapped.

Enzo threw his head back and laughed coldly, "Royal, your statement alone shines a guilty light on you."

Hagan waved his son down, still sneering at Enzo, "Where is your proof?"

Tom stood, "We had our analysts talk to every shipyard owned by a member of the Thirteen. They each reported missing shipments. All except for Hagan's. They reported having a larger count of shipments than expected."

Some of the men at the table nodded silently. As if agreeing that their shipments had indeed been stolen. Enzo knew this already, he also knew that they would never admit it lest they appear weak, so he'd sent people to the docks in disguise to gather the information for him.

It didn't matter what family a lower pier worker was aligned with, if there was a shipment issue, they got mad. Usually they would seek an open ear which is what Enzo had given them.

"Circumstantial at best," Narciso scoffed.

The other men at the table murmured, putting their heads together. Chairs creaked when their occupants moved to whisper to the next person. It only took a few minutes before silence returned to the room and eyes were on Enzo again.

"You need a unanimous vote for the Hagans to be removed from the table, Berardi," Costa spoke up, "And you don't have my vote."

Enzo nodded to the man, "And I don't begrudge you for it. If the Commission doesn't come to a vote, I will respect it."

"Mature of you, Berardi," Hagan raised his brow.

Enzo shrugged. He had accomplished his goal and even without the vote, he was pleased with the result. Every man in the room would now be paying closer attention, and Hagan knew it too. He was now the center of attention for the Commission and his every move under scrutiny. Enzo had planted a seed of doubt and indignation.

Enzo stood from the table and buttoned his jacket, bid the men goodbye, and left. Tom followed closely, already working on his phone. Enzo had no idea what the man was doing this time. Something that required enough focus that Tom didn't see the pillar in his path. He walked right into it with a *thump*. Tom's phone went flying and he had to struggle to maintain his balance.

Enzo let out a roar of laughter before scooping up the fallen phone and handing it back to its owner. Clapping Tom on the shoulder he told him, "It happens to the best of us."

His own phone suddenly blared quite loudly as his analyst's name popped up, with a sigh Enzo answered, "Matteo, what can I do for you?"

"Berardi, we may have caught a break with the mole," He exclaimed, "You need to get back to the manor!"

"Ten minutes," Enzo hung up the call and pulled out of the parking lot. The tires screeched at the sudden speed and turn. Matteo knew that the drive was much longer than that but hung up anyway.

The drive was less than thirty minutes at the speed he went, so Enzo took the opportunity to run up the stairs and change into a suit instead of the tuxedo he wore for the meeting. The black three piece fit him like a glove having been tailored to perfection. Running a comb through his hair to pull the wayward strands of his eyes, Enzo took a moment to breathe and set a mask in place before going down into the basement to meet with his team.

Matteo, Luke and Tom were waiting for him in the observation room. Their eyes fell on him the moment he stepped into the room, commanding the attention like a king. The door to the interrogation room was shut tightly and a tablet on the table displayed a man tied to the chair inside.

The man was a thin balding man, what little of his hair remained was the kind of blonde that was more of an absence of color than anything else. He was wearing a work suit, a deep blue color stained with black spots that might've been grease. Berardi guessed he was a mechanic of some kind or worked in a similar field. He was pale and his eyes were deep set and a dull blue color, his hands were covered in smudges from the same black substance that stained his clothes.

"Berardi, meet Bill," Luke said, "One of our field teams caught him in his workshop talking about how the Hagans have a spy. He was using rather colorful language that would make a sailor blush."

Matteo smirked, "From what we were able to tell, he knows something about the situation, possibly even who it is. It wouldn't be too hard to believe that he's pretty high on the Hagan payroll. I figured you'd want to talk to him."

Enzo nodded, "Anything else I should know?"

Matteo shook his head, "Go ahead and talk to the guy. I don't think we have much else. We're working on getting into his bank records to see what Hagan's shell company name is."

"Okay," Enzo put his hand on the doorknob, "Tom, let's go talk to the guy."

Tom shrugged and sauntered in after his boss, hands tucked into his pockets casually. He leaned against the wall, glaring at the man tied to the chair. Enzo pulled a chair from the corner easily and sat on it. Leaning forward and propping his elbows on his knees, he stared, waiting.

The mechanic stared back, after a moment he pulled at one of the ties on his wrist but was unable to loosen it. He looked back at Enzo, his discomfort starting to show, a bead of sweat ran down his neck. His Adam's apple bobbed in his throat as he swallowed, nervous.

Finally, he broke the silence, "What do you want with me?"

"What do you know about the Hagans?" Enzo asked, his voice level and deadly.

"Wh-what? I don't know anything about no Hagan!" Bill exclaimed wildly. His eyes were wide and wild.

Enzo sat back casually, "See, I don't believe that. My guys heard you talking about them, not only that, but talking about them like you knew something about them."

Tom spoke, his voice low and nonchalant, "You really should be more careful with your words. You never know who is listening."

"I don't know anything! Please!" Bill pushed his feet into the floor, trying to push away from the Italians.

"Okay, say I believe you, why would you brag about knowing the Hagans if you didn't know anything?"

Tom walked around the room to a shelf on one side of the room. He began to pick up and inspect the tools on it. An ice pick, a hammer, needles, scalpel, and three different sets of pliers. Eventually he settled on an intimidating knife and came to stand behind the mechanic. He set the blade to rest on Bill's shoulder.

Bill gulped, "Look, all I know is that they said you're going to be ripe for the taking soon! That their spy is doing his job well and is going to be rewarded soon!"

Berardi looked over the shaking man in front of him and made eye contact with his man. Tom frowned and shook his head; he didn't believe that was all this man had to say. Tom stroked the edge of the blade over the interviewee's cheek, softly, not cutting him, but making him aware that it could happen.

"You're lucky, Bill, you know that?" Berardi chuckled menacingly, "My usual interviewer isn't here right now. Dante is a lot nicer than she is. If she were here, you'd already be a pincushion, don't make me call her in."

Tom raised an eyebrow at the bluff but said nothing. He yawned behind Bill's head like he was completely bored with the situation, "I'm growing tired by the lack of information, Bill."

"They're hosting something at the Cruz mansion soon! A wedding for the sister!" The man yelled, trying to lean away from the knife.

Berardi rolled his eyes, "You are quickly running out of reasons for me to keep you alive, we knew that already. Give me something I don't know and maybe I'll turn you over to local authorities instead of letting Dante have fun."

"Hagan's got a secret son who is supposed to finally make his appearance! I don't know anything about him except that they refer to him as 'R' and he's got a mean streak!"

"Well, an initial is technically more information than we had," Enzo patted the man's knee mockingly, "Now you hang tight in here, Dante and I are going into the other room."

Amelia Cruz: Betrayal

Amelia managed to escape the meeting and get back to the *hacienda* before her brothers or future in-laws caught up with her. The Commission meeting fell apart after Enzo and Tom had left. The remaining twelve Family Leaders had started throwing accusations around the table. Wild theories and stories claiming either Berardi or the Hagan families were hellbent on destroying the Commission or trying to take over it completely. Two wildly different sides of the spectrum.

Annoyed with the theories, Amelia had slipped out of the room unnoticed. As she hopped into a cab, she half wondered if she had time to get into the sealed envelopes in the study.

Amelia snuck into the study when she got back only to find the envelopes had vanished. The drawer they had been in previously was unlocked and most of its contents were gone. Only blank pieces of paper and fast food receipts remained. Perhaps her brothers were onto her. She rolled her eyes and left the study to wander the house, listless and bored.

The house was uncomfortably silent and left her alone with her thoughts. Not even the staff was making any noise. She found herself pacing her room waiting for something to happen. Amelia groaned and snatched her phone from the desk next to her to shoot off a text message, hoping that she might finally get a reply. The previous string of messages was entirely on her side and it was beginning to irritate her.

Amelia: Lance? Hey, I heard about your family. I hope everything is OK. I miss you.

Amelia: Love? Are you okay?

Amelia: Lance?

Amelia: Please answer me, I'm worried about you. I love you.

Amelia: They're trying to marry me off. If you hear anything about it, please know it's a ruse. I wouldn't do that to you.

Amelia: There was a Commission meeting today. I had hoped to see you there.

Amelia: I'm worried. There's a lot brewing in the city. I wish you would answer me.

Amelia: I miss you.

Flopping on her bed, she waited for his response. Nothing. Again. Why was she trying anymore? For the first time she understood why people used the phrase 'absence makes the heart grow fonder… or forgetful.'

Was he forgetting his love for her? Was she forgetting her love for him? Was it worth it to keep fighting for their relationship when he wasn't doing the same? Were Tom and Enzo right that the relationship wasn't healthy anymore? The idea made her skin crawl. She hated being wrong.

And now to add to her frustration and hurt, the Cruz brothers' voices were heard from the lower level.

The door slammed and Angel bellowed through the house, "Amelia Rose Cruz! Get in here now!"

Amelia propped herself on her elbows and raised a brow. She was suddenly feeling very stubborn and uneager to obey her brother. She knew who she was and it most certainly was not their pawn. Unfortunately, they didn't seem to get the memo.

Angel stormed up the stairs and blew through her door. The wooden frame splintered from his force. Fury was written all over his face, a vein popped in his forehead and his eyes were crazed.

"Woman," He sneered, "You have a lot of nerve. First, you show up at the Commission against my explicit instruction. Then you proceed to humiliate your future in-laws and my partner. And then you ignore me, AGAIN! I've killed men for less, why do I keep allowing you to live?"

Amelia scoffed and stood up, approaching her brother, "I came to those meetings even when I worked for Berardi, if he couldn't stop me, what makes you think that you could? And you haven't killed me because you need me."

At this point Benjamin and Camilo were watching from the doorway, waiting to see what would happen next. Angel seemed to realize he had an audience now as well. He raised his hand and slapped Amelia across the cheek with the backside of his hand. Amelia's head whipped to the side and her own hand came to cover her cheek. She could feel exactly where his signet ring had met flesh. The spot smarted and burned, already turning red. She stared at Angel, wide eyed. He'd never raised a hand to her before. Their father had. But Angel had always shown more restraint. Until now.

He pointed a finger in her face, "Do not ever disrespect me like that again, *mija*. The punishment will be worse."

"If you resort to slapping, you are no better than our father!" Amelia snapped, "You used to say you'd be better. You're just as disappointing as he was."

He lunged, catching her by the hair and brought her close enough to hiss into her ear through grit teeth, "Your behavior caused so much of a scene, Mr. Hagan has decided he needs to speak with you tonight as well. If you blow this for me tonight, I swear to every known deity, you will suffer the consequences, Amelia."

"Bite me!" She spat into his face. She thrust her elbow into his stomach making him release his hold on her, "I will go to your stupid little meeting, but you should be the one making sure your deal doesn't fall through, not me. If I feel the urge to speak my mind, I will. Now, get out."

She crossed her arms over her chest and waited, giving her brothers a pointed look. Camilo retreated first, holding his hands up in surrender. Benjamin took a step back too but kept his eyes on their brother who was still trying to catch his breath. Angel had dropped to the floor, the wind knocked out of him when Amelia hit him. He was desperately trying to regain his composure.

Eventually he managed to wheeze out, "One hour. You have one hour to be ready. There's a package for you downstairs, Hagan sent it. He insists you wear it."

He slowly walked out the door, arm wrapped around himself. Benjamin shot his sister a glare before pulling the door shut once he and Angel were clear of it. Amelia let out a sigh when they disappeared.

A few moments later, a knock sounded on the door causing Amelia to shout, "Angel, I swear, if you've come to lay another hand on me it will be the last thing you do with said hand!"

She swung the door open to find Mrs. Byrd standing outside with a box. She wore a bemused expression, "You plan to remove your brother's hand? Come now, you know your mother wouldn't want that level of violence."

"Mrs. Byrd, he slapped me!" Amelia explained, "My mother would understand. She knew the world we lived in. She knew it would be impossible to keep me out of it."

Mrs. Byrd hummed, "Well, your revenge will have to wait. This is your dress from the Hagans for tonight. I'm sorry that your mother and I couldn't keep you out of this."

"It's not your fault. Or hers," Amelia sighed, "I was born into this world. It was inevitable."

The elderly woman gave Amelia a soft smile and set the box on the bed, "Amelia, dear, your mother was under no illusion that you would escape this life without a body count. She only hoped that you would keep a semblance of morality."

Amelia rubbed her face and looked out the window. It wasn't the first time she'd speculated about her mother's opinion of her work. But it was the first time she'd had a conversation about it with someone who'd known Maria. Mrs. Byrd left the room after setting the box on the bed, leaving Amelia to stare outside and consider her words.

Ding!

Lance: I'll see you soon.

*****

The Hagan home was an eerie Grecian style mansion. The white washed pillars stood stark against the black painted walls behind them. The door frame and window sills were all painted an awful maroon color that made the house look like it was bleeding. At the start of the path up to the house stood two horrific gargoyles guarding the house. The wrought iron gate that encircled the property had a security hut with a sentinel inside who glared at the Cruz's cars as they approached.

"This looks friendly," Amelia commented dryly.

She was riding in the same car as Angel who chuckled cruelly at her words, "It'll grow on you, I'm sure."

He was acting like nothing had ever happened, like there had been no altercation. Neither Benjamin or Camilo had said anything either leaving Amelia feeling irritated and on edge. Before they'd left the house she'd sent off a message to Matteo and to Luke, hoping one of them would get her location to Enzo just in case something happened.

She'd replied to Lance but he'd gone back to radio silence. She almost wondered if she'd imagined it. She'd gone back to look at his message about a dozen times. It was there.

"I doubt it," She replied to her brother, watching him from the corner of her eye. She slipped her phone back into her clutch.

The car came to a stop and she stepped out, smoothing her hands down her bright orange silk dress. It was not her choice of color, it had been demanded by the Hagan groom to be, as well as the way she wore her hair. It was loose and hanging down her back, ending at her hips. Because of its length she usually chose to wear it up. It got in the way when she was working. And if she was in a fight, she preferred to not give her opponent the opportunity to grab it.

But she was playing a part, so she'd complied with the demands. Every bit of her ensemble screamed 'used,' nothing about it was her choice. It was a manipulation tactic. But for who she wasn't sure anymore.

One thing she had refused was the jewelry, choosing her own gold pieces. She did, however, continue wearing the engagement ring. Amelia couldn't wait to be able to take it off, especially since the belt on the dress that she'd been given matched the ring. The silver claddagh belt dug into her waist, like it was purposely trying to make her uncomfortable. She would have marks on her skin when she removed it later.

Benjamin and Camilo approached her and their brother having gotten out of their own car. They both looked dapper in their suits, Benjamin wearing maroon and Camilo wearing teal. Angel had gone for a traditional black suit rather than a colorful one. They'd all foregone the usual Cruz colors for the evening it seemed. Perhaps to show their loyalty to their new ally.

"Are we ready?" Benjamin asked while straightening the cuffs of his jacket.

Amelia sighed, "As I'll ever be."

The four Cruz siblings stepped up the door. A garish 'H' knocker rested on the wood above an embossment of the family's crest. Amelia rolled her eyes, of course they had a family coat of arms and of course they displayed it. So it wasn't just the mystery groom who took pride in the family heritage. The whole family did.

Camilo reached for the brass piece and banged it several times. Not a moment later, a tall, lean man opened the door and allowed them to enter. He introduced himself as the butler and led them to a parlor where Narciso and Royal sat, drinking whiskey from crystal tumblers. Both men were draped casually across the furniture, laughing with one another.

Upon seeing the sibling enter the room, Narciso hauled himself into a standing position, and greeted them, "Welcome! Welcome to our home! And your future home, Miss Cruz."

He gave her a slimy smile and tried to take her hand. When she snatched it back, the large man's expression faltered for a moment but he recovered quickly. He ushered them into the room, offering the men whiskey. When he didn't offer a glass to Amelia, she poured one for herself and raised it mockingly to the men, earning a glare from everyone.

"My other son will be here shortly. He got held up running an errand for me," Narciso explained as he handed Benjamin and Angel their glasses.

Amelia moved to sit in the furthest possible place, watching every person in the room warily. She gripped her clutch tightly, grateful she'd had the forethought to grab one of the bugs from the office. Having no other way to make sure she could relay information, she hoped Matteo was listening to the transmitted audio.

"How long do you think he'll be?" Benjamin asked over his glass.

"Not long," Royal replied, he was eyeing Amelia like a predator watching its prey, "I hope that you didn't have too much trouble after the Commission meeting."

"Not much, plenty of yelling from other parties and snapping sisters," Camilo chortled.

"Sisters are an unfortunate part of reality," Royal said sympathetically.

"How would you know, Royal? As far as anyone is aware there are only boys in your family," Amelia rolled her eyes. She leaned back in her chair and crossed one leg over the other, tilting her chin downwards, challenging Royal.

Narciso chuckled, "You will learn that all is not what it seems, Miss Cruz. My children, for example, I have more than my two sons. I also have a daughter. She is married and thankfully someone else's problem now."

"'Problem?' You really don't hold women in a very kind light do you? No wonder you've been one upped every time you've gone against one of the families," Amelia said, "They don't hold to this archaic mindset."

Angel glanced between the two, feeling the tension rising and interrupted the conversation, "So, Narciso, will we have the pleasure of meeting your wife tonight, as well?"

"Unfortunately not, she isn't in state at present," Narciso swirled the liquid in his glass.

"She's been out of state for some time," Amelia muttered under her breath, "One might think."

"I beg your pardon, my dear?" The obese man asked, his eyes dark and angry, "One might think what?"

Benjamin spoke up, glaring at his sister, again, "Ignore her, please. She's been in a mood lately."

"One might think that she left you. Or you simply disposed of her. It wouldn't be the first time your family has been suspected of it," Amelia shrugged casually.

"*Hermana! Por favor!*" Benjamin snapped, exasperated with his sister, "My word. I truly have no idea how our father never killed you. Or even Berardi."

Angel turned to the Irishman, "I am so sorry, Narciso. Truly."

"Women," Narciso said and shrugged, like it explained everything, "They're much like brood mares. Filled with fire and spite until you teach them otherwise."

"Precisely," Angel groaned, rubbing his eyes tiredly.

Amelia rolled her eyes at her brother and looked around the room. The furnishings were either black or silver or a mix of the two. On one side of the room stood a floor to ceiling shelf full of liquor of all sorts. The entire thing had been designed to show off the family's wealth and prestige, nothing looked like it was actually meant to be lived in.

"Miss Cruz," Narciso called, gaining her attention, "I would like to speak frankly with you. After your performance earlier today at the Commission, I realized that we had not yet laid down expectations for you yet. So, for now, I am willing to forgive your impudence. But we will be laying down some rules to help you understand what's expected of you."

"How gracious," Amelia scoffed. She sipped her whiskey and used a certain finger to dab at the corner of her mouth.

Royal glared, "You really do have a mouth on you, don't you?"

"I do pity your brother, Royal. Having to deal with her for the rest of her life," Angel groaned, "She's been a menace all day, not just at the Commission."

Narciso chortled, "She will learn quickly. And if she doesn't, it means more fun for my son. He really doesn't like his women to talk back."

"I'm still here," Amelia snapped and proceeded to let out a litany of uncouth names in Spanish, "And if your son has a history of abusing women, he will meet a sticky end, which I will happily provide."

While she was speaking to Narciso, Amelia didn't hear the door open. She didn't hear the steps approaching her or the deep familiar chuckle. It wasn't until he finally spoke that she realized that Narciso Hagan's second son had finally made his appearance.

"Hello, Lia."

Amelia's back stiffened and her hair stood up on end. She was suddenly very aware of her surroundings and that all eyes were on her. She looked up, facing the man who spoke and felt her heart break into a thousand pieces. All of the sudden, everything made sense. The spy, the stolen shipments, the ability to stay below the radar for so long, the ability to obtain private documents from Berardi's office. Unknowingly, she'd been the one who had helped Narciso plant his spy, and not only that, but she'd gotten him into the inner circle. It was her fault.

He came to stand in front of her, gone was his usual beer stench, replaced with an expensive cologne. His hair had been brushed back into a neat half up half down style, and the ragged jeans and t-shirts replaced by a perfectly tailored suit. This was a different man than the one she'd grown to love over the past years.

She breathed, "Lance."

Amelia Cruz: A Broken Heart and Trust

Lance turned away from her and moved to greet the other men. First his father and brother before he moved to speak lowly with Angel, introducing himself to him. Angel seemed rather pleased with finally meeting Hagan's second son, but Amelia could barely breathe. He moved on to introduce himself to Benjamin and Camilo, shaking their hands confidently and firmly.

Somehow Amelia managed to have the presence of mind to remove the bug from her clutch and stuff it into the seat cushions while the men were distracted. Never once did she take her eyes off Lance. Tracking his every movement and feeling like a knife had been plunged into her heart with each smooth and elegant step.

"I trust there was no trouble this evening, Ray?" Narciso asked. His question was pointed at Lance, but the use of a different name caught Amelia's attention. It seemed the Hagans had naming traditions like the Cruz family. Alliterations.

"'Ray?'" She whispered just loud enough for him to hear.

Narciso seemed to understand her reaction because he laughed maniacally, "Miss Cruz, you should have no issues with your betrothed now, don't you think? You've already been with Ray for a couple of years now, yes? Although, you knew him as 'Lance Alexander.' There's not a drastically large difference between the two personas."

"Wait, sorry, I'm a little confused, could you explain exactly what is happening?" Camilo interjected, "Amelia knows him already?"

Poor Camilo, he had not fully caught up with the situation having been more focused on refilling his whiskey glass. He was looking from Narciso to Amelia to Lance/Ray. His brow creased as he tried to puzzle out what was happening.

"Of course, Mr. Cruz," Narciso seemed oblivious to Camilo's genuine confusion, "My son, Ray, infiltrated Berardi's organization several years ago. He worked his way into the inner circle by getting your dear little sister here, to fall in love with him. He's been passing information ever since."

"Yes, thank you for that, Lia," Ray turned and smiled at Amelia, "I doubt I would've gotten into the inner circle without you. Berardi was always a touch too suspicious. But you, you darling, played your part so beautifully, so unknowingly. It was perfect."

Amelia's mouth fell open. He'd played her from the very start. He'd used her to get close to Enzo and she'd fallen into his trap.

"She's speechless," Angel observed, "Incredible. I didn't think that was possible."

Ray threw his head back and laughed, "Mr. Cruz, when you manage to get someone to love you so unconditionally that they're willing to do anything for you, speaking out of turn is hardly a problem. Your sister learned not too long ago that she had to earn approval. She would stay quiet if I wanted her to. Getting her to submit was never the issue."

Amelia swore and jumped from her seat, "Don't. Just don't. You were never able to control me. You know that."

"Uh-huh, and how many times did you sleep on my couch waiting for me to give you just a shred of approval? How many times did you have to justify yourself to Berardi for being with me? Lia, you were never in your own control. It was always me."

"I- uh," She stopped, realizing the truth in his words, "Bastard."

"Maybe so, but you fell for it, so what does that make you? Gullible? Naive?" Lance or Ray, whatever his name truly was, approached her. A smirk spread across his lips, "And you should know, darling, of all people, that when someone is underestimated, it's easy to take control of the situation."

Benjamin stood in awe, "I'm impressed, Hagan. Genuinely impressed. This is incredible!"

Narciso tented his hands and chuckled, "You say our ideas are archaic? Outdated? Dear girl, our ways are exactly the reason that we could never fall into the same trap as Berardi did."

"Berardi allowed himself to be read like an open book. He practically handed me his weakness on a silver platter!" Ray added on to his father's explanation, "Berardi's weakness was easy to exploit, darling. You were and *are* his weakness. The best part was you genuinely had no idea! It was almost comical! He is so in love with you that when he was worried about you, every other defense was down."

Amelia's heart pounded in her chest, his words were harsh and unforgiving, barbed, and venomous. He suddenly grabbed her upper arm, and dragged her towards the door, "Now, I think it's time you and I had a frank discussion. Privately. We're going to go to a different room for a bit, Father."

Narciso waved his hand dismissively. The Cruz brothers turned away from their sister to continue asking questions, to dig into the how of Narciso's plan. Benjamin was grinning, eager to hear the details. Angel had leaned forward, desperate to understand every bit of information from Narciso. At that moment, the Irishman had the upper hand in the coming war.

Royal snickered and threw his brother a mock salute, "Enjoy her, little brother."

Ray made a rude gesture at his brother as he pulled Amelia from the room. Camilo waggled his fingers at Amelia and Ray just before they exited. Amelia had hoped that maybe her brothers might actually speak up and help her for once, but of course, none of them had. They were too enamored with Hagan's master plan.

Amelia struggled against Ray's hold on her arm, but it was too strong for her to pull out of. Ray never once looked at her while he dragged her down a hallway. Their footsteps echoed in the hall, his determined steps, and her scuffling shoes.

"Amelia, if you don't stop resisting, I will throw you over my shoulder and carry you the rest of the way," He finally turned and snapped at her.

Amelia stopped moving, "I trusted you."

"Yes, and that was a mistake, now move!" He snapped at her. He turned away, muttering under his breath.

"Was it all a lie?" She whispered.

Ray groaned and grabbed her by the hips and lifted her over his shoulder. His grip was harsh, leaving marks in her skin. He moved quickly and refused to answer her until they got to a set of double doors. Ray set her down long enough to open the door and shove her through. He followed and locked the door behind himself.

Amelia looked around and found herself in a rather large bedroom. Any décor was in shades of gray or navy blue. An image of the Hagan family crest hung on the wall above the bed, standing out, the orange bright against the other monotonous colors. The bookshelf against the wall had not one tome on it, instead it was filled with weaponry ranging from handguns to axes.

"Yes, Lia, it was a ruse," Ray sighed, as if he had been explaining it over and over again to a child, "I had been trying to get into Berardi's good graces, unsuccessfully, for a year before you came along. He trusted me with small things that would never give me the information I needed. Then you showed up, like a perfect little gift from Fate. He immediately trusted you and brought you into his fold. All I had to do then was get into *your* good graces. And you were so desperate for love, to be loved, it was perfect."

"So, I was simply a tool," Amelia could feel the sting of tears behind her eyes.

"Nothing more than a pawn. As you should have always been," Ray tucked his hands into his pockets, "But you can't truly be disappointed with your betrothed, after all, you do love me. The messages you've been sending me, begging for a response, saying that you do."

"You are not the man I love, that man is a myth, a figment of imagination. He never existed," Amelia seethed, "And *you*? I am not marrying *you*. Never in a million years. Not if you were the last man on earth."

She backed away from him, a small subtle step. Amelia hoped that she might be able to pull a weapon to defend herself in case he crossed the distance between them. Ray smirked, eyes sparkling with mirth. He threw his head back, cackling like a maniac.

This section contains mentions assault.

"Darling, the contract is binding. You're mine, to have and to hold. To do whatever I want with," Ray did indeed cross the distance, but his long legs had him in front of her before she had fully pulled her knife from her sheath hidden beneath her dress.

He gripped her wrist, keeping her from moving the blade, "You will need to give these knives up when we're married. It's a nasty habit, darling. I can't have my wife trying to murder me in my sleep."

"That's all I would try and do if I was your wife," Amelia spat, "You would find your end at my hands, one way or another."

Ray plucked the knife from her hand and tossed it across the room and pushed her backwards until her knees hit the foot board of the bed. He shoved her down until she was sitting on the edge. Gripping her jaw and moving her head from side to side, examining her face like one would inspect a piece of fruit or cut of meat. Amelia snarled at him and tried to bite at his hand. His response was immediate, a swift smack across her face, the same cheek her brother had hit earlier. Ray's hand encircled her throat, effectively limiting the amount of oxygen she could pull in.

"Woman, I am warning you, this behavior will get you nowhere," He slapped her again, this time across the other cheek.

Amelia saw red. She brought her knee up into his groin, making him drop like a sack of potatoes. She swung her elbow down into the spot where his neck met his shoulder, forcing him to stay on his knees. He reached for her ankle to bring her down, but she leapt over his hands. Ray managed to pull himself up off the floor and lunged for Amelia. He caught her by the ends of her hair and reeled her in. Using her hair as if it was a set of reins, he pushed her to the floor and tilted her head back.

"That, my dear, was a massive mistake," He spat on her face. With his free hand he reached for his necktie and pulled it off. He started binding her hands together with it. When he leaned down to pull her up by her wrists, Amelia headbutted him. The pain from the impact radiated through her own skull, but Ray's nose had gotten the worst of it. Blood spurted from it, the cartilage crooked and broken beneath his skin.

"You'll pay for that," He swore. His eyes widened as he tore at the belt around her waist and threw it across the room.

She continued to struggle against his hold but with her hands tied, she wasn't able to do much. Ray growled and wrapped his hand around her throat again and squeezed. The edges of Amelia's vision started to blur, and her limbs began to feel heavy. She could feel Ray picking her up and throwing her over the mattress before she blacked out.

*****

When Amelia came to, her body was sore and bruised. Ray wasn't in the room and she wasn't sure where he went nor was she sure how long he would be. Quietly, she moved from the bed and abruptly realized her dress was torn and hanging off one shoulder. There were angry red marks on her thighs and neck. She could see bruises beginning to form on the base of her neck and around her collarbone. Every part of her ached and she felt as though she might fall into a thousand pieces. She felt violated, hurt, angry and exhausted all at once.

Torn fabric from her dress was draped across the bed like Ray had thrown it away. She didn't know what he'd done to her and that thought alone make her physically sick.

Amelia dropped to the floor, retching. After the contents of her stomach had been emptied, she stayed bent on all fours, heaving.

"*¡Dios mío!*" She whispered, tears slipping from her eyes.

Violent section is over.

Amelia looked around the room searching for something to replace her tattered clothes. Her eyes landed on the closet. Inside were perfectly tailored suits made of the finest linens. The kind of clothes Lance had never worn but apparently were the preferred clothing choice of Ray Hagan. The two-timing bastard.

She found a button-down shirt and threw it on over the remains of her dress hoping to preserve some of her remaining dignity.

Making her way back into the bedroom, she found her shoes and clutch had been thrown across the room, thankfully both were intact, usable and unopened. Searching her clutch, Amelia let out a sigh of relief when she found her phone. Finding Tom's contact she sent him a brief message.

Amelia: Help. Luke's.

Leaving the room and creeping through the house was a little harder since she didn't know the layout well. When she found the main staircase leading to the exit, a clock chimed somewhere in the house telling her that it was close to three in the morning. She realized her brothers had probably left her thinking she was spending the night with her fiance. How wrong they were. He'd left her on the bed after he'd finished with her, going who knew where.

The door blessedly had no chimes or alarms connected to it when she opened it. Peeking outside to the driveway, Amelia sighed, her suspicions were correct, her brothers' cars were gone. But sitting in the drive was a motorcycle. It was painted the horrible Hagan orange but at that moment it was the most beautiful thing Amelia had ever seen.

The bike was a small racing model, likely used by Royal when he decided to join the races once in a blue moon. Amelia straddled the vehicle and reached for the wiring beneath the keyhole. A moment later the bike roared to life, and she was off. The Hagans left their gate open overnight leaving

Amelia's path to freedom open. She drove like she'd never driven before. Adrenaline coursing through her body, egging her on, encouraging her to keep moving. A sentinel in the guard house watched her leave through the open gate and reached for a walkie-talkie but she didn't stop.

The further she got from the mansion the more she felt the physical pain from the evening. Her throat ached from the pressure that had been put on it and taking a breath felt like drinking fire.

"Just a bit further," Amelia whispered hoarsely to herself, "Move! Move! Don't stop."

It felt like an eternity had passed before the bridge to Manhattan Island came into view. Relief flooded through Amelia when she saw it and she urged the bike to go even faster. Weaving through the cars that always filled the roads, avoiding the cyclists and pedestrians. The lights of the city seemed to light her way to Luke's shop.

When she finally showed up to the door Luke was already outside with Fae waiting for her. Tom apparently had already called them. They both rushed towards her and helped her dismount the bike and into the shop. Once the couple had deposited her onto the couch inside the shop, Luke went back outside to wheel the motorcycle inside.

"I am going to enjoy stripping this of parts," He muttered through grit teeth. He pushed it to a corner where it would wait for him to bring a wrench down on it, effectively ending its life.

"Now isn't the time for that, Babe," Fae whispered. She had brought blankets to Amelia who was starting to nod off. Exhaustion catching up with her. Her head spun and ached, her eyes growing heavier with each passing second.

Amelia smiled gratefully at the couple and urged them to go back to their bed and sleep, "I'll be alright."

"Are you sure?" Fae asked gently, "We can stay down here if you need."

"Go, get some sleep," Amelia nodded at the steps leading to the upstairs apartment the couple shared.

They nodded and left Amelia alone, whispering to each other as they went up the stairs. She pulled the blanket up to her chin, letting the tears finally slide down her cheeks. Embarrassment, humiliation, and heartbreak tore through her like a raging fire and the sobs broke free.

*****

Amelia wasn't sure when sleep took her, but when she woke up, she could hear urgent hushed voices from somewhere in the room. Luke and Fae were downstairs again, this time joined by Enzo and Tom by the sound of it. Amelia stayed still, hoping they wouldn't notice that she'd woken up. She simply lay there, listening to the words of her colleagues and boss.

"What happened?" Enzo hissed angrily.

"We don't really know. Tom called us and said to be ready for her, she was pretty beat up when she got here," Luke explained.

"Tomaso?" Enzo growled. Even though she couldn't see him, Amelia knew he was running his fingers through his hair.

"She sent me a message saying 'Help. Luke's,' that was it," Tom said quickly, "I called Luke to be ready for her."

"She's shaken, Berardi, be gentle," Fae whispered, "I've seen her come into the shop with black eyes from fights before, but this is a whole different level of abuse. She's not going to want to talk about this."

Both Tom and Enzo spoke at the same time. "What kind of abuse, Fae?" Tom asked.

Whereas Enzo said, "Whose hands am I taking?"

Amelia whispered, "Lance Alexander's."

All four heads whipped around to see her. They rushed over, asking questions. Wanting to know if she wanted anything if she needed anything. Enzo reached her first, carefully sitting in front of her on the couch. His hands were gentle when he touched her face and examined the bruises. He brushed the hair from her face to see her better, concern written on his face. Tom and Luke stood behind the couch and Fae at the end of it.

"I'm fine. Please, just leave me alone," Her eyes met Enzo's. A deep worry and sadness filled his brown eyes, and a softness she wasn't used to.

"I'm not leaving you alone, Amelia. I did that already and look where it landed you," He told her.

"Enzo!" Amelia groaned and buried her head in the couch cushions.

Tom spoke up, "What did you mean when you said 'Lance Alexander?' He did this? I thought he was with his family?"

Amelia spoke but no one could understand her with her face still buried. Enzo reached out and stroked her hair gently, "Say it again please, Amelia?"

She lifted her face, "He *was* with his family. They just happen to be the Hagans."

Enzo Berardi: Failing

Enzo had gone to bed hours early, but was unable to rest. His dreams were filled with haunting images of his people being killed in brutal and bloody ways. Slit throats. Bludgeoned heads. Execution style shots. It was his fault they were being killed. In his dreams he saw Tom being shot, Amelia's throat slit, Luke being blown up by his own explosives. Fae slowly choking on poison, Matteo being beaten with baseball bats covered in barbed wire. Over and over and over again, non stop. It was a never ending montage that kept going as he tossed and turned, tangling the sheets around himself. It was a vivid prediction of their future if they failed. If he failed at protecting his team, his family.

bang! Bang! BANG!

Enzo sat up in a cold sweat with a gasp. His heart was pounding in his chest and his hair stuck to his forehead. A glance at the clock told him that he'd been out for several

hours. It was the early morning now, and someone was now emphatically banging on his door.

"Berardi!" It was Tom, "Enzo, get up! Now!"

He pulled the damp sheets away from his body and stumbled to the door. Yanking it open to find his friend in front of him, wearing an unnerved expression. Enzo stared bleary eyed for a moment before asking, "What happened?"

"It's Amelia. She's been hurt."

"Come again?"

Tom sighed, "I don't know what happened yet, but she's been hurt. It doesn't sound good. She just made it to Luke's. He said it was bad."

Enzo swore, "I'll be there in a minute. Get the cavalry. We're going to get her."

The second in command nodded, "I'll see you in the car."

The Italian closed the door and took a steadying breath. Someone had just poked the bear and there was going to be hell to pay.

Enzo rushed down the steps minutes later, yanking a jacket over the double shoulder holsters. He'd pulled on actual clothes instead of his pajama bottoms and t-shirt. He had also grabbed several guns and even a set of brass knuckles. One of his sentinels was waiting at the door for him, he followed behind the boss. Closing the door behind them and hopped in the car after Enzo was seated on the passenger side of one of the several cars waiting.

Tom was sitting in the driver's seat, white knuckling the steering wheel. His face cold and calculated; furious. Utterly furious.

"Drive," Enzo commanded as soon as his door closed.

In the early morning hours the traffic through the city was easier to drive through than during the day. Tom wove between the lanes and around the few cars, pushing the gas pedal down as far as he could without flipping the car. Enzo went from watching the clock to watching the road and back again, tapping his heel against the floor.

"Somebody tell me something!" He demanded, drumming his fingers on the door.

The sentinel in the back seat cleared his throat, "According to Matteo, she sent her location close to nine o'clock last night. She also took a bug from the Cruz house with her."

"Where did she go?"

"The Hagan mansion in the Bronx," The sentinel answered quickly, his voice wavered, his nervousness getting a hold of him, "She was supposed to be meeting Hagan's other son."

"Thank you, Luca," Tom said. He was still white knuckling the steering wheel and clenching his jaw.

Enzo could feel his own fury reaching a boiling point and nausea rose in his throat, "Someone has signed their death wish tonight. There will be blood tonight!"

Tom nodded and pushed down on the gas pedal, speeding up even more, "Are you officially ordering a death warrant?"

"No, I want the person brought to me. Someone in my circle gets attacked, I will deal with them personally," He gripped his gun tightly in one hand, the door in the other needing something to hold on to.

Tom's phone dinged in the center console and Enzo picked it up. He read the new message from Luke and swore. He put the phone back and stared at the road for a moment.

"How much longer?" He asked.

"A couple more miles," Tom responded, "Why, what happened? What was the message?"

"Amelia didn't have her weapons on her when she got to Luke's, the bastard who attacked her knew where she hid them."

Tom swore, "We're a couple of minutes out. I'd love to kill her brothers for this."

"I don't care if it was them or the Hagans, we're destroying both families completely," Enzo looked out of the window, "Send word out to our allies. Everyone who we have even the smallest favor to call in, prepare them for war."

*****

Enzo didn't wait for the car to stop moving when they pulled up to Luke's shop. He sprinted to the door and pounded his fist against it. Seconds later, Fae stood in the doorway. When she saw him, she stepped aside to let him in. Tom was right on his heels having handed the car off to the sentinel.

"Where is she?" Enzo demanded.

Fae held her finger to her lips and shushed him before whispering, "She finally fell asleep about thirty minutes ago. She was sobbing pretty heavily after we went upstairs. I don't think she wanted anyone to be around for that."

Luke came treading down the stairs wearing superhero pajama bottoms and monkey slippers. He noticed Tom giving him an odd look for his wardrobe and shrugged. Luke shook Tom's hand in greeting and motioned for the two men to follow him. Luke led Enzo to the VIP lounge he kept in the shop. On the sofa was Amelia. Even from the door, Enzo could see some of the bruising and could tell her face was red and puffy from crying.

She was curled up in a ball with the blankets pulled all the way up to her chin. Light tremors were running through her, Enzo assumed it was the aftermath of the sobs and trauma.

Fae touched his shoulder gently, "Be careful."

"What happened?" He hissed, running a hand through his hair.

"We don't really know. Tom called us and said to be ready for her, she was pretty beat up when she got here," Luke explained. He leaned against the wall and wrapped an arm around Fae comfortingly.

"Tomaso?" Enzo growled, again, he ran a hand through his hair. Then he pulled on the cuffs of his jacket and shifted from one foot to the other.

"She sent me a message saying 'Help. Luke's,' that was it," Tom said quickly, "I called Luke to be ready for her."

"She's shaken, Berardi, be gentle," Fae whispered, "I've seen her come into the shop with black eyes from fights before, but this is a whole different level of abuse. She's not going to want to talk about this."

Both Tom and Enzo spoke at the same time.

"What kind of abuse, Fae?" Tom asked.

Whereas Enzo said, "Whose hands am I taking?"

Amelia's voice came suddenly, gaining his attention, "Lance Alexander's."

Fury rose within him. Of course it had been Lance. His abuse was no longer purely verbal. He'd finally laid a hand on her. Enzo had hoped and prayed Amelia would get out of the relationship before it happened. When they had gone their separate ways during her deployment, Enzo wanted to believe it would end. Lance had left for a family emergency and she was staying with her brothers, they'd had no contact that he was aware of. When had Lance gotten back? When had he had the opportunity to attack Amelia? Especially when she was supposed to be at the Hagans'. The questions ran through his brain but Enzo didn't focus on them. He rushed to Amelia's side, carefully sitting next to her on the couch. The rest of the group followed him, encircling the couch, their concern palpable.

"I'm fine. Please, just leave me alone," Her eyes met Enzo's. Pain and hurt laced her expression. A vulnerability he wasn't used to seeing in her.

"I'm not leaving you alone, Amelia. I did that already and look where it landed you," He told her, his own heart ached for her. He'd been the one to put her in danger and he wasn't the one with the consequences, she was. How he wished he could trade places with her.

"Enzo!" Amelia groaned and buried her head in the couch cushions.

Tom spoke up, "What did you mean when you said 'Lance Alexander?' He did this? I thought he was with his family?"

Amelia spoke but no one could understand her with her face still buried. Enzo reached out and stroked her hair gently, "Say it again please, Amelia?"

She lifted her face, "He *was* with his family. They just happen to be the Hagans."

"You're kidding," Tom's jaw dropped.

Amelia shot him a glare, "Why would I joke about this?"

Tom looked at her then at Enzo, "How about I go get the car ready?"

Enzo called after him, "Get Dr. Smith on the phone. Have her meet us at the house."

"No! I do not need medical attention!" Amelia shoved Enzo's shoulders to get him to look at her.

"Yes, you do," He said softly, "Amelia, I'm sorry it got to this point. I'm sorry I couldn't protect you. You didn't deserve this, please let me help. Let me make something right."

Fae came and touched Amelia's shoulder, "Get the help. What's the worst that could happen?"

"A lot could happen, but fine," Amelia moved the blanket and tried to stand up on shaky legs, "Since none of you will leave me alone if I don't."

Enzo's eyes darkened, her dress had been torn from hem to hip. There was a mark on her thigh, like something had been torn across it. He realized with a start that it was her thigh holster. Lance had torn it from her body.
   Enzo looked up to find Amelia watching him. She sighed and grabbed one of the blankets and wrapped it around herself. Enzo stood abruptly and wrapped his arms around her shoulders and guided her to the door. He noticed when they got close to the door that she had started leaning on him rather heavily, so he bent and tucked one hand under her knees and picked her up.

"Enzo!" She exclaimed, her eyes wide, "What are you doing?"

"Starting the process of making amends," He said, "Relax. You're safe and

I'm taking you home."

She didn't argue with him, instead, just dropped her head to his shoulder. Enzo walked to the car where Tom was waiting. He opened the door so that Enzo could gently set Amelia into the passenger seat. Once the door was closed he spoke lowly with Tom.

"What's the word?"

"The doc will come to the house in a bit. Thankfully, it isn't too early to call anymore," Tom said.

Enzo glanced at his watch and realized that several hours had passed since they first got the news of Amelia's attack. He nodded at Tom, "Okay. Thank you."

"Want me to take another car?" Tom asked.

Enzo nodded and Tom chuckled humorlessly, "You know, we both wanted their relationship to end, this wasn't what I had pictured."

"I agree. This... this is," He sighed, "Something else. However bad I thought it was, this is worse. To attack the one person who always fought for him. I can't imagine what she's going through."

Tom nodded, "I can't even begin to express how *I* feel so, yeah, trying to imagine what she does... Enzo, this can't be left unanswered."

"It won't be. I swear it on my father's grave."

Enzo looked down through the glass window, Amelia had leaned her head against the door and closed her eyes. He could swear there were tears running down her face. But in the rising sunlight, he couldn't tell.

"Get her home, boss," Tom clapped a hand on his shoulder, "We'll take care of the rest later."

*****

Enzo watched Amelia the entire drive home from the corner of his eye. Any bump in the road that made her wince he would slow the car and check on her. He realized when he pulled into the driveway that he had probably checked on her over fifty times.

"I am so sorry, Amelia," He whispered under his breath, over and over again.

He carefully pulled her off the door so when he opened it she wouldn't fall. He shut his door as quietly as he could so he wouldn't wake her and rounded the car. He eased the passenger door open and scooped Amelia into his arms. Turning to the house, Enzo carried her inside.

He took her up the steps, ignoring the burn in his legs when he reached the top. It was a short trip to the young woman's room, he would survive.

"Hey," He whispered kindly, making her open her eyes, "Why don't you go take a shower and change clothes really quickly. Doctor Smith is going to be here soon."

She nodded hesitantly and he lowered her feet to the ground. He kept his hand on her shoulder to keep her steady for a moment before she turned and limped towards her closet. Enzo's eyes never left her, he took in every movement, every wince, grimace and flinch. He would have a pound of flesh for each one.

Amelia exited the closet, holding clothes tightly to her chest. Her lip had stopped bleeding but the shadow of bruises were forming around her neck. Her fingers rubbed at the marks gently, like she was trying to rub them away. Slowly making her way in the bathroom to shower off the day's events just barely holding herself together.

Berardi watched the door shut and once it had, he dropped into the desk chair, head in his hands. Taking deep breaths to calm himself down took significant effort. He tried to lower his heart rate, knowing his anger was the least useful thing to Amelia. He heard doors opening and closing downstairs followed by the deep tone of Tom's voice. He couldn't quite make out the words at first but as the voice drew nearer, he began to decipher them.

Tom was apologizing for calling on the doctor so abruptly, she was chastising him for that and continued on by saying, "I am *not* a medical doctor! I'm not even a qualified nurse!"

Pushing open the door to Amelia's room, Tom replied, "You were a CNA while you were working on your BSA and psychology degrees. You're qualified enough for what we need."

He stepped inside the room with a petite woman, her curly hair piled on her head and held up with a pencil. Glasses sat on the bridge of her nose, highlighting her round eyes. In her hands was a duffle bag that Enzo assumed held medical supplies. She wore an irritated expression on her face.

He nodded in greeting, "Audra, thank you for coming. She's cleaning up right now, but by the looks of it, he roughed her up well."

Audra Smith sighed, "Will I ever be able to convince you to see an actual doctor?"

Enzo chuckled dryly, "Probably not, but I also think that Amelia isn't going to need one as much as she'll need you. This was someone she trusted at one point, who should've had her back and so much more. She probably would've taken a bullet for him at one point. The betrayal is going to leave an emotional scar."

The doctor crossed her arms, "From what your man here told me, I'd say that even if it was a stranger, it would leave that kind of scar. Assault isn't something many people recover from in the blink of an eye."

The running water in the bathroom shut off, silencing the conversation for a moment. Dr. Smith took her bag and set it on the desk and began to pull out its contents. A roll of gauze, medical tape, some tubes of cream, pill bottles, and the usual stethoscope and blood pressure cuff.

She lined everything up neatly on the desk before turning to the men, "I'll need you to leave now."

Amelia stepped into the room at that moment, her wet hair was leaving marks on the gray shirt she was wearing. Her face was clean of the smudged makeup from earlier. She wore comfortable leggings and thick socks, like she was trying to cover as much of herself as possible, creating a layer of armor.

She glanced at Enzo, making eye contact, slight panic filling them. He stepped close to her and brushed a strand of her hair behind her ear, "I'll be right outside if you need me."

Amelia nodded and Enzo wondered if he'd imagined her leaning into his hand. He stepped out of the room with Tom on his heels. They looked at one another for a moment before Enzo jerked his head in the direction of his office. The two men stayed silent until the door to his private office had shut behind them.

"Want a drink?" Enzo asked. He poured himself a generous glass of whiskey. Tom nodded and he proceeded to pour another. He handed the glass over and took a seat on the couch.

"How did we miss Lance?" Tom asked. He looked exhausted and distraught,

"How the hell did we miss him?"

"I don't know," Enzo groaned, "I don't know and it's killing me."

"We're going to kill him, right?" Tom asked so nonchalantly, he might've been asking about the weather.

Enzo shook his head, "We're going to bring down the entirety of both families for this."

"'So, it is to be war between us.'" Tom said, quoting an old famous opera.

"Indeed it is. I held back, waiting until we had enough information. Now, I don't care. I will burn them to the ground for this."

Enzo Berardi: The Aftermath

"This isn't something you're going to be able to fix with violence," Dr. Smith was explaining to Enzo and Tom, "You're going to have to give her time. She's questioning her capability, judgment, and even her worth right now. She will inevitably believe she deserved it or that it was her fault."

"That's ridiculous!" Tom exclaimed, "It's not her fault! Why on-?"

Enzo held up a hand, silencing his friend, "Let her continue."

The doctor smiled in thanks, "It doesn't matter that it wasn't her fault, she's still going to rethink and relive it for a while, wondering what she could've done differently. She knew the person, you two warned her about him and she didn't listen. Amelia is incredibly lucky to have you on her side, but you need to be prepared for her to emotionally withdraw. This will take time. There will be good days where it seems like the pain is a thing of the past, and there will be days where it's just as raw and painful as the day it happened."

This time it was Enzo who interrupted, "What kind of 'prepared' are you talking? Let her withdraw from the world? Or be prepared so we can pull her back into the world?"

"She's going to want you to leave her alone, and for the first little bit, you'll need to let her process," Dr. Smith sighed, "But it's your job to help her step back into the world. You cannot help her reclaim the power she lost, but you can support her through the healing process. Reclaiming her power is a choice that she will have to make when she's ready to."

"And what if she says she'll never be ready?" Tom asked worriedly.

"Healing isn't linear, frequently it's two steps forward, one step back, but healing isn't impossible, especially because you are her support system," The doctor stood from her chair and picked up her bag, "Just know that everything needs to happen at her pace. Don't push her, especially on the good days."

Dr. Smith left the room leaving Enzo and Tom sitting in the office alone.

"I don't know if I've ever felt so helpless and useless in my life," Tom dropped his head into his hands, "I can't imagine how you feel."

Enzo nodded in agreement, "I'm at a complete loss."

Tom looked up, "Actually, I can think of a time. The Massacre. When we lost our fathers. That's the only other time I felt so powerless."

"And Narciso Hagan was behind both that and this," Enzo growled, "We need Amelia to help us. But I can't push her, I have no idea how to help."

"Maybe we get Fae talk to her?"

"That's not a bad idea, but are they close enough?" Enzo rubbed his chin tiredly and sighed, "I'm going to check on Amelia. You go and rest. We'll reconvene in the morning."

Enzo didn't wait for Tom's response before leaving the room but he was stopped by his friend calling after him, "If she isn't close enough to Amelia, the best person to talk to her is you!"

Enzo looked back at Tom for a moment, "No way."

"Come off it, Enzo, you love her more than anyone else in this world. Who would be better?" Tom rolled his eyes, "No, your romantic love for her isn't going to make it all better. But your protective love, your love for her as a member of this family, might help. Just think about it."

Enzo nodded and made his way down the hallway to Amelia's room, tapping on the door quietly, he poked his head inside. Amelia was sound asleep, unable to fight the effects of the sedative the doctor had given her. He could see that her eyes were red and puffy from crying again, her hands clenching the blankets tightly to her chest. Enzo could feel his heart breaking in his chest for her yet again.

Scooting a chair closer to the bed, he reached for her hands and gently loosened them from the fabric. Once her hand was removed from the blanket, it wrapped around his hand tightly.

Enzo's breath hitched in his throat. He closed his hand around hers, "I'm not going anywhere. I've got you, I swear."

With his other hand he reached up to stroke her hair softly. It was still damp from her shower earlier, carefully he lifted it away from her neck knowing how much she hated it when it lay there, she would say it was too hot or overstimulating.

"I know this is going to take time, but I will be here," He whispered softly and pressed a kiss to her brow, "While you find your way out of the darkness, I will hold your hand and stay by your side. You will never have to fight alone."

Amelia shifted in her sleep but didn't wake up. Her face was scrunched up like she was having a bad dream and her grip on Enzo's hand tightened.

"Rest, Beloved," He whispered.

A tap on the door broke the quiet surrounding the room. Tom stood in the doorway, he'd tucked his hands into his pockets. He looked exhausted.

"I'm not leaving either. But I doubt I mean it in the same way you do. I'm sorry I snapped earlier," He said, "Are you ever going to admit you love her to her face?"

"It's okay, I get it," Enzo shook his head, "No, I won't. Not until she's ready for it."

Tom nodded, "I'm heading to bed. Let me know if you need anything."

Enzo watched his friend leave before turning to face the girl on the bed. For the first time he was understanding what his father had meant when he talked about finding one's partner. There was a difference between a business partner and a life partner. Enzo had known he'd loved Amelia for years, but it wasn't until the fear of possibly losing her forever had struck him that he understood how deeply he loved her. She had always been the sadist in their relationship, teasing, poking, angering, and challenging. But Enzo had been the masochist, every time she pushed, he had fallen further. He realized it was exactly like his father had said; once one finds someone to love the rest of their life, it's impossible to let go.

He thought back to when he started seeing the signs of Lance's true nature. He wondered why he hadn't been willing to say something then. He had stopped getting on Lance as much in the most recent months. Maybe it was his way of trying to stay on Amelia's good side, maybe he'd grown tired of fighting with the man. Whatever Enzo's reason was, he felt shame writhing inside for having grown complacent.

Two and a half years ago:

Amelia watched on as Enzo and Lance exchanged blows in the boxing ring, Tom standing with her. The men in the ring danced around each other on the balls of their feet, Enzo correcting Lance's form every now and then.

"Lighter on your feet, Alexander!" Enzo called and swung his foot out, pulling Lance off his feet as demonstration, "You're off balance and heavy footed."

Lance grunted in frustration, "Yeah, yeah, I get it."

Enzo offered a hand to help him up, "You've got to get it if you want to be able to join on stealth missions."

Lance rolled his eyes and walked away, tearing at the Velcro on his gloves, "I can do stealth, you're just not willing to let me. You're too busy letting the girl sleep her way into the desired positions."

Enzo was on him in the blink of an eye, before Lance could react, he was pinned to the floor. His face pressed into the mat; arms pinned down by one of Berardi's feet. His knee pressed into the small of Lance's back.

Enzo leaned low to speak into the other man's ear, "Disrespect will get you nowhere in my company. Shape up and be a gentleman."

Amelia whistled sharply to get the boss' attention, "Leave it alone, Berardi. He's lashing out because of his own self-pity. I don't care nor am I offended."

Enzo got off the man, "You're lucky, she's nicer than I am."

Tom laughed and shrugged when Lance glared at him, "I warned you at one point what would happen if you pulled crap like that."

Amelia shook her head, "Come on Tom, our turn in the ring."

Tom followed her into the ring and pulled his gloves over his hands. She followed suit, securing the Velcro around her wrists. She bounced on the balls of her toes, preparing for the spar. Tom held out his hand and as best as he could with the thick glove on gave her a 'come at me motion.'

Their boss watched intensely from the side, ready to critique their form. He followed their movements, their footing and even their breathing. Knowing that perfection was needed in the ring, Enzo pushed them towards it. He reminded them constantly that when put into a real life scenario, a person was more likely to revert to their lowest training. He didn't want that for his team, he wanted them ready and prepared for anything.

Lance stood with Enzo outside the ring, watching the two. Tom lunged first, a center jab at Amelia's chest. She moved aside easily and swung at Tom's head but he blocked the hit with his arm. With her arm up, he took the opportunity to smack her torso landing a solid hit that sent her stumbling back for a moment.

As Amelia regained her footing, she shot Tom a glare, "That wasn't very nice."

He shrugged, "All's fair in love and war."

Enzo chuckled at their banter before calling, "Watch your arms, Amelia. You're dropping them too low, you're leaving your head exposed."

She spared him a quick glance and nod before turning back to her opponent. Tom raised his hands back up and swung rapidly several times. Jab, rear hook, left uppercut, cross, jab again. Amelia managed to put up her defense and block them before launching her own counter attack. Tom expertly dodged her barrage of hits, bouncing lightly on his feet as he moved away from the hits.

Enzo clapped a hand on Lance's shoulder, "That's what it should look like."

The boss walked away from the group, heading towards the showers. He didn't look back over his shoulder to see Lance's glare pointed at him and then Amelia and Tom. Lance dug his hands into his pockets, still watching the two in the ring as they wrapped up their sparring session.

Now:

Sleep had taken him prisoner, he wasn't sure for how long. When he woke up, Amelia was awake, looking down at him. Her hair was frizzy from sleep and her shirt was wrinkled, but in that moment, Enzo had never seen anything so beautiful.

She was there and she was alive.

"Amelia! Hey!" He jumped up and sat on the edge of the bed with her, "How are you feeling? Can I get you anything?"

"Coffee?" She croaked.

Enzo chuckled, "How about water first?"

She glowered at him, "I've been beaten and bruised. I want coffee."

"Coffee it is! After a glass of water. And the meds the doc left," He stood and held a hand out to her to help her up, "Deal?"

Amelia sighed, "Deal."

She placed her hand in his palm. Enzo moved as close to the bed as he could so if she needed help balancing, she would have it. He wrapped an arm around her shoulder unsure whether it was for his sake or hers.

He led her through the house to the kitchen. When they got there, he pulled a bar stool out for her but she hopped onto the counter. Enzo stared at her sitting cross legged on the marble and gave her an amused expression.

"Really?" He asked with a small smirk.

"Deal with it," She told him, crossing her arms.

He shrugged and walked around the counter to the coffee bar, "Don't let the housekeeper catch you on the counter."

She frowned and stuck her tongue out at him, "Mrs. Janis has given up on keeping me off the counter."

Rolling his eyes, he turned the coffee machine on. The whir of the grinder briefly filled the kitchen. He poured the grounds into the machine and filled it with water. The next sound was the gurgling of boiling water and the drip of coffee into the metal pot. Minutes later the machine clicked off by itself. A delicious aroma filled the air as he removed the pot from its place.

Enzo took a cup and filled it with Amelia's preferred ratio of coffee and creamer. She thanked him with a small smile. She turned to look out the window, watching the birds in the yard. Enzo, however, kept his eyes on her a moment longer before returning to the coffee pot to get his own morning wake up.

"How are you feeling?" He asked her.

"Sore," She admitted, "Happy to be home though."

"I'm glad you're home," Enzo smiled at her. It was the truth.

"What are you planning?" Amelia asked softly, "I know you. You've already got some plot in your mind."

"I am going to kill the Hagans," Enzo stated so casually, he might have been talking about the weather.

She nodded, "I'm first in line for actually taking a blade to Lance, I mean, Ray. I know there's a line of people who want to punch him, but I'm the one he hurt the most. I call dibs on being first in line."

Enzo chuckled, "Fair enough. I'll even tie him down for you."

Amelia smiled, "We're at a turning point, aren't we?"

"Yeah, I think so. The Hagans have laid it all out on the line. They probably think they're untouchable now," Enzo ran a hand through his hair and glanced out of the window.

"No one is ever truly untouchable," Amelia mused softly.

"No, they're not," Enzo agreed.

The two heard footsteps descending the stairs a moment later, signaling that Tom had woken up and was joining them for coffee. The man entered the kitchen bleary eyed and groggy. He was still wearing the same clothes from the night before, rumpled and disheveled.

Enzo nodded to the coffee pot, "There's caffeine."

Tom grunted in response and moved like a zombie to the pot. Enzo moved out of the way and went to sit at the table. Amelia silently slid from the counter and followed. Enzo watched her take the furthest seat from where he was sitting. She pulled her knees to her chest and balanced her coffee mug on her knee. Tom joined them at the table a moment later with his own steaming mug.

"This is cozy," Amelia commented mildly.

Tom hummed in response, taking a long sip.

Enzo glanced between the two before setting his mug down and leaning forward, "Amelia, can you tell us a bit about what happened? You said Lance is a Hagan?"

She sighed, "Yeah, although he's been using an alias."

Tom frowned, "What's his real name? I assume Hagan is his last name?"

"Ray."

"The 'R' name," Tom realized, eyes wide.

Enzo nodded, turning to watch the sun through the window, "I keep thinking back to when the team and I were going through files, trying to figure out who the mole was. Everyone from the day you were hired and the year following. He wasn't even on the radar."

Amelia frowned, "He was before me."

Enzo's head snapped back, "What?"

"Yeah, he was here before me. Not the other way around," Amelia explained, "Maybe a year or so."

"Then the Hagans were lying!"

"You're surprised by this?" Amelia remarked dryly.

"No, not at all, but think about it! Your brothers were convinced the mole came after you, that it was because of the broken contract," Enzo's eyes widened as he started to put it together.

Amelia dropped her feet to the ground and leaned forward, "If Ray was here longer than me, they've been planning this longer than we originally thought."

"Considering the assassinations that happened years ago," Enzo told his colleagues, "Just about every family got hit. But you know who didn't? The Hagans. Of course they've been planning this for a long time."

Amelia's eyes widened in realization. Tom nearly spat his coffee out across the table. Just like when Enzo had figured it out, the pieces fell into place with the other two.

"The Hagans are going to try and usurp the Commission," Enzo declared, completely confident in the conclusion now, "They've got control of the Cruzes and their allies. They're going to try and turn some of ours and they think they will have everyone's support."

"But you tried to expose them before, what if nothing changes?" Amelia asked.

"Everything has changed," Enzo grinned, "They attacked someone who is under the direct protection of one of the Big Three. That is a violation of the most sacred of Commission laws."

Enzo saw realization dawn on Amelia's face. She glanced down at her wrist where her initiation tattoo rested. The beautiful script that had been placed out of tradition was what now helped their cause. Tom seemed to realize the implications as well and looked at his own tattoo.

"We may actually be able to pull this off," Tom said, "Except for one thing, Amelia was betrothed. How do you plan to get around that aspect? It would negate the protection order."

"We can't exactly come right out and say I was a mole," Amelia groaned.

Enzo grinned again. A plan forming in his mind, "I have an idea. Possibly. But we're going to need to pull a few strings at the courthouse."

"I like the look in your eyes, Enzo," Tom said, a smile plastered onto his own face, "It usually means blood."

Amelia Cruz: The Next Step

octor Audra Smith was not a medical doctor, but she'd been a nurse's assistant and had spent several years cleaning up injuries of Berardi's men. She was, however, a psychologist. She was a good one too and sometimes the members of the organization would actually come to her for therapy which made a nice change to the frequent bloody knuckles and noses. Her primary job however, was running the Shelter. A sanctuary built by Leon and Lucia Berardi. The multilevel Shelter helped people of every demographic. From children in foster care to adults escaping abusers to widows seeking companionship. The Shelter was a place of peace and healing.

Amelia sat on the edge of her bed picking her sleeves nervously. After showering she hadn't let a single tear come and refused to let them come while in the presence of another person. But they'd come when she was in the shower, she'd been seen as vulnerable and it had given someone the opportunity to attack. She wasn't going to let it happen again.

The doctor had pulled the desk chair in front of Amelia and was now sitting across from her, "I'm sorry that I have to ask this, but you know I do. Did this happen at the hands of someone currently in the house?"

Amelia shook her head, "No."

Dr. Smith continued, "Do you feel safe at home?"

"Yes."

"Did you know your attacker?"

"Yes."

"What is his name?"

"Ray Hagan, formerly known as Lance Alexander."

The psychologist sat back and looked Amelia up and down for a moment, "This was the first time this had happened?"

Amelia shook her head, "He had been using my hair as a way to move me around lately. He never hit me before today."

"So this was the first time he'd physically struck you?" Dr. Smith asked gently.

Amelia nodded, "He'd been part of the organization longer than me. Recently he'd started acting differently. More smug, less air headed, it was all different than what we were used to."

Dr. Smith nodded along, "And tonight, what happened?"

"He revealed himself in his family's home and assaulted me," Amelia sighed and fell back across the bed, "He choked me until I lost consciousness."

"We can stop anytime you need to, Amelia," The doctor said calmly. Her eyes looked sad, like she felt Amelia's pain as though it were her own.

Amelia shook her head and continued, "Everything I know how to do: throw a knife, shoot a gun, punch or jab, I couldn't."

Dr. Smith hummed in thought for a moment, "Are you familiar with the fight or flight response?"

Amelia sat up and frowned, "Of course I am."

The doctor nodded, "In reality there are three responses. Fight, flight, and freeze. The first two are when your body releases adrenaline and cortisol in your brain, causing your heart rate to speed up and give your major muscle systems what they need to get you moving. However, when you freeze, your heart rate can drop, you may hold your breath, like you're waiting for the next move. This is the body's way of avoiding conflict and protecting itself. And, it isn't your fault."

"It kind of feels like it's my fault," Amelia admitted softly, "I did pull a weapon."

"I know. And it probably will for a long time. You will ask yourself why you didn't move or use that weapon. The truth is, when in danger, people can blank out and forget how to fight, especially in cases where they knew their attacker," Dr. Smith looked at the young woman, gauging her reactions, "Subconsciously, you might have also not wanted to hurt him because you knew him, which, again is *not* your fault."

"But he was a threat! I've faced threats worse than him before and never froze! Why now? Why this attack?" Amelia demanded. Pin pricks of tears erupted and she furiously wiped her eyes, "Can I even do my job if I couldn't do something about this?"

"Perhaps because he was familiar, you processed it differently," Dr. Smith replied calmly. She watched Amelia try to regain her composure for a moment before standing and searching through her duffle bag. She removed a needle and a small glass bottle, "Amelia, I want to give you a sedative to help you get some rest so that you'll be able to process when I come back tomorrow."

"No way!" Amelia exclaimed, "I've had enough control taken tonight."

The doctor came in front of her and spoke with kind words, "I know. Which is *why* I want you to rest. That is your first step to reclaiming your control and power; getting rest and not letting him take your health away too. I want you to sleep tonight knowing you are safe and protected. He cannot get in here."

Amelia hesitated then extended her arm so the drug could be administered. As sleep overcame her, she watched as Dr. Smith packed away her bag and left the room quietly. Once the door had shut, she let the tears fall.

Guilt wracked her body as she shuddered from the full body sobs. She felt unclean and wanted to crawl out of her skin. She could still feel Ray's fingers on her arms and his weight on her chest. As she drifted off, she made a silent vow to never allow herself to be in such a vulnerable position again.

*****

Enzo grinned again. A plan forming in his mind, "I have an idea. Possibly. But we're going to need to pull a few strings at the courthouse."

"I like the look in your eyes, Enzo," Tom said, a smile plastered onto his own face, "It usually means blood."

Amelia left the table abruptly after Tom's declaration, "I need a minute."

Nausea rose in her stomach, hitting like a freight train. Stumbling against the railing of the stairs, Amelia's breath began to increase. Hyperventilating, the walls around her seemed to close around her. She needed to get out.

Amelia managed to crawl to her room and find running clothes and shoes. Slipping it on quickly and taking a steadying breath she fled the house. Reaching the street she ran. And ran for miles, until her legs and lungs burned. Until the echoing voices of people in her head faded in her mind and the feeling of hands clawing at her skin slipped away.

The trees surrounding the road slowly turned into a neighborhood. The few people outside waved hello when they saw her, but Amelia kept going. Feet pounding the pavement, pushing and increasing the distance between the mansion and herself.

The houses changed back into trees as she passed through the suburbs. She didn't know how long she ran before her legs gave out and she dropped. Deep shuddering breaths wracked her body, she squeezed her eyes shut. She flopped onto the grass regaining control of her breathing when a car rolled up beside her. The door opened and closed before footsteps approached.

"I had a feeling you might need a ride home," Tom said, looking down at her, "You ran like someone was chasing you."

Amelia opened an eye and saw her friend and colleague staring at her with concern, "You followed me. Doesn't that make you the person chasing me?"

He shrugged and offered her a hand up. She took it gratefully and he hauled her to her feet. The sudden change of position gave her a brief moment of vertigo but he held her steady until it passed.

When they were both seated in the car he looked at her, "Do you want to talk about it?"

"Not really," Came the reply.

"Okay," Tom turned back to the road, the trip back to the mansion was much shorter than her run had been, "Just so you know, Berardi isn't at the house. I'm not staying either. You'll have the place to yourself for a bit.

Although, I believe Dr. Smith is coming back to check on you in about an hour or so."

"Where is Enzo then?" Amelia queried.

"He's gone to meet with some of our captains. He's having them deliver declarations of war to both the Cruzes and Hagans."

"We're officially at war?" Amelia's jaw dropped, "Why?"

"Amelia Rose!" It was a good thing Tom had pulled into the driveway and stopped the car already otherwise he would've either slammed the brakes or swerved the car off the road, "Why on earth would we not be?"

"Because it isn't that big of a deal! I'm not that big of a deal! It's a hazard of my job!" She replied, throwing her hands into the air.

"Dear lord, Amelia, please tell me you don't really believe that!" Tom looked heartbroken.

Amelia stepped out of the car without replying and ascended the steps to the door. She could hear Tom jumping from the car and following her. He pulled her away from the door and closed it, preventing her from entering the house without finishing their conversation.

"Look at me!" He told her, "Amelia, you are a vital part of our team, that alone makes the attack personal to all of us. Secondly, you are *family* and we defend our family, you know that just as well as I do. But thirdly, and, Amelia, if you tell Berardi I said this, I will deny it. Enzo Berardi loves you."

Amelia was taken aback, "You're still on that?"

Tom sighed, "He loves you, Amelia. He always has. But he was never going to tell you."

"Why not?" She breathed.

"I think originally it was because he wanted you to be free to make your own choices, now it's because of the attack," Tom explained gently, "Honestly, the ball is in your court. You can pretend we never had this conversation, or you can talk to him, when you're ready."

Tom stepped back and gave her a minute to think. She looked at him, trying to detect any lies and found none. And Amelia realized she didn't need to search for falsehoods in the words, she could feel the truth ringing in them. Perhaps deep down she'd known as well but had always denied it. And now, now she was broken and hurt, what could she offer Enzo?

"I- I need to go," Amelia whispered.

Tom nodded and opened the door for her, "Just remember, you are worth fighting a war for. No matter what. I love you like the sister I never had, Amelia."

Amelia watched him close the door behind her. She stood staring at it for a few moments, processing Tom's words. Somehow they both made sense and didn't, like her mind was at war with itself.

Enzo Berardi was her boss, maybe even her friend. He'd never shown interest in her, right? Amelia remembered how he had been by her bed when she'd woken up. How his hand had been outstretched, like he'd held onto hers all night. How throughout the years, he'd been the one to make sure she was safe. Enzo had constantly checked in on her, listened and been a constant. Maybe there was something of substance in Tom's words.

Amelia looked around the house, she was the only other person who lived there besides Enzo and Tom. She'd never questioned it until that very moment. Yet somehow it made sense that he might really love her.

*****

An hour later, after showering, Amelia found herself sitting across from Doctor Audra Smith again. The young doctor had a yellow notepad on her lap and was taking notes as Amelia answered the questions asked. Large glasses perched on her nose so she could look over and through them. They were borrowing Enzo's office, sitting on opposite couches. Amelia was trying very hard to not think about her earlier conversation with Tom.

"I'm not sure seeking revenge is the best choice," Doctor Smith said slowly after hearing that Enzo had gone to declare war, "I don't believe that it's necessarily conducive to healing from trauma."

The doctor was wearing professional clothes a therapist might wear rather than scrubs, which surprised Amelia for some reason. She had simple flats on, comfortable shoes for the work she did in Berardi's clinic and safe house. It wasn't a wonder she had the answers for the kind of trauma Amelia had endured. She faced it everyday.

Amelia cracked a small, half hearted smile, "In my defense, I wasn't the one who declared war. I just happen to be on board with the idea."

The psychologist sighed and pushed her glasses on top of her head, "Most of my patients are not gang members, I don't usually have to talk people out of going to war or picking fights."

"First of all, we are an organization, not a gang. Gangs deal primarily in drugs and weapons, we don't. I mean, we do deal in them, but we mostly keep it in the lower levels to prevent detection," Amelia scowled, "Secondly, we are only responding to their attack."

"Setting aside the drugs and weapons, wouldn't it be better for every party involved to move on?" Dr. Smith asked, a genuine curiosity in her voice.

"I don't really know what's better. It would be great if we could just leave it in the past. But I don't see that happening here. Especially when you consider the broken trust. Not just mine, but my boss' and teammates' as well," Amelia looked away, "Honestly, I think I would prefer a war. It's better than the cat and mouse game we've been playing for years."

"How do you feel about the impending conflict? Do you think you're ready for that so soon after the attack?" The doctor sat back, her hands together in her lap.

"Isn't facing our fears inevitable? And even necessary?" Amelia asked. She fidgeted with the hem of her shirt uncomfortably, still avoiding eye contact.

"It depends on the fear. Do you really think you're afraid of him or are you afraid to trust your judgment again?"

Amelia stared at the doctor, mouth slightly open. Stunned by the question and unable to answer, "I- I don't know."

"From what I know about you, Amelia, I think it's the latter because up until now, you've believed in the choices you've made. Now you're questioning them and your ability to make them," Dr. Smith said gently but pointedly, "Just because you wanted to believe the best in someone does not mean that the attack is your fault. That was his choice, a choice that you are not responsible for nor will you ever be."

"What about the panic and fear caused in other people? Who is responsible for that?" Amelia demanded, she felt the tears pricking at her eyes again, "He put them in jeopardy and I could've stopped it. I could've listened to them in the beginning rather than allowing it to progress."

Amelia looked away, wiping her eyes furiously. She sniffled a little, trying to stop herself from crying anymore than she already had. Ray was not worth the tears, his actions were not worth the tears. Right?

"Amelia, everyone is going to feel this attack personally but that still isn't your fault. Their friend and teammate was attacked and they were helpless when it happened. Of course they're going to feel some type of way about it. In some parts of their brain, they wanted to take your place and protect you, and the fact that they couldn't hurts them," Dr. Smith explained, not reacting to the outburst from the other woman. Knowing it was a result of the pain and guilt she felt, "You have to understand that they're going to take it personally because they love you. They're all asking themselves the same question you're asking yourself, 'how could I have stopped it?'"

"I wish I could rewind the clock and have him booted before any of this happened," Amelia whispered. She looked up at the ceiling, blinking rapidly, "I was so stupid."

"I know you feel that way, but for now, what you can do is lean on the people who are here for you as you heal. Let them help you and try to help them," Dr. Smith said kindly. Before she could continue talking, her phone started to ring shrilly. Picking it up, she sighed disappointedly, "Unfortunately, that's all the time I can give you today. I have to go into the office now. But please, come by at some point and book an appointment."

Amelia stood and shook the woman's hand, "Thank you, Audra. Seriously. I am grateful for your help. I know our organization annoys the crud out of you."

The doctor laughed, "You all have interesting ways of dealing with injuries and trauma, but I don't mind. I'm always here to help. I hope you actually take my advice and make an appointment. I think given your family history and now this, it could be beneficial."

Amelia tucked her hands into her pockets, "We'll see. I'm pretty busy."

"You owe it to yourself to make time to heal," With that last tidbit of advice, Dr. Audra Smith left the Berardi mansion.

Amelia stared after her, frozen momentarily. She was unsure what the right response to this woman's words was. It felt like the psychologist had been able to read the darkest parts of Amelia's mind, pulling the insecurities and questions to the forefront and into the light. The young woman shook her head and moved from her spot on the floor.

"It's an odd thing to owe to yourself," Amelia said to no one in particular.

She turned to face the rest of the house. She was still the only person home and the silence was heavy. Wandering the halls trying to find something to do, she eventually pulled out her phone and sent a text to her friend.

Amelia: Hi

Fae: Well, well, well. I was beginning to think you'd started enjoying not having something to do.

Amelia: It's been less than a day since I got home.

Fae: Uh-huh. You can't sit still to save your life. Get your butt to the shop. Everyone's here anyway.

Amelia: Fine, you got me. I'll be there soon. Need me to get anything?

Fae: Pizza's on the way, so food is covered. Maybe grab a fire extinguisher?

Amelia: Luke's there?

Fae: Yup.

Amelia: Oh dear, yeah, I'll grab one.

Fae: We got a new one last week. It didn't last long.

Amelia laughed, Luke's penchant for explosives was well known. If she was being asked to grab a fire extinguisher, it was likely he'd already blown something up a couple of times. She would find out soon enough. Amelia went searching for her keys and helmet.

Amelia Cruz: Running

Matteo's shop appeared empty when Amelia arrived. After exploring it a bit and examining some of the newer cameras, she ended up making her way to the basement. As she came down the steps, she found her team already at work.

Matteo with earbuds in, frowning at his computer screen and tapping on his keyboard or clicking the mouse. Fae was looking at a poisonously green textbook, her face was more neutral than her boyfriend's but still concentrated and focused on the task at hand. Luke was reading from a manila folder and highlighting part of whatever was inside with a red marker with a scowl on his face. Tom and Enzo were leaning close, heads bent over another folder. They spoke quietly, gesturing at things on the paper as if trying to emphasize a point.

"Hey," Amelia greeted, breaking the concentration at the table, "What are we doing?"

Matteo pulled his headphones off, resting them around his neck, "Trying to clear up the audio from the bug you planted. It's a bit distorted since it's inside cushions."

"Sorry about that. I didn't have a chance to place it properly," Amelia took her seat at the table, grateful to be in the familiar environment.

The Hispanic waved her off, "It's fine! It's better than nothing. I've got it mostly clean anyway."

Amelia nodded as Tom spoke up, "We're going over Lance's file and every mission he was ever part of. Seeing how it lines up with his time off and other times he wasn't where he said he was going to be."

Enzo handed her a stack of files, "These are the main people Lance would take if he was leading. They've already been let go. Or will be once they arrive at Petrov's."

"I just want to check with you guys," Luke interrupted, "It's cool if I blow up the Hagan house when all is said and done, right?"

"We'll raid them first, but absolutely. Blow it to hell," Enzo grinned wickedly.

Fae gave an exaggerated shudder, "And people wonder why they're told to stay away from you all."

"Who says that?" Amelia grinned, enjoying the momentary levity, "I'm an angel."

Tom sniggered, "Yeah right, and Berardi's a saint."

"Do you two know what you're called out on the street?" Luke asked, mischief written all over his face.

"Enlighten me, Datar," Enzo said. He wasn't fully paying attention to the table, his eyes roamed the file in front of him, like there was something interesting about it that had caught his eye.

"Um," Luke looked back and forth between the two, "Suddenly, I'm not sure it's a good idea."

"No, I'm curious, go on," Amelia leaned back, crossing her arms over her chest.

"Umm, well, Berardi is the Bear. But he knew that. You're the she-bear, Amelia," Luke ducked behind Tom's chair as he told them their nicknames.

"Where did *that* come from?" Amelia rolled her eyes.

"Let's put a pin in that for a moment," Enzo said, "Amelia, take a look at this guy. You've worked missions with him before. I want to know your thoughts."

She nodded and took the file from his hand. Inside was the photo of a man who she'd worked with before. He hadn't been significant enough to stick out in her mind before, she handed the file back shaking her head, "I don't know, he was decent enough. Nothing to write home about, why?"

"He had been particularly chummy with Lance, sorry, Ray," Enzo explained, "It's going to take a moment to get used to that."

Matteo held his hand out for the file, "I'll run a search to see if I can find anything."

"Don't bother Matteo, just put a hit out on him," Amelia shrugged, "I'm not risking leaving any trace of the infestation. We kill them all."

"OK, well, while you're doing that, I think I cleared up the audio enough to listen to. You might want to listen, it's pretty entertaining," Matteo pulled his headphones off and set them aside and turned his computer's audio up so they could hear.

"'Entertaining'?" Amelia raised a brow, "How so?"

"Just play it," Enzo said harshly. A frown now deep set in his brow.

The audio recording started with the scraping of cushions from when Amelia had hidden it. After came the brief introduction of Lance as Ray Hagan and Amelia's recognition, and Royal's jab. There was a door slam when Ray had pulled her from the room then laughter.

Enzo reached a hand over and gripped Amelia's shoulder comfortingly.

The audio continued:

"This'll be interesting," Royal sniggered, "He's a pretty dominant guy."

Angel sighed, "Royal, please, a little decorum. She's going to be your family."

"Like you speak any better of her, or any other female family member of ours?" Benjamin jabbed. It was evident the conversation wasn't a serious one because both men roared with laughter.

"Excuse my interruption," Camilo cleared his throat, "How did you get Ray into the Berardi organization?"

"Ah, that was difficult," Narciso chuckled, "We took a page out of law enforcement's book, we created a new identity from scratch."

"It helped that he stayed out of the public eye for years prior to going undercover," Royal slurped his drink loud enough it was heard through the bug.

"What's your big goal with them?" Angel asked, shifting in his seat.

"Are you familiar with Berardi's main form of income? Why he's as powerful as he is?" Narciso questioned, "Why the family has been so powerful for years?"

"Information and land," Camilo answered proudly, excited to have the answer.

Narciso scoffed, "That's certainly part of it, but definitely not the whole of it. He works in imports, hidden under the guise of bringing over car parts, kitchen appliances, and similar items. But the real money is in the weapons he smuggles in with them. He owns the largest ports and the land around it. Security, protection orders, and fences."

"That still doesn't explain your plan, Hagan," Angel sighed, "Get to the point, please."

"We know how the operation works now and we're going to undermine it and take it from him. If we control the ports, we make bank," Narciso claimed proudly, "And with our alliance, we will have more power than any of the Thirteen. We will own the streets. Berardi's allies will leave him and he will be left with nothing. He'll be exiled from the city."

Matteo turned off the audio and turned the computer back, "So that's some of what they'd been talking about. But they also thought it would be fun to take you down a few pegs, Enzo."

"How did they plan to do that?" Enzo crossed his arms over his chest, an amused look on his face.

"With her," Matteo gestured towards Amelia.

The amused expression dropped from Enzo's face and he hummed thoughtfully, "Perhaps we ought to pay them a visit and give them an example of what happens when they mess with our circle."

"What are you planning?" Tom asked.

"Let's call a meeting with both of them, at the Speakeasy. All of us are going, so put on your game faces, we're putting up a unified face," Enzo announced, "They want to monologue? Let's give them the opportunity."

Amelia's jaw dropped, "You want me to face them again? Already?"

Almost immediately Tom began rushing Matteo, Fae, and Luke out of the room. Amelia and Enzo stared at each other until the door at the top of the steps had slammed shut and the voices of their team had faded. Amelia swallowed uncomfortably, unsure of how to start. Enzo rubbed the back of his neck and looked anywhere but at her.

Finally he said, "Amelia, it's entirely up to you. If you can't face them yet, that's fine. I won't judge you. I spoke without thinking and I'm so sorry."

Amelia held her hand up, silencing him, "I don't know how I can face them. Especially Ray."

"We don't know that the Hagans are going to bring him into public yet," Enzo said.

"Enzo! That isn't the point! Everyone else is complicit, it isn't just about him," Amelia snapped harshly, "My brothers sat by while it happened! They signed my life over to him! It isn't just about Ray. It's about my brothers too."

She watched hurt and understanding flash across his face. He nodded softly then held his hand out, offering it for her to take. She took it, apprehensive and hesitant.

"If you decide to come, I will be there for you and if you want to leave, say the word. I will take my cues from you," Enzo told her gently, "The ball is in your court. Only you can decide what you're capable of or what can tear you down. And while I will support your decision, I think that you should consider making an appearance, if only to show them you aren't broken and they can't break you. Just food for thought, Amelia."

Amelia flashed back to her earlier conversation with Tom. He was using the exact same words. It struck her how different Enzo and Lance were. How different they had always been.

   During her time with Lance, or Ray, she had never been given the choice, maybe the illusion of a choice, but it was never really hers. In the end, Ray had always gotten what he wanted. Enzo had never guilt tripped or manipulated her decisions. Even when speaking with her and others within the organization, his speech has always been different. In their arguments or teasing there had been an effort to make her feel heard. Nothing had ever been said to tear her down. It was a strange realization for Amelia, especially having been such an advocate for Ray. It was funny how quickly the tables turned.

"Do you promise you'll be there the whole time?" She whispered nervously.

"I won't leave your side unless you tell me to," He replied solemnly, squeezing her hand gently.

"Tom was right," Amelia suddenly laughed lightly.

Enzo gave her a puzzled look, "What do you mean?"

She smiled, "I would tell you to ask him but he said he would deny it if I said anything."

This time Enzo held his hand up, "Never mind, I know exactly what you mean. Would you excuse me? I am going to have a quick conversation with my second in command."

Amelia nodded and watched Enzo take the stairs two at a time. When he disappeared, Fae's head popped into view. She trotted down and took Enzo's deserted chair.

She gave Amelia a raised brow before saying, "Spill. What was that all about?"

"Really? After everything in the past twenty-four hours, *that's* what you're interested in?" Amelia scoffed, "My conversation with our boss?"

Fae shrugged, "I mean, I'd like to know what happened at the Hagans but I figured you had already told a million people and wouldn't want to tell another person."

Amelia dropped her head on the table with a groan, "It's Berardi. There's something strange with the way he's been acting. I can't explain it."

"Strange how?" Fae asked, propping her chin on her hand, "Strange like he's not acting like himself or strange because you finally realized he's in love with you?"

The Hispanic woman peeked up at her friend, "Did everyone but me know?"

Fae threw her head back and laughed, "Seriously? You're kidding right? Amelia, he looks at you like you hung the moon in the sky. He listens to you like you are speaking the greatest poems ever written. He's waited years for you to realize it. Now his competition is with a memory. It's an impossible battle! Only you can choose the victor."

Amelia sat back up and stared, jaw open. Her friend's words were unwavering and sincere. But even she didn't know how to fight the ghost of a memory that would be plaguing her for who knew how long. It was a battle she wasn't ready for.

"Fae, I have to go, I can't do this right now. I'm not ready," Amelia grabbed her phone from the desk and ran up the stairs, calling behind, "Tell Enzo that I'm sorry!"

Luke and Matteo were leaning on one of the glass counters when she got to the shop. Their conversation stopped when they saw her but she didn't stop to say anything to them. She made a beeline for her motorcycle and revved it quickly. The beautiful machine carried her away from the camera shop and away from the people she had worked with for so long. She needed to escape.

Find somewhere to lay low for a bit and maybe even stay permanently. The conflict of emotions inside of her were overwhelming. She wasn't ready to face them and she wasn't ready to face other people.

Checking her fuel gauge, she urged the bike to go faster. The full tank could get her roughly two hundred miles out of the city and she was going to take every inch she could possibly get.

Wind whipped at her clothes and might have stung her face were it not for her helmet. It both shielded her from the elements and from people recognizing her.

The city grew smaller in the rear view mirror and the road became less crowded. It became easier to weave in between the cars and speed up even more. The further she went the less the pressure on her shoulders felt.

Why did her team choose to tell her something so monumental after being attacked by someone she had trusted? What was the purpose? Was she supposed to suddenly get over the betrayal? The pain that had been caused was already unbearable, to put this on her as well? Amelia couldn't breathe. She hoped that maybe taking some time off might help her see more clearly.

Enzo Berardi: Another Short Meeting and an Explosion

Enzo wasn't surprised when Amelia didn't show up at the Speakeasy. He wasn't even surprised when she didn't answer a message from him. He'd spoken to Tom about what he'd told Amelia. While he had sworn he would deny it, Tom told his friend what he'd said. Enzo glared at his under boss for quite some time after hearing everything but ultimately decided not to dole out any punishment. This time. Enzo would need Tom by his side that night at the Speakeasy.

They'd sent out the request to meet with the Cruzes and Hagans earlier that day and had gotten a prompt reply: they would be there.

It wasn't just Tom who would be at his side tonight, Luke, Fae and Matteo had gone with him too. Enzo gave them each a once over. Luke had gone with slacks and a red button down, contrasting his usual style. He had kept the sneakers though apparently not caring what anyone thought of them. Fae had gone with a 50's style evening dress the color of blood. She looked terrific and her boyfriend seemed to agree since he couldn't take his eye off her. Matteo's suit was black as night, everything, from his shirt to his shoes was the same color. Except for his tie, it was a vibrant shade of crimson.

Enzo nodded approvingly when he realized that each member of his team had worn the Berardi color. They were displaying their alliance proudly. They all stood tall, ready to follow him into battle and Enzo was honored to work with them.

Enzo straightened his shoulders and led his team into the Speakeasy.

The only sound inside the shining halls were their footsteps. The usual jazz band and murmur of guests was absent. There was no clinking of glasses and bottles at the bar. It seemed as though the Cruzes had cleared their establishment for the evening.

The Italian mobster thought it might end up being better for them. If things turned nasty, there wouldn't be any bystanders hurt. Not that many civilians chose the Speakeasy as their preferred nighttime haunt.

Enzo rounded the corner into the main dining hall and found himself in the presence of six men. Narciso Hagan and his two sons sat at one table, each wearing something with the signature orange of their clan. Narciso had a baby blue suit and orange tie, simple and classy. Royal had gone for a gaudy orange sport coat and he seemed rather proud of it. Ray's clothing was closer to his father's, with baby blue slacks. He didn't appear to have a coat to hide the neon color of his shirt though.

Seeing Ray made Enzo seethe. He had to fight every urge in his body not to lunge for the man or shoot him right there. A muscle ticked in his jaw as the only sign of his rage. He forced himself to look at the other three men who sat behind a table next to the Hagans.

The Cruz brothers. Just as responsible for Enzo's anger, just as guilty for the abuse dished out. Angel and Benjamin both had simplistic suits in their family color whereas Camilo had again gone for a crushed velvet look. But what stood out the most to Enzo was the complete lack of concern for their sister. The pure dismissal of her.

"Gentlemen," He drawled. Enzo motioned to his team, "I trust introductions are not in order?"

He pulled a chair from a table and plopped down into it. His team fanned out beside him, taking seats of their own. Enzo tented his hands, staring at Ray, daring him to make a move or mistake.

"So, Berardi, you called us here," Angel started the conversation, "Why?"

"I hardly think I need to explain why, or did Mr. Hagan not explain what he did to your sister?" Enzo said so casually, one might think he was talking about the weather.

Angel nodded slowly, "If by you are referring to him spending the night with his betrothed, I gave my blessing. And it hardly seems like your concern, after all, she left you."

Enzo hummed, "Did you also give him permission to assault her? She came to me after that night, covered in bruises, bleeding and beaten, so forgive me if I show some concern for her. Especially when her family seems to care so little."

"You violate the laws of the Commission, Berardi," Narciso told him angrily. He tried to cross his arms over his chest, but his numerous rolls prevented him from fully being able to.

Enzo's brows rose, "Really? How so? The last time I checked, if a person came seeking shelter, on neutral ground, anyone could give sanctuary."

"Not only that, but Miss Cruz still bears the mark of the Berardi family which would guarantee safety in perpetuity," Tom added.

"Ah, yes, there is that little matter as well. You attacked a member of another family, unprovoked. So, tell me, Mr. Hagan, who is really violating the laws of the Commission?" Enzo said, the tone of his voice amused but lined with violence.

The Hagan men glanced back and forth between each other. Enzo might have thought they were nervous if it weren't for the pleased smirk on Ray's face. The man leaned forward and whispered to his father and brother, not caring that there was an audience.

Camilo groaned and stood from the table. Sauntering over to the bar and hopping up to sit on it, he reached for a bottle of vodka. He poured out a shot and threw it back without a wince. He repeated this twice more before he set the bottle down and let out a belch that distracted from the conversation. All heads turned to him with disgusted expressions but Camilo merely shrugged. He lay back on the bar and drummed his fingers through the air to music that only he could hear.

Enzo watched him with curiosity before he turned back to the Irishmen. They had finally stopped whispering and faced him again as well. The elder Cruz brothers watched their ally with wariness, ready to follow their lead.

"It seems we are at an impasse, Berardi," Ray chortled, "I had every right as she is my betrothed. If I believed she needed punishment for her loose tongue, it was my prerogative."

"I would agree with you, if, and only if, you were married. But alas, you are not and therefore, the impasse is nonexistent," Enzo replied evenly, "Don't get me started on your espionage, Ray."

"I never did anything wrong," Ray shrugged, "Technically followed the rules."

"Bull," Fae said, covering the word with a fake cough.

Enzo smirked but looked over and held a hand up to tell her not to do it again. She nodded respectfully and shot him an apologetic look. Her boyfriend leaned and whispered something in her ear, making her smile and cover a chuckle with another false cough.

"I didn't come here for an argument over the rights and wrongs of the past weeks or even years. I came here to tell you face to face, we are at war," Enzo grinned, "But I will offer you a choice; apologize and start honoring territory lines and pay back what you've stolen, or you will see what really happens when you poke a bear. You have twenty-four hours to decide. I do hope you make the right choice. But if you don't I have a line of people waiting to carve your son up."

"You challenged me first at the Commission, now you take us to war? Berardi," Narciso clicked his tongue at the Italian, "Your father would be so disappointed in your failures."

Enzo didn't move or twitch, but Tom did. He was standing from his chair in an instant, gun drawn, "Don't you dare make another sound, Hagan."

"Put a leash on your dog, Berardi!" Angel snapped. "Dante," Enzo said quietly. He gave his friend a pointed look that said 'later.'

Tom growled and put his gun away, "Mark my words, Hagan, you will pay for all your family has done."

"I think we've made our point. Have a good evening gentlemen," Enzo stood from the table and turned to the door.

His team followed him out to the parking lot, waiting for him to say something. He leaned against his car and ran a hand through his hair.

"All of you, go home. Take some time before the morning, this is the only rest we get for a while," Enzo told them, "They aren't going to make a decision we like but we knew that coming in."

Tom suddenly held a hand in front of the team as they started to walk away, effectively stopping them, "Luke, did you bring any C-4?"

Luke looked offended, "Is that even a question?"

Tom grinned maniacally and Enzo was reminded why his friend was also his second in command. Tom may be calm for the most part, but mess with his team? There would be hell to pay. And insult Leon Berardi or Alessio Dante? A person bought themselves a one way ticket to the grave.

Before Amelia had taken over the interrogations for the organization, Tom used to do them. His vicious streak had always shown then. Most of the time, Amelia's techniques didn't actually involve weapons, but with Tom, he would pull out the medieval methods. Tom's cunning and wisdom had been one of the keys to Enzo's success in the organization.

Enzo watched the mechanic pull open the trunk of his car. He reached inside and fiddled with something for a moment before handing what looked like a lump of clay to Tom. Luke pointed at one of the cars then beckoned for Annabelle to come grab another lump of clay. He kept sending the group around the parking lot for a few minutes, placing lumps of C-4 in the cars sitting in the lot.

Finally he brushed his hands off and turned to his boss, "I wasn't sure which cars were theirs, so, all of them are rigged except ours. We should go. Like, now!"

Luke rushed to the driver side of his car and jumped inside, Fae on his heels. The engine turned over and he sped away from the parking lot. Matteo was right behind him. Tom rushed to the car he and Enzo had both ridden in. They jumped inside and disappeared into the night.

Behind them an explosion went off, rattling the ground and lighting up the sky with flames. Smoke billowed up, hardly diminishing the light from the city. Windows shook in their frames and car alarms went off. Enzo glanced over his shoulder and laughed.

"That was genius," He told Tom.

Tom looked over, a mischievous glint in his eyes, "I have no idea what you're talking about. Fate must have stepped in to repay them for an insult."

Enzo shook his head, amused. He looked down at his phone wondering whether or not he should check in with Amelia. Against his better judgment, he sent her a message.

Enzo: How are you feeling?

Amelia: …

Enzo: That doesn't tell me anything, you know.

Amelia: I'm taking some time off to recover.

Enzo: Do you need anything from us?

Amelia: No.

Enzo put his phone away before relaying the conversation to Tom. The two men sat in silence for the remainder of the car ride. The Berardi mansion welcomed them with dark windows and an eerily empty feeling.

"Drink?" Enzo offered, walking up the steps.

Tom tucked his hands into his pockets, "Sure."

Enzo led them into the study and flicked on the lights. The liquor cabinet was well stocked with several kinds of whiskey his father and grandfather had collected but he reached for his tried and true favorite. Pouring generously into two tumblers, Enzo downed his rather quickly and refilled it before actually giving Tom his glass. The second nodded his thanks and took a seat on the sofa.

"We're at war, we're down two men, we're losing shipments left and right, what more could go wrong?" Tom groaned.

Enzo sighed, "I'm pretty sure Amelia left the city. So there's that."

"You're kidding. Why?" Tom flopped his head back to rest on the sofa.

"Probably because it wasn't just you who said something to her. Fae did too. And it was all too soon after the attack," Enzo said, "I told you not to say anything!"

"I'm sorry. Seriously, I didn't mean to spill it," Tom sipped his whiskey, "She asked why we had bothered to go after her and I couldn't stop myself. Enzo, she's like my sister, I hate how broken she seems right now. I was trying to make her understand how valued she is."

Enzo nodded in understanding, "How do you think I feel? If I hadn't held her in such high esteem, Ray wouldn't have targeted her. She wouldn't have suffered the years of abuse. It's my fault."

"I think that might have been inevitable," Tom said thoughtfully, "Growing up in a home like hers, it would make sense for her romantic relationship to resemble it. That's what she knew. Even if she was determined to make her own choice, she still sought out what was familiar. It doesn't necessarily mean that everyone who grows up in a bad home will end up in an abusive relationship nor does it mean that they will become abusive themselves. It's just a higher chance. In short; don't beat yourself up. Just be better for her when she's ready."

"What the hell, Tom! Where did that come from? Have you been spending time with Dr. Smith when you aren't at work?" Enzo laughed incredulously.

Tom raised his glass, "Majored in psychology, nimrod."

Enzo grinned, "I forget about that you went to college sometimes."

"Really? I couldn't tell," Tom's sarcastic tone and face made Enzo grab a wad of paper from the table and chuck it. He missed his friend's head resulting in Tom taunting, "You missed me by a mile."

"Yes well, I've never been the better shot," Enzo held his glass up in salute.

Tom mirrored him, "To the war to come, may we be victorious and richer for it!"

*****

Enzo's phone woke him up a couple of hours after his conversation with Tom. Luke's name flashing on the screen.

"Hello?" Enzo answered, groggily.

"Hey…" Luke started, "Um so, I didn't go home."
   Enzo sat up, "What did you do, Luke!"

"It wasn't just me!" Luke cried defensively, "Tom's here too!"

The Italian swore, "What did you do?"

"We haven't done anything. Yet," Luke paused, "But we're at one of Hagan's buildings in the Bronx. He runs a lot of business out of it. It would be a shame if it weren't here in the morning."

Enzo grinned, "Such a shame."

"Do we have permission to continue?" Tom's voice came through the speaker.

"Don't get arrested, don't get captured by the Hagans," Enzo hung up, "I have an errand for the two of you after you finish."

Enzo flopped down on his bed for a moment, cackling like a fool. The Hagans were getting hit hard that night. First their vehicles, now the heart of their business. They would suffer for the pain that they had caused the Thirteen and their retribution was starting.

He hauled himself from the bed and got dressed. He was still grinning, enjoying the formulating plan of humiliation for the Cruz brothers.

Shortly after Enzo had pulled his motorcycle off the road near the Speakeasy, Luke and Tom pulled up in their car. They were laughing and smelled like gunpowder. Smug expressions lit up their faces when they greeted their boss and friend.

"Evening. Or rather, morning!" Enzo nodded in greeting, "Camilo Cruz should be leaving the Speakeasy soon. Likely drunk off his butt. I want you to throw him in the trunk."

Tom shrugged his coat off and threw it into the backseat of his car, "Are we imprisoning him or sinking him?"

"I haven't decided yet," Enzo shrugged, "Maybe just holding onto him to make a point."

Luke opened the trunk of the car and rifled around. Moving tools from the trunk to the backseat, removing anything that could be used as a tool or weapon. He pulled a roll of duct tape out and held it up for approval from Tom and Enzo. When they gave him a thumbs up, he slammed the trunk and started tossing the roll up in the air and catching it again.

"I am going to enjoy this," Enzo admitted, "I'm going to enjoy embarrassing the Cruz brothers."

"I want a pound of flesh from all of them," Tom rolled his neck.

"Here he comes!" Luke told them.

Camilo Cruz was sauntering out of the Speakeasy. His cheeks were pink and his steps uneven, drunk as predicted. Luke trotted up to him with a smile and tapped his shoulder. The Hispanic turned and began slurring at the mechanic.

"You're one of Berardi's!" Camilo tripped over his words, "Why are you here? Come to ruin more of our stuff? I liked that car!"

Enzo rolled his eyes, "He isn't the sharpest knife in the drawer but at least he can recognize people."

Tom shrugged, "It's probably part of his job. He has to know which family people belong to when they're in the Speakeasy."

Enzo nodded, "Possibly. Let's go."

The men walked up to Luke and Camilo. The latter glared at Enzo when he got close enough to be recognizable. He tried to swing at the Italian but ended up lurching forward, off balance. Tom laughed and grabbed the man, twisting his arms behind his back to duct tape his wrists together. Luke took a strip and tried to put it across Camilo's mouth, a task which proved difficult. Camilo was sticking his tongue out and licking at the tape and Luke's fingers, trying to to prevent being silenced.

"Heaven have mercy," Enzo pulled his gun from his pocket and pistol whipped the curly haired man, knocking him unconscious, "Put him in the trunk. I don't feel like dealing with him just yet."

"What are we going to do with him?" Luke asked after Camilo was secured in the trunk.

"We could put him on a cargo ship and wave goodbye," Tom suggested, "With his drunkenness and flamboyant behavior, it would be believable that he would do it himself."

Enzo considered his friend's words, "It might just be humiliating enough. Camilo isn't the main culprit in his family's sins anyway. It seems unfair to take it all out on him, no?"

It was agreed that Camilo Cruz would be dropped off with Petrov's harbor master and placed on a ship leaving the city that night. It wouldn't be long before he was back, but it would get the attention of the brothers and the Commission.

Enzo Berardi: A Battle at the Docks

Enzo wasn't sure if he actually appreciated the ongoing conflict, nor was he sure if his men appreciated it. Or really any of their business ventures did. Each day brought a new casualty of the war, whether it was a ship or even a building. The streets of New York often were filled with sirens on a regular basis already, but even the civilians had picked up on the rise in flinging bullets and smoke. The Hagans weren't pulling punches, they had doubled down on their thefts and active campaign against Berardi. The Cruz brothers had retrieved Camilo from the cargo shift he'd been on after paying a hefty ransom Petrov had decided to set simply because he could.

The brothers were doing their best to wreak havoc on Enzo's businesses as payback. For the most part though, they'd stayed in the shadows, hidden and sending their men to do the work for them.

One night the Italian family had gotten word from one of their own spies that the Cruzes had brought in a large shipment and their main harbormaster would be present.

They had taken a group to invade the dock and find him. Enzo sighed, looking out at the group in front of him, he was about to lead them into the Cruzes' shipyards and

commandeer their supplies. This particular shipment was coming from the Cruzes' connection in Mexico. Their cousins in the cartels were sending them plenty of *cocaína* to keep them in business for the next month and Enzo was about to destroy it all. He wondered if the Cruz brothers knew their cousins in Mexico did not hold to the same mindset as them. While the brothers believed women couldn't hold seats of power in New York, their counterparts in Mexico were being led by some of their female cousins. Enzo had already sent word down to Mexico and was working to sway the women leading to support his organization rather than their cousins'.

"Gentlemen, I hope you are ready," He called out to them.

A rallying cheer flew up into the night air without a care of being heard. Somehow knowing they were coming, Angel Cruz had two different Families guarding his docks, the Garcias and Floreses. Neither family was large enough to really contend with the Berardi men. But Enzo wasn't going to gamble with his men's lives and had brought a second family as well. The DeLucas had been all too eager to join the battle. They were a bloodthirsty bunch which was why Enzo liked to use them as his guards or soldiers, and that night, they would be let off their leash.

"Take it all!" Enzo yelled over their eager murmurs, "Take it all, and enjoy it! The spoils of war are yours to use as you want!"

Like they had been shot from a gun, the group of men that had stood at attention were suddenly running towards the docks. Violent screams and calls for death and destruction rained down. The rattle of gunfire filled the air followed by the potent odor of gunpowder.

Tom stepped up next to Enzo, "Not joining this round? That's unlike you."

"In a moment," He replied, "I want them to weed out the leader first."

"Do you remember the first time we saw our fathers come home from a battle?" Tom asked, crossing his arms over his chest, watching the carnage.

"Of course," Enzo smiled at the memory, like it wasn't a gruesome and bloody thing, "Territory dispute over our docks. Again."

Twenty-five years ago:

The front door opened, letting in two laughing men. Alessio Dante and Leon Berardi stepped into the entryway. Their shirts were soaked in blood, even their hair was slicked back with it. But the worst injury on either of them were a couple of bruises or scratches. The men shook off their shoulder holsters, setting them on the table by the door, not realizing they had an audience.

Lucia Berardi was standing further in the room with her hands on her hips. Not a hair out of place, flawless makeup, wrinkle free clothes. And a dubious expression.

"So," She said, gaining the attention of the two men and two boys hidden at the top of the stairs, "This was the reason for your early departure from the gala tonight? And late arrival home? No phone call, no note, car gone, you could've died for all I knew!"

Alessio and Leon stood like deer in headlights. They could face down mobsters any day, but an angry Lucia Berardi was a different beast. Even mobsters knew 'happy wife, happy life,' were words to live by, especially if said wife knew how to use a revolver.

"Darling!" Leon threw his arms open and stepped towards his wife.

She held a hand up, "No. Not until you shower."

His arms dropped, "As you wish, my darling."

Leon trudged up the stairs leaving his friend and second in command to face the wrath of his wife alone. Alessio audibly gulped when he realized he was being abandoned to Lucia.

"Leon! Get back down here!" He called, "You might be the scary lion but everyone knows the lioness is worse! Don't leave me alone with her!"

Leon paused on the stairs and might have gone down to help his friend if he hadn't spotted their sons in their hiding spot, "Well, well, well, what do we have here? A couple of spies who are supposed to be in bed."

This got Lucia's attention away from the men and focused on the boys, "Lorenzo, Tomaso! If I have to come up there!"

Like they'd been shocked with a live wire, both boys jumped from their hiding spot and bolted. Their fathers' laughter followed them down the hallway. They rushed into Enzo's bedroom and slammed the door, leaning on it as if their combined seven year old body weight might keep out even one of their parents. Enzo looked over at his friend and they fell to the floor, bursting into giggles.

Now:

"How did they get *that* soaked in blood?" Tom asked in wonder.

Enzo shrugged, "We can always find out by joining the fray. I see the leader."

He jumped from the box he had stood on for a vantage point and ran towards the battle. He pulled his pistols from their holsters and aimed them at the first enemies he saw. Enzo didn't care whether or not his own shots were fatal or not this time, his only concern was to ensure that he stayed alive through the battle. He continued to pursue the leader who was trying to escape.

From the corner of his eye, he saw a large man in dock worker's coveralls bringing a rifle to his shoulder to shoot at him. Enzo raised his own guns and fired quickly, hoping he was fast enough to stay alive. The man dropped like a rock, his rifle falling from his hands.

Enzo blew over the barrels of his guns, "That's right, my bullets are faster than yours."

"Nice shot, Berardi!" Tom called. He came running up to his boss, he'd lost his coat somewhere between their starting point and now. His rifle was slung over his shoulder casually, like they weren't in the middle of a war zone.

Together they ran towards the storage containers they had seen the leader slip behind. Enzo motioned for Tom to walk one side while he took the other. He hoped they would be able to pin the leader and pull the information they needed from him. If he wasn't willing to give up what Enzo wanted, well, it was a good thing he had a Plan B.

The floodlights from the docks cast long shadows over the metal containers and challenged Enzo's sight. Carefully he put one foot in front of the other, trying to stay quiet to not alert the rat he was trying to catch. The further he got from the main dock the more the angry sounds of the brawl faded, soon the loudest sound was the click of his shoes on the pavement.

"Come out out wherever you are!" He called mockingly.

A shadow bolted on his right. The man ran as fast as he could, weaving in between the containers, trying to get away from them. Tom appeared chasing behind him, grinning like a mad man.

He was chanting a song Enzo had never heard before, "I peek around the corner, shoot you in the head, now you're gonna stumble, fall over dead!"

"Tom! Man, we're not killing him yet!" Enzo hissed.

"I know, it's just a warning for later," Tom laughed and pointed down an aisle for Enzo to go down. He was still focused on flushing the man out.

"I do not want to die tonight!" A Hispanic accent called from somewhere in the maze of shipping containers.

Enzo exchanged a glance with his friend, "Then come out and tell us what we want to know!"

He listened for the scrambling footsteps giving away the man's position and quickly followed. Enzo was growing tired of this cat and mouse game they were playing. Taking a glance at his gun and ensuring there was a round in the chamber, he shot it down the aisle in front of him. Three things happened in quick succession, first, the gun let off a bang, then the bullet hit a metal container somewhere down the aisle. Finally, the Hispanic man screamed bloody murder.

"Okay! Okay!" He cried, "I am coming out! Please don't shoot me!"

Slowly he came out of the shadows with his hands over his head in surrender. Enzo identified him as Gabriel Flores, the Head of that Family. He smirked, what a beautiful turn of events.

"Señor Flores," He said in greeting. His expression was a cat-caught-the-canary look causing Flores to swallow nervously, "This *is* a pleasant surprise."

"Berardi," He replied in greeting, "What are you doing here?"

Tom came around the corner, tossing a grenade up in the air and catching it again, "He didn't really ask that, did he?"

"Tom, put that down before you kill us all. How you can be sane and insane at the same time is a bewilderment to me," Enzo rolled his eyes. The wheels in Enzo's head turned as an idea began to percolate, "Flores, you are not a stupid man. Usually. You have been thoughtless in your choice of Leader though, haven't you?"

"I don't know what you mean," Flores sputtered indignantly.

"Sure you don't," Enzo leaned against one of the containers and tucked a gun into a holster and spun the other by the trigger well, "Where are any of the Cruz brothers? I don't see anyone actually related to the family. It seems to me that they're willing to risk you and not themselves. Cowardly, if you ask me."

Mischief glinted in Tom's eye, he rounded the Hispanic man so he could be face to face, "In case you didn't notice, the Berardis don't play that way. First in, last out."

Flores looked between the two rapidly, "What are you getting at?"

Enzo shrugged, "You can always switch your allegiance and have actual protection, more money, more property, the list goes on. Simply help us win this war we're in."

Flores sputtered again looking aghast, Tom looked utterly delighted with the turn of events and Enzo simply shrugged. He pretended to check the sight on his gun, aiming it at the Hispanic while waiting for his response. The threat was subtle, but Enzo had never intended for this to be an offer he could actually turn down.

If he could pull support from most of the families, the war would be easily won and perhaps maybe even pave the way for larger profits. The Floreses were a Family known for being able to hide certain powdery substances in the form of other things, an ability that could prove useful. If he could pull the support of the Garcia, Murphy and Connor families, the Hagans and Cruzes would be wildly outnumbered. They would be forced to surrender.

"Okay, okay!" Flores yelled, "We'll swear fealty to you!"

"Excellent," Enzo smirked, "I want you to meet with Héctor Perez, be a good man and try to convince him to join our cause, won't you?"

Flores nodded, whimpering softly, "I will! I swear!"

Tom glared at the man, "The Garcias are here too, you'll aid them in making the right choice as well. If not, I'm happy to spill blood tonight. I wouldn't be disappointed with pouring yours to the ground."

Again, the Hispanic nodded, "I will, please let me go!"

Enzo sniffed the air and wrinkled his nose. The stench of ammonia was wafting off the man. He'd soiled himself in his fear.

"Man, that is disgusting!" Tom gagged, realizing the same thing as Enzo.

Enzo approached the man, "I will be willing to forget this little mishap, just remember our deal."

He patted the man's cheek twice and didn't wait for a response before walking away. He heard Tom confiscating Flores' gun and trotting to catch up with him. He disassembled the gun as he walked, throwing the parts left and right. The fight was still going strong when they approached the main dock, bodies littered the ground, blood watered the pavement. The guttural sounds of knives entering flesh surrounded the men, bones crunched, shots echoed in the night air.

"I think I understand how our fathers got so covered in blood," Tom mused, looking around the chaos.

Men swung at each other with makeshift weapons as well as their real ones. Blood soaked the ground, pouring from open wounds. Some men had knives sticking out of their shoulders but it didn't slow their attack. They fought with their other arm, refusing to be defeated. Fallen bodies lay across the gravel or hanging over the edge of the ships, having been shot. A bullet whizzed by Enzo, missing him by inches and embedding itself in a light pole behind him.

Enzo nodded in agreement. He took his own gun and looked around until he found what he was looking for. A propane tank sitting on the deck of one of the ships. It sat next to a metal shipment container waiting to be unloaded. He nodded to himself, it would work. He fired off two rounds; one into the tank and the other to scratch the surface of the container, causing sparks. The sparks ignited in the gas, causing the canister to explode. All eyes turned to the fire spreading across the deck of the ship. While the fighting had momentarily ceased, Enzo fired one more shot into the sky, gathering the attention of every man, Flores or otherwise.

"Gentlemen, I commend you on a battle well fought," He called out, "Flores men, your Head has decided to call off this fight to protect you. There is now an alliance between our two Families. All I ask tonight, is that you destroy the remaining cargo on these ships. Then, go home. Rest. Recuperate. The battle is over tonight, but we all know the war will continue to rage on."

Tom stepped up, "Garcia family, the same offer extends to you. Swear loyalty and you are free to leave. Decline our offer, well, you may join others beneath the waves."

The DeLuca and Flores men let out a unified cheer, clapping each other on the shoulder, as if they hadn't been fighting to the death moments earlier. It was certainly one of the stranger things about the mafia family dynamic. Camaraderie could born and burned in seconds. Loyalty was treasured of course, but when there was a chance to survive, even the most loyal of men would turn in seconds. The Garcia that remained approached Enzo, reaching to shake his hand and swear fealty. Another victory for the Berardi Family.

Enzo watched the men climb aboard the docked ships, seizing fire axes and wooden beams. They broke windows and crates, snapped locks on the metal containers and threw grenades inside. The decks rattled and the vessels rocked, the water churned underneath, chaos grew with every explosion. The Cruzes were going to take a considerable loss from this night. Part of him wondered how they would reply, another part of him didn't care, naming this as partial revenge for their treatment of their sister. He still hadn't heard from her. Amelia had vanished off the face of the earth.

Tom stood on his right side, gone was the maniacal expression replaced with one of considerable thought. He was likely wondering the same thing as Enzo. Considering the repercussions to come. The Cruz brothers weren't as bloodthirsty as their father had been, but they had considerable power still. Severely diminished power now, due to the change of allegiances that night.

"Somehow, this feels like it goes deeper than the past couple of weeks," Tom expressed suddenly, "Like this is also for the damage caused by the callus behavior of the families in the years since the assassinations."

Enzo nodded, "War has a way of pulling out ugly memories and making us remember the violence of the past and relive that hurt."

The men started to file out of the dockyard. The new alliances already making friends of once enemies. They helped the wounded to cars so they could get medical care. They retrieved fallen weapons and returned them to their rightful owners if they could. Nods of appreciation were shared and words of welcome extended.

"At this rate, you'll take over the Commission through allegiances faster than Hagan will with force," Tom observed, "You already have most of the Thirteen on your side now. If you don't count Hagan and Cruz."

Enzo agreed softly. It had never been the intention to take over the Commission. His desire had always been to maintain balance, but in wartime, intentions and desires change. He sought revenge. Not peace.
He sought revenge for his father.
Revenge for Alessio Dante.
Revenge for Amelia.
Revenge for every of member of his organization who had lost their life.
Vengeance for his mother, who had lost so much of her life to the grief of losing her husband. Of watching her son lose his childhood.
Enzo would have his revenge.

Amelia Cruz: The Shelter

melia hadn't been able to leave the city. She got about seventy miles away from the city before she'd turned around and gone back. But she hadn't been able to go back home either. So, instead she'd gone to the shelter that Enzo's parents had founded.

Doctor Smith ran the shelter and welcomed Amelia warmly. The first two weeks had been hard for Amelia. She hadn't been able to do much but hated sitting still. She had meetings with Dr. Smith and she went to group meetings but not much beyond that. It had taken Dr. Smith a long time to convince Amelia to even attend one of the group meetings. She was sure those would be particularly difficult because no one would understood the kind of work she did and how it had played into the attack. But surprisingly, the people there had related. They'd helped her through.

The whole shelter was built underground to stay hidden. The only thing that was above ground was a little recreation center that middle and high school kids liked to play basketball in. The parts underground were built similarly to a hotel. Several rooms with single bathrooms, a shared meal space on the lower level, offices for refugees who were working remote jobs. There was a small library for the children doing homework or if anyone simply wanted a book.

During non-meal times, the dining space was the group meeting place. People mulled about and chatted with one another like one might see at a family reunion.

Dr. Smith had forced Amelia out of her room to go at one point, saying, "I will tell Enzo Berardi where you are if you don't start acting like you're here to heal rather than hide out. This is not a place to ignore the world, Amelia!"

That was how Amelia found herself sitting in a circle with a group of men and women of varying ages. Most of them greeted one another pleasantly and comfortably, like old friends. One of the older women had shaken Amelia's hand kindly and offered her the seat immediately next to her. The woman wore a perfume that made Amelia think of her *Abuela*. The woman was shorter than her with curled white hair and large pearl earrings. She was the picture of a welcoming grandmother.

Amelia was surprised when no one called the meeting to order like the movies she'd seen. The people just chatted amongst themselves, catching up on day to day life. Some were talking about books or the weather outside. Others, like Amelia, just observed. Until the woman next to her tapped her shoulder with a smile and introduced herself.

"I'm Dorothy, what's your name, dear?" She asked sweetly. "Um, Amelia."

"What a delightful name! So pretty! Your mama chose well," The woman smiled and clapped her hands together in a short round of applause. Amelia was surprised when no one looked over, it must have been a regular occurrence.

Unsure of what to say, Amelia just said, "Thank you."

"Why are you here, dear?" The woman folded her wrinkled hands in her lap, waiting for Amelia's response patiently.

"I didn't know where else to go," Amelia admitted, "I have the ability to go literally anywhere, but I couldn't seem to pull myself away from the city. It's like a magnet, always pulling me back."

Dorothy nodded understandingly, "You came to the right place. Lucia, the dear woman who used to own the shelter, used to say this wasn't some halfway house. It was a place of rest and where one could find direction. It was a place of healing too, for those of us who needed it. Somehow, I have a feeling you're here for that too, aren't you?"

"I-uh," Amelia stuttered, uncertain of what to say. Dorothy took her hand and squeezed it gently, nodding to encourage Amelia to find her words, "Someone who I loved very much, betrayed me. And hurt my family. And what my family doesn't know is that I don't have much money anymore because of him. I have a little. Enough to get me away from the city if I wanted, but he took most of it."

"Oh my," Dorothy sighed sadly, "Unfortunately, that is a story I hear all too often here. Many of the people in this group have experienced something similar. While everyone's story is unique, sometimes it's helpful to know that not everything is completely exclusive to you. Now, let's see. Marcus over there, has been here for about three months now, his ex- fiancee cleaned him out and ran off with someone from Wall Street. He's a bright young man though, he's working on a remote job and rebuilding so he can come back stronger." Dorothy pointed out the man she mentioned. He was a lean figure, shaggy brown hair in need of a trim. He was conversing with an older gentleman who saw Dorothy looking at them and waved. She waved back and blew him a kiss with a girlish giggle.

"That's Donny, my husband. He and I met here about three years ago now. We were both mourning the loss of our spouses, and let me tell you dear, after forty years of marriage, you begin to feel like the world can't go on without them. But then sometimes Fate has a little surprise for you and brings a second chance along," Dorothy looked at her husband lovingly, "So take that to heart, dear, just because your heart has been broken one way or another, doesn't mean that it's not still lovable."

Amelia stared at Dorothy in wonder, "How do you- do you read minds?"

Dorothy's laugh was like a bell, light and airy, "No dear, but I know the look in your eyes. I've seen many people come through here with that look. So did Lucia when she still worked here. Bless her, she was truly a delight. I wonder how her son is doing. Oh, anyhow, people who've been wounded frequently feel unworthy, unlovable, and incapable. You're not. I promise. It may take some time to see it from a different perspective, but the beauty of this place is that you have time."

Dorothy patted Amelia's hand and stood from her chair. She toddled around the circle, greeting people and chatting with them here and there. Eventually she made her way over to Donny who took her hand and kissed it. He looked at her with such love in his eyes it made Amelia hope that maybe Dorothy was right.

"Dorothy came and knocked your socks off I see," A young woman, maybe Amelia's age, plopped down in the elderly woman's abandoned chair. She stuck her hand out, "Hi, I'm Sophie."

"Amelia," She replied, "Yeah, does she always begin conversations that way?"

The girl chuckled, "Yeah, but she's harmless. She's really sweet actually, she and her husband knew the old owners of the place and like to stay and volunteer here everyday."

"They knew the Berardis? Do they know their son?" Amelia asked abruptly, cutting Sophie off.

She frowned, "Not that I know of, they practically live here, I would be surprised if they know anyone who lives outside of the building. Why?"

"Um, no reason," Amelia hesitated, unsure if she should share anything about Enzo down here.

"Hey, it's okay, if you're hiding from someone, the rule is that we can't tell anyone you're here. No matter what. I'm sorry if I pushed too soon," She placed a hand on Amelia's shoulder apologetically.

"He's not the reason I'm here but I certainly don't want to see him right now," Amelia whispered, "He's so confusing. I can't think when I'm near him."

Sophie gave her a small smile, "It's okay. You don't need to be ready to see anyone. This is a safe haven. From whatever and whoever."

The meeting seemed to wrap up a few minutes later, leaving Amelia alone. Sophie had left her alone with the promise of seeking her out later to check in. Dorothy and her husband had waved farewell to her before wandering away.

Amelia looked around the empty dining facility and stood with a sigh. The lack of purpose was going to catch up to her down in the shelter if she didn't find something to do first. Perhaps she could find something that would distract her mind.

Luckily for Amelia, Luke's machine shop wasn't very far.

The red awning over his shop only stood out to Amelia among the New York life because of its familiarity. The bell over the door jingled merrily when she stepped inside, the pungent odors of oil and new rubber assaulting her nose. The clerk saw her and waved, greeting her like an old friend.

"Hey Ramone! Is Luke here?" She asked with a wave.

"Hey! Bike girl! Yeah, he's in the garage, want me to call him?" Ramone asked. He was a dark skinned man who could only be described as 'jolly,' his attitude was always pleasant. He was quick with a joke and a bit of humor, when he laughed, his whole belly shook.

"No thanks, I'll just head back there," Amelia smiled at the friendly man.

"You're staying out of trouble, right, Bike Girl?" Ramone called after her.

Amelia turned, walking backwards towards the garage doors, spreading her arms innocently, "Now where's the fun in staying out of trouble?"

Ramone's laughter followed Amelia into the garage. Shaking her head Amelia stepped out of the air conditioned store and into the concrete garage. Two out of the three bays had cars in them, the third held a couple of motorcycles. Amelia recognized hers among the lineup, the beautiful piece of machinery had been polished and its red paint sparkled. She longed to run her hand over it, to feel the vibration of the engine as it roared to life.

Just as she was going to go inspect it, something clanged from underneath one of the bays. Luke's voice suddenly filled the garage with a string of words in a trucker dialect that would make a sailor blush. Then the loud popping of something misfiring in one of the engines.

"Need a hand, Luke?" Amelia bent down and looked below one of the cars. There was her friend, covered in grease, holding a wrench in one hand and a bucket in the other, "How did it make that sound when you aren't messing around with anything that sparks?"

"Hey! Amelia! Where'd you come from?" He looked up revealing a grease smudge on his forehead.

Amelia quickly turned her laugh into a false cough, covering her mouth with one hand, "I just stopped by, I was in the area. But do me a favor in advance, don't tell anyone I'm here. I'm trying to keep a low profile, even from Berardi."

The mechanic nodded, "Sure thing. Want to help with this lunatic's oil change?"

She frowned, "An oil change had you swearing like a sailor? What the hell happened?"

She shucked her jacket and tossed it aside, Amelia popped the hood. The engine inside was covered in leaves and different engine liquids. Remnants of coolant had crusted to the radiator, and the oil wand was bent at a ninety degree angle instead of put away properly.

Luke realized she was looking into the engine and laughed humorlessly, "This guy probably would believe blinker fluid was a thing. There's sugar and cooking oil in the engine and it seized. Duh."

Amelia groaned, "An oil change isn't going to fix that."

"Nope. But the customer gets what the customer wants," Luke sighed, "You can't fix stupid."

"Not most of the time," Amelia sighed, pulling her hair up and digging into the mess of an engine.

The next couple of hours were spent clearing the engine of its oily mess. Replacing some of the broken pieces and trying to fix it. But as Amelia predicted, when the customer came for his car, it wouldn't start. He shouted at Luke and Amelia until Ramone escorted him out of the shop. After that Amelia bid the two men goodbye and made her way back to the shelter.

*****

Not long after her visit with Luke, Dr. Smith had asked Amelia to come to her office. As Amelia trudged up the steps to the office, she felt like a child called to the principal's office. She was just grateful that Audra Smith wasn't nearly as scary. Yet.

She tapped on the door and was welcomed in a moment later by Dr. Smith's light voice, "Come in."

The psychologist was sitting at her desk typing away on her computer when the woman came into the room. She held up a finger to ask for a moment. Amelia looked around, little potted plants sat on a window sill near the desk, shelves of medical and psychology books sat against the wall. It looked like a normal therapist's office which surprised Amelia, although she wasn't sure why. Possibly because of how close the woman worked with a crime syndicate.

"Amelia, why don't you take a seat?" Dr. Smith looked up from her computer and gestured to the couch that had escaped Amelia's notice.

"I'm not in trouble, am I ?" Amelia asked curiously.

Dr. Smith gave her a confused stare, "No. I just wanted to check in with you after your first couple of weeks. I know they're a little unconventional and Dorothy can be, how should I put this? Intense?"

"She's like a walking soundbite," Amelia chuckled.

Dr. Smith took a chair opposite to Amelia and stared at her for a moment, "Okay, how are you really doing? You're not just telling me you're fine to get me off your back, right?"

"Is that really professional psychologist talk?" Amelia raised her eyebrow.

"Or deflecting the question," Dr. Smith said, unamused.

Amelia sighed, "I don't think I'm ready to talk about it."

"You don't have to be, you may never be. Some people process through their actions. If it would help you to help others, I have volunteering opportunities around the shelter. We can check in once a week and see how you're doing. What do you think?" Dr. Smith asked gently, "Helping other people frequently helps us."

"Let's try it," Amelia smiled back, feeling lighter and hopeful for the chance to do something to help others.

That was how she found herself volunteering with the middle and high schoolers everyday. Whether it was helping with their homework, fixing a car, or throwing a baseball for them, she was involved.

Amelia found herself falling in love with herself again, coming alive. Being ready to face her day head on instead of hiding out in the shadows. It wasn't an easy process, it had taken weeks to even be willing to work in conjunction with one of the other volunteers. It had taken longer still to be willing to try and work on something by herself. But eventually, she gained the childrens' trust and gained confidence in what she was doing. Soon Amelia was looking forward to volunteering as much as she had ever looked forward to dancing as a young girl or reading a new book or tormenting Enzo.

She became close with a young boy in foster care. He spent everyday at the shelter, doing his homework and learning how to play sports. He loved talking with Amelia and listening to her stories. She had ended up showing him to replace the chain on his bicycle after he'd walked from his school to the shelter when it broke. Hudson was the kind of boy who wanted to know everything. He asked questions and genuinely listened to the answers.

Amelia even taught him to cook simple meals. He became her shadow. Following her to Luke's shop and asking the mechanic questions too. Luke took it all in stride and took the boy under his wing. Soon Hudson was changing the oil in cars faster than Amelia.

Everyday she was astounded by what the children could teach her about the world. Each one had their own story of pain or grief, but everyday they showed up to the shelter. They wanted to overcome and be better than their past. Amelia worked hard to encourage all of them, to teach them how to pursue what they wanted and how to defend themselves.

As Amelia volunteered with the children, she vowed to be the person she wished she'd had growing up. She would advocate for them. She would show up for them. When they all graduated school, she would show up and cheer. They deserved to have someone sticking up for them.

*****

"Hudson! Run to home!" Amelia shouted at the boy she'd been working with. He was standing on third base watching the ball fly into the outfield.

He heard her voice and bolted for the base, pumping his arms and moving as fast as he could. The boys on his team cheered him on, urging him to run faster, urging the player on second to steal third. The other team realized what was happening and scrambled for the ball but it was too late. Hudson slammed his feet onto the rubber plate and threw his arms in the air, celebrating his victory.

Amelia watched with a smile, of all of the boys she'd started working with, he'd improved the most. His grades had skyrocketed and he was interacting with his peers. The shelter, she had come to realize, wasn't just about hiding out, it was for growing and learning. These kids came for a safe place to be during the afternoon hours and found friends and a support system, much like the adult underneath the after school building.

Someone walked up next to Amelia to watch the game, "I think that working in the program helped, what do you think? You're not moping around anymore."

"Dr. Smith," Amelia greeted, pausing to cheer for the boys playing their game, "I never understood why this place meant so much to Lucia when I first started working for Berardi. But watching the light in these kids' eyes,

I get it now. Not just for them, but for people like Dorothy and Donny. For Sophie."

The psychologist smiled, "Amelia, I'm so proud of you. I know this isn't an easy process, I know even physically being around people was hard for you at first, but you've made so much progress."

"I couldn't without your help, so thank you," Amelia hugged the woman who had turned from doctor to friend for her.

A cheer from the baseball field caught their attention. The game had ended and both teams were celebrating the win. Amelia laughed and cheered right along with them, leading them back to the gymnasium at the shelter. Just outside of the gym were tables being set up with a summer picnic for the baseball teams. Residents from the shelter and after school participants alike were gathering around and grabbing plates.

"This can't be good," Dr. Smith said, watching three black sedans pull into the parking lot.

Amelia followed her gaze and felt her heart sink in her chest, "Audra, get everyone into the shelter, now."

Amelia Cruz: Facing Fears and Returning Home

"¡Ándale!" Amelia called, pulling a handgun from her waistband. Catching Dr. Smith's admonishing look, she shrugged, "Old habits die hard. GO!"

"I'll chastise you later," Dr. Smith called over the chaos, waving the children into the building. The residents helped move them along, glancing over their shoulders at the cars nervously.

"When you get inside, call Luke Datar at the machine shop down the road," Amelia instructed Dr. Smith, "Lock the doors. Go."

The woman nodded as the sedans' doors opened and out stepped Royal and Ray Hagan. They smirked when they realized who stood between them and the shelter doors. Royal glanced at his brother, a gleeful expression on his face while he waited for his brother to say something to the woman. He still wasn't doing his own thinking it seemed.

"This is an odd place for you, isn't it?" Ray called, leaning on the hood of his sedan. He motioned at the other cars, signaling them to fan out, "What, did Berardi kick you to the curb when he realized you were damaged goods?"

Hagan's men spilled out from the sedans, each armed to the teeth. Machine guns, handguns, some even had chains wrapped around their fists. Amelia was wildly outnumbered. Fifteen men had emerged, forming a crescent shape around her. Guns in hand and looks of hatred pointed at her.

"How many clowns did you bring to fight your battle today?" She called back, ignoring Ray's comment. She adjusted the grip on her gun to reassure herself that it was still there.

"Someone's gotten bold since the last time we met," Ray chortled. He crossed an ankle over the other casually. His brother propped a hand on the top of the car, watching the interaction like it was Christmas morning.

"Royal, wipe the drool off your chin, your stupidity is showing," Amelia braced her feet and adjusted her grip on her gun.

"Cute, did you get that from your mother?" Ray scoffed, "Oh, wait…"

Amelia rolled her eyes, "That was childish, even for you. Now, do you want to leave or do you want to see what happens when you start a fight on neutral territory? It won't end well."

Royal rolled his eyes, "You really are a lot of trouble. Definitely not worth the trouble we've gone through to procure you."

"*¡Dios mío!*" Amelia groaned, "Ray, control your brother. Or are you incapable of doing that too? I'm going to say this one more time; attacking here is a mistake. Consider the laws you'd be breaking."

Ray seemed to pause and consider her words, he looked at his brother who shrugged. Neither of them would honor the bounds of territory or the laws of the Commission, Amelia already knew that. She hoped Dr. Smith had made the call to Luke and that backup would come, she just needed to keep them talking or out of the shelter until it arrived.

"Lia, let's not be stupid, put the gun down," Ray grinned, "Maybe I'll even reconsider the marriage contract."

Anger rose in her chest but somehow she managed to keep a neutral face. She shrugged and sauntered over to the picnic table, carefully setting her feet, she glared at Ray, "For the last time, it's 'Amelia,' not 'Lia!'"

She tipped the table onto the side, giving herself a bit of blockade. Checking the slide on her gun to confirm a bullet in the chamber, she jumped to her knees and fired over the top of the table. Amelia watched three bodies fall to the ground in rapid succession. Ducking back down and taking a breath to steady herself, she waited, listening. Confirming that the men hadn't drastically moved from their original places. The clicks of their guns seemed to echo through the air. They hissed instructions back and forth trying to formulate a plan.

Again, she was back on her knees, firing over the table. Another two men fell. That took care of a third of her problem, only one third. Fifteen men. Fifteen bullets. She could not miss a single shot. So far, it hadn't been an issue, but now the men were firing their own guns and the table she was hiding behind was not going to keep her safe for long. Wood splintered over her head, falling into her hair and over her shoulders.

"No wonder you needed Daddy to arrange a marriage for you, Ray! You were never going to get a girl to marry you with these anger issues!" She called, baiting him.

The gunfire ceased, his pride forcing him to defend himself, "That's not what you said when we were together, or don't you remember? 'I can't wait to marry you.' Your exact words."

"I remember someone who wasn't worth the breath it took to say those words, but please, prove me wrong, or do you need your men to do it for you?" Amelia held her breath. It was like waving a red flag in front of the bull, her only hope at this point was to buy the shelter enough time to call for help, "Will you let them fight your battle for you?"

Footsteps stormed close to the table. She crouched to face it, ready for someone to either move it or come over it. Ray chose the latter option, hoping over the top. Landing in front of her, a sneer on his face, fists curled at his sides. Amelia gave him a quick once over trying to assess where his weapons might be.

"We came here to make a point to Berardi, but how much more of a point would it be to destroy it and leave your mangled body here for him to find?" He taunted.

Amelia stood, gun in hand, "Leave the shelter out of this, Ray. It's on neutral ground. There are innocents in there!"

"I'll think about it," He put a finger to his chin, pretending to ponder for a moment before saying, "Not a chance."

Amelia didn't give him the chance to strike first like she had last time. She jumped forward, slamming the butt of her gun into his temple. He crumpled but remained conscious. He began crawling towards Amelia, swiping at her feet.

He waved his men on, "Go, go, go! Take it!"

Amelia watched in horror as Hagan men rushed the shelter. She raised her gun again to try and stop them, but Ray reached out and yanked her ankle. She plummeted to the ground, barely keeping her head from hitting the pavement. Her gun went flying to some unseen place.

Ray was suddenly on top of her, his knee on her chest limiting her breathing. Gasping for breath and swinging as hard as possible with the limited range of motion, her fist connected with his crotch. He groaned, falling to the side, releasing Amelia. Scrambling away, gasping for breath, she scanned the area for her gun. The gunfire from inside the shelter was causing her heart to rise in her throat and panic to bubble up.

Before she could locate the weapon, Ray was back. He stood over her, grabbing her hair to lift her from the ground. A snarl ripped from his throat at the same time a cry of pain escaped her lips.

"Your hair always has been a useful tool to hold you, hasn't it?" He mused. With his free hand he gripped her neck, "I won't be so gentle this time."

"You won't get the chance to be rougher," Amelia reached for the knife on his hip, "And too bad it's the last time you'll get to pull my hair."

She held the blade as close to his hand and as far away from her head as she could reach. With a sudden forceful movement, Amelia sliced through her hair. She dropped to her knees, instinctively reaching to feel the ends of her hair, the sudden loss of it felt foreign. It was choppy and fell below her shoulders, a safer length for physical combat.

Ray gaped at the hair in his hand before dropping it in disgust. He swung his leg forward into Amelia's ribs. She dropped from the force, the air forced from her lungs.

"That certainly wasn't your finest moment," A new voice said from behind Ray.

Ray turned and was immediately pistol whipped but none other than Tomaso Dante. He stood there like a golden haired hero in a movie. He held a hand out and helped Amelia up, handing her a sheath of knives and a new gun, "Cutting your hair off was a bit dramatic."

"So was that entrance," She nodded gratefully at the weapons and ran off, calling back, "Took you long enough to get here!"

"Hey, it's not my fault that traffic was a mess at four o'clock on a Monday! You couldn't have picked a better time to be ambushed?" Tom replied, "Get inside!"

Amelia saw her friend turn to Ray, rolling his neck and preparing for a fight. The Irishman eyed his new opponent nervously. His fists came up to shield his face. Tom seemed to see what Amelia also saw; Ray had never learned from sparring with Enzo. He still dropped his guard and left his balance uneven.

Tom swooped in and caught Ray's leg. With one leg out of commission, Ray bounced on one foot momentarily before Tom wrapped an arm around the man's neck and took him to the ground. Ray was struggling against the Italian's hold even as he wheezed from the impact.

The spray of gunshots pulled Amelia's attention back to the shelter and the people inside. She ran to the door of the shelter to find bodies on the floor. Someone had shot these men already. Slowly, with her gun raised, Amelia crept through the door. Another body on the steps, shot as well. There was a trail of Hagan's men but no sign of the shelter residents or children. Lights flickered on the ceiling, their wiring hit by stray rounds. The empty halls drowned in shadows without the fluorescent lighting.

"Audra! Sophie!" Amelia called into the shelter, hoping someone would answer, "Where are you? It's safe to come out now!"

Something clattered in a nearby room, startling Amelia. Whirling the gun around she found Hudson standing in a doorway looking frightened. His hands shot into the air when she faced him.

"Hudson!" She gasped, putting the gun in her waistband, "*¡Dios mío!* Are you okay?"

She rushed to him, hands on his shoulders looking him up and down. Aside from trembling like a leaf he seemed uninjured. Without warning he embraced her, sobbing like the terror was only just setting in. He clawed at her shirt, trying to get closer. Amelia wrapped her arms tightly around him wishing she could give him courage and peace.

"Hey, hey, it's okay. The bad guys are gone and there are good people outside to help," Amelia wiped the tears from his cheeks, "We're going to be alright."

"What about Dr. Smith?" Hudson asked her, rubbing his eyes to rid himself of the tears.

Amelia frowned, "What about Dr. Smith?"

"She went to her office and got a gun when we got inside. She shot the bad guys," Hudson explained softly. Amelia led him to sit against the wall and take deep breaths while he continued to talk, "But something happened. She's got blood on her and she isn't moving. I think the bad guys shot her."

"Take me to her!" Amelia jumped from the floor, pulling the preteen with her.

He took her hand and led her down a hall and knocked on a closed door. Inside the room were the rest of the residents and children. Many looked petrified, mothers held their children close. Brothers and sisters held each other, and those without anyone rocked back and forth in a corner or sat by themselves. Some held scratched knees or elbows, the worst of their injuries thankfully. Dorothy and Donny seemed to be taking care of most people and keeping order.

"Help is here," Was all Amelia could muster the strength to say. Having grown up around violence, it never shocked her anymore, dropping bodies didn't bother her. But these people hadn't signed on for this kind of psychological trauma.

"Hudson!" Dorothy exclaimed when she saw the boy, "Where did you go! You could've been hurt! We didn't know if anyone else was out there."

The elderly woman reached for Hudson. He jumped from Amelia to the woman and hugged her. The young Hispanic felt a lurch in her heart as their embrace. She patted Dorothy's shoulder as she passed, leading the people from the room.

Slowly the people filed out of the room to go back to the gymnasium upstairs and that's when Amelia spotted the doctor. She lay on her back in the corner. Someone had propped her head up and put a blanket over her. Her skin was pallid and gaunt. Amelia ran across the room and dropped to her knees, feeling for a pulse.

"Audra!" Amelia didn't recognize her own voice, "Audra! Look at me!"

Kneeling over the woman, Amelia pulled the blanket back. Leo had been right. She'd gotten shot several times. Her stomach was peppered with holes, the shreds of her shirt soaked in blood. There would be no coming back from this, the damage was too extensive.

"Audra, please, look at me!" Amelia tapped her friend's face gently, hoping she was still trying to hang on.

"Amelia," Dr. Smith managed to whisper, "Take care of them."

The young doctor whimpered slightly and shuddered. Blood continued to pour from the wound onto Amelia's hands. She was pressing against the entry wound trying to stop the flow. The effort was futile though, the sheer amount of the fluid on the floor told Amelia the bullet had hit an artery.

"You don't get to leave me with just that!" Amelia demanded, "Come on, hold on, we'll try to get you to the hospital."

"Don't, let me go, Amelia. We both know I wouldn't make it there. Take care of the shelter. Promise me," Audra reached out a trembling hand and squeezed Amelia's.

"I promise," She whispered.

The psychologist closed her eyes, nodding her head gently. Slowly her breathing slowed and rattled from the damage in her lungs. Amelia's finger's sought the pulse point on the other woman's wrist. She could feel Audra's heart beat for a final time, releasing its hold on life.

"No, no, no! Audra!" Amelia wept, "Not yet, please, not yet! I'm not ready to lose another person."

"Amelia," Tom entered the room, clearly looking for her, "She's gone. We have to go. I'm so sorry."

Amelia set her friend's hand down and stood from the floor, tears running down her face, "You're not the one who needs to be sorry. Hagan will pay for this tenfold."

Tom nodded. He seemed to realize her anger was not at him, "Are you coming back then?"

"It was already time to, this is just proof of that," Amelia looked at Tom, "The war has been waging, but until now, everyone played by the rules of the game. I'm done doing so."

"Good. So is Berardi," Tom nodded, "Let's go talk to him. He's going to want to hear about this anyway."

"We can't leave her like this," Amelia stated.

She looked around the room until she found what she was searching for. A closet with spare sheets. Pulling one out, she handed one end to Tom and together they carefully draped it over Audra Smith's body. The white fabric stained instantly from the blood. It spread quickly through the woven fibers, outlining every spot the poor woman had been shot.

Tom reached an arm around Amelia's shoulder and squeezed her close, "We have to go. I'm so sorry."

"You're not the one who owes an apology," Amelia squeezed him in return.

Amelia walked silently behind, taking in the abandoned halls of the shelter. This once safe place had been violated. Who would come there now?

The damage extended far beyond the current residents and children. It impacted those who had not yet made it there yet. Those who were still gathering their courage to escape. Amelia would be damned if she didn't resolve this. If she didn't recreate the safe space. Tom opened the door of his car for her, wearing a solemn look.

"The Hagans need to be ready for hell," She told Tom when they got into his car.

"They will be, I let Ray go with a warning to his father," Tom told her and started the car, driving them off towards Enzo's home, "Royal crawled out of the shelter shortly after you went in and followed his brother. Those two are like cockroaches. They can survive just about anything."

"I should've killed him," Amelia growled.

The rest of the drive to Enzo's was quiet. Tom occasionally looking over to check in on his friend, but mostly keeping an eye on the road. Soft music played from the radio, keeping the actual silence at bay.

In the safety of the car, Amelia let tears flow freely, mourning the loss of another person in her life. Not just in her own life, but in the life of those who lived in the shelter. Those who sought out the doctor for aid and comfort now had no one. How would the Shelter survive?

Tom pulled the car into the parking lot at a grand building in Manhattan. He led Amelia inside and to the elevator, taking her to the top floor. When the doors opened, the duo were greeted with armed guards lining the hall. They gave them a nod as they walked past to one of the many doors. Like a gentleman, Tom opened the door and allowed Amelia to enter first.

Inside was beautiful and the young woman was suddenly very aware of her disheveled appearance. Her clothes might stain the immaculate furniture. The doors to a large balcony overlooking the city stood open.

Amelia's breath caught in her throat. Enzo was standing on the balcony. His back to her, unaware of her arrival.

Enzo Berardi: Admissions

The response from the Hagans and Cruzes was swift and harsh after the fight at the docks. A rather large cardboard box had been left at the guard house overnight containing the weapons of two sentinels from some of the Rossi Family. The bodies weren't recovered. They assumed they'd been dropped into the harbors but had no proof.

Enzo had taken the weapons to the sentinels' families. He mourned their loss with them and received support from the Rossi Family for the war. They called for repercussions, wanting to avenge the deaths of their men. Enzo had readily agreed to seek vengeance, adding it to the never ending list of sins committed by the Hagans.

For several weeks there was a tit-for-tat game between the Families.

A death blow dealt by the Hagans or Cruzes, retaliation from Berardi or his allies. Back and forth it went. Allegiances were shifting, control and power shifted too. Some days it looked as though the Hagans were on top. Other days, Enzo was riding high.

The city was starting to feel the turmoil. News stations were picking up on the rising death count. Armed guards surrounded the shipyards and were even on board the vessels coming in. For the first time in almost a century, the mafia families were out of control.

Meetings had been called at the Commission but none had ever been useful, some hadn't even happened for fear of being assassinated. Most of the Families refused to even show their faces at the meetings. They might send a representative, but it was hardly beneficial.

Enzo stood on a balcony in Manhattan watching the cars below. These weeks of chaos had laid a heavy weight on his shoulders. He was more tired than he used to be, late nights, early mornings, they all took their toll. He'd abandoned his family mansion after one of the rogue Garcias had rigged a particularly nasty bomb at the Cruzes' request. Some Families were divided in alliances, the Garcias among them.

Since then, he'd lived in a penthouse his grandfather had owned in Manhattan. It often reminded him of the first time his father had brought him there.

He'd told Enzo that Manhattan was primarily run by civilians or Families who'd sworn fealty to the Berardis. If they ever wanted to, they could shut down any of their enemies' work on the island. For the first time, Enzo was considering doing so. Or perhaps offering an ultimatum, fealty to him or lose their stakes in Manhattan. There were very few lines he wasn't willing to cross anymore. With the amount of dead bodies piling up, he was losing patience.

Enzo groaned and hung his head. He was leaning on the balcony railing. He was having trouble thinking clearly with the lack of sleep and perpetual turmoil. He had no idea if it would be feasible to form alliances with the other families. The alliances went back generations, would they be willing to break from tradition to stop a war?

"You look like hell," A voice said behind him.

Enzo turned and his mouth fell open. In front of him stood Amelia. She'd cut her hair to her shoulders and was still wearing tattered clothes, but it was her.

"Shut your mouth, you'll catch flies," She rolled her eyes at him.

"You're here?" The question came out barely above a whisper.

"I can leave if you'd prefer," She gestured to the door and made to leave.

Enzo rushed forward and stopped her by grabbing her wrist, "Don't."

He suddenly realized Tom was there as well. Arms crossed and covered in scratches, smelling like smoke. He and Amelia both. They'd been in a fight.

"What happened," He dropped Amelia's wrist and stepped back to look them up and down.

Tom and Amelia looked at each other before the former spoke, "The Hagans attacked the shelter."

Enzo reacted without thought, his fist slammed into the drywall, leaving an impressive hole. Amelia winced at the impact but said nothing. He began to pace back and forth, swearing under his breath. He faced his employees looking half crazed and half furious. He ran his hand through his hair causing it to stick up on end.

Amelia cleared her throat, "That's not all."

"What? What else could you possibly add to this, Amelia?" Enzo growled.

"They killed Audra too," She sighed, a tear slipping down her face. She wiped it away quickly.

Enzo stormed further into the apartment, down the hall into the kitchen. Mrs. Janis, his housekeeper, had come with him to the penthouse and was determined to keep the kitchen perfectly organized, so it took Enzo very little time to find a cup. Even less time to find a bottle of whiskey and pour a shot and slam it back.

"It's a little early, Enzo," Amelia said gently, having followed him into the kitchen with Tom.

"I really don't care," Enzo snarled, "I don't understand why you do."

"Enzo, man, don't," Tom warned, "Let's not do this right now. We're all mourning. Amelia was first on scene. She felt the impact more than either of us. Hell, she was fighting Ray when I got there."

He poured another shot and slammed it back, "I really don't care. Get out."

"So that's it then? You're giving up?" Amelia pressed further, "What happened to 'don't poke the bear?'"

"Why do you care so much, Amelia? Your parents didn't build the shelter, mine did! Your parents tried to set up an arranged marriage and when they died your brothers tried to continue that, so tell me, why do you care so much when you left?" Enzo's eyes were red and crazed. Guilt ripped through him for yelling at his friends but he couldn't seem to stop.

Tom took a step back, placing a hand on Amelia's shoulder like he was trying to pull her back with him. Enzo watched her shrug it off and step closer. The angry expression on her face encouraged him to step forward and meet her in the middle.

She glared up at him and he at her.

Finally she whispered dangerously, "I was there, *pendejo*. I held Audra's hand when she took her last breath. I fought with Ray Hagan, trying to protect the residents and children inside. I lived there for weeks as a resident myself. I couldn't fully bring myself to leave, Lorenzo Berardi. I never left you. If you had truly needed me, I would've been here."

"I do need you, Amelia! I have always needed you!" Enzo yelled, surprising the woman in front of him. Surprising himself too. He wasn't sure when he'd made the decision to finally admit how much he wanted, no, needed this woman.

The tension in the air was palpable. Neither of them moved, breathing heavily, staring at one another. Inches separated them instead of the miles that had kept them apart for the last few anguishing weeks. He looked down, seeing her lips, parted ever so slightly. Enzo had to fight the urge to lean down and close that distance.

"And that's my cue to leave," Tom broke the silence. He rushed from the room like it was on fire, calling over his shoulder, "Good luck!"

Enzo jumped back like he'd been shocked. Amelia turned around and braced herself on the counter. He watched her tip her head back, blinking rapidly.

"I'm sorry. I didn't realize you'd been staying there," Enzo hung his head, ashamed at how he'd treated them, "My parents built the shelter to protect people who've been hurt, like you. I just wanted to protect their legacy."

Amelia turned around, "Their legacy lives on, not just in the shelter, not just in you, but in the people who stay there, who volunteer there. If you talk to Dorothy at the shelter, she has nothing but praise for your mother. The legacy isn't the building but the purpose behind it."

Enzo sighed, letting tears form in his eyes, "I'm sorry." The ache in his chest grew and he was suddenly gasping for breath. One hand bracing himself on the counter, the other clawing at the buttons on his shirt. Yanking at the collar and sending buttons flying across the room, Enzo tried to gulp down air. His vision blurred and it seemed like cotton filled his ears, preventing sound from getting through.

Somehow, Amelia's face came into focus in front of him, worry written all over her face. She cupped his face with both hands, demonstrating deep breaths for him to copy. Enzo tried to copy her but his knees began to weaken and he sank to the floor. To his surprise, she sank with him, staying right in front of him, never breaking eye contact.

Enzo forced himself to follow her breath as close as he possibly could in his frenzied state. He watched her shake her head and mouth something but whatever it was, he couldn't hear. Amelia wrapped a hand around the back of his neck and pulled his forehead down against her own, letting her breath fall across his face. The physical stimulation of it somehow triggered his body to comply and copy without him even trying. Slowly, the world came back into view. The cotton in his ears disappeared and his breathing slowed until it returned to normal. His heart rate was still elevated when he finally pried his eyes open.

Amelia was still there. Hands wrapped around him, eyes closed and pressing her forehead to his. She was close enough he could see the light smudges of her makeup and faint freckles on her nose. A few strands of hair fell around her face, framing it just so.

"Amelia," He whispered hoarsely, tears slipping from the corner of his eyes, "I'm sorry. I'm so sorry."

She looked up at him, "Stop apologizing. Panic attacks aren't your fault."

"Are you staying for good then?" He asked hopefully.

"Are you ready for me to be back? I'm pretty sure Tom calls me a sadist when I'm around you," She teased lightly.

"Please, stay," Enzo pleaded.

Amelia nodded, "I'll stay."

Enzo couldn't help himself, he grabbed her and embraced her closely. She returned the embrace tightly, pressing her face into his chest. Enzo pressed a kiss onto the top of her head without thinking. Somehow this woman seemed to fill the cracks in his broken heart and make it whole again, against all odds. So they sat there, wrapped in each other's arms on the kitchen floor.

Amelia looked up at him, "I want you to tell me everything in your own words. Not what you think I want to hear and not a repetition of Fae or Tom's words."

"Everything about what?" Enzo refused to make eye contact. He knew what she was referring to, but he didn't know how to reply to that question.

"You know exactly what I'm talking about," She said.

Enzo sighed, "Some of what you were told is true. But, I never moped like Tom probably said."

Amelia laughed, a beautiful sound that Enzo had missed sorely but hadn't realized how much until that moment, "He never said that! But now I'm inclined to think you did. But seriously though, were your stupid arguments with Lance because of how you felt about me?"

"Ah, should have seen that one coming," Enzo leaned back against a cabinet and crossed an ankle over his knee, "I think it was both because of that and because on a purely instinctual level, I didn't trust him. I couldn't figure out why though."

Amelia nodded and looked away. In her next sentence her voice was mildly surprising to him, "He never got the initiation tattoo."

"I had a feeling," Enzo replied, "Franklin never saw him come into the shop and he always said he'd gotten it done on his chest, right?"

She hummed in response, seemingly losing herself in thought, "Yeah, but eventually I saw the proof that he never got it."

Enzo shuddered. He didn't want to know when she had learned that particular fact. Ray's behavior already made him hate the man, but each time something new came up, it fueled the fire.

"What are you thinking about?" He asked as casually as he could, trying to distract from the conversation.

"Nothing."

Berardi chuckled softly, tucking a loose strand of hair behind her ear, "You know I don't believe that."

Amelia sighed, "I was thinking about all the times I made excuses for Ray. Wondering if I could've done something different."

"Don't go down that road," Berardi said sternly.

"Like you aren't going down it yourself," She stared pointedly.

He raised his hands in surrender, "Okay, you got me on that one. But I still don't think you should go down that path."

"It's hard not to," She admitted softly.

"Are you sure you're ready to be back?" Enzo asked her nervously.

Amelia looked at him sharply, "I left for what, four, five weeks? And you declared war, moved to Manhattan, our profits are down and the city is in chaos. Oh, and the Hagans decided it was okay to attack on neutral ground. Tell me again you don't need me."

Enzo watched in awe as the fire in her eyes lit furiously. While he knew she was being sarcastic, her words rang with truth. She was calling him out and he needed it. He couldn't count the amount of times he and the team missed Amelia's skills and mind.

"You'll stay forever then?" He cringed internally for how desperate that sounded, but he wanted to know.

"Finish answering my earlier question and we'll see."

"Amelia, despite what they said, I didn't always love you. I don't believe in love at first sight, but I do believe in true love. I saw it everyday with my parents. They loved fiercely and I want nothing less in the future," Enzo started talking and it felt as though the words he'd wanted to say a thousand times over finally came pouring out, "I fell in love with you while getting to know you. By the time I understood what I felt, you were already taken by someone else. So I settled for any interaction I could get, the teasing, the poking, even the bloody arguments! Because all I wanted, all I desperately wanted, was you."

"And would you have me now? Damaged as I am from the attack? From the years of abuse?" She whispered, her eyes glistening.

"Beloved, I would have you any way you would let me," Enzo admitted wholeheartedly, pressing another kiss to the top of her head.

She stared at him in wonder until he reached forward and pulled her from her spot on the floor. Enzo guided her across the short distance between them and pulled her down onto his lap. Wrapping his arms around her, Enzo held on, like he might prevent her from leaving again. He could feel the tension and nervousness ease from her body as she relaxed into his hold. Her head fell back onto his shoulder, eyes closed, lifting her face to the ceiling. Enzo couldn't help himself, he pressed a gentle kiss to her temple.
Enzo couldn't believe that in all of the chaos of their world, they finally managed to find their way to each other.

"You want to tell me what your plan is?" She murmured, eyes still closed, "For winning this war?"

"I will end the Hagans for touching what is mine," Enzo declared, his voice barely above a whisper.

"'Yours?'" Amelia opened her eyes and turned her face to him, amused, "That an awfully bold statement."

Enzo took her wrist in his hand and turned so her own initiation tattoo was lifted for them to see. Underneath the words was a small bear print, similar to the one on the back of his own hand. The only people Enzo had allowed to get the paw print were Tom and Amelia. It was the symbol of her rank within the Family. It was also his way of adding an extra layer of protection over them. He'd grown his circle, but he had only wanted the two people closest to him to have the mark. Tom and Amelia, his two closest companions, friends, his family. It was a mark reserved for those directly related to the Berardi Family and them alone.

"I'm a selfish man, Beloved, I don't have any intention of letting you go now that I've got you," His lips pulled into the smile. Realizing the words he was saying and how long he'd waited to say them.

Amelia looked up at him, "Enzo, I don't think I'm very good at having relationships. I need you to be patient with me. There are habits and even trauma responses that I need to break free of, not just from Ray but from my family. I want to take this…I don't think slow is the right word, I don't want slow. I already know that if this is anything like our lives, it's going to be a wild ride. And I want that. But I need control. I need to be able to have control sometimes."

"Whatever you need," Enzo intertwined their fingers, "Whatever you need, whatever you want."

"I don't even know what a real first kiss is like," She laughed incredulously, "My first kiss was because *he* wanted to. I wasn't even ready for it."

Now Enzo pushed back so he could see her better, "If you didn't say yes, you didn't do it."

"That simple?" Her brows rose and a half smile appeared on her face.

"That simple."

Enzo watched her face, he could see the thoughts passing through her mind, reading her like a book. He tucked a strand of hair behind her ear gently, waiting for her to say something. Amelia moved from his lap back to her own spot on the floor and looked at him. He leaned towards her. She matched his position, challenge glinting in her eyes, like she was daring him to continue. He allowed a small smirk to grace his lips.

"A kiss isn't meant to say 'I want to.' A kiss is supposed to say 'I want *you*,'" He whispered softly, leaning closer still.

"What's the difference?" She asked, her eyes half closed, her head tilting closer to his. She nodded almost imperceptibly but just enough for him to know, she was giving him permission.

"Oh, Beloved," Enzo breathed, "Everything. The difference is everything."

He closed the distance between them, finally.

Enzo Berardi: Coffee Makes Dangerous Plans

As much as Enzo would have loved to stay in the blissful confines of the penthouse with Amelia, there was a war that required their attention. There were people who needed vengeance and men who needed to be punished for their crimes. He, and now Amelia, were done playing, it was time to end the whole affair once and for all.

Enzo stood on the balcony connected to his bedroom sipping a cup of coffee. The early morning light was creeping over the top of the New York skyline. The people going down to the subways or fighting the traffic were perfectly clueless of the underground war. He watched as the city came alive knowing full well it would be the last morning many would see.

A soft sound from behind him drew his attention back to the bedroom. Amelia had shifted in the bed, sheets falling down her back putting her shoulders on display. Her hair was fanned out over the pillow. Enzo had gone with her the previous evening to have the ends trimmed and tidied since her abrupt cut with a knife had left rather jagged edges. The new length suited her and Enzo had enjoyed running his fingers through it.

She was still asleep but Enzo could see her starting to wake. He crossed the room and sat on the edge of the bed. Brushing a strand of her hair from her face, he sat and admired the beautiful woman, marveling that she somehow had chosen him.

Amelia seemed to sense she was being watched and opened her eyes, peeking up at him. A soft smile spread over her face as she turned over to look up at him, "Good morning."

"Good morning, Beloved," He whispered, leaning down to kiss her forehead.

"Is that coffee I smell?" She asked hopefully, reaching for his mug.

"It's black," He warned.

"How very disappointing," She sighed dramatically.

Her hand dropped and she shot him a pouty look. Amelia sighed again and pulled herself from the bed, walking to the closet and rustling around inside. Enzo chuckled and left the room to go and make her coffee. If she didn't have her morning coffee, they may not need an army but he would rather not face that level of crankiness.

He watched out of the window as he prepared another pot of coffee. The morning was going to change rather drastically soon. Tom would show up at some point to hear the plan and update him on anything that had happened during the night.

A knock sounded on the door.

Tom had shown up sooner than he anticipated. Enzo groaned and added more grounds to the pot before going to answer the door. To his utter lack of surprise, there stood his second in command.

Tom smiled sheepishly, "I didn't want to just walk in this time. I don't know what you two have been up to."

Enzo rolled his eyes and gestured for the man to come inside, "Good morning, Tom. I hope you rested well."

"Oh, so we're not cranky anymore?" Tom snarked, stalking into the kitchen. He wore a smug look at his friend's light tone and lack of scowl.

"I may not be, but someone is. She hasn't had her coffee," Enzo closed the door and followed his friend back into the kitchen.

"So we all have a death wish this morning?" Tom called over his shoulder.

Tom was already scowling over a cup of coffee when Enzo caught up with him. Whatever had happened after he left the day before had not been good if it warranted this mood. Retrieving his own mug, Enzo raised it to his friend before giving him a questioning look.

Before Tom could speak Amelia walked in wearing one of Enzo's button downs over a pair of leggings. She kissed Enzo's cheek gently before pouring herself a cup of coffee and hopping up on the counter. She looked back and forth between Tom's stunned face and Enzo's enamored one.

Enzo cleared his throat, trying to get his friend's attention, "Great, glad that you're here. Tom, care to explain your cranky tone this morning?"

Tom's jaw was on the floor when Enzo spoke and he had to physically shake himself to focus, "I know I've teased and pestered you for years about getting together, but I never thought it would really happen. What did I miss?"

"Thank you for the vote of confidence," Enzo said dubiously, "Glad to know my oldest friend has such faith in me."

"Leave him alone, Enzo, even I didn't think this was possible a couple of days ago," Amelia kicked a leg at him halfheartedly.

"What did you have to share, Tom?" Enzo pinched the bridge of his nose.

"We found the Cruzes again," He said, "They went back to the *hacienda* finally. I think they missed their staff because the first thing they did was order for their laundry to be done and a meal made."

Amelia rolled her eyes and whispered insults in Spanish before looking at Enzo, "The staff at the *hacienda* can't be hurt. I want them safe. Especially Mrs. Byrd. My brothers don't deserve them, but the staff don't deserve to lose their livelihood because of the morons I am unfortunately related to."

"What do you want to do then?" Tom leaned forward, "Do you have a plan, Enzo?"

Enzo looked at them, fire in his eyes, "It's time to bring them to their knees. Exterminate them. I hadn't planned on taking the Commission over, but I'm past the point of playing by the rules. I don't really see the point in them anymore, all things considered."

"So what's the plan then? Don't keep us in the dark," Amelia grinned, ready for him to lay it out. Spending time away had been good for her, she'd healed a lot, but she needed the action and Enzo knew that. She was a violent thing.

"Call the team. We're meeting at Hernandez's," Enzo grinned evilly, "Oh, and call Fae. It's time to put her knowledge of poisons to use."

*****

Enzo escorted Amelia into the room, watching her face light up when she lay eyes on their team. He was glad she was ready to be home, the group operated better together, more like a family than a team. And now that family was whole again.

Ray's chair had been thrown in the dumpster out behind the shop and a simple office chair had been pulled up for Fae. The snack basket was filled with bags of pretzels and fruity cereal, sour candies and chips, they were set up for a sugar high. In spite of everything they were preparing for, they all seemed to be in high spirits, feeding off of the mischief, giddiness, and depravity they all shared.

"Fae, I know you didn't originally want to be a part of this world permantently, but we need you," Enzo started to say.

Fae gave him a raised brow, head tilted, waiting for him to continue explaining. It had taken three people on the phone with her to even get her to the meeting. He knew she was going to need some convincing.

"We need your poisons. All you have to do is make them. Amelia will deliver them," Enzo explained.

"I will?" Amelia looked surprised.

"You will," He confirmed, "Fae, it's time to end this war. We just need something to paralyze someone. Not even to kill them. Yet."

Fae crossed her arms, considering for a moment, "Fine, there's something I can make. But only because I have a feeling I know who this is for and this war needs to end. I keep getting knives pulled in my shop and I'm sick of it!"

Enzo winced, "I'm sorry about that. Do you want a guard posted?"

"And confirm my mafia involvement?" Fae retorted. Enzo gave the woman a blank stare. Everyone knew she was protected by his family already, surely she realized that. He looked over at Amelia to see what she thought, she only gave him a bemused look.

"Fae, babe, you're sitting in a mafia war meeting, I'd say you're pretty involved," Luke said, resting a hand over the back of her chair.

She huffed and glared at him before kissing him, "If I'm permanently part of this craziness, can I get the tattoo at least?"

Enzo pinched the bridge of his nose, suddenly reminded that both Luke and Fae were at least ten years younger than him. They both still had immature tendencies that would show up at the most inopportune moments, yet they were still some of the most useful people. He waved his hand at her as a way of telling that she could indeed get the Berardi initiation tattoo. Shaking his head and turning back to address the rest of his team, Enzo took a breath.

They were about to further disrupt the traditions of the city that went back nearly a century. Whatever happened, he needed to get this group out of it alive.

"Boss, another thing I meant to mention this morning is that the Hagans called for a Commission meeting. They're calling for your removal without provocation," Tom piped up, "A little bit like the way you called for Hagan's."

Instead of disappointing or surprising him, Enzo realized that this worked perfectly for them, "Not helpful, Tom. But, is everyone going to be there? All of the Thirteen?"

"The plan is that it will be everyone but you," Tom confirmed.

Matteo leaned across the table, eager to hear the plan. Each person was waiting eagerly for the plan he had falling into place in his head.

"We've held back, up until now. We are the largest Family in the city, it's time we act like it. Tomorrow, Luke, Matteo, Tom, you three will take a group and ensure the Cruzes make it to the meeting on time, no matter what. They need to get there, the Hagans however will need to be late. Think we can handle that?"

Tom gave him a mock salute, "Yes, sir. What else?"

"Fae, those paralytics need to be strong. Like 'holy hell, I just chugged an entire bottle of vodka' strong, we need to be able to move them without a problem," Enzo pointed at the woman he was speaking to. Suddenly even he was excited and ready for what was to come. Enzo had never claimed to be a good man, he hadn't been raised to be and now it was time to show the Thirteen why he led the largest family.

*****

Enzo dismissed the meeting not long after laying out the plan, sending them all off to prepare. He was watching the monitors on Matteo's computer, the video feed showing him the Cruz household. He wasn't sure why he was still watching it when they hadn't gotten much useful from it. It had simply been a means to an end, in a way, the cameras had provided Amelia with the safety she needed when spying. He frowned, and wondered what his father would say if he were there. Years previously, when the assassinations had first started, Leon had sat Enzo down to discuss what was happening in their world. He'd only been twelve at the time, but his father wanted him to be prepared just in case. It ended up being a good thing that his father thought ahead given that he was killed the following morning.

Twenty years ago:

"Lorenzo, listen," Leon sat his son in the chair in front of his desk, "In our line of work, strife is inevitable. It's inevitable everywhere, no matter where you are. To overcome it, you need to understand every perspective. If you refuse to listen to another person's point of view, you will not succeed as a leader."

"What if I know I'm right?" Enzo interjected.

"You still need to listen. Try to find every angle possible."

"Why?"

"Son, there is a conflict happening in the city, men are falling over dead. No one can figure out who is responsible because they refuse to think about what other groups have to lose and who has the most to gain from the deaths of certain people," Leon explained.

Enzo frowned, "Does that mean you know who's responsible?"

"I believe I do," Leon nodded, "But now is not the time to discuss who it is because it will lead us into a conversation about the why. And your mother will be home soon and have my head if you aren't in bed. Off you go!"

"Dad!" Enzo whined as his father shooed him from the office, "Why won't you tell me?"

"Because, Enzo, you are still growing. You know the world I operate in is a violent one, but I will protect you from it as best as I can. You aren't ready to be subjected to the betrayal and politics happening right now," Leon rested a hand on his son's shoulder, "It isn't because I don't want you to be a part of this one day, I know you will be better than me, but you should enjoy being a child while you can. But, learn to listen and see things from other people's viewpoints. Understand?"

"Yes, sir," Enzo nodded. He turned and ran up the stairs, hurrying to get into bed before his mother came home.

Now:

That conversation had stayed with Enzo for years, it was the last conversation he'd gotten to have with his father. The assassin got him in the early morning hours near one of their docks. Enzo devoted himself to the art of strategy afterwards, hoping to see from every angle and perspective like his father had encouraged him to. Seeking revenge for his father.

Enzo crossed his arms, still watching the screens aimlessly when he felt something on his back. Looking over his shoulder, he found Amelia, tracing a pattern on him with her fingernail. She came up next to him and leaned her head against his shoulder. Enzo wrapped an arm around her and didn't let her stay at his side, instead moving her so that her back rested against his chest. He embraced her with both arms, setting his chin on her head, still staring at the screens.

"What are you thinking about?" She whispered softly, still tracing patterns on his arms now.

"My father," He admitted, "The night before he was killed he told me he knew who was having the Heads killed. He never told me who though. He wanted to shield me from the violence for a bit longer. It's a shame that it lasted less than twenty-four hours."

Amelia leaned her head back to look up at him, "Enzo, you asked me if I was ready earlier. Are you ready now?"

"I've had twenty years to get ready, Beloved," Enzo looked into her eyes, "I'm more than ready."

"Then let's get the bastards," Amelia pushed off his chest and left the room, presumably to get what she needed.

"Amelia! We have to wait for Fae to make the poisons!" Enzo called after her with a chuckle. He followed her out of the room glad for the distraction to pull him from the computer monitor and from his thoughts.

Amelia was waiting for him at the top of the steps, "Enzo, right now it's just the two of us here. And the Hernandezes, but they're working. We have time, and you need to let some of the tension go before we mount any sort of attack."

"Did you have something in mind?" He asked, waggling his eyebrows.

Amelia rolled her eyes, "Get your head out of the gutter."

She held up his motorcycle helmet and shoved it at his chest. A grin spread across her face as she grabbed her own helmet and ran outside. A moment later Enzo heard her bike start and rev. He ran out after her. His own motorcycle was standing against the side of the building, hidden from plain view. Dragging it out, Enzo brushed the leaves off the seat and mounted it. He started it up, listening to the purr of the engine and feeling the motor hum underneath him. He could feel his heart rate starting to increase, excitement rising.

"Ready?" Amelia asked.

"Is this really the right time, Amelia?" Enzo glanced back at the shop.

"Enzo, blow off steam before we go so that the rest of us know you're level headed. If you aren't even keeled, how will the rest of us function?"

She didn't wait for a response before speeding off into the street. But Enzo had to admit she was right. If he didn't straighten his mind out, what use would he be for the team? They needed him to watch their backs and trust that he would guide them. So he shrugged and chased after the Hispanic woman. The feeling of riding without direction was unbelievable. Nowhere to be, just the ability to go and leave it all on the road. He was reminded why he preferred riding his motorcycle in the first place. The freedom it offered, the speed it could go, it seemed to pull everything right off his shoulder and fill him with adrenaline. The feeling was euphoric; addicting even.

He swerved through traffic, watching the building and sparse trees go by. He avoided the traffic cameras and wove through the lanes, bobbing this way and that as he balanced the bike. Somewhere between 122nd street and 125th street, Enzo lost sight of Amelia, she'd gone on ahead of him somewhere. He continued to drive, knowing she would likely find him before he found her on the streets.

Each mile he put between himself and the camera shop seemed to help lighten the load on his shoulders. Amelia reappearing also helped ease the tightness in his chest as they rode. He spared a glance at her on her crimson bike and knew that whatever happened would all be worth it because somehow, he got to love her. As long as they were both still alive at the end of it.

Amelia Cruz: Using the Poisons

Fae had called them to the coffee shop about an hour into their ride. She had prepared the paralytics they would need. Amelia had waved down Enzo and had him follow her all the way to the shop. They only stopped to drop their bikes in Luke's shop for safe keeping while they went to retrieve the poison.

Fae stood inside the shop wearing a canvas apron and a sour expression. Her hands were on her hips as she glared at the two people walking into her shop, "You two owe me. I had to close the shop down for the day to do this."

"Fae, you're being initiated into the organization properly, isn't that enough?" Enzo rolled his eyes, earning himself and eye roll from both women and a pinch on his arm from Amelia.

The blonde held up three glass vials, "This should be more than enough. But I made extra just in case one of these broke or something."

Amelia nodded and took them gratefully. Fae handed her three medical needles for administering the paralytic later. All of it went into a small pouch and was slung around Amelia's shoulder.

"Do not, and I repeat, do not give more than the specific dose for each person," Fae warned them as she walked them to the door, "This will paralyze them for up to twenty four hours, but too much could either cause permanent paralysis or death."

"Neither of those sound wholly unwelcome," Enzo told her.

"Amelia, I need you to understand this, even a milliliter too much could lead to death, and we aren't there yet," Fae had told her, "Be careful not to have any air bubbles in the syringe or you'll cause an air embolism."

"Enzo, go get on your bike," Amelia waved him off, turning to the other woman, "Thank you for all of your help. Not just with this."

"Of course," Fae hugged her friend tightly, "Be safe."

"We'll try," Amelia said, following Enzo across the street and back to their backs.

Behind her, Fae called one last encouragement, "Bye-bye! Have fun storming the castle!"

*****

Amelia made her friend repeat the instructions three times and made sure she could recite them back. The goal was to kidnap, not to kill. At least not kill yet.

Now she was making her way to the Hagan mansion. Enzo was riding behind her, weaving through the traffic, not wanting her to go alone. Tom was waiting for them at Berardi mansion. He'd risked going back so they could use the interrogation room below. Adrenaline rushed through Amelia's veins leaving her with a sadistic excitement.

They slowed their bikes as they approached the mansion, pulling to a stop not too far away from the guardhouse. Enzo pulled a specialized tranquilizer gun from the back of his bike much like the one Tom usually carried.

Amelia watched him carefully set the sights and fired a silent dart into the guard's neck. He dropped like a rock, leaving the house open for the taking. Amelia darted to the guard house and counted the on duty guards from the security cameras before shutting down the system. The gate started to slide open, its motor screeching, breaking the silence of the night.

Enzo stood by, waiting and watching for trouble. Amelia pointed out where the guards were for him before she darted off to the house. She trusted he would shoot the guards before they caused her any issues. Carefully, she crept into the house. She remembered the layout perfectly, embedded in her brain from that horrific night. What she didn't know were which rooms belonged to Narciso and Royal. She would need to search quickly.

She figured their rooms were on the same floor as Ray's which significantly lowered the number of possibilities. It didn't mean she found them right away though, the first few rooms were empty, but on her fifth attempt she found Royal. He was sprawled on his bed shirtless, freckles peppered his pasty back. The sheets twisted around his lower half, just barely leaving something to the imagination.

Amelia removed a syringe and vial from her pouch, carefully she measured out a single dose of Fae's paralytic. She tapped out the few air bubbles before tiptoeing to the bed. She looked down at the sleeping man, an evil smile gracing her lips. Jabbing the needle into his neck woke Royal up, but it was too late. The paralytic took effect and silenced him, leaving the look of horror frozen on his face.

Amelia knelt down and whispered, "This is for the people you like to call collateral damage."

Enzo's voice filled her ear on the comms, "Nice touch."

"Thank you, I thought so too," Amelia moved from the room and down the hall to the next one, "Are the guards taken care of?"

"Do you doubt me, Beloved?" Enzo asked in mock offense.

"Never," Amelia chuckled softly.

She found Narciso's room nearby but found the door locked.

She scoffed at the simplicity of it. A couple of seconds and two hairpins later, the door swung open. Narciso's snores sounded like a tractor was in the room, she could practically smell the gasoline. Amelia was surprised that the windows weren't rattling in their frames. With a shake of her head, she removed another syringe and measured the perfect dose for the man. She and Fae had needed to recalculate the poison for him due to his immense size.

Much like with his son, Narciso woke up when the needle pierced his skin. Eyes wide and mouth agape. Amelia looked down on him, pitiless. Knowing he wouldn't be able to identify her later gave Amelia a smug bit of satisfaction. Once she was sure the paralytic had taken full effect, she walked away.

"No quippy comment for him?" Enzo teased.

"My previous statement goes for all of them, I see no need to repeat myself," Amelia shrugged.

She stood in front of Ray's door and took a breath. Panic and bile rose in her throat. It took her a moment to force it down. She could do this, she already had, at the shelter. And she was doing this not just for herself, but for every person he had harmed when he attacked the shelter. For every person he had harmed in the past and for every person he was actively trying to harm.

Steeling herself, Amelia opened the door and stepped inside. The room was dark but she was able to creep through without tripping over anything he left on the floor. Lumps on the floor indicated he did not usually do his own laundry. Much like his brother, Ray did not sleep with a shirt on. As she got closer, Amelia noticed a large tattoo on his shoulder, the Hagan family crest. How had she never seen that?

Amelia couldn't help the chuckle that escaped her. It was the perfect ending to their story. Without hesitation or mercy, the needle slid into his skin smoothly. The poison slipped into his veins with ease. She could see his joints stiffening as it took effect, somehow his eyes stayed closed. He seemed to sleep through it, unlike his family.

"Ready in here for you, Enzo," She told her counterpart over the comm.

Moments later, Enzo strode into the room with a couple sentinels. He instructed them to take Ray and put him in the trunk of their car and meet them at Berardi mansion. Amelia watched the sentinels lug Ray's body out of the bed and out of the room.

After watching them leave, she turned and looked at Enzo who was already watching her. He reached out a hand and pulled her in close. Amelia rested her cheek against his chest a moment and felt the weight of his chin on her head.

"Are you ready to go?" He asked.

"More than," Came the swift reply.

They left the house and Amelia was surprised to see Royal and Narciso laying out in the grass on the front lawn. Along- side them were the guards Enzo had taken out with his tranquilizer gun. They all looked like they might have purposely been sleeping outdoors with the way they'd been arranged.

"We nearly needed a forklift for Narciso," Enzo told her with a chuckle, "The others were easy enough though."

"Why bring them out here though?" Amelia asked.

"Because, my dear, we are taking them with us. 'Prisoners of war,' I believe is the expression. Besides, I need to make sure they arrive late to the meeting, remember?" Enzo held her helmet out to her, "And I'm sending Luke later. He wanted to blow up the house."

*****

Tom stood at the door waiting for the couple when they got back to the house, "Fae administered the antidote not too long ago, he should be awake now."

Enzo nodded, "Good, and the rest of the team is here I presume?"

"Yes."

"And their own tasks are done?"

"Yes."

"Let's go down and greet our guest then," Enzo offered his arm to Amelia and escorted her inside.

It was obvious someone had been inside the mansion, the furniture was on its side, there was even graffiti on the wall. The orange and navy spray paint gave away the perpetrators of that crime. Amelia could see the pain on Enzo's face when he saw his family home in shambles. She squeezed his arm comfortingly and guided him to the basement door. They could hear chatter from down below, leading them directly to their circle of friends and teammates.

"Berardi!" Luke called when they entered, "Or is it Berardis now? Did you two elope in your afternoon off?"

Amelia laughed, "No, definitely not."

Enzo gave her a curious look before clapping his hands together and gathering the room's attention, "We have a guest in the interrogation room. I am sure you are all eager to go in there and give him a piece of your mind or a knuckle sandwich, but for now, let's just see what he has to say about his family's plan."

Amelia let her hand slide out of Enzo's as he walked towards the interrogation room, "I'm not ready to go in there yet."

He nodded and kissed her hand before nodding toward the observation room. She walked in with Fae, Luke, and Mateo following along behind them. She watched Tom and Enzo enter the interrogation room through the small one way glass. In the metal chair sat the man she might have said she loved once. Ray. He looked groggy, like the lights weren't fully on upstairs.

Tom leaned against the wall, a maniacal look on his face. He enjoyed getting to be in these meetings. Enzo crouched in front of the red haired man and patted him on the face a couple of times to get his attention.

"This will be interesting, don't you think?" Mateo asked.

Amelia nodded, "I think that it will be enlightening."

Together they watched the scene unfold in the next room. Ray seemed to wake up more when Enzo smacked his face. He looked around the room wildly, utterly confused by his surroundings.

"Berardi! What the hell? Where am I?" He demanded.

"You can't be that stupid," Tom scoffed from his spot on the wall.

Enzo chuckled, "Glad you're awake, ponytail. We have a couple questions."

"Like I'm stupid enough to answer you," Ray spat at Enzo's feet.

Amelia sighed, "That was a mistake."

Luke laughed, "His mistake was thinking he could get away with even half of what he did."

Amelia glanced over her shoulder at her friend. He was fiddling with some metal contraption and quietly explaining what it was meant to do to his girlfriend. She turned back to the window to watch. Enzo had traded places with Tom which was never a good sign. The latter was rifling through a set of drawers behind Ray while Enzo was giving him a smug look.

"Ray, you know that Tom can be, what's the right word?" Enzo grinned, "Ah, deranged. Are you sure you don't want to be compliant?"

"Go to hell!"

"Your choice," Enzo shrugged, "I'm going to ask the questions and you have the choice of answering them or not. If you decide not to answer them, Tom will use whatever method of extraction he likes."

Tom pulled a few different devices from the drawers and laid them on the shelf to prepare them. As he removed his coat and rolled up his sleeves, Amelia identified them and internally winced. Ray was in for a rough evening entirely of his own making. There were pliers, a cat of nine tails, a hammer, and what looked like a spool of wire. No, this was definitely not a pleasant evening in the making.

"What is your father's plan for the Commission? His intention is to take it over? Yes?" Enzo started casually. He was inspecting his nails, not even looking at Ray.

Ray spat at Enzo again and was rewarded with a swift hit of Tom's hammer to his hand. He let out a guttural yell as the bones in his hand crunched. Tom swung the hammer around, tossing it up in the air, whistling a tune without a care in the world.

Enzo sighed, "Ray, I've played nice up until now, but I'm getting rather tired of it, so please, answer the questions. Same question stands."

Ray simply glared. Tom swung again, this time at the other hand. The bones crunched and he let out another yell.

Fae grimaced, "I don't have much sympathy for him, but seriously, if he doesn't start talking soon, he's not going to have many more bones to break."

Amelia didn't even look over her shoulder when she told her friend, "There are ways of extracting information without breaking bones. Sewing needles into nerve bundles works wonders."

"Holy hell, Amelia, that's terrifying. Remind me never to tick you off!" Fae laughed incredulously.

Mateo looked over at her, "Oh, yeah! You've never seen her work there, have you?"

"Nope!" Fae replied, popping the 'P'.

Luke grinned, "Be glad, it's bloody, terrifying, and brilliant."

"It's fun," Amelia said, turning around and looking at her friends, "There's an art to extraction. Tom likes brute strength and fear. It works but causes a lot of damage. But if you use the more graceful forms of it, well, let's just say it's a lot easier, a lot faster, and a lot simpler."

"And you're not in there now simply because of who it is, right?" Fae asked.

"Yep," Amelia leaned against the wall, watching again.

Ray's nose was bleeding now and he was glaring at Enzo and Tom. That last part wasn't new. It had been a favorite pastime of his when he'd worked for the organization. But he usually had done it from the safety of their relationship. Now he had nothing to hide behind and it was putting himself in dangerous waters.

"I missed what he used for the nose," Amelia mused quietly.

"Brass knuckles?" Mateo guessed. He came up to the window to watch with her, arms crossed over his chest.

Luke stepped up to the window to watch, "Maybe, but wasn't that Lance's favorite weapon? Not Tom's?"

"It would be a cruel irony to use his preferred method," Amelia hummed. She suddenly straightened and walked toward the door.

"Where are you going?" Luke called after her.

"To add a touch more irony."

Amelia walked into the interrogation room surprising Tom and Enzo, and surprising herself most of all. Ray's hanging head lifted at the sound of the door, a sneer spreading across his face at the sight of her. She merely rolled her eyes at him and turned to face Enzo.

"Go out," She instructed.

"Are you sure?"

Amelia nodded, "It's work. He's no different than any other moronic henchman I've had in the chair."

Enzo touched her cheek for a moment, staring into her eyes as if trying to decide if she really meant what she said. Finally he kissed her forehead and beckoned Tom out of the room. Just before the door closed behind them, he turned to say, "We're right outside if you need us."

"I know," She gave him a soft smile.

Amelia took a breath, steeling herself and turned to face Ray. He was glaring at her now with a disgusted look. Not unlike his interactions with Enzo, he spat a mouthful of blood at her.

"So, you *were* sleeping with him."

"So, *you* were giving information to the enemy," Amelia retorted, "Are you sure you want to go down that road? I will win, I assure you."

"You think that, if it gives you comfort," He laughed cruelly.

"And what gives you comfort, Ray? Is it the destruction of shelters for the abused? Is it simply abusing people? I'm curious," Amelia leaned against the wall with her hands tucked into her pockets.

"Go to hell, woman," He seethed.

"Eh, not interested, thanks," She shrugged, "But if you don't have anything useful, I think I'll go ahead and get started. What do you think?"

She didn't wait for his response. Slowly, Amelia put away Tom's torture devices and pulled out her own, purposely making clanging sounds when he couldn't hear her. Slamming drawers and clinking metal together.

"Battery, clamps, wire, needles, hose," She checked a list off, barely loud enough for the man to hear.

Amelia could just imagine Enzo's smirk and Tom's grin as they watched the scene unfold. Taking the water hose and turning it on, the young woman sprayed it all over the Irishman tied to the chair. Immediately he struggled against the ropes holding his hands and ankles down, his unsuccessful attempt in escaping brought a laugh bubbling out of Amelia as she watched the futile effort.

"Same question still applies, when that one is answered, Berardi will ask another one through the intercom, understand?" She came around in front of him pulling rubber gloves on to protect herself from the voltage she was about to administer.

"You are a sadist," Ray told her.

"Thank you! That's the nicest thing anyone's ever said to me!" She said mockingly, placing a hand over her heart, "Shall we begin now?"

Now waiting for a reply, Amelia clipped the cables to the car battery and tapped them together sending sparks flying. Her eyes looked frenzied at the sparks and yet, everything else about her remained in perfect control.

"We'll start small. On your ankles, maybe?" She reached down and connected the cables to his soaking jeans. The electric current flowing through the wet material didn't stay in his lower extremities. She didn't leave it going for very long, just long enough to leave him sagging in the chair, panting and swearing like a sailor.

Amelia clicked her tongue lightly, "Language, language, Mr. Hagan, there are ladies present!"

"You're no lady!" He growled. His usual gusto was lost in his fatigue.

She let out a light laugh, "I didn't mean myself, I meant the young lady watching on the other side of the glass. Now, what do you think? Are you ready to answer some questions? What is your father planning?"

Ray groaned, "I won't tell you anything. Two-faced she-beast."

Amelia raised a brow, "'Two-faced?' Really, Ray? You want to talk about being two-faced, let's talk about your time here in our organization, shall we? First, you lied about your name. Secondly, our entire relationship was a lie. Thirdly, you passed information onto another family. Do you want me to continue? This list is a mile long."

Ray remained silent so Amelia shrugged and grabbed one of the sewing needles and carefully inserted it underneath his fingernail. He grit his teeth but resisted crying out until she held the jaws of the jumper cables to it. He shook in his seat, rattling the bolts that kept the chair on the floor.

"He's taking over the Commission! There's a meeting this afternoon!" Ray screamed out.

Amelia removed the cables and jerked the needle out. Kneel- ing down in front of him she demanded, "That's old news, what else?"

"My father intends to call for Berardi's removal on grounds of Commission violations," Ray admitted, "He told the Commission the thefts were committed by Berardi's men, any deaths were under his orders. And the assassinations from years ago were because of Enzo Berardi. He plans on ruining your beloved Berardi."

Amelia Cruz: Confronting the Commission

Enzo was waiting for Amelia in the hall outside of the interrogation room, leaning against the wall, hands in his pockets. Seeing him felt like a breath of fresh air. The dichotomy between him and Ray was so incredible, Amelia wondered why it took her so long to see it.

She didn't hesitate to wrap her arms around Enzo upon coming out of the room. Resting her head on his chest to listen to his heart beat and take comfort from him being there. One of his hands wrapped around her waist, the other around the back of her head ever so gently.

"Are you okay?" He whispered to her, resting his chin on her head.

"Yeah," Amelia pulled away and shook her shoulders out. Noticing a dark patch on Enzo's shirt she groaned, "I got your shirt wet! I'm so sorry."

Enzo chuckled, "It's okay. It's just clothes. Come on, I've got a plan."

Amelia took his offered hand and followed him into the observation room. The rest of the team was waiting for them. She noticed that someone had turned off the light in the interrogation room so they couldn't see the person on the other side. Enzo pulled a chair out for her at the table before stepping to the front of the room, everyone's attention on him.

"Do you remember when I said the Cruzes needed to show up on time?" Enzo asked, "We're going to make every part of their day look like Lady Luck has her eye on them. I want them to think that even *we're* on their side. All the way up until Amelia claims leadership of the Cartel."

"I'm sorry, what?" Amelia held a hand up, pausing him, "That won't fly with the Commission. They're pretty strict about the line of succession."

Amelia watched a smirk slither over Enzo's face. Shivers went down her spine. Whatever he was planning, she was going to be on the receiving end of some very hateful slanders from at the minimum her brothers and the allies they had left.

"The line of succession calls for the eldest to take ownership after the Head's passing," Enzo said.

"Enzo, I am well aware of the laws," Amelia rolled her eyes.

The team's heads bobbed back and forth between the two, like they were watching an interesting tennis match. Back and forth, back and forth. They stayed silent waiting for the couple to finish their little argument.

Amelia realized what he was planning a moment later, "You're about to turn Angel's greatest fear into reality, aren't you?"

"I have a plan, Beloved. Trust me, please," Enzo implored her.

Amelia frowned, "As you wish. I think it's risky though."

"I know. And I don't think you'll like some of the plan," Enzo shrugged sheepishly.

"That worries me immensely," Amelia crossed her arms.

*****

When Enzo had said she wasn't going to like the plan, she didn't realize how much she wasn't going to like the plan. She was suddenly sitting with him in the back seat of one of his tinted out sedan staring at a back-dated marriage license. On her finger was a gorgeous ruby, set in a gold band, surrounded by diamonds. She knew the ring well. It was *the* Berardi family heirloom ring, Enzo's mother had worn it, his grandmother had worn it, it followed the family all the way back to their roots in Italy. Somehow in the midst of their war, Enzo had asked his mother to send the ring back over from Italy.

"They're going to charge me with infidelity!" She hissed at him for the hundredth time.

Enzo reached across the bench and grabbed her hand, "They can't for several reasons. The first being because we'll claim that it was under my instruction to weed out the mole. Secondly, it isn't like a lot of them are perfectly faithful to their spouses either, that alone is leverage. It'll be fine, Beloved."

"This wasn't some scheme of yours to make sure I couldn't run away again, was it?" She sighed, resting her head against the seat and covering her face with her hands.

"Amelia, I would have preferred to give you the wedding you deserve. Believe me, this was not my preferred method of giving you my last name, although that had always been my intention," He kissed the back of her hand, "Trust me, please?"

"You know I do. It's the Thirteen I don't trust."

"Well, thank goodness it's not all of them. The Hagans are imprisoned in the basement in our home," Enzo grinned maliciously, "For now."

Tom looked back at them from the driver's seat, "Sorry to interrupt the happy new Mister and Missus, but we're here."

"Tomaso!" Amelia warned. He'd been teasing since they'd left the courthouse.

He grinned at his friend and stepped out of the car to open the door for her. He handed the keys to one of their lower level sentinels to and whispered something to him before following the couple into the hotel. For a hotel lobby in New York City, it was shockingly quiet. For the lobby of a hotel the Thirteen were meeting in, it was concerningly silent. Staff nodded at the trio walking through and carried on with their duties. A few civilian businessmen nodded as they passed by, exiting the building.

Amelia assumed the majority of the Commission was already upstairs in the boardroom. They were probably wondering why the Hagans were yet to arrive. Waiting for the elevator to descend, she rubbed her palms nervously against her violet colored dress. Enzo seemed to sense her anxiety and reached for her hand.

"Relax, we'll be fine," He leaned and kissed her temple as the elevator doors opened.

Inside the elevator were a few sentinels from the Walsh family, one of the Hagans' allies. Recognition dawned on their faces when they saw Amelia next to Enzo. Immediately they stepped forward and blocked the door to the lift.

Amelia sighed and reached into the slit in her skirt, removing a hooked knife from the hidden holster and holding it up, "Let's not do this gentlemen. This is a new dress and while I'm not afraid to get blood on it, I'd prefer to keep it clean for at least a full day."

Enzo chuckled, catching their attention. He raised his hands up, "Don't look at me, she's the one who will gut you like a fish. I'm not going to help you unless you swear fealty to me instead of the Hagans."

The men looked at the knife and murderous expression on Amelia's face and seemed to reconsider. They moved aside, allowing the couple and Tom to enter the elevator. They continued watching until the doors closed. At least her reputation was still intact. For now.

"That was a peculiar interaction," Tom commented lightly.

"There will be more. They're here to remove me from the Commission. They didn't expect me to actually show up though," Enzo replied mildly.

Amelia replaced her knife and straightened out her skirt. She tossed her hair with huff. She had not yet fully forgiven Enzo for blindsiding her with the marriage, especially when he wouldn't tell her the full plan. He only said that she wasn't there to represent him or the Berardi family in spite of her new name.

Tom looked over at her with an amused look. She had cornered him at the courthouse and asked if he'd known the plan. He swore up and down he hadn't, but she wasn't sure if she believed him or not.

She had been reminded of her first meeting with Tom and Enzo. It felt like more than three years had passed since then. But she could still remember Tom telling her the day Enzo looked for a marriage contract, hell would freeze over.

It appeared that hell had frozen over.

The elevator dinged open, depositing the trio into the hallway near the conference room. Just a few yards away stood a guard at the door. Amelia rolled her eyes, not a lot of muscle for a group of paranoid mafia men.

Enzo offered her his arm to take as they made their way to the meeting.

The guard followed their approach and planted himself firmly in front of the door, rifle across his chest. He glared at them as they stood in front of them and set his jaw, like he was determined to bar their entrance.

"Let us into the meeting," Enzo told him.

"What meeting?" He said. His voice wavered just a touch, revealing his own apprehension.

"Oh my -," Amelia scoffed, "Tom, tear his arms off."

Tom moved towards the man with a gleeful look but he darted away from the door, "Go on in!"

The door opened smoothly, Enzo went in first, followed by Tom. Amelia hesitated just a moment before stepping through. The rest of the Thirteen sat at the table, some surprised by the appearance of Enzo and not the Hagans. However, many of them looked smug when they saw Berardi enter. They sat straighter, an air of confidence suddenly surrounding them. Their boost seemed to give Amelia what she needed to hold her head high and walk with purpose and authority. They had allies and a lot more than she had originally thought.

Enzo smiled at her and pulled a seat out for her to sit in. At his right hand. Tom gave her a subtle nod of approval when she took her place. Enzo was making a public declaration of her importance to him.

But of course, the moment was broken by Angel Cruz.

"She is not allowed in the meeting, Berardi. Never has been and we're setting our foot down. Please have your *puta* removed," Angel waved his hand dismissively at his sister.

While she somehow managed to keep a straight face, Amelia sat there shocked by her brother's blatant vulgarity. She knew he hated her, but that was new. But she didn't have to jump to her own defense. Several people from the Garcia, Perez and Flores families all interjected, calling him out. Angel had just put his foot in it. The Families that hadn't been allies to Berardi when they walked in seemed to consider it now.

Flores was the first to speak, "Cruz! Control your tongue, man! We still honor the laws of the Commission! She is under the protection of a Family and therefore should be treated as such."

"*¡Cállate!*" Garcia snapped, cutting Flores off accidentally.

Perez had reached over and pounded his fist on the table in front of Angel. The impact vibrated through the whole table, all the way down to where Amelia sat. Benjamin and Camilo stood behind their brother, unsure of what they were meant to do in the sudden chaos. Angel sat flabbergasted at the turn of events.

"What is the meaning of this?" He demanded, "Since when do you question one of the Big Three at the Commission table?"

"Since they are no longer aligned with you, Cruz," Enzo stated bluntly, "But, before you ask, no. They're not aligned with me."

Puzzled expressions filled the room. Amelia watched her new husband, curious as to what bomb he was about to drop on the table. He paused, letting the tension build. He reached a hand out, intertwining his fingers with Amelia's.

"They are in an alliance with the new Head of the Cruz Cartel," Enzo finally revealed.

Amelia's breath caught in her throat, letting the announcement echo through the room. Angel's biggest fear was her taking over the Cartel, claiming birthright as the first born from another woman. And here was Enzo, usurping his position and giving it to her. With the support of allies! Amelia stared at Enzo in awe. The plan was brilliant. Silence filled the room, everyone held their breath, waiting for the reveal of who was taking over. Angel whipped his head to Benjamin who shook his head. It wasn't him. He looked at Camilo who shrugged, just as confused as his brothers. That was when Angel seemed to come to the correct conclusion. His sister was removing him from his seat of power and taking it for herself.

He opened his mouth to speak, but she stood from her seat, "I am Amelia Cruz, firstborn daughter of Antonio and Maria Cruz. I am claiming my birthright as the Head of the Cruz Cartel."

Héctor Perez was the first to respond. He stood and crossed his arm over his chest and nodded to her, "The Perez family recognizes Miss Cruz's claim. I've seen you work, You're not someone I'd want to cross but someone I'd want fighting with me."

Garcia followed, acknowledging her claim. One by one, each of the Heads stood and offered their endorsement. Finally, Enzo was the only person who had not given it. All heads turned to him, waiting.

He had been watching Amelia throughout the whole ordeal and when he realized all eyes were on him, he gave a mock gasp, "Do I really need to be asked? Of course I support the claim to the Cartel. I was the one who helped arrange the transition after all."

Amelia laughed lightly at his performance. It had gone over much easier than she'd expected. The Cruz brothers had lost their power in a matter of minutes and there was nothing they could do to stop the shift. They'd lost the respect of the Thirteen in their behavior towards their sister and how they handled their business. The Cruz brothers were drowning.

"What's in this for you Berardi?" Angel snarled.

"Well for starters, it gives me great pleasure to bring you and your brothers down a few pegs. Secondly, this meeting was never going to vote me out of the Commission, the entire reason for it happening was to boot other people. You and your brothers were the first," Enzo smirked, tenting his hands on the table, "I would recommend clearing your things from the *hacienda* before the eviction notice arrives tomorrow."

"I am not leaving, Berardi, you may have convinced the smaller families to back her, but you forget I am still aligned with the Hagans. Two out of three will overturn this ridiculous proclamation!" Angel jumped from his chair, sending it flying backwards. Camilo had to jump out of the way to avoid being hit by the flying furniture.

"Ah, yes, about that," Enzo said, "The second order of business, charging Narciso, Royal and Ray Hagan with their heinous crimes and finding a punishment befitting them."

Amelia couldn't help herself, she laughed out loud. Each point Angel made, Enzo was ready. He had prepared for every twist and turn, proving yet again why he was the most powerful of the Heads. The most influence, the most men, the most money, the most land. And her stupid brothers had thought themselves on equal footing and had been proven wrong, publicly. The Thirteen seemed to have forgotten who Enzo Berardi was and they were watching Angel relearn the hard way.

"Angel, give it up. Stay if you like and listen to the proceedings, but you have been outmaneuvered," Amelia laughed. She lifted and dropped her hands like she couldn't think of anything else to say, nor was there anything that her brother could do.

"Now, Señor Cruz, relinquish the chair to the Señorita," Garcia demanded firmly and politely. He stood from his own chair, as if he would force the man to move from where he sat.

The Commission had a tradition of setting the table in a 'T' shape, with the Big Three at the top, looking down at the remaining Heads. Angel was sitting on the right this time, with Enzo on his left. The empty chair on Enzo's left was originally for Narciso Hagan who, of course, was not going to be there.

They never maintained the same order like the rest of the Thirteen did. The goal had always been for the Big Three to be equal with each other. But once a person tastes power, they are loath to relinquish it, much like Angel.

Perez stood, again offering support to Amelia's claim by asking Angel to move as well. To her surprise, the head of the Walsh family expressed similar sentiments. The people who endorsed her rise to Head were now assisting her in physically taking her place. Amelia looked at Enzo a little unsure. He gave her a wink and squeezed her hand comfortingly.

"Any time now, Señor Cruz," Tom rolled his eyes, "There are other things that need to happen today. Unless you would like to stay and watch the trial. But then you might be implicated and we have a plan for you if that happens."

Benjamin's eyes widened and he bent to whisper to his brother. Angel glowered at his sister but got up. He walked to the side of the room and took a seat, his brothers following.

Camilo looked nervous and leaned to whisper to Angel, loud enough they could all hear, "Angel, are you sure we shouldn't leave?"

"They have no real reason to implicate us in any sort of crime," Angel sneered, "Be still and wait."

"Don't we?" Amelia asked. She was standing next to Enzo's chair, moving to her new seat. She glanced down at him, wondering if it was the right time to play their next card.

Enzo's eyes glinted when he nodded. He waved Tom over and murmured something in his ear. The blonde man left the room quickly as Amelia settled in her chair. The view was different now, if only because of the power connected to the position.

"Angel, why don't you join us back at the table?" Amelia gestured to the empty chair at the foot of the table. The chair where a man would sit while on trial. She smiled innocently at him when his jaw dropped in horror.

Enzo cleared his throat, "I'm going to enjoy this, Cruz. I really, really am."

Angel took the trial chair, hands shaking as he placed them on the arm rests. Benjamin watched, a bead of sweat rolling down his temple. Camilo mostly looked confused.

"Angel, I can think of several things we could charge you with," Amelia started, "Starting with not respecting a protection order."

Several Heads looked over at Angel who'd gone white as a sheet, "I didn't!"

Enzo lifted Amelia's wrist and showed Angel the bear print tattoo, "This is a mark of protection in my Family. Everyone is aware of it. You disregarded it."

"How? She sought shelter in my house! How did I ignore a mark of protection?" Angel demanded, sweating profusely now. The Heads watched, some terrified of what was to come, others eager to see.

"You really should've left when you had the chance," Enzo chuckled, "You violated a protection mark when you tried to marry my *wife* off to someone else and let them lay their hands on her. My WIFE!"

Enzo Berardi: The Trial

The announcement had the desired effect.

Angel jumped up to defend himself, men stopped him from lunging towards the Big Three seats. Benjamin however, managed to evade the men and threw himself across the table at his sister. He crashed into her, sending them both flying to the floor, hands clawing at her face and throat. Amelia shoved against him, pushing him away as best as she could.

Enzo was up in an instant, pulling the man off Amelia by his collar. He threw him down on the table and pulled a knife from his waistband. Benjamin lay there, wide-eyed, the edge of the blade against his Adam's apple. Blood beaded around the blade and ran down the Hispanic's neck.

"Don't you ever lay a hand on my wife again," Enzo growled. Hair fell into his eyes and a vein pulsed in his neck. Fury was coming off him in waves.

A soft hand wrapped around his wrist and gently pulled the knife away, "Enzo, he isn't worth the salt to season his food. Let him go."

"As you wish, Beloved," He murmured.

Amelia forced herself in between him and Benjamin, making him look at her. Her emerald eyes pleading with him. Enzo let his hold drop, releasing Benjamin to the sentinels who escorted him from the room. He placed a hand on her cheek and turned her head to examine the angry red marks forming along her jawline.

"You're lucky my wife is more forgiving than I am," He called after the Cruz brothers as they exited the conference room. He turned to address the room, "Does anyone else have any issues they would like to present? Or can we proceed to trying the Hagans?"

"What will happen to the Cruzes?" One of the Heads asked.

Many people turned towards Amelia. As the Head of her family, it was her choice what happened to them. She looked at Enzo for a moment, he shrugged, trying to tell her that it wasn't up to him.
  She looked out over the table and towards the doors her brothers had gone out of. Enzo watched her, trying to figure out what she was planning. He saw when the idea came to her, she looked back at him with an evil grin, making him hope that whatever she was planning wasn't something she could enact on him if he made her mad.

"My brothers will be sent down to Mexico to our cousins there. A list of their crimes will go with them and whatever happens, happens. I can't imagine our relatives will be pleased all things considered. They're a bit more progressive with leadership down there. I'm quite certain they'll enjoy dishing out your punishment."

The other Heads nodded and returned to their seats, casting fearful looks at Enzo. He wanted to continue sending a message of what he was willing to do to people who stood against him, but he'd promised Amelia. Enzo nodded when she finished her declaration and sent a message to Tom before sitting as well. Blood was still rushing in his ears, his foot bounced up and down and his pulse still persisted in beating faster than necessary. Again, Amelia reached over, this time she was the one offering comfort. Threading her fingers through his, uncaring of their audience, she started taking deep breaths. He mimicked her as she intended for him to, calming himself with her aid.

Someone rapped on the door sharply. Connor called out in response, bidding the person to enter the room. Tom stepped in, nodded at Enzo and waved for someone to follow him. Several sentinels escorting Narciso Hagan enter the room. They led him to sit at the designated place at the foot of the table. He still seemed groggy from the paralytic he'd been given the night before. The sentinels strapped him to the chair so if he became fully aware, he wouldn't be able to cause any damage.

Tom smirked at the obese man before walking up to the head of the table and plopping himself down in what would've been Hagan's seat were he not on trial. Shockingly, not a single person said anything, although he did earn himself an amused look from Amelia.

Enzo pounded the table with his fist, gaining the attention of everyone, "Narciso Hagan, you are here to be brought up on the charge of violating the Commission Laws as well as murder of the Heads. You are responsible for the deaths of Costa, Flores, DeLuca, Perez, Antonio and Blas Cruz, Alessio Dante, and Leon Berardi during the Commission Massacre twenty years ago."

The man grunted, "Go to hell."

"Sir, you are already down at least four allies, maybe more, I wouldn't push your luck," Enzo rolled his eyes, "The first charge, violation of the Commission Laws, you attacked a shelter designed to keep civilians safe from abuse. You stole their safety and home. Hagan, there are three easy Laws to follow, declare your alliances, respect a protection order, and don't attack on neutral ground. Somehow you crossed all three lines in a matter of weeks."

The Heads started murmuring with one another and their second in commands. A Berardi sentinel passed a stack of photos around as proof of the crimes. Among the stack was documentation of Ray's spying in and thus, infringing on another family's territory, proof of orchestrating the thefts. The final paper was a copy of one Enzo had found in his father's files. Images of Narciso Hagan meeting with a known hitman, money passing hands. There was a photocopy of the contract between the two, naming not just the people who had died but some who had simply disappeared. As the Heads read through the evidence in front of them, they gave cries of outrage at the actions of the Irishman. Narciso Hagan lost the rest of his allies at the sight of the one single photo. A reputation was everything and Enzo had found a way to shatter the Irishman's.

Enzo was proud of his team who had managed to find proof of Hagan's involvement in the thefts, of all of his crimes, he'd covered that the best. The Heads now had an itemized list of the shipments the Irish family had stolen from them and a calculation of the money he'd robbed them of.

As the men started to discuss and deliberation over the charges, Narciso started to pull at his handcuffs. Muttering inanities under his breath. He drew the attention of his former allies.

"Hagan! Be still!" Walsh demanded. He had once been one of the most loyal of allies to Hagan, but the tides were turning, "Berardi, I don't suppose you are open to new alliances?" Enzo nodded, "You are welcomed, although allegiance is not just to me."

Walsh crossed an arm over his chest and bowed his head to both Enzo and Amelia.

Amelia turned to Narciso, "There are smart alliances, and then there are dangerous allegiances. You should always choose the latter, they tend to be a touch more loyal."

"Narciso Hagan, you are hereby stripped of your title and your land is henceforth removed from your ownership. It will be given to the person who you most egregiously wronged. I believe the Commission stands united in the decision to give that land to Amelia Cruz, as she was assaulted at the hands of your son," Murphy stood, delivering Narciso's sentence like a death blow, "You will also remove yourself from the city and are prohibited from entering its limits again. If you do, you will be put to death."

"Forgive the interruption, Murphy," Amelia said sweetly, "I have plans for Hagan if you don't mind. We have a lockup I want to put him in."

Murphy chuckled humorlessly, "Only if his sons go too. I don't want this filth anywhere near my land!"

Enzo looked up from fiddling with Amelia's hand, "As long as I live, they will be imprisoned. You have my word. I'm going to enjoy seeing them suddenly live without all of their riches."

*****

Narciso had been escorted from the room and Royal brought in. His trial went much the same as his father's. He had no title or land to lose, so he, like his father, was to be imprisoned by the Berardis. He had tried to talk in his defense during the trial, but it had not ended well for him.

"You can't blame me for following the orders of my father!" Royal claimed, "If anything, I'm his number one victim for making me part of his plan. He and my brother were the masterminds behind it all! I didn't know what I was doing. You have to believe me! I am an innocent man!"

After saying that, Amelia, Tom, and Enzo all spoke simultaneously.

"Isn't it dangerous to use your entire vocabulary in a single sentence?" Tom drawled.

Amelia rubbed her forehead, like she was trying to rid herself of a headache,

"Thank you for that litany of nonsensical thoughts. I am sure we are all dumber for it."

Enzo retorted with, "Has anyone ever told you that you are an astute young man? No? Yeah, I didn't think so."

Amelia continued, "You threatened me with assault several times, so forgive me if I don't believe your innocence."

Royal had stood there, unsure of the right response. He wasn't given the time to come up with anything as he was promptly escorted from the room. That was the last time Enzo ever saw the man out of a prisoner's jumpsuit.

*****

The third and final trial was Ray's. Enzo had already planned for it, ready for any of the jabs he would send their way. He steeled himself, straightening his spine as the doors opened to allow sentinels to bring in Ray. He was going to do his best to deflect any barbs away from Amelia.

Unlike the last time Enzo had seen him, Ray seemed put together. His hair had been neatened and his clothes were very clearly not the same ones from the interrogation room. He snarled at the head of the table as the sentinel attached his cuffs to his chair.

"How'd he get clean clothes?" Enzo whispered to Tom.

"Dunno, but where did the other two, as well? We captured them in their pajamas I thought? Doesn't really matter. We have men making sure they make it to our prison where the clothes will soon be ruined anyway," Tom whispered back.

Petrov pulled a paper in front of himself and began to read from it, "Ray Hagan, you are charged with violating all of the Commission Laws. Do you have anything to say in your defense?"

"Do you enjoy going behind people's backs, Lia?" He smiled at the woman. It didn't quite reach his eyes, leaving him looking rather cold.

Amelia turned her face away, choosing not to answer. Enzo leaned back, draping an arm over the back of her chair and kicking one ankle over the other leg. His own casual behavior seemed to relax Amelia enough to lean into his touch. She took a breath and straightened her spine, not allowing Ray's words to get to her. Or trying not to.

"Traitor," Ray laughed, "You have the gall to charge me, sitting up there on your high horse, but you and I both know you're just as guilty, if not more so. Shall we count off? No attacking on neutral ground? You shot first at the shelter. Second, you didn't share that your allegiance had never changed when you went to your brothers, did you?"

Enzo looked over at Amelia gauging her response. To his surprise, her expression was hard and stony. She was taking great care to not react. He watched her close her eyes for a moment, steadying herself.

"The biggest mistake you made, Ray, was thinking you could violate the most beautiful thing this vicious world has ever created, and get away with it," Enzo drawled even though Ray seemed determined to get through his entire spiel.

"I can still go on! The final law is respecting someone under a protection order! You fired at me while under the protection of the Hagan crest! So correct me if I am wrong, you should be on trial as well!"

"Silence yourself, Mr. Hagan, or you will be removed while we deliberate," Flores warned.

Ray just laughed, "You, Lia, are as guilty as the rest of them! Don't sit there acting like a victim on your throne!"

The door had opened behind Ray as he was speaking. Luke and Fae stepping into the room midway through his rant. Their lips curled in disgust at the man and that might've been why Fae pulled a syringe from her bag and measured something into it. Carefully creeping up behind him, she stabbed Ray in the neck with it, administering whatever drug it held. His head dropped to his chest. Completely unconscious and no longer running his mouth.

Fae looked up at the Thirteen, suddenly realizing who her audience was, "I am so sorry! But that was getting rather disgusting."

One of the Heads waved a hand then rolled his neck, stiff from the hours in the same position, "Please, don't worry about it. I really couldn't stand listening to him for another minute. That was probably the most useful thing anyone has done during this entire meeting."

"Same punishment as his father and brother?" Rossi asked the table.

Murmurs of agreement rose up fairly quickly. Everyone was tiring of the proceedings and seemed ready to go home. The new faces didn't seem to care one way or another, but they hadn't experienced the entire Commission meeting. They hadn't had to deal with the rants of three disgustingly violent men.

"Luke, why are you here?" Tom asked suddenly. Dropping his feet from the table to the floor, staring at the silver haired man with concern.

"Oh, yeah!" Luke snapped his fingers like he was remembering something he needed to say, "I made a wee bit of a mistake that I thought you should know about."

"Understatement," His girlfriend commented under her breath. She rubbed her eyes, clearly annoyed with whatever the mistake was.

Enzo looked at Amelia and whispered to her, "This isn't going to be good."

She shrugged, "With these two, you never know. It could be that she added too much sugar to a cookie or he grabbed the wrong sized bolt. It isn't always bad."

"It isn't always bad enough to interrupt a Commission meeting to tell us," Enzo tilted his head pointedly, knowing he was making the winning argument.

Amelia opened her mouth and closed it again. She did get a chance to reply before a massive explosion went off in the distance. Car alarms started going off from the Bronx to Queens. Cats yowled in displeasure, dogs barked and people were yelling on the streets. Sirens immediately wailed on their way to a tower of smoke in the distance.

"*¡Dios mío!*" Amelia exclaimed, jumping from her chair to look out of the window.

Enzo and Tom stared at Luke who was looking anywhere but at them. He slowly stepped behind Fae who looked offended that he was using her as a shield. Enzo sighed, pinching the bridge of his nose again.

"Luke, please tell me that your mistake doesn't have to do with that explosion," Tom warned.

"No! No it doesn't!" Luke looked relieved and stepped out from behind his girlfriend.

"Then what was your mistake?" Enzo asked, since the danger of the explosion seemed to be contained to a singular area, he was finding himself less concerned with it.

"I gave the wrong date to people. They're already showing up," Luke explained.

Enzo's face dropped in relief and he swore under his breath, "Okay, thank you, Luke."

He nodded and took a seat on the side of the room to watch the rest of the meeting. Enzo wondered how he hired this chaos monster in human form sometimes, but he couldn't think about that. They needed to officially call the meeting to a close and quickly.

"Are we in agreement on all sentences?" Enzo asked the table, the men seemed to realize he was in a hurry and quickly nodded, not wanting to cross him or the woman at his side, "Good. If there is nothing else we need to discuss, my wife and I have an incredibly important event we must attend."

He grabbed his jacket from the back of the chair, shoving his arms through it as he moved towards that door. Amelia and Tom followed quickly, trying to match his strides. Some of the Heads were shuffling in front of the door, slowing him down.

"I truly wonder what that explosion was," Murphy mused aloud as he ambled into the hallway.

"The Hagans' mansion," Luke told him with a grin.

Enzo whirled around, "I thought you said the mistake didn't have to do with the explosion?"

Luke held up a finger, "Ah, ah, ah, I said that the explosion wasn't the mistake, I never said I didn't make it."

The argument lasted all the way up until they got to the car. Fae was telling Luke he should've told them about the explosion. Luke said he thought it was fine because Enzo had given him permission. Tom laughed and asked what kind of explosives had been used. Amelia seemed to enjoy the conversation, occasionally sharing her thoughts on the matter. Enzo had needed to assure several of the Heads that no, his mechanic was not actually insane, just excitable.

While waiting for the car to be brought around, Enzo and Amelia received vows of fealty from the remaining Heads. The final person who stepped up to them was the head of the Connor family. He greeted the couple kindly and almost apologetically.

"I am sorry for everything you've endured at the hands of the Hagans. Truly. I wish I had not been a part of their organization," He told them.

Amelia smiled softly at the man, "Connor, I can't recall a single time when you or your family treated me without respect. You don't owe me an apology, I won't accept it."

Enzo wrapped an arm around Amelia's shoulders, "We will, however, accept your loyalty."

Connor barked out a laugh, "If I'm not mistaken, with my family now in alliance with yours, that makes you two the Heads of every family in the city. I certainly wouldn't want to be your enemy."

"It seems that for the first time in Commission history, we are unified," Garcia overheard the comment and chuckled, "Hail the king and queen of the New York Commission!"

Enzo looked down at Amelia, "Do you hear that, Beloved? We're royalty."

Enzo Berardi: One Last Surprise

The Thirteen seemed to think the new titles were fitting for Enzo and Amelia. Tom and Luke also thought the titles were amazing. They'd bowed so low that their noses touched their knees. Fae had even joined in and given an exaggerated curtsy just as the sentinel pulled their car around.

"Finally!" Enzo muttered even though he was truly amused by the antics.

Even though his wife was pestering him and asking where they were now heading to, Enzo refused to answer. He stared out of the window, watching the buildings whiz by as Tom drove them to their destination. He could feel the annoyance rolling off Amelia since Tom wasn't answering her either, just chuckling.

"I'm getting pretty tired of being dragged around and told to show up at places without information, Lorenzo!"

"I know, Beloved, but trust me, you will enjoy this surprise. I swear it isn't some awful surprise marriage contract again," He teased her with a smile.

"I never said the marriage was awful, I said being blindsided by it was," Amelia pouted, crossing her arms over her chest.

"So I don't need to worry about you petitioning for an annulment?" Enzo grinned. He reached over and unbuckled her seat belt. He then pulled her across the bench so she was close enough he could wrap his arms around. She rolled her eyes but leaned against him anyway.

Amelia scoffed at him as she pulled her seat belt back on, "No, you don't and I'm offended that you would ask such a thing."

"I never know with you, Amelia, you jump from family to family," Tom quipped from the front seat, "First the Cruzes, then us, then the Cruzes again, then engaged to one of the Hagans, now the Cruzes *and* us! Tsk, tsk, you really can't make up your mind."

Amelia kicked the back of Tom's seat, "Don't begrudge me for my family, that isn't fair. Need I remind you that you two are the reason that I suddenly am one of the Thirteen. That is a position I never needed or wanted."

Enzo laughed, "Beloved, you don't have to run the Cartel. All of the men already swore allegiance to our family, I'm quite certain we can trust them to keep things going. Your job will remain the same; continue being the scariest thing to walk this earth. And run this place."

They had pulled up in front of the Cruz *Hacienda*. Several cars were already parked out front, people milling about around them. Enzo recognized some of the people immediately. Some he was only familiar with their faces and others he didn't know at all.

"Why are we at my brothers' house?" Amelia asked as Tom pulled the car in next to the other vehicles.

Enzo didn't get a chance to answer Amelia. As soon as she was out of the car, a boy barreled into her chest, wrapping his arms around her tightly. An elderly couple looked on, pleased and loving smiles plastered on their faces. Amelia looked down at the boy and immediately wrapped her arms around him, spinning him around in a circle. She definitely knew the people there. She approached the elderly couple and embraced them sweetly after setting the boy down.

The person that caught Enzo's attention was not the couple or the boy. It was the olive skinned woman in a maroon dress walking towards him. She had the same color and shape of eyes as him, the same hair, no one would look at them and not see that this woman was his mother.

Lucia Berardi had returned from Italy.

He stepped away from Amelia and wrapped his mother in a tight embrace. She held onto him tightly, like she was trying to make up for the years spent away. Lucia pulled back and placed her hands on his cheeks, tears in her eyes as she examined his face.

"You look just like your father," She finally whispered, "I am so proud of you, my son."

"Mother," Enzo could hardly believe she was there. He looked at Amelia who was watching him with love shining in her eyes, one arm draped over the shoulders of the boy and the other around the waist of the older woman, "I'm sorry I couldn't protect the shelter."

"My darling boy!" The older Italian woman exclaimed, "It was never about the building! It was about the people. And Dorothy here, has been telling me you saw that. So why are you apologizing?"

Enzo wrapped his mother in a hug once more before pulling away and reaching a hand out to Amelia. He gently pulled her closer, "I want you to meet the woman who helped me see that. Mother, this is Amelia, my wife."

"'Wife?'" Lucia screeched, "You got married? And you didn't invite your poor mother to the wedding! Aye! *Mio Dio*! Why would a son insult his mother so?"

Enzo turned red at his mother's dramatic reaction and tried to step away but she held him back and wrapped him in another hug. Behind him, Amelia was cackling and Tom was leaning against the car to hold himself up. He was laughing so hard he was wiping tears from his eyes. Even the boy, who Amelia introduced as Hudson, was laughing at the woman's theatrics. The elderly couple, Donny and Dorothy looked amused as the display.

"I like your mother," Amelia told him, "Maybe she can convince you to tell me why we're at my brothers' house now?"

Enzo didn't have to look at his mother to know her hands were on her hips. He sighed and led Amelia up to the door of the *Hacienda*. The Cruz brothers had already been forced to vacate according to Tom, so they were able to go right inside. He stopped in the courtyard, smiling when he saw the Cruz housekeeper, Estelle Byrd, standing on the stairs, waiting for them. He'd gotten a little time to get to know the woman and knew she had a fondness for Amelia and her mother. When he'd asked if she would stay on for Maria's daughter, she'd told him that as long as Amelia was around, so would she.

"Mother, Amelia, Dorothy, Donny, Leo," Enzo turned to address his audience. He spied the Hernandezes standing in the corner and nodded in greeting, "The shelter meant something to all of you. I don't know if I will ever truly understand its significance because I wasn't there, but I don't need to. Since the Cruzes will no longer be able to use this property and Amelia lives with me, this house would stand empty and useless, unless we do something about it."

Amelia gasped, clasping her hands over her mouth. She had figured out what he had been working on and why Dorothy and her husband were there with Hudson. Lucia was beaming at him with pride, giving him all the encouragement he needed to continue speaking.

"With Dorothy and my mother's help, and of course, Mrs Byrd, this *Hacienda* will stand in place of the underground shelter. No more hiding from the world," Enzo gestured to the courtyard as he spoke, "Instead, let's give people the ability to take their power back and reclaim their place in this world."

Hudson let out a whoop causing the adults to laugh and applaud. The boy took off, running around the courtyard excitedly. When no one stopped him, the others took it as a sign to disperse and look around. Enzo stepped towards his wife who still had tears in her eyes. With a light chuckle, he embraced her and kissed her forehead.

"There's more," He told her.

"What else could you possibly do to top this?" Amelia looked up at him, "This was amazing."

Enzo turned her to watch Hudson who was running around, now playing a game of tag with Luke. Fae was laughing with Mrs. Byrd, snippets of their conversation drifting over to them. The list of baked goods the place was apparently about to offer was already quite long. Dorothy was chatting excitedly with Lucia, their hands clasped between the two of them. They seemed excited to be reunited after so many years. Mateo, Annabelle and Tom were also already lost in conversation though Enzo didn't know what about.

"Hudson was adopted," Enzo told Amelia, "Donny and Dorothy adopted him."

"That's even better than the shelter," Amelia admitted. "My mother will stay here at the *Hacienda* to help run it,"

Enzo explained while wrapping his arms around Amelia and resting his chin on her head. She was the perfect height to let him, making it one of his favorite things to do, "I don't think Dorothy is going to leave this place anytime soon either. She's been a staple of the shelter for as long as I can remember."

He and Amelia stood there watching their family enjoy themselves. For the first time in months, they were able to relax, to be human.

A person can only stay rigid for so long before they snap and Enzo had been pushing that limit. He was infinitely grateful for his team, they had worked without question. They had devoted their time and energy to a battle that wasn't theirs originally. But they made it theirs, fighting for their team.

He was glad to give them the chance to rest and step away. To have a reason to celebrate that they'd made it through the dark tunnel.

"Mother and I decided to rename the shelter," Enzo whispered into Amelia's ear. She turned in his arms to see his face, "The Audra Smith Memorial Shelter. She dedicated so much of her time to the shelter and even died defending it. It seemed it was the best thing we could do to say thank you."

"You are wonderful," Amelia whispered with a smile.

Someone turned on music, playing it loud enough to hear in every corner of the *Hacienda*. Amelia pulled out of his arms and grinned mischievously. She took his hands and dragged him to the center of the courtyard, moving her hips with the music.

"Dance with me!" She demanded, "It hasn't been a traditional wedding day, so at least give me a first dance."

Enzo smiled and wrapped a hand around her waist. He moved with her, dancing to the upbeat music. Amelia was certainly better than him, having grown up dancing to the Mexican music pumping through the speakers.

He'd known that she'd enjoyed dancing, but seeing her enjoy it without the pressure of anything else happening was a completely different level of understanding. She was graceful and carefree, moving with the melody of the song. A soft smile graced her lips and Enzo couldn't help but lean down to kiss her.

They moved across the floor, enjoying being with one another. Some of the guests smiled, watching the newlyweds move across the floor.

Out of the corner of his eye, Enzo noticed Donny leading Dorothy onto the floor. As he watched them dance, he sent up a silent prayer to whoever was listening, hoping that he and Amelia would look like the elderly couple one day. Enjoying music and the simplicity of life together.

Matteo was trying to get Annabelle to dance with him, and Enzo had to give her credit. She was trying. She just wasn't very good. Enzo watched his mother drag Tom to dance with her, making him blush the color of a tomato. Fae and Mrs. Byrd had ceased their whispering and disappeared somewhere into the house leaving Luke alone with Hudson. Their heads were bent over something, hiding it from view with their bodies. Enzo could sense the trouble coming but didn't care too much. He had a beautiful woman in his arms and he was determined to enjoy the time with her.

The music changed to a slower song and Enzo changed their pace accordingly. No, it certainly wasn't the wedding he would've given to Amelia, but now he wouldn't change anything. Their closest friends and family close by, enjoying the fading daylight. Amelia hummed contentedly against his chest and he held her just a touch tighter.

Fae and Mrs. Byrd caught people's attention by bringing out food and laying it out on a nearby table. Amelia managed to slip from Enzo's hold to assist them in carrying out the meal. He shook his head, unsure of how they'd managed to make so much food in such a small amount of time. Soon the table was groaning under the weight of the food, a mix of both traditional Mexican and Italian dishes. Enzo's mouth watered as he eyed the fresh focaccia. He realized, Fae must've told Mrs. Byrd to prepare for their arrival. So much for secrets. He spotted Amelia rolling a cart out of the kitchen, a large stone bowl on it. She picked up a knife and began slicing avocados while chatting with Hudson who was watching and asking questions. The boy was incredibly curious as he watched Amelia make a large bowl of guacamole for the party.

Enzo turned away to see his mother also helping dish out the food. Several of the kids from the original shelter had formed a line to receive their food. He couldn't help but laugh and jump in to serve them. He was starting to understand why the shelter had been so important.

A while later, Tom came over and nudged his shoulder, gesturing to the back door. They quietly grabbed plates of food for themselves and slipped from the courtyard. Outside Enzo found Amelia with a small cooler next to her. She already had a plate of food and was sitting at a metal porch table. She smiled widely at him and used her foot to push out a chair for him.

"Sit," She commanded.

He dropped a kiss on her cheek and took the offered chair. Tom sat across from him, a light smile on his face. Amelia turned her face to the fading light, enjoying the sunlight dancing on her skin. Enzo placed a hand on the back of her neck, gently rubbing out the tension knots. The focaccia that was making his mouth water tasted better than it looked, soon there wasn't any left on his plate. Amelia chuckled softly and handed her slice over to him without a word, Tom however, wrapped his arm around his food jokingly protecting it from Enzo, lest he be tempted to take his as well.

"What's in the cooler?" Tom asked her, breaking the silence.

She handed it to him, "Nothing super expensive or nice like we're all used to, but it's a family tradition. My uncle used to say 'every proper Mexican celebration needs a Mexican beer.' I figured it was alright to keep some traditions from my family, even if they weren't the best. We still had some enjoyable moments."

Tom opened the cooler, revealing three bottles of a popular Mexican beer.

He opened each and passed them around. Enzo took his gratefully and held it up in a toast. Amelia and Tom held theirs up, waiting for him to actually make a toast.

"Don't worry if you don't like it, I have wine for later," Amelia teased.

Enzo shook his head and ignored the comment. "To family and the dangerous allegiances we made along our journey," Enzo nodded to two closest people in his life, listening to the chatter inside, "*Saluto*, my family."

Epilogue

A**melia Cruz-Berardi:**

Amelia was throwing things into a suitcase at the request of her husband. He'd come home from wherever he'd been working that day, and urgently told her that she needed to pack immediately. As usual, he had chosen not to tell her where they were going, only saying it needed to be a mix of clothes. That alone had told her they weren't in imminent danger, but something was definitely brewing. She'd tried to interrogate him but he'd remained firmly closed-lipped.

She tossed a few dresses and matching shoes into her suitcase before stepping into the bathroom to retrieve her toiletries. A small sticky note on the mirror caught her attention as she searched for a hairbrush. Enzo's morning message he'd taken to leaving her when he left before she woke. This time it read 'I love you, Beloved.' Very simple and to the point, but it was perfect.

"Amelia, Beloved!" The man in question called, "Are you ready?"

She grabbed the remaining items and stuffed them into the hardback suitcase. Zipping it up and setting it on the floor she looked around their room. Nothing else stood out as a must bring item for this mystery trip, so she made her way into the hall.

"I'm ready," She called back, "Are you ready to tell me where we're going?"

"The airport, let's go." Enzo grabbed her suitcase and ran out the door. He didn't wait for her to catch up.

"What in the world?" She wondered aloud, following him out to the car.

Unsurprisingly, Tom was waiting at the car ready to drive them. He grinned at her and opened her door. She eyed him warily. The mischief in his eyes told her everything; he knew.

"Lorenzo," Amelia warned as she got into the car, she refused to sit immediately beside him so that she was able to see him.

Tom flopped into his own seat, starting the car, "Amelia, you've been married for a year and worked for him for three years before that. Do you seriously think you can get him to tell you what he's planning?"

Amelia crossed her arms, "Are you going to tell me then?"

"Nope," Tom laughed. He might've been her best friend, but he was Enzo's brother. He wasn't giving up a secret.

She kicked the back of his seat in response. Neither man seemed to care about her annoyance. Enzo watched her with amusement, he was clearly enjoying himself.

"Enzo, I can hold something back from you," She warned him a second time, "Don't think I won't."

He had the decency to flinch, "Sorry, Beloved, you're going to have to wait and see. I love you though!"

*****

Enzo Berardi:

Enzo watched his wife with amusement as she tried to figure out what he was planning. Even after being married for a year, he still managed to pull the wool over her eyes every now and then. He doubted she would completely figure out what he had planned.

Thankfully and luckily, the drive to the airport was short and she trusted him enough to follow.

A chartered jet was waiting for them. The crew was already on board, everything was ready for them. It was time.

Enzo was grateful they were able to avoid going through security. The last time he'd sent Amelia through security, she'd had to go back through at least three times. But it wasn't nearly as bad as Tom's record. The man had gone through ten times due to hidden weapons he'd forgotten about. Since then Enzo had sworn to use chartered only.

The crew took their luggage and carried it on board for them with a smile.

Enzo took Amelia's hand and led her up the steep steps onto the plane. The interior seating was cream colored leather, buttery smooth and soft. A silver bucket sat on a little table, a bottle of champagne inside and two flutes next to it. Amelia raised a brow as Enzo popped the cork, pouring into the two glasses. He handed her one and set the bottle down. Picking up his own and gently tapping the crystal against her glass he pressed a kiss to her forehead.

"We're going to Italy, Beloved," He finally told her as the crew shut the door and instructed them to take their seats, "It's our anniversary so I thought it was time to take that honeymoon we never got."

Amelia stared at him for a moment before laughing, "You are so lucky I love you."

"I am well aware," Enzo returned her smile, "Are you still going to withhold that other thing you mentioned?"

Amelia kicked at his shin just to have her ankle caught by him, he pressed his thumb into it and stroked up and down, "No, I'm not. But you knew that already."

"I did," He confirmed, continuing to rub her ankle softly, "I love you, Amelia Berardi."

She leaned forward and whispered, "That's Amelia Cruz-Berardi, to you, sir."

She pressed her lips to his. Enzo pulled her glass from her hands and set it down before pulling her into his lap, deepening the kiss. He thanked his lucky stars that somehow this woman loved him and he got to love her. And to think it had all started with a dangerous allegiance.

II

Acknowledgments

There are many truths throughout this book and nods to people in the author's life. Without the following people, this book would not exist. Thank you all for everything, words cannot fully express the author's gratitude and love for each person listed.

Ryan and Kristy Durso

Deborah and Kevin Durso

Reese Durso

Wayne Janis

Audrey and Christopher Sowers

Michael and Kristin Durso

Ethan Smith

Joanna Warner

Enrique Franco Martin

Hayley Prashar

Christopher Giorgio

Alexa Guerra